keep her SAFE

Q.B. TYLER

Copyright © 2023 by Q.B. Tyler

All rights reserved.

No part of this publication may be reproduced, distributed, or transmitted in any form or by any means, including photocopying, recording, or other electronic or mechanical methods, without the prior written permission of the publisher, except in the case of brief quotations embodied in critical reviews and certain other noncommercial uses permitted by copyright law.

This is a work of fiction. Names, characters, businesses, places, events, and incidents are either the products of the author's imagination and used in a fictitious manner. Any resemblance to actual persons, living or dead, or actual events is purely coincidental.

Kristen Portillo—Your Editing Lounge
Developmental Editing: Becca Mysoor—Fairy Plot Mother
Paperback Cover Design: Emily Witting Designs
E-Book Cover Design: Pang Thao
Interior Formatting: Stacey Blake—Champagne Book Design

Playlist

Kill Bill—Sza
Hold Up—Beyoncé
Essence—Wizkid (ft Justin Bieber & Tems)
Never Felt So Alone—Labyrinth
Comfortable—H.E.R.
Get You the Moon—Kina
Where Have You Been—Rihanna
I Have Nothing—Whitney Houston
Lost in the Fire—Gesaffelstein & The Weeknd
Good As Hell—Lizzo
A Sunday Kind of Love—Etta James

*To all the women who wished that the movie
The Bodyguard had a different ending.*

keep her
SAFE

Prologue

Shay

THE FLASH OF A CAMERA IS SO BRIGHT IT ALMOST BLINDS me, and for the first time in years, I put a hand over my face to shield them from the tears that are building in the back of my throat. Tears I *never* shed in front of paparazzi. I've rarely even cried aside from the times I had to for work. I can count on one hand the number of times in the last five years, but watching my life fall apart in front of my eyes has the tears building from deep within like I'm preparing to exorcize years' worth of demons.

I'm used to being in front of the camera. I've never been shy. Even at a young age, there are videos of me performing musical numbers for my stuffed animals and talent shows I put on for anyone and everyone in the neighborhood where I grew up. There are hundreds of VHS tapes in boxes in my basement of practice auditions and dramatic readings and singing and even more of me learning all of the skills that were on the resume glued to the back of my headshot.

Ballet, horseback riding, tap dance, archery, gymnastics, and the list goes on.

There are hundreds of Polaroids and pictures taken with disposable cameras that were once glossy and shiny but have faded over time in dozens of photo albums and shoe boxes because my mother could never take just *one* picture.

I'm used to being on the red carpet where thousands of cameras are pointed at me; where I'm trying my best to focus on each of them, trying to give my attention to everyone at once.

Smile. Turn. Change pose. Smile. Turn. Sexy smile. Sweet smile. Wink. Flirt with the camera. Walk to your next mark.

It's as easy as breathing. Of course, there were moments when I felt anxious. The moments when I didn't feel my best, or I didn't feel pretty, or I felt the pang of regret over skipping a workout. A fleeting worry that maybe I hadn't been standing straight so a camera caught me at a bad angle. But I learned to take those moments in stride. I'm not perfect and having to be *on* twenty-four-seven is impossible. I've watched as it destroyed fellow actresses' mental health and how quickly it could send them into a spiral.

As often as I'm in front of the cameras, I'm rarely in front of them for the *wrong* reasons. I stay out of the drama and the scandals and I'm one of the few child actors that hasn't spent a night in the drunk tank. I'm considered unproblematic, genuine, kind, and according to the last issue of *People Magazine*, one of America's Sweethearts.

Unease washes over me and a sinking feeling in the pit of my stomach tells me that my days of not being associated with drama are over. I want nothing more than to run. Run away from the room where I had a front-row seat to my worst nightmare and from the man that starred in it.

My man.

But running from this room like it's on fire will raise questions and the last thing I want is to answer them for the paparazzi before I have a chance to answer them for myself.

"SHAY!" His voice booms after me and I try to ignore him just as I notice the movement of a group of girls pulling out their phones and holding them up towards us. I was the star of a hit television show in a relationship with Hollywood's newest "IT" actor who was predicted to take home the Oscar for Best Actor in just a few months. So, it's rare for the cameras not to be on us which is why I'm very confused as to why he put himself in a situation to literally get caught with his pants down. Even if he hadn't been caught by me, which I know he wasn't expecting given that this trip was a fucking surprise after weeks we'd spent apart, it was stupid for him to assume that he'd get away with fucking his co-star in the back room of a club without anyone finding out.

His hand grabs my elbow and I pull out of his grasp as gracefully as I can, wanting nothing more than to scream at him for what I just walked in on, but I can't do that.

"This is not the place to do this, Pax," I tell him through narrowed slits while also trying my best to appear unphased. He knows my looks, so he should be able to read the one I'm giving him that says *don't fucking push me* but might be unreadable from a stray picture taken by anyone at the club. His brown eyes are worried and it irritates me more than I care to admit that he keeps darting his eyes around the room to see who is paying attention to our interaction.

Don't cause a scene.

Right now, it probably just looks like we're in a lovers' quarrel.

"Trouble in Paradise?" the headlines will read.

But responding the way I want to will cause a domino effect that I'm not prepared for without talking to my PR team and getting a plan in place first.

My job doesn't allow me the luxury of acting based on emotions. Everything has to be practical. Pragmatic. Calculated.

I fucking hate it sometimes.

I'll take the media outlets reporting that it's just an argument versus headlines exposing his affair though. The ones that would speculate that I knew he was fucking other women despite our committed three-year relationship or even that I engaged in it.

No. Fuck all that.

I refuse to look weak.

For now, I have to keep things cute.

"Baby…" he starts, running a hand through his dirty blonde hair that he'd highlighted for this most recent part—*that I'll admit I do not particularly love.*

"No." I shake my head at him. "How could you?" I feel the tears building and I refuse to let them fall here. Not now. My eyes dart behind him and I pray the woman I found him with, his whore of a co-star—*who's a really shitty actress for what it's worth*—doesn't emerge. That would just alert everyone in the bar that Shay Eastwood just caught her boyfriend of three years cheating on her.

I turn my head, searching for Damian, and just like always, I don't have to search far before our eyes lock from across the room. Even with the low lighting, I can see his face transform from impassive to something dark and almost angry and then he's a man on a mission, tearing through the crowd towards me. His long legs eat at the space between us and just as Paxton goes to touch me again, Damian is at my side towering over us both. "Everything okay, here?" His voice is low and I detect a hint of anger in it probably brought on by his instincts that everything is definitely *not* okay.

"I'm ready to go." I glare at Paxton. "Alone."

"Baby, please just let me explain. Let me come with you. We can talk, *privately*." *What the fuck could he possibly explain? That I didn't just catch him fucking his co-star? That I'm seeing things?* He pulls at his suit jacket, probably trying to straighten how disheveled he still looks from having to get dressed so quickly to follow me out of the room.

Don't cause a scene.

Don't cause a scene.

Paxton doesn't wait for me to respond; he just looks at Damian in the way a man looks at another for their co-sign when they think a woman is being unreasonable. I can almost hear the, *you know how she can be…*in the two-second glance. "Can you give us a second?"

I go to respond when Damian beats me to it. "No. When she wants to talk to you, she will. Back off, Paxton." Damian turns his back to him, putting himself between me and my soon-to-be ex-boyfriend, and ushers me out. Like every other time, he doesn't touch me, but I can feel his hand hovering at the small of my back.

"What the fuck? Shay!" I hear Paxton call after me but I keep walking towards the entrance of the club and I'm grateful there's a long-enclosed hallway before we get outside granting me a second of peace before I have to face the paparazzi.

I'm even more relieved that Paxton didn't follow me.

I stop walking when I hear the door close behind me, leaving Damian and me alone in the long corridor. He's a few steps ahead of me and I don't know when he realizes I've stopped walking but moments later, I see his black Tom Ford loafers that I'd gotten him for Christmas—I practically had to beg him to keep them. *Something about them not being practical.*

I'm staring at the ground, the adrenaline slowing down and the reality of what the fuck just happened settling in, when I hear his voice, smooth and even as it washes over me like the warm shower after getting caught in a freezing rainstorm. "Shay, look at me." My gaze darts up to his obediently and his blue eyes, that were previously cold and angry, are soft. "You cannot cry right now." I blink away the unshed tears that are pooling in my eyes and nod in preparation to wade through a sea of flashes that will scrutinize every facial expression I make while I walk to the car. "You have a few seconds before we're out there and you're in front of the cameras and the paparazzi are going to have questions especially if you're leaving alone when they know Paxton is here. Don't let them see you cry. You can cry once we get in the car." He leans down so that we're at eye level. "Don't give them that."

Chapter ONE

Shay

Five Years Ago

"I DON'T UNDERSTAND. I ALREADY HAVE SECURITY," I tell my father, pushing my sunglasses to the top of my head as he, my mother, and my manager are now blocking me from the sun where I'm sunbathing beside the pool at my parents' house.

My father stares down at me with a look I haven't been on the receiving side of many times and I blanch under his narrowed gaze. Tall and slender but with a muscular build after years of college sports and a few years of playing semi-professional basketball, my father is now a lawyer at one of the top entertainment firms in the state. "That you ditch constantly to get into trouble with Veronica. They are both way too easygoing for our taste. You need someone that isn't so easily manipulated."

Veronica chirps from the other side of me. "Hey, what did I do!?" She peeks up over the latest issue of *Vogue* and lowers her sunglasses to the bridge of her nose before pushing them back into her cornsilk blonde hair. "I hardly call going to the mall, brunch at the Grove, and going to the occasional bar getting into trouble. Come on Mr. E."

"You're not twenty-one!" my mother exclaims, crossing her hands across her chest. They're both tanned to a rich mocha and glowing from their recent trip to Mexico on what was probably their fourth honeymoon, a trip they had to cut early because of what happened last week.

I knew this was coming, just not this fast.

Veronica looks at my mom with a surprised expression. "So what, you think we'll get arrested?" The humor in her voice is evident and despite the irritation that was previously flowing off my father, he chuckles.

"Not. The. Point." She points between us before smacking my father's arm. "Do not encourage her." She turns back to Veronica. "Your parents put us in charge while you're out here and I do believe you promised them that you'd behave."

Veronica's parents live in Chicago with her younger siblings and a medical practice her father isn't prepared to leave until he retired, so when she signed on for the spin-off to the television show we'd been on for five years, she moved out here permanently to live with me. We'd been best friends for years, about as long as our characters had been, making us more like sisters.

"Look, I'm not going to get on you about going out. I've gotten you this far without any scandals and bullshit. You're eighteen now and I can't make you stay out of trouble," my father starts. "If you want to tarnish the reputation that you've built to become the clichéd child star turned party girl, by all means." He waves his hand and I roll my eyes at the reverse psychology. "But being eighteen means you have different eyes on you now, and after what happened last week, I'm not taking any chances."

I'll be honest; the situation last week did shake me up a little. I was used to the paparazzi. I was used to fans. Fans that told me they loved me, fans that wanted to be my best friend, fans that wanted me to sign things for their daughters and nieces and granddaughters.

Boys *my age* that would tell me they loved me or slide in my Instagram DMs asking me to go to their proms with them.

What I was *not* used to was grown men that were fans. Grown men that were now *legally* able to engage with me.

I was out shopping one day, admittedly alone because I had ditched my security. I was just at the mall, and was rather incognito when I was approached and then followed around for most of the day by this guy that may or may not have been trying to lure me into a windowless van. I texted one of my guy friends from the show a very panicked SOS and when he showed up with three of his friends in tow, it led to a swarm of paparazzi because *"An 'LA Days and Ways' reunion!"* It also led to a rumor that we were dating that lasted for two news cycles.

My parents eventually caught wind of what happened when I had to explain to them that Bryan Whitlock—*Hollywood's bad boy and not in a good way*—and I were not dating and why I called him in the first place. This opened the floodgates of the "fan mail" they'd evidently been keeping from me. And by fan mail, I mean pornographic letters of what men and some women wanted to do to me.

Sometimes *while I resisted*.

"You're meeting him tomorrow morning, so be in my office at eleven," my manager, Cooper Jennings, from the time I was just doing Pampers commercials, speaks up. Cooper has always been on my side and takes my feelings into consideration more so than my parents do sometimes. He'd backed me up in arguments when I didn't want to go for certain auditions and even convinced my parents that getting highlights and a nose ring wouldn't be the worst idea. *Sure, the nose ring lasted about five minutes but principle.*

"Wait, you've already chosen him!?" I sit up completely and my eyes widen, shooting to Cooper who I always thought reminded me of a young George Clooney without the mullet. "Really?!"

"We've been holding interviews all week." My father gives me a look that says, *do you have a problem with that?*

"Shouldn't I have been allowed to sit in? Ever heard of a screen test? What if we don't get along?!" I screech thinking about some of the friends I have who can't stand their bodyguards. The ones that treat them like their prisoners and don't even allow them to go to the bathroom alone. The ones that sit one table over from us at brunch making it impossible to talk about anything personal. The ones that report on every single move they make to their parents and agents.

"You will get along great with him. He's very nice." My mother speaks up as she tucks a strand of her new sleek bob haircut behind her ear. "And he comes highly recommended!"

"By who?"

"A guy from work," my father says. "He was on the security team for one of our top clients."

"Why isn't he anymore?" I ask, immediately conjuring a story in my head that he was fired for something scandalous.

"How should I know? The guy's an asshole, so maybe Damian got sick of his shit. Who knows?"

You do. I think.

I go to respond when my father points at me. "You're asking a lot of questions. Tomorrow, at eleven. Do not be late."

I'm not late, but I'm also not early, which earns me a look from Cooper as I stroll into his office at the stroke of eleven with a vanilla latte in my hand, somewhat surprised my new security isn't waiting in his office.

"So, where is he? I have a meeting with my trainer at one." I drop to the chair in front of his desk, crossing one leg over the other, and push my sunglasses to the top of my head.

His office is huge, twice the size of the office he'd started in all those years ago when I was just a toddler running around with pigtails and overalls and Converse sneakers. I smile, thinking about how far he's come. *How far we've come together.* "Janine took him on a tour of the floor, he should be back shortly," he tells me referring to his assistant. He eyes me from behind his desk and sends a hand through his chocolate brown hair that is graying at the temples—*thanks to me because he only has two sons and they don't give him half as much stress.* "Listen, I know you're not thrilled about this, but we just want to keep you safe. Your mother is a bit shook up about all of this. So is your dad." He swallows and lets out a sigh. "So am I." He leans forward. "For what it's worth, I would be really sad if something happened to you." He blinks a few times before turning to his computer. "And not just because you're my biggest client." I roll my eyes and his green irises find mine. "I'm serious Shay."

I wave a hand dismissively. "I know, I know, I'm the daughter you never had blah blah blah."

"Never *wanted*, but that's neither here nor there." He gives me a side smile just as a knock sounds on the door.

"Ah, this must be Damian." He stands and adjusts his suit jacket just as the door opens behind me, and when I turn around all of the air leaves my lungs and I can feel my heart hammering in my chest as I take in what is possibly the best-looking man I've ever seen in real life.

And I have seen a LOT of good-looking men in real life.

Dressed in a black suit without a tie making him look like he just stepped of the runway, Damian has to be somewhere over six feet because I'm five seven and I can tell he will tower over me once he gets closer. He has dark hair, cut short, blue eyes, and a square jaw hidden by a light dusting of stubble. My eyes trail down his form quickly. Broad shoulders. A trim waist. Muscles I make out under the suit. A hint of a tattoo peeking out from under his suit sleeve on his hand.

Holy fuck.

"Hello." I finally speak, and I'm not sure how much time has passed but Cooper doesn't miss a beat so maybe I wasn't ogling him as openly as I thought.

"Shay, this is Damian Hunt." He nods towards him and then back to me. "Not that she needs any introduction, but Shay Eastwood." He points towards me before moving back to his desk and my cheeks heat.

Damian holds out his hand and I slide mine into his, shaking it slowly. His handshake is firm and when I look down, his fingers completely envelop mine making me feel small and feminine next to this big, muscular man. He has this air of ruggedness while still being very clean-cut, and a vision of him lifting me into his arms and pushing me against a wall as my legs wrap around him flashes through my brain.

"It's nice to meet you, Miss." His voice is smooth, rich, deep, and sexy as hell.

Fuck.

I absolutely cannot have a crush on my new bodyguard.

"You too," I squeak, yes actually fucking squeak, and I clear my dry throat not knowing what else to say.

I'd been given his file last night, to learn a little bit more about his background, so I don't know what to ask him that I don't already know at this moment. Thirty years old. An undergraduate degree in computer engineering. A tour overseas with the Army, followed by security once he retired. A black belt in karate and a whole laundry list of fighting techniques, not to mention a self-defense teacher and still a trainer for the military when needed.

No one is getting by him and the thought makes my toes curl in my shoes.

"So, with this being a trial period, I was thinking he'd accompany you for the rest of the day and all week and we'll see how it goes."

I realize that Cooper has been talking this whole time and I turn around to face him. "What?"

"You're not on set this week, so we thought this was the perfect time for you guys to get to know each other a little." We were on a recess for the spring, and we wouldn't be back to filming for another two weeks which means I have more free time than usual. Veronica, some of our cast mates, and I were even toying with the idea of a trip to Vegas this weekend.

"Okay, sure." I turn my gaze towards him. "I...have to meet with my trainer and then I'm meeting some of my friends for lunch and maybe some shopping." I wince, suddenly feeling juvenile and immature to this worldly man that has spent the last ten years being noble and heroic.

He nods and pins me with a glare that both annoys me and turns me on a little. I raise an eyebrow in question, wondering why he's looking at me like that when he speaks. "I would advise that you don't try and give me the slip, Miss Eastwood. If I can't trust you, you'll have to switch to shopping online or having brunch at your house. You're also not twenty-one, I would advise you not to try to order a drink."

Okay scratch being turned on, now I'm just annoyed.

My mouth drops open and I turn towards Cooper who is fighting a grin as he types away on his computer avoiding my eyes completely. "Oh, you can go now."

"Cooper." I glare. My back is to Damian, so he can't see the look of rage I am giving him.

"Bye, Shay!" He salutes, effectively dismissing us.

Chapter TWO

Shay

Present Day

I'D BARELY TOUCHED DOWN IN LA FROM MY VERY QUICK TRIP to Canada when it was decided that I had to go straight to Cooper's office, despite it being five in the morning.

I didn't want to go; I wanted to sleep for the next week. Crawl into a hole and disappear until I need to be back on set in a few weeks to begin the final season. I could feel the tension in my shoulders and spine. My head and back ached. My heart ached. The last thing I wanted to do was go to my manager's office with my entire public relations team to do *damage control*.

After hours of going back and forth on how we were going to "spin this" for appearances, we are finally pulling into the gated community where I live in Beverly Hills and the exhaustion from being on the go for almost twenty-four hours, including a flight to another country, is hitting me hard. Coupled with the feelings of annoyance over where things are forced to stand between me and Paxton, makes me feel like the walls are closing in. We make it through my private gate and up the driveway and my eyes flit to Emmett, my gardener, trimming the hedges that line the driveway and I give him a wave through my window. When my door opens, Damian, who's been quiet ever since we left Cooper's office, stands next to it just as he always does.

For the first few months that he was the head of my security, he wouldn't even let me into my own house when I returned from being out without doing a thorough sweep of the property to make sure I wasn't in danger. But after he had a top of the line security system installed that he could access twenty-four-seven through his phone and a gate you needed a perfectly clean background check and fingerprints to get through if you weren't already on my carefully approved list, he backed off.

I slide out of the limo, push my sunglasses to the top of my head, and narrow my eyes at him.

"Why are you being so quiet?"

He's still wearing his sunglasses so I can't see his eyes. I'm not surprised he doesn't take them off, though I know he's looking at me.

"What would you like me to say?" he asks before turning and walking away. "I assume you're not going anywhere right now?"

I fall into step with him and he enters the code to my front door. I leave the door open so the driver can bring my bags in, but I follow Damian towards the kitchen which is located in the back part of my house. "No. I don't have any plans to go anywhere."

We walk into my state of the art all white kitchen, and he stops, placing his hands on the island in the middle of the room, and lets out a sigh.

"So, you're staying with him?"

"I am not staying with him," I scoff. *Though I kind of am, I suppose.* He removes his sunglasses and shoots me a look that says he's not buying whatever I'm selling, giving me that one arched eyebrow that is both sexy and annoying. "It's not that simple, Damian."

"Isn't it?" A scowl finds my lips and I think he regrets his choice of words because his eyes soften slightly. "He's cheating on you, Shay."

"I know that Damian. I saw it with my own two eyes, remember?"

He nods before turning to face me head on and I see the sincerity in his eyes but I can still sense his irritation. "You deserve better than that, you know."

My heart squeezes in my chest hearing his words, knowing that he's right, and also that maybe *he* wants better for me. "I know, but my PR team is not advising me to stay with him forever."

"Let me guess, just through award seasons?"

I hate how transparent this all seems and how obvious it is as to why I would stay with him. "It's not just about that. Being with Paxton has opened a lot of doors for me professionally and to their point, I don't want to risk blowing up a relationship that might be directly connected to me landing a role in a movie or my next potential project." *My father did always say it isn't what you know it's who you know,* and as of late, Paxton knows a lot of people.

Right now, it seems that my team is on the same page that he owes me.

"You don't need him, Shay. You're very talented. People are beating down your door to work with you. You're up for an Emmy this season. Your career is at an all-time high." I push away the smile that is pulling at my lips after hearing what I believe to be his version of praise. *He thinks I'm talented?*

I stop myself from going down the rabbit hole of what his words mean and remember why he felt the need to say them. "For television, sure," I argue, "but there's a whole different world that I have yet to break into and with *LA Dreams* going into its final season, I want to keep my options open. I haven't decided what's next and the idea of movies does seem like the logical next step. I've been doing television since I was thirteen and I'm twenty-three. I just want to see what else is out there. I've been playing the same character for ten years across two different television shows and there's a lot of pressure and speculation and excitement surrounding what my next project will be."

My parents always wanted me to have a well-rounded portfolio. They always said when *LA Dreams* ended, *pending it ended on the studio's terms and not for getting canceled,* movies would be the next natural step. They didn't want me to risk getting typecast into the role I had been playing for years: the popular, quirky, loveable, and very outgoing girl that everyone had come to love. A flicker of pain moves through me that this is the first major decision I'll be making without them.

"So, you're using him?"

I blink rapidly recalling the very same question I asked my PR team when they laid out this plan. "They want me to use the situation to my advantage," I say repeating back the very words they had said to me. Damian rarely has much to say about my career unless it directly affects my safety. There were times he'd advised against appearances or parties, of course, but that was the extent of it so for him to have this much to say is out of the norm. He doesn't reply. "Are you judging me?"

He shakes his head. "No. That's not my job." He lets out a sigh. "I just don't know who you have looking out for your personal interests and I wouldn't want you getting forced into something you don't want. Maybe this is the right thing for your career, but is this the right thing for *you*?"

I let his words wash over me as I move towards my refrigerator to pull out a bottle of San Pellegrino. I'm grateful my assistant went shopping while I was on my five-minute trip to Canada because there was hardly anything but takeout in here when I left. I grab a container of strawberries and pull them out.

"I don't know," I tell him honestly. "Do you think this is a bad idea?" Damian is smart and perceptive and can see things most people can't. *Obviously, with his line of work.* He can see a million different ways something could play out within a second.

"I don't think he should get away with what he did or what he's doing."

"He's not getting *away* with anything. We aren't together. We were never a couple that engaged in a ton of public displays of affection and he's in Canada so it's not as if we would be spotted out socially anyway for the next few weeks. There are a few events we're scheduled to appear at together over the next few months and then *my* PR team will re-evaluate with *his* PR team over what comes next. I don't even need to talk to him except while we're in public."

I don't respond and he doesn't say anything else. He just stares at me, his blue eyes are emotionless and hard and I frown at the way he's looking at me.

"Don't look at me like that," I whisper before turning around to grab a glass from my cabinet. I'm preparing to hop on the counter to grab it when I sense his presence, and when I turn around, he's standing behind me. He grabs the glass that was just barely out of my reach and pours the sparkling water into the glass for me. I narrow my gaze at him. *That's…new.* I was used to him doing things for me but not usually things I could easily do for myself and rarely while I was home.

"I don't like it," he says, breaking me from my thoughts. He slides the glass to his right for me to grab. "I like order and organization and I think this has the potential to bring chaos and a lot of drama to your life and I work very hard to avoid that for you. This is going to make my job harder, you know."

"I do." I hop up on my counter so I can be closer to his eye level and take a sip of the water. "Don't be mad at me. How about a raise?" I give him my best cheesy smile and slide a hand under my chin.

He shoots me a glare. "I'm not mad at you and you know it's not about the money. I worry about you, okay?" His eyes dart to mine from where he was staring into space. "Someone has to." His nostrils flare angrily and I can hear the implication. My parents would be livid over Paxton cheating on me.

They went to war over me for much less. Shitty directors, rude co-stars, and news outlets they felt didn't treat me with the respect they thought I deserved—my parents were there to let anyone and everyone know what wouldn't be tolerated.

So, a potential cheating scandal and a man who broke my heart? They'd be out for his blood.

And his reputation.

And probably monetary compensation for emotional damages—my dad was a great lawyer.

His words slither down my spine and I hate the way it makes me feel. *Almost like they'd be disappointed.* He doesn't wait for me to respond before he's moving out of the room and towards the front door without another word. Damian stays in the guesthouse that sits just to the left of my house. There have been times he's stayed in the main house, but for the most part, he has his own space. The door slams behind him just as I meet the familiar hazel eyes of my best friend, Veronica Walters.

"What's his problem? He almost ran me over coming in." She points behind her as she pulls her sunglasses off and tosses them in her bag before moving around the island and pulling me off the counter into her arms. "Hiiii." She envelops me in a hug, squeezing me hard. I texted Veronica everything that happened from the plane and I had to beg her not to call Paxton and cuss him out. *I am still not one hundred percent sure she listened.*

"He has some thoughts over the fact that publicly I'm not breaking up with Paxton yet."

She lets me go and leans against the island. "Probably because he's in love with you."

I shoot her a look, tired of that same narrative she's been spewing for years. "He is not."

"Have you seen the way he looks at you?"

He's my bodyguard, of course he's got his eyes on me all the time. "Like he'd take a bullet for me?"

"Exactly!" she squeals.

"That's his job."

"That's not how he looks at you."

I roll my eyes and my lips form a straight line. "What?"

She puts her hands under her chin and beams from ear to ear flashing me her hundred-watt smile that has scored her countless toothpaste commercials and print ads. "He looks at you like you're his reason for breathing and *that's* why he'd take a bullet for you not because of what you pay him."

"V, he is not in love with me."

"I don't know why you're fighting my theory so hard like you haven't been horny for him since the first time he looked you dead in your eyes and told you *no.*"

I wince remembering that night and embarrassment flares through my body in memory.

"First of all," I hold a finger up, "it was before that," I joke, "and secondly, it was a harmless crush when I was eighteen. Can you give it up? Besides, don't you remember what happened the one time I tried it?" Before I'd met Paxton, I'd tried to channel my inner Whitney Houston from The Bodyguard—*yes, I realize how cliché that sounds*, and let him know that I was interested by not so subtly asking him out. He was definitely not having it and we definitely did not end up in bed together.

I would say that movie gave me unrealistic expectations, but I know quite a few people that have fucked their bodyguards.

Unfortunately, I am not one of them.

"Because he knows that being with you in that way would get in the way of protecting you! Hello? Besides you had the whole dead parents thing going on for a while and he's all you had and kind of took on a parental role." She bounces up and down on the balls of her feet excitedly. "It's actually quite romantic."

I blink at her several times. While she's the only person who can get away with using humor to talk about my parents' deaths *because it's the way I cope with it*, I'm a little irritated that she's making it a part of this theory that Damian has feelings for me. "You're actually *quite* annoying." She shrugs and moves around me to open my refrigerator and goes straight for the bottle of rosé in the door. She grabs two wine glasses and I put a hand up to stop her from pouring me a glass. "I'm jetlagged and exhausted and haven't eaten much. I am not getting wine drunk with you right now." I shake my head knowing that one glass of wine with Veronica could quickly turn into two bottles.

"You just found out your boyfriend is cheating on you and you don't think getting wine drunk is the answer?" She points at me before snapping like she'd just gotten another idea I'm sure I'll like even less than wine. "You know what? You're right. Tequila is the answer. I'll rally the troops for tonight. Imagine how he'll feel seeing you out in the streets without a care in the world. Maybe we should stage a run-in with someone. I'll see what everyone is doing tonight."

"V..."

"Shay." She shoots me a look. "You wouldn't have told me if you didn't want this."

She's right that I had expected this, but I tell Veronica everything, and keeping this from her wouldn't have lasted a day because we can read each other easily. "I told you because you're my best friend."

She doesn't say anything for a moment, and I hope that means she's getting over the idea of going out tonight for me to drink my sorrows.

She pulls out her phone and begins scrolling. "That girl is hideous by the way."

"No, she's not." I sigh. "A terrible actress, yes, and the only reason she got that part allegedly is because she fucked the executive producer, but you know what? That's hearsay so who knows if it's even true? Maybe she got it because she was fucking Paxton." The back of my head prickles forcing tears back into my eyes and I do my best to blink them away. "But she *is* pretty and it's pissing me off." Sparkling green eyes and tanned skin and gorgeous long wavy dark hair. I spend hours and thousands of dollars to get my hair to do what hers does naturally. *It's fucking irritating.* And now she's had my man inside of her.

I flex my fists picturing taking a swing at her *and him* once. I'm not violent and my parents are probably turning over in their graves at the thought of me hitting anyone, but I was *furious*.

"You looked good when you left. Not a ton of questions as to why you left early. Of course, some, but nothing with any substantial proof. It seems Paxton left shortly after you did and he was alone. Do you want to see?" She holds out her phone and I see him emerging from the club in the Valentino suit I'd picked out.

Was he thinking of me when he pulled off the clothes I'd bought him? Did he look down at his wrist and see my initials he'd had tattooed on him when he'd wrapped his hand in her hair? Was he reminded of me and just didn't care?

Did he ever care?

"No." In this moment, I care less about what everyone thought and how anything is being perceived and more about how badly it hurts and how I'm ever going to get through this. How, in two weeks, I'm supposed to begin the press tour for the final season of the dramedy that made me famous. A show that might get me my first Emmy nomination after this past season. *How am I supposed to play someone who's generally happy when I feel like there's a hole in my chest?* Paxton and I had several upcoming appearances and parties we were supposed to attend together, and when you're in the limelight it isn't as simple as "not showing up."

Not showing up to commitments makes a woman look difficult, undependable, and overall, *a diva*. In this situation, it could look like I've let personal problems affect my job or my responsibilities. As a black woman, the speculation could potentially be even harsher depending on the news outlet.

"Did you actually walk in and catch them?"

"Yes, and I see it every time I close my eyes."

She scrunches her nose in disgust and shakes her head. "I am shocked. Shit, Shay, I'm so sorry. I thought…" She trails off.

"I know, I thought it too." I thought we were moving towards more. I'm twenty-three now but we started dating when I was twenty, and in Hollywood, a three-year relationship with no drama or scandals is a lifetime.

Every other day, news outlets questioned if we were engaged or if I was pregnant. They were always camped outside of my house or his to see where we'd stayed the night before when we were both in town. I was constantly on baby watch and there were always pictures zoomed in on my left hand in search of an engagement ring.

Not that we'd really discussed marriage…but again, perception.

And the perception is that we are this gorgeous, successful, talented power couple that is very much in love and very happy.

Ugh.

The worst part about all of this is I thought the same.

"I still think we should go out tonight," Veronica says interrupting my thoughts. "A night out with your best friend who is also friends with a lot of guys from a very popular LA basketball team! And a baseball team…and hockey."

I chuckle in response. "Let me take a nap and see how I feel."

"Nap by the pool." She motions towards my backyard at my gorgeous pool.

"Is that your way of saying you're staying over tonight?"

"Obviously!" She pads down the hall towards my staircase.

My house has ten bedrooms, one of which is Veronica's whenever she stays over.

When I make it to the foyer, I see my house manager, Annette has moved my suitcases, and when I make it to my room, I see the open empty suitcase on my bed indicating that all of my clothes have been put away.

My bedroom is one of my favorite places in the world. It's located at the back of the house overlooking my terrace and my pool as well as my large backyard that sits in front of a small forest of trees. There's a gate that goes around the back to keep people out, but my backyard is the length of at least two football fields. I have a huge bay window and bench built in for me to sit and read or just stare out the window and think about everything *or nothing*. I have two bookshelves built into the wall that are separated by a fireplace set between them that I love reading in front of but my bed is the best part. A king set a bit off the ground that sometimes I needed to run and jump to get on to especially if I've had a few drinks.

I know Veronica wants to relax by the pool, but I want my soft, satin sheets and my blackout curtains. I want to shut out the world and forget this whole shitty day ever happened.

I begin pulling off my clothes to take a shower to wash the travel off of me when anger begins to spike in my veins. *How the fuck could he do this to me? Paxton pursued me. For months!* Showing up to set under the ruse that he was coming to see some of the guys he was friends with, sending flowers *constantly*, liking and commenting on my social media posts. He'd even done an interview where they'd asked about his love life and he'd explicitly said he was holding out for me.

Looked straight at the camera and said, "Shay Eastwood, please go out with me."

I believed he'd staged more than one casual run-in so we could spend the night talking and getting to know each other better. It wasn't as if I wasn't interested. Paxton is gorgeous and charming and talented and a laundry list of other positive attributes.

We can take loyalty off that list.

I was just busy and we had such different schedules and I was just starting to feel like myself again after losing my parents so suddenly. I wasn't trying to throw something as unknown and unstable as a high-profile romance into the mix. So, I'd made him wait months for a date. Months for me to claim him publicly and probably a full year before I'd slept with him.

Now I'm questioning everything. *Was he doing this the whole time?* My fingers tingle with the urge to text him and ask him that very question. *No. Don't do it.*

He'd probably lie anyway.

Paxton had been blowing up my phone since I left Canada. Texts, emails, voicemails. My boxes were full of messages of him apologizing and trying to explain. Telling me he loved me. That she didn't mean anything. That it was just sex. It was just one time. *Yeah, okay.* That he was drunk. What a cliché.

By the time I get in the shower, I'm pissed. I scrub my skin almost raw as I argue with Paxton in my mind. Then I argue with Cooper. Then with my PR Team.

Then with Damian.

And I don't miss the way my nipples harden slightly when I think about his chiseled and hard jaw clenched as his blue eyes bore into mine. I bite my bottom lip trying my best to think of my opening line of our argument when I remember how he was in Canada. I'd been on the verge of breaking down when he'd said, *"You can't cry right now. Don't give them that."*

I don't think he has feelings for me, but I do think that he cares for me on a different level than other clients. I think when I lost my parents, he did step into a protective role that went beyond his job, and now the lines are a little blurry because this is my first-time experiencing heartbreak and betrayal and I think he wants to beat the shit out of Paxton for that.

Not because he had feelings for me but because like my parents, he didn't want to see anyone fucking with me.

That's all it is.

"You sure about that?" I hear his voice in my head and instantly my nipples harden again and goosebumps erupt on my flesh. It isn't unheard of that I get off on Damian's protectiveness, but I am a little surprised that I feel turned on amidst this mess with Paxton. It's something I've struggled with and I admit that I've felt a bit of shame for thinking of Damian when I touch myself while having a boyfriend, but I couldn't help it. Sometimes it was the only thing that got me off.

"God you're fucking beautiful, Shay. He's an idiot," I imagine him saying. *"Don't let that get to you. Let me touch you. I'll make it better. You know I can,"* he murmurs.

I moan thinking about him between my legs. His fingers. His tongue. His dick.

No, Shay.

Chapter THREE

Shay

Two Weeks Later

"RISE AND SHIIIIINE!" THE VOICE OF MY BEST FRIEND rouses me from sleep at god knows what hour because not only am I wearing a mask over my eyes, but I've been sleeping with my blackout curtains which I rarely do. I hate the feeling of not knowing what time it is when I wake up and only use them in desperate times like when I'm jet lagged or have been awake for a considerable amount of time.

Or when I'm sad.

I slide my silk sleep mask up over my eyes to rest on my forehead. I can barely make out Veronica's form as she moves through my room to one of my large floor to ceiling windows. She presses the button to open it, letting a considerable amount of light stream into the room.

"Go away," I grumble.

"I've allowed you to hole up in here for the past few days, but you're done." She marches over to the side of the bed and puts an iced coffee on my nightstand and motions towards it. "I ordered us breakfast and if you're feeling up to it, I made mimosas. I would love to get you out of the house, but I would settle for getting you out of this room." She's dressed casually in high-waisted, holey, wide-leg jeans and a tank top sporting a tan that I'm fairly certain she didn't have the last time I saw her.

In true best friend fashion, she'd spent the first week staying with me. Ordering takeout and binge watching television shows, namely *Sex and the City* to commiserate over all their terrible boyfriends. I'd let her force me into working out two of the days after I spent one day consuming nothing but cinnamon ice cream from my favorite local shop. I'd also made a visit to my physician to be tested for anything that Paxton could have potentially given me over this past year. Thankfully, I'm not leaving this relationship with any unwanted parting gifts.

Paxton is still in Canada, but he's been calling non-stop and has sent hundreds of flowers since I left, and while the press circuit is quiet, there's still some speculation about why I left Canada so hastily. Some theories are true, some have parts of the truth, and some were way off base, but most of them surmised that Paxton and I were on rocky terms, especially since I haven't been spotted out anywhere.

I'm not a party girl, but I am someone that usually makes appearances at social events and I haven't been anywhere. I sit up, reaching for the coffee, knowing that after sleeping for what felt like the past twenty hours, I probably need some caffeine.

"How are you feeling?" Veronica asks as she sits on my bed in front of me.

I'm not sure how I feel. I've experienced loss on such a visceral level this almost feels inconsequential. Paxton is still alive, he just isn't going to be my boyfriend anymore. Once you go through the worst thing you can go through, it makes everything else seem not as bad. Right?

Should I be more upset?

I haven't cried yet, surprisingly. I'm too angry, too humiliated, and just too much in shock. Those feelings haven't reached my tear ducts yet and so I haven't shed a tear, but I know the second I let that first one trickle down my face, I won't know how to stop.

I've been with him for three years and I haven't cried yet; what does that mean?

"I think I'm still numb."

She nods. "He was still in Canada as of yesterday." Veronica has been my eyes and ears because I've been avoiding all social media including my burner accounts. "Spotted going to get groceries looking like a tool." She says with a look of disgust.

I get out of bed, stretching my legs with each step, and move into the bathroom with Veronica right on my heels.

"Do you want to go out tonight? The guys have all been trying to get together." I shoot her a look and she shakes her head. "I haven't told them anything. It might be good to get out though." I begin brushing my teeth as she continues. "We don't have to do anything crazy. Maybe just to *Rush?*" she says mentioning one of the more lowkey clubs we frequent. "We start the press tour next week, so it's the last bit of time we all have together before we go back."

I spit and stare at her through the mirror. "Sure, but lowkey, V. Just the guys."

Me: Veronica and I are going out in a little while.

I stare down at my phone knowing that I'm about to be hit with a mass of questions in response to my vague text message and sure enough, the bubbles appear instantly.

Damian: Where exactly and what time?

A smirk pulls at my lips knowing he's probably a little irritated with me because he hates when I'm vague with details. I go to respond when Veronica comes into my room carrying two glasses filled with a clear liquid and cut-up strawberries swirling amongst the ice that I assume to be something with vodka. Her makeup bag that she never leaves the house without sits under her other arm while her hairbrush is held between her teeth. She's still in a white silky bathrobe but her hair is blow-dried and pin-straight hanging down her back.

She hands me the drink and I take a sip before shooting Veronica a look over the rim of the glass that is filled with more vodka than tonic. She winks at me before she speaks, not even addressing the strength of the drinks she made. "How dressy are we thinking tonight? I brought all kinds of outfits. Also, should I curl my hair?"

"No leave it, you look hot." I turn back to my phone when I feel it vibrate in my hands.

Damian: Are you planning on meeting anyone?

Damian didn't love when Veronica and I went out with the entire main cast of the show. The six of us are like family and we tend to get a little more reckless when we're all out together. With it being the last week before we enter into our final season of taping, I'm sure he's predicting us to be in rare form when and if we're together.

Me: I think we are just going to Rush or any of our usual spots downtown. Maybe in an hour? Probably just Jeremy and Derek.

I rattle off the answers to his questions and I'm already preparing for more when my phone begins to ring in my hand. I swipe my finger across the screen, and before I can even say hello, he speaks. "Think, maybe, and probably," he repeats. "Do you have any definitive plans? Are you sure you even want to go out?" It's a question, but the bite in his tone makes it sound more like, "*Why would you want to go out?*"

"Yes, I need to get out."

"Are you sure about that?" I can tell he wants to say more but he doesn't and I've now caught Veronica's attention as she emerges from my closet holding up my brand new Jimmy Choo boots that I haven't even worn yet. I shake my head and mouth NO at her and she rolls her eyes and stomps her foot before retreating into my closet.

"Tell Damian to RELAX!" she yells.

"Did you hear that?" I ask him, knowing that Veronica's voice carries and that he more than likely did.

"Tell Veronica that I will certainly not relax and that Max is sick of her shit." I chuckle over the fact that Damian has developed a sort of friendship with Veronica's security because of how often we're together, and I do believe that her bodyguard, Max, is probably sick of her shit.

"Damian, I'm fine."

"Are you? I don't think this is a good idea." *And?* I think to myself.

"Okay, well I don't recall taking a poll. I'll see you in an hour," I snap before hanging up the phone and tossing it over my shoulder. I should be able to go out with my friends without it being some huge inquisition, especially after the past two weeks I've had. *And even if I do get hammered and embarrass myself, so long as I'm safe, how is that his problem?*

"You sound pissed." I hear Veronica's voice from inside my closet.

I'm about to respond when a hard knock on the door startles me and my eyes snap to it knowing not many people would be knocking on my door like that. "What?!"

"Open the door." His voice is low and Veronica comes out of my closet wearing wide-leg leather pants and a strapless lace top both of which are mine, earning a look from me. She puts her hands together under her chin to say *please* and I roll my eyes before opening the door. "Did you hang up on me?" The first thing I notice, like always, are his eyes. Icy blue and narrowed with anger. His lips are pulled into a scowl and his arms are crossed over his chest. He'd changed out of his suit into black jeans and a black t-shirt that isn't particularly tight but still seems to highlight his very muscular forearms and his chest, the sexy sleeve of tattoos, and if he lowered his arms and I looked hard enough, I could make out his eight pack.

God, he looked good like this.

Despite my obvious ogling, I remember that I'm irritated. "You were being unreasonable, Damian. We are just going to *Rush*. Can you relax?" I put my hands up letting him know I'm not in the mood for a back and forth.

He cocks an eyebrow at me like he's surprised at my annoyance before he nods. "Fine. I'll see you both in an hour. Please text me where you're planning to start and a tentative plan for the rest of the night."

He turns around without another word and the anxiety builds in the pit of my stomach over his demeanor.

This wasn't the first time we didn't agree about me going out. We'd argued before, many times, but only over my safety. We'd yell, I'd stomp out of the room after he'd told me he was putting his foot down. There were times when I was younger, that I'd throw a tantrum and *sometimes* he'd give in. But I hated arguing with him. I knew he only wanted to keep me safe and I know sometimes I can be reckless. But this feels different. We're going to the same lounge we've been to a hundred times. A lounge, where we have our own booth in our own section away from everyone else. It's a super exclusive club, meaning there aren't usually a ton of fans and he won't be thwarting attempts of people getting too close. And while there are paparazzi, they're minimal and usually pretty respectful of our space.

At most, Veronica and I will take too many shots and I'll be ready to go by midnight. I'll fall asleep in the car on the way home and wake up just in time for the pizza to be delivered that I would have ordered before we left the club.

This is about the new revelation in my personal life. He's worried about me going out for the first time and drinking too much and having a meltdown over Paxton.

Fair.

But I'll be fine. I know how to keep it together. I knew how to turn on the charm for the cameras and smile and wave and pretend like everything is fine even when my insides are screaming in pain. I've been doing it for years.

Five to be exact.

When I'd almost shed a tear at the club, it was simply a moment of weakness. A kneejerk reaction to walking in on who I thought to be the love of my life fucking another woman. I've had time to get my emotions under control.

I'll be fine.

Veronica raises an eyebrow at me as she closes the door. "You guys have so much sexual tension, Shay, oh my god." She hops on my bed and leans back, crossing her ankles.

"No, we don't. He's like an overprotective brother who's a pain in my ass half of the time."

She raises her eyebrows up and down and reaches for the drink she'd set on my nightstand. "Like a hot stepbrother that wants to fuck you?"

My lips form a straight line, not wanting to go further down this line of questioning. "I'm going to do my makeup."

She follows me into my large bathroom and leans against the counter as I begin moisturizing my face. "You're telling me that there are no feelings there now?"

I swallow. I don't want to have this conversation with Veronica especially while I'm newly single and vulnerable and potentially consuming alcohol at a quick velocity tonight. I don't respond as I reach for my foundation, and she must take that to mean something because she pulls the makeup from my hand and looks at me. "Shay."

"What?"

"You know you can't lie to me."

"Oh my god, Veronica. I didn't have feelings for him. I had a harmless crush because he was hot and I was vulnerable and then he just...went above and beyond the call of duty during a really tough time in my life. I tried to act on said crush and..." I pause trying to figure out what I was thinking when I tried to hit on the man hired to protect me, "he wasn't having it. Then I met Paxton." I roll my eyes at the ease with which his name falls from my lips. "Case closed."

"Hmmm." She narrows her eyes at me and takes a sip of her drink. "I don't buy it but fiiine." She exaggerates the last word. "The guys are already on their way there and said they'll get our table."

I shoot her a look, knowing exactly who she means when she says "the guys." Two of the guys from the show, Jeremy and Derek and maybe one of the project assistants who became a part of our circle despite not actually being a cast member. "You talk about me. Are you going to invite Derek back here later?" I cock my head to the side as I refer to Veronica and Derek's on and off relationship.

"We decided that we aren't going to do *anything* until after the season and I guess the show for that matter is over. You remember season four."

"Ah yes, the season you two were literally at each other's throats so bad that they had to write an actual breakup in the show for the two of you because your chemistry fucking sucked?" I give her a smug grin. Like their real-life relationship, on the show, they were also on again and then off again, but that year they were *off* in their real-life relationship and it was a nightmare. They were miserable to be around and everyone fucking hated it. *Except for the fans. They lived for all the angst and drama and it made it one of the most talked about storylines that year.*

I finish my makeup and finally decide what to wear, landing on a black, low cut, and short tuxedo dress that makes my legs look a mile long in my favorite black pumps. *Not to mention my tits look great.* I'd curled my dark brown hair before pulling it up into a loose ponytail while allowing some strands to frame my face. I know I'll be photographed tonight and I want to ensure that any pictures that make it across Paxton's phone are drop-dead gorgeous.

"You look like sex on a stick." Veronica praises as she takes a long sip through her straw now that she has on cherry red lipstick. "Let's post something. I'm sure within five minutes, he'll have seen it."

"Okay fine, just one thing, and then I'm not posting anything else the rest of the night."

"Brilliant. He'll be stalking your page and probably mine too all night and it will be radio silence on our end." She claps before wrapping an arm around my neck and snapping a selfie. After a few pictures that she posts and a cute video of us clinking our glasses together in a cheers, we head downstairs and I see Damian in the foyer with his phone to his ear.

There are moments that I forget Damian is my security. I think in those same moments he forgets he's my security too. Those moments are usually when my legs are completely bare and out on display. I could be in full glam preparing for the red carpet wearing a six thousand dollar couture gown and I wouldn't get a second look. But if I'm going to the grocery store in a pair of shorts? His eyes will rake up my legs slowly until he meets my eyes and in that moment, he remembers himself. That his eyes aren't meant to look at me like that.

Though a part of me lives for those fucking looks.

He blinks away quickly just as he always does and I'm grateful that I can see Veronica staring down at her phone and therefore not a witness to our eyes locking for just the briefest second. That would only give support to her theory that there's a spark between us.

"I called Tony," he says referring to the head of security at the club. He speaks so coolly like he hadn't just set my skin on fire with his gaze. "There's a lot of paps by the entrance to *Rush*, so we're going to bring you in through the back, if that's okay? Unless you want the attention?" He asks and I'm somewhat surprised that I'm even given the option.

"That sounds good." I nod.

Veronica, who still hasn't looked up from her phone, chimes in, "I'm grabbing a spiked seltzer for the road, do you want one?"

"Please," I tell her as she walks towards my kitchen.

I'm grateful for the privacy because I want to talk to Damian about what happened upstairs. I don't want him to think I was mad or didn't appreciate his intentions.

He takes a step closer to me and lowers his voice. "I'm sorry for earlier," he says before I can speak. "I didn't mean to come off like an asshole or unreasonable. I'm just worried about you being thrust into the spotlight before you've really processed everything. But if you say you're good, I believe you."

My heart melts at his words even though I know he doesn't believe me. "So, you're adding 'therapist' to your list of duties now?" I joke and he gives me a smile that doesn't reach his eyes, almost as if he is trying to find humor in my words but can't. "I appreciate it." I smile and he nods just as Veronica returns with two cans of grapefruit-flavored spiked seltzer.

We head out of the house, Veronica's arm linked with mine as

Damian trails behind us, locking the door. Max, Veronica's security arrived not long ago and will trail in the car behind us. We opted to go more lowkey and didn't request a limousine for the night. Instead, we decided to take a Range Rover since it would only be Veronica and me. Damian will sit in the front, of course, while Veronica and I sit in the back.

The ride to Rush is quicker than usual despite LA traffic and we are there within about twenty minutes and just as the manager, Tony, had told Damian, the entrance is crawling with paparazzi. We circle the block before going down the back alley towards the employee exit that is very much covered so that if anyone happens to be back there, they wouldn't see who is going into the club. It's one of the reasons so many people like coming here when they want to be incognito.

Before long, we're inside and heading towards our table, nodding and waving as I pass by friends and acquaintances.

"About time you got here," Derek says, immediately sliding a hand around Veronica when we slide into the booth and pressing a kiss to her cheek. I roll my eyes because *I know how this is going to end*. I can already see it in her eyes, and the second he flashes her his hundred-watt smile complete with those dimples she'll be in the bathroom gagging on his cock.

She slides his arm from around her. "Miss me?" She grabs a glass of champagne from the center of the table.

"Obviously." He smiles, just as Jeremy, who must have been at the bar, comes around and slides next to me in the U-shaped booth. Jeremy, who happens to play my love interest on the show, is probably one of the best friends I have other than Veronica. Maybe because we had to become very comfortable with each other very quickly, given that our romance begins after a one-night-stand on my first night in the city in the first episode of season one. It's been six seasons and a lot of love scenes and we are slated to get married in the series finale according to the vague outline of the season I received last week.

Although we have chemistry on the show and spend about twenty hours a week making out, there's actually nothing between us. He's ten years older than me and when he started the show, he was engaged to someone else whom he truly loved and was kind of fucked up for a while when things didn't work out. By that point, he and I had established such a strong friendship that neither of us ever wanted to ruin that. We truly are like brother and sister.

Of course, there was always some buzz around us. Fans love us on the show and shipped us as a couple relentlessly much to Paxton's annoyance. There was a night that Jeremy had a party at his house and I ended up staying over that led to weeks and weeks of people speculating that we were in a secret relationship. *It didn't matter that half of the LA Dreams cast stayed over. Nope, it was just the fact that I was there.*

"Thank god, you guys showed up. Derek is being a whole pain in my ass," he says grabbing his beer and pulling it to his lips as I grab a glass of champagne.

"Because he wants V's ass?" I joke loud enough for them to hear and Jeremy nods in agreement.

Veronica flashes me her middle finger just as Derek raises an eyebrow and cocks it at her. "We had a whole conversation about this. No, Derek."

"Whatever." He rolls his brown eyes and narrows them before pointing at me. "By the way, why have you been so MIA and what happened in Canada with Pax? I saw you were there for all of five seconds." While Derek is obviously closer to me due to all the time we spend together, he is friendly with Paxton. I had told them all I was going to be in Canada for a few weeks when Derek had brought up going to Napa Valley for one last weekend before shooting started.

Veronica flashes a look at me and I prepare the lie to fall from my lips. I will probably end up telling Jeremy but Derek talks way too fucking much especially when he's drunk. He never knows what's appropriate to share in mixed company and I don't want him blabbing all of my business to everyone in our circle.

"It's a long story," I say, waving him off. "We had an argument while I was there and I left. I have so much shit to do before we go back to filming anyway so I wasn't going to spend it arguing with him in another country." The lie is seamless and Veronica nods in agreement.

"Plus, she missed me, obviously." She tosses a blonde hair behind her ear before giggling into her champagne.

"I guess he wants to clear the air," Jeremy says and I look at him wondering what he means by that when he nods towards the entrance to our section where I see Paxton making his way towards us.

Fuck.

Chapter
FOUR

Shay

"Hey, baby." The words are out of his mouth the second he gets to the table as he stands in front of us. I am hyperaware of Veronica tensing in my periphery and I can sense her focus on me. My eyes dart around him searching for Damian as I try to plan my exit strategy. I didn't want to talk to Paxton. Our PR teams didn't want *or shouldn't want* me to talk to him either. *Especially in public.* I find Damian instantly, not too close, but close enough that he could get to me if I was really in trouble, standing next to the bar. His eyes are on me and I give him a slight shake of my head letting him know that I'm okay and to give me a second.

I glare at Paxton, annoyed that not only is he here but he's wearing this very particular gray suit that he wears when he wants all my attention. Objectively, he looks good and it pisses me off.

"Pax, sit—" Derek says and he starts to get up to shake Paxton's hand when Veronica wraps an arm around his shoulder and presses a kiss into his neck, effectively keeping him in place and distracting him from inviting Paxton to sit down. I'm pretty sure she's only doing it for my benefit, and I wince internally, knowing it's setting her up to be in a position she's trying to avoid which is ending up in bed with Derek later.

I put on a smile, *that I'm sure everyone at the table knows is fake.* "What are you doing here, Paxton?"

"I thought we should talk?"

I stare at him, confused, blinking twice. "About...?"

"Do you want me to move so—" Jeremy starts and I cut him off, grabbing his arm to keep him in place.

"No." I look at him and five years of friendship allows him to read my face. *I don't want to talk to him and I need you to stay here as a buffer.* "Paxton and I have nothing to talk about."

"Shay, please. It's not..." His eyes dart around the table to the three other people and he lets out an exasperated breath. I know it's because he doesn't know what to say or how to say it. "It's not what you think."

My lips pull into a thin line and my eyebrows furrow in question. "You can't be serious. I don't *think* anything. I'm not assuming or speculating. I saw it with my own two eyes, Paxton. Don't even try to play with me right now."

Jeremy tenses next to me probably reading between the lines and his eyes flash to Paxton's in disappointment.

"Shay, can we talk in private, please?" Paxton asks as he avoids Jeremy's gaze.

"No. You ambushed me while I'm out with my friends so you can try to force me into talking?" I flash him another smile and bat my eyelashes at him. "You really tried it." I snort. "Not going to happen!"

"If I walk away from this table without you, they're going to know we're fighting."

"They already think that," Veronica interjects. "Paxton, just stop. She's not getting up and to quote a classic movie *you can't sit with us.*"

"So, this is how it's going to be after everything?"

The fake pleasantries fly from my body and anger flashes across my face. "Are you serious?"

"Paxton, Shay, can we get a picture?" I hear Jeff, one of the nicer and more polite paparazzi from just beyond the velvet rope at the entrance to our section. It isn't unheard of for paparazzi to be floating around or to actually ask us to pose for pictures rather than just snapping potentially unflattering ones. My eyes pull from him and give Paxton a look because if I had to guess, I'd say Paxton told him we'd give him a picture if he asked just to force me into it.

I grit my teeth, narrowing my eyes at him before looking at Jeremy. "Can you move so I can take this bullshit picture?" I say through a perfectly composed smile and Jeremy nods before letting me out of the booth so I can stand next to Paxton. Immediately his arm wraps around my hip and slides down. I turn to face him, putting my back to the camera. "I would think again." I think he realizes he shouldn't fuck with me right now because when I move back next to him to prepare for the picture, he doesn't touch me.

A few more people have realized that we are posing for a picture and I hear more clicks from around the room. I already know it's going to be a race to who can share it first.

"Five minutes, Shay," Paxton pleads and I can see the sadness in his brown eyes. I'm not sure if he's already mourning our relationship or mourning the part of him that will get eviscerated when the public finds out what happened, but the pain in his brown orbs is evident. "Please."

"Fine." I nod. "But only because they're going to just stay there taking pictures for the rest of the night until you leave. And make no mistake, you *are* leaving after we talk."

He swallows and nods before following me towards the back where we can be alone except for Damian who is no more than thirty feet away. His back is turned, disallowing anyone to interrupt our moment of privacy and his large body takes up most of the entrance so it would be difficult for anyone to get a clear shot of us behind him.

"I fucked up," Paxton blurts out, obviously thinking that I'm going to hold him to five minutes.

"No shit." My lips flatten. "How long?" I ask the one question that's been eating at me since I saw his dick thrust inside of her and his quiet hesitation has me wanting to throw up. "Are you kidding me?"

"Shay…"

"We talked about the future. We talked about what *our* future would look like when *LA Dreams* was over and the whole time you were fucking another woman?"

"Not the…whole time."

"ARE YOU ARGUING SEMANTICS?" I scream and immediately I ball my hands into a fist digging my fingernails into my palm to try and quell the rage building inside of me. There is a dull roar in the lounge but if I keep getting louder, I'm sure they'll be able to hear me. I notice Damian looking over his shoulder before turning around to face the room again. "You and I are done. Do you understand me? Done."

He lets out a sigh and rubs his forehead. "You and I both know it's not that easy. Your PR team already talked to my team and they want us to stay together. And I want that too." He reaches for my hand and I snatch it back.

"Stay together while you keep fucking her and whoever the fuck else? Pass."

"I'm not going to be sleeping with anyone anymore. It wasn't… she doesn't mean anything."

Anymore. That word is a bitter pill because it means he's only stopping because he got caught. Not because he's worried about hurting me. Just his reputation. "That's all you have to say? She doesn't mean anything? That means I should put up with this?"

"Shay, I'm sorry. We hadn't seen each other in a while and—"

I put a hand up silencing him. "You can get the entire fuck out of here with that. We've been together three years and you threw it away for what? Because you needed your dick sucked? My God, you're pathetic." I snort. *He threw us away for a fling? I was half expecting him to tell me they'd been hooking up for months. That he was in love with her or she was in love with him. That there were feelings. But for nothing? He risked us for nothing? Is that all I meant to him?*

I can tell I've struck a nerve with my insult because he narrows his gaze at me and I raise an eyebrow daring him to test me. "I want to know how long you've been cheating on me."

He lets out a breath. "I want to be with *you*. None of them meant anything, Shay."

The word slices through me and I take a step back. "*Them?*"

He lowers his head shamefully, unable to meet my eyes. "Yeah."

Rage begins to build again, causing my heart to race. "You want to be with me while you sleep with half of Hollywood? Are you crazy? How many? And how fucking long, Paxton? I'm not going to ask you again."

"I don't know."

I feel like a masochist. I know the answers will only hurt me, and yet I'm desperate for them. I want to know how many and when and how and *why*. "You don't know how many women you've cheated on me with?" The tears are building from deep within but there's a zero percent chance I'll let him watch me shed even one.

He shakes his head. "No."

"That…many?" I shake my head and he forces his hands into his pocket and looks over his shoulder towards Damian, probably a little worried that if my bodyguard hears him, he might actually do him physical harm.

How had he flown under the radar for so long? My God, who knows how many of his team members knew and helped him hide it. Humiliation washes over me that so many of them know and yet constantly smile at me and hug me and tell me how cute Paxton and I are together. *He turned me into a fucking joke.*

"The whole time?" I ask.

"No. Not the whole time." He clears his throat. "Last year things just…changed."

Last year, he'd blown up. More roles, more opportunities, more women probably throwing their panties at him and sliding into his

DMs with their phone numbers and explanations as to what their mouths do. His career had changed overnight and evidently, I'm the last to know that it also changed how he saw our relationship. The sound of a cheer from the lounge reminds me that we are not completely alone and I don't want to delve deeper into this conversation.

I'm not sure if I want to go home or stay and get drunk with my friends but I know for a fact I'm done talking to Paxton.

"Listen to me very carefully." I take a step closer and although he towers over me, I know I'm the one with all the power. "I don't care if they want us to smile and pose for pictures and wave for a few months until they release some bullshit press release that we've grown apart but we'll always be friends and wish nothing but the best for each other blah blah blah, fine. I'll play along *for now* because of what that could mean for my career. But *we* are done. Don't call me. Don't text me when you're horny or lonely because those women don't know shit about you and you can't be yourself with them. Don't call me to ask me which pants go better with what shirt or when you can't figure out what tie matches best. Don't call me when you need someone to vent about your father and how he doesn't approve of your lifestyle choices. Don't call me bitching about your agent or that you feel like you can't trust anyone in your circle. You could trust *me*, by the way, but you already knew that." I shake my head at him. "When we are in public, don't attempt to kiss me or touch me in any way other than platonically. You and I are through. And I swear on my parents' graves if you don't play by my rules on this, you will wish you never met me."

He lets out a sigh and nods. "Okay. Shay I—"

I hold up a hand. "There's nothing left for you to say here. I loved you and cared about you and only wanted the best things for you. I was always in your fucking corner. You destroyed us for *this?*" I narrow my eyes at him hoping he can see the disdain in them. "I hope it was all worth it."

I turn on my heel to walk towards the bathroom I know to be tucked back here and push my way into the room and into a stall, grateful that it's empty. It gives me a second to get myself together.

I'm glad I had the oversight to grab my clutch before I left the table because it means I have my phone with me.

I bypass the text from Veronica and one from Jeremy, both asking me if I'm okay, and open the text message thread I have with my parents. My parents were always the first people I told when something happened. Whether it was good or bad, this text thread housed all of my big moments.

Even after five years, for the moment just after I would press send, I can imagine they're here and I'll receive their response. My mother would always reply with a bunch of emojis and exclamation marks and my father with a perfectly constructed text with correct punctuation. Both of them excited for me in their own ways.

It has been a while since I texted this thread, as most of my big moments had been going to Paxton or sometimes Veronica. I stare at the last message I sent which was a screenshot of the rumor that I might be nominated for an Emmy this year followed by about twenty exclamation marks because I am truly my mother's daughter.

Me: Hi.

Me: I wish you were here.

Me: I miss having people I can trust wholeheartedly.

Me: Sometimes, I just feel so alone.

My phone vibrates with one of the alerts I have set up for myself and the picture I'd just taken with Paxton flashes across my screen and then another and another followed by the headlines *"Trouble in Paradise?"* and some terrible puns about us being a "dreamy couple" as a play on the title of my television show.

The feelings of being betrayed by the man I loved and being betrayed by the universe for taking my parents from me way too soon overwhelm me. Coupled with the alcohol I consumed tonight, the familiar tingle of tears build in my throat, and before I can stop it, one slides down my face.

Fuck.

I try to stop but a second one falls and then a third and soon

I'm having the breakdown I've been avoiding for the past two weeks in the private bathroom of *Rush*. I wipe my face just as more form and spill down my cheeks.

Me: I'm ready to go.

Damian: Whenever you're ready. I'm outside of the restroom.

Me: I can't stop crying.

The bubbles that show he's typing appear and then disappear instantly and then I hear the sound of the door opening. I assume it's Damian but I hold my breath in case it's not. I let it out when I hear, "It's me." His rich baritone floods my ears and I unlock the door and open it to find him standing in front of the stall.

His eyes are soft and empathetic and it spurs more tears. "He… he…" I stamp my foot. "FOR A YEAR!" I yell.

His nostrils flare angrily and he starts to say something but stops himself. He looks away from me and his eyes slowly close before turning back to me. "We are leaving." His tone is even and calming and just those three words have my heart rate slowing. *You're fine, you're okay. You're with Damian and he would never let anything bad happen.*

"What about Veronica?" The tears have slowed and I'm able to blink the ones forming out of my eyes as I wipe under them to collect the ones that have fallen.

He takes a step to the side to let me exit the stall. "Max is here, she'll be fine. And *you* are my only concern." His words send goosebumps all over my flesh. They make me feel safe and guarded and the thought that he'd never let anyone get to me overpowers the feelings of my now ex-boyfriend who'd just made me feel anything but safe.

I stop walking, unsure of what's on the other side of the bathroom door. "Is anyone in the hall?"

"No and you are not going back to the table. We are just going to go out the back and no one is going to see you."

I turn around and look up at him. "Did Paxton leave?"

"I'm not entirely sure. Once I saw you come in here, I followed you. I couldn't really give a fuck what he did as long as he was away from you."

I nod and take another deep breath. "Thank you."

He moves to walk in front of me. "Why are you thanking me?" he asks without turning around to look at me.

"I—" *Because you're here? Because you can protect me from anything? Because you're the only person I feel like I can trust?*

"This is my job, Shay," he says before I can finish and I snap my lips shut before alcohol and my emotions convince me to say anything else.

Chapter FIVE

Shay

THE RIDE HOME IS QUIET. I IGNORED ALL THE PHONE calls from Veronica and Jeremy but texted them to let them know I was fine and that I would see Veronica whenever she got back. Veronica wanted to come home immediately but I told her to enjoy her time and that I was going to bed because honestly, I'm not in the mood to rehash it with her. Now, I'm sitting in the back alone, staring out the window while the faint sounds of Rihanna play through the speaker.

My mind recalls all of the good times I had with Paxton and it's really not the time for that so I try to recall the bad ones instead. The times we'd argued or the times he'd promised to show up for me but didn't. Unfortunately for me, *right now*, there weren't many occasions where Paxton was a shitty boyfriend. Screwing everyone and their mother behind my back aside, he had been a good boyfriend to my face. *Somehow, and I'm not sure why, but that makes me feel fucking worse.*

The fact that on the surface it seemed like he was the perfect boyfriend makes me feel like I did something. Like this was my fault or I hadn't been a good girlfriend.

I pick up my phone to scroll through social media to see the pictures of us that were posted and anything being said. My personal life is a shitshow, but I hope the entire world doesn't know that. My door opens just as I pass the tenth picture of us from tonight and I make my way out of the car to follow Damian up the path to my door.

"Do you want to know what happened?" I ask as he lets us in.

He turns to face me. "Do you want to tell me what happened?"

I nod. "Yes."

"Okay. If I end up killing him, that makes you somewhat culpable, you know."

A smile tugs at my lips at his joke. "Cute."

"That wasn't a joke. I am allowed to kill for you." I follow him down the foyer towards my kitchen. "Are you hungry?"

"No," I tell him as I move to my bar and grab one of the bottles of whiskey. "What are the chances you'll have one with me?" I cock my head to the side. I've never known Damian to drink in all the time I've known him. I'd asked him a few times here and there and he said he didn't drink alcohol while he was on the job. "I'm not going anywhere."

"That's not the only reason I refrain from drinking, Shay."

"No one is getting in either! Veronica will probably show up in a few hours but she has her own code to get in the gate." He gives me a look like he's thinking it over but needs more convincing. "Please." I pout. "I don't want to drink alone and I just had my heart broken tonight."

He narrows his gaze and moves towards me, removing the bottle from my hand. "Tonight?" I can hear the question in his voice. *Didn't you have your heart broken when you walked in on him in Canada two weeks ago?*

"Oh yes, I learned quite a lot tonight. Turns out there's much more to the story."

He pulls two highball glasses from my cabinet and puts a few ice cubes in each. A thought hits me as I prepare to tell him what I learned tonight. Damian is perceptive. He misses nothing. Had he...? "You don't miss anything." I bite down on my bottom lip as he pours the amber liquid into my glass and slides it across the counter.

"Okay?"

"You're perceptive in ways that I'm not. You can read...everything." He blinks a few times as if to say, *and?* "Did you know?"

He looks down at the empty glass in front of him, refusing to meet my eyes. "Know what?"

I huff because I know he knows what I'm asking. "That he was cheating on me, Damian. Cheating on me with god knows how many women for a fucking year?!" He doesn't respond.

"Answer me and don't lie to me."

He pours himself a glass and fills it much higher than he did mine. The liquid is almost to the brim. He looks down at it for a long beat like he regrets pouring such a full glass before his blue eyes meet mine. "I didn't know."

"I'm sensing a but..."

He takes a long sip of his drink before he speaks. "I never thought he was good enough for you," he tells me. "There were times he looked at you and I sensed his mind was somewhere else. There's a look in a man's eyes when he truly loves the woman he's looking at, and...I didn't see that when he looked at you."

My mouth drops open. "What! How could you say—" I start when he holds his hand up.

"To be fair, there's a look a woman has when she's truly in love and you didn't have it either."

"Excuse me?"

"You cared about Paxton and probably even loved him, but... you wouldn't have married him."

"How do you know?"

He shrugs. "Instincts."

"And you couldn't have told me this...a long time ago?"

"I can't force my thoughts on you. You have to figure things like this out for yourself. But believe me, I didn't know he was cheating on you." He cocks his head to the side. "I promise."

"A year, he told me. He's fucked countless women over the past year. He couldn't even give me an exact number."

"Asshole," he grits out.

I hold my glass up. "Cheers to that," I scoff before taking a long sip. "Probably cheated on me with supermodels and A-list movie stars and pop stars and women so much prettier than me." I move off the stool towards one of my living rooms that's just off the kitchen and drop to the couch sliding my four-inch heels off in the process. Damian follows and sits in the adjacent loveseat.

"You can't possibly think that."

I lean my head against the back of the couch and stare up at the ceiling as defeat washes over me. "Oh, I do."

"Who's prettier than you?" I lift my head slowly and look at Damian and can't stop the heat from shooting up my body and rushing to my cheeks.

"You're sweet." I smile.

"Shay, he's an idiot and he knows it. You are…perfect."

He's never said anything remotely like that to me before and I briefly wonder if it's brought on by the alcohol that he never consumes around me. My cheeks are still hot and a tingling feeling dances up my bare legs. I cross one leg over another and it draws his attention to them. I watch as his eyes trace up my legs quickly and suddenly, I'm hyper-aware of how short my dress is. I'm still covered, but I need to be mindful of how I shift while I'm seated.

I don't know how to respond to his comment, but something he said earlier intrigues me. "How do you know what a woman looks like when she's in love? You said I didn't look at him a certain way."

He takes a sip of his drink and leans back in his chair, his large body making the loveseat seem much smaller than usual. He spreads his legs slightly and the movement draws my attention to his groin, but I look away instantly. "I was in a relationship," he starts. "Years ago."

This is the first we've ever really talked about his past. I don't really know much about Damian other than what was in his background checks and the little pieces of information he's given me over the years. For the most part, he's a mystery to me. The idea of learning something new is as intoxicating as the drink in front of me. I nod wanting him to go on.

He shrugs. "It didn't work out."

I blink. *That's it?* "Well obviously." I giggle. "I think I would know if you had a girlfriend or a wife after five years. What happened? How long were you together?"

"You ask a lot of questions." A smirk pulls at his lips and my eyes drop to them, tracing them like he'd just done to my legs. I've always had a thing for a man with a nice smile, nice lips, facial hair, and if he has a dimple, I'm a goner. Damian doesn't have dimples but a man that has three out of four is still sexy as hell in my book.

I raise my eyebrows as if to say, *well then?*

"We were together for three years and…it was just tough. Being with someone when this," he says pointing back and forth between us, "is what I do." He swallows. "She loved me and she probably would have stayed but I wasn't being fair to her. She wanted kids and I didn't."

"You don't want kids?" I can see why he may not want them but that seems like a shame because I'm sure he'd make an amazing father.

"Again, not while I'm doing this. I have my reasons, but if and when I'm ready to start a family, whenever that may be, my focus will be on protecting them."

"Going to leave me high and dry at some point, huh?" I tease but I feel a pang of disappointment at the thought of not having him in my life down the line.

"Rarely do I stay with the same assignment. Usually, every few years I change it up."

I frown. "You've been with me for five years."

He takes another long sip of his drink. "You're different."

I tuck one of the strands framing my face behind my ear, which is my nervous habit that I'm sure he's picked up on. "Why am I different?" He leans forward, resting his elbows on his knees, and gives me a look that I'm able to read. "Right. Because my parents died?"

"I wasn't ready to leave you on your own after three years."

"I'm an adult, you know. I would have been fine." I turn away slightly embarrassed that he feels like he has to babysit me because of the trauma I've been through. A memory of collapsing into Damian's arms when I'd learned that my parents were killed in a car accident flashes through my head. "I'm stronger than people give me credit for. Including you, apparently."

"That's not how I meant it."

I look down at my drink. "Sure." I get up, planning to go upstairs and change into sweatpants and wait for Veronica to show up when he says my name. I turn around and I'm shocked to see him right behind me even though I know he can move stealthily and quickly. He's rarely been this close to me except in extreme circumstances. I smell his cologne and it's sexy and clean and I find myself pressing my legs together because a vision of me laying between sheets that smell like him flashes through my brain. His eyes move across my face from my eyes to my nose to my mouth and I briefly wonder if he's going to touch me when he takes a step back. I let go of the breath I hadn't realized I was holding.

"That's not how I meant it," he repeats. "I know you will be fine and you are stronger than any person I've been assigned to." He narrows his eyes and sucks in a breath before looking away. "I just… care about you and I don't know very many people that I would trust to watch out for you."

A tiny gasp escapes me before I sink my teeth into my lips to quiet the sound. "I—well, that's nice."

He clears his throat and for a moment I think he's nervous. Part of me wants to press him to see what he's thinking, but that's also the part that just got her heart broken and is a little needy for male attention.

"So, you're in for the night?" I nod. "Right, well you know where to find me. I'll probably come by again to check on everything once Veronica gets here."

He starts to walk away. "You could stay, you know." He freezes in the doorway and turns around. "I mean, I'm going to change but I was probably going to come back down here to wait for V."

His sharp jaw tightens, and again he seems like he's at war with himself over what to do. "I have some things I need to do tonight," he says and while it's not cold, his tone is definitely more clipped than it was moments ago.

"Oh okay." I nod. "Sure."

"Some other time," and then he's gone without another word.

Chapter Six

DAMIAN

Jesus Fucking Christ, Hunt. Get it together.

I'm outside heading towards my house when I decide to do a walk of the perimeter. I don't often anymore since I've taken all the measures to ensure the property is secure at all times, but the past hour has me more keyed up than usual and I could use the distraction. I walk down the long driveway towards the gate and grab the flashlight that is stowed at the entrance.

I can't believe that little fucker has been cheating on her. I stomp along the boundary of the gate, searching for anything that seems out of place. *How the fuck could he do that to her?*

Seeing those tears in her eyes when we were in the bathroom of *Rush* fucking gutted me. It's so rare that she cries and seeing those tears stream down her face felt like someone had knocked the wind out of me.

And then…back here. *Why the fuck had I said all of that?* Calling her pretty and perfect and even telling her about my ex-girlfriend, Simone? I had never told any of my clients anything personal. I kept everything professional. No lines were crossed. Even the times that I was assigned to a man, I never allowed him to think we were friends. I was there to do a job and nothing else.

It has been years since I've even thought about Simone. I'd thrown myself into work when I ended things and found a new assignment guarding a man in the running for senator that may or may not have had a dicey past. I was with him for a few years before I'd essentially been recruited by his lawyer—the father of television star, Shay Eastwood.

It shocked me how much I liked her instantly. She was fiery and had this energy that was different than anyone I'd ever known, let alone guarded. Despite being eighteen, she was pragmatic and mature and while she liked to go out, she rarely got into trouble. I saw the way men looked at her. The way their heads turned and ran their gazes all over her. I'd seen the pornographic fan mail and the emails and the way some men would even touch themselves when she'd walk by. It was fucking ridiculous that she'd become so numb to it all that it barely fazed her.

She was and is beautiful and she knows it, but she doesn't come off arrogant. She's confident which is a fine line to walk and it's sexy as fuck.

She is sexy as fuck.

And it drives me fucking crazy.

I had never been attracted to anyone that I was protecting before. I knew the trouble that came with getting involved with a client and I had made it my cardinal rule to keep my distance and not get too close.

It's why I didn't touch her unless I absolutely had to.

I make it to the back of the house and my eyes immediately go to her bedroom. Her curtains are drawn but I see her light on and for a brief second, I wish she'd left it open. She faces nothing but miles and miles of land so there is no risk of anyone seeing her unless someone is in her backyard. Someone like me. I could walk by and see her just for a second.

No, Hunt.

Feelings of shame wash over me thinking about her.

Naked.

I grit my teeth trying to temper the feeling of my dick thickening in my pants as I think about her. I walk through her garden, checking for anything out of the ordinary and take a seat on the bench wondering what the hell I'm going to do now that she's single. It was much easier to manage this when she started dating Paxton. She'd stopped flirting with me and it seemed like the tension between us came to a halt while she focused on her relationship with him. Frankly, I was grateful for him. It solidified the thought that I couldn't have her.

But before that? When I had just started my assignment? And right after her parents died? She was very clear that she'd wanted something to happen between us and I had to be the responsible one to tell her that wasn't going to happen.

Five Years Prior

It's been six months since I got this job protecting Shay Eastwood who might actually be the most beautiful woman I've ever laid eyes on. All of the magazines and media say that she is one of the most beautiful people in the world, but seeing her through my eyes is something completely different. I saw her fresh from sleep, without a stitch of makeup, or right after a shower when her naturally curly hair is pulled into a bun. I've seen her when she's sick and throwing up from one too many tequila shots with her friend Veronica and I've even seen her cry once after an argument with her father.

She was beautiful in all of those times.

But that's a problem. It's a problem that I think she's beautiful, smart, charming, and talented. *Fuck,* I could go down a laundry list of all the things that make Shay Eastwood the star of every one of my thoughts while I fucked my hand.

I've kept things professional, but my resolve is weakening especially when she walks around in those tiny little shorts that make her smooth legs go on for fucking miles. I love a woman with nice legs and hers are fucking phenomenal. They are toned with muscles from ballet that I'd thought of more than once wrapped around my waist while I drove into her.

I've played with the idea of resigning. I could get another job easily. One where I don't feel so distracted half the time by a woman I can't even escape in my dreams. A job where I'm not hyper-aware of every move they make for reasons other than the fact that I'm hired to protect them.

I'm sleeping in the guesthouse that is just to the right of Shay's house tonight. There are some nights I do stay in her house, but it's been a very quiet few days and I believe her assistant and Veronica are both staying over as she has an early photoshoot tomorrow morning. I'm mindlessly flipping through the channels when my phone pings with a text message. I reach for it, assuming it's Shay but not sure why she'd be texting me at almost one in the morning, and sure enough, I see the alias I have her under flash across my screen.

Winter: Hi, I need help!

I sit up, wondering what she needs help with but am also pretty sure that it's not an emergency. I have her stored in my phone as *Winter Green*. Mainly because of the disgusting wintergreen Lifesavers she eats all the time but also because of her love for snow and skiing and everything associated with winter.

Me: With?

Winter: Please!

Me: You haven't answered my question. What do you need help with at one in the morning?

Within seconds my phone starts to ring and I bring the phone to my ear. "Yes?"

"Can you please stop being difficult and just come here, please?"

I can hear the alcohol in her voice and I let out a sigh as I pull on my shoes. "If I get all the way there and it's nothing, I am going to be irritated, Shay."

"You're always irritated," she mumbles.

"What was that?"

"Stop being so cranky with me all the time. I am a fucking deliiiight and you are RUDE," she says as I make my way out of the guesthouse.

"Is that so?" I chuckle because the tone of her voice is almost comical.

"Mmmhmmm." I hang up and make my way into the house. I climb the stairs towards her room and I wonder if Hillary and Veronica are with her, but I don't hear anything as I approach her door. I knock and when the door flies open, I fight the urge to groan when I see Shay standing in front of me wearing nothing but a tank top and boy-short underwear. The tank top has a high neckline so I don't see any cleavage but I can tell she isn't wearing a bra because her nipples are poking through the material. So much smooth skin the color of a rich caramel is on display and it's fucking painful to drag my eyes away from her.

I clear my throat. "Is there a reason that you've summoned me to your bedroom?"

She bounces on her toes and points towards the corner. "There's a bug."

I shoot her a look, momentarily ignoring that she's wearing next to nothing so I can show her how irritated I am. "Are you serious?"

"It's gross." She wiggles her fingers and scrunches her nose. "A spider."

I stomp across the room, grabbing a tissue from her nightstand and pick up the very tiny reason I'm living my worst nightmare slash fantasy before tossing it in the toilet of her ensuite bathroom.

She gives me a smile and two thumbs up. "Thank you!" She bats her eyelashes at me. "You're the best!"

"You're welcome. Anything else?" I ask, and the twinkle in her eye lets me know that I'm about to regret that question when she hops on her bed making her tits bounce deliciously.

FUCK. I have to get out of here.

"Well, actually there's one other thing."

I cross my arms over my chest, balling my hands into fists in the process, and begin running through every unsexy thing I can think of to calm my dick that is about to start rising. "Mmmhm." I raise an eyebrow at her.

"So, there's this party next weekend?"

I lean against the door jamb. "Go on."

"No paparazzi. They're even making us check our phones at the door." This isn't new. There are often parties she goes to where they want celebrities to feel safe to let loose without the fear of someone leaking a photo so no phones are allowed inside. Usually, security waits outside so we can keep our phones and we have access to some sort of landline.

"But I was thinking…maybe you'd want to actually come."

"Of course, I'll come. I'll be outside like always." I nod at her.

Her lips form the most adorable fucking pout and I lower my gaze at her. "I mean, like come in…to the party. Have…fun with me?"

Well, shit. "Shay, you don't pay me to have fun."

"Okay, well what if I gave you the night off, then will you?"

"If I had the night off, I wouldn't be going to a party with you. Kind of sounds like work."

She scoffs and tosses a hair over her shoulder. "Some say hanging out with me is fun."

"Well, I'm not one of your friends."

"God, you sound like my parents. You're not that old, Damian. Don't you ever let loose?"

"Not while I'm on the job."

She huffs and puts her hands under her chin as if she's praying. "Damian, pleeease! I think you'll have fun, and Veronica and Derek are in their 'on' phase and third-wheeling with them is really fucking irritating sometimes." She rolls her eyes dramatically.

"Shay, I'm not here to entertain you. You have plenty of friends you can go with."

"Well…yeah, but none of them…are you." She sinks her teeth into her bottom lip almost to drive her point home that she's asking me out.

Holy shit.

The most gorgeous woman I've ever met just essentially asked me out and I have to tell her no. "Shay."

"I think you would have fun. I mean I'm fun." She points at herself. "We would have fun together. I said 'fun' a lot, didn't I?" Her lips form a straight line as she looks up towards the ceiling as if the answer to her question will fall from it.

"Shay, I can't…we can't go down that road."

"It's just a party."

"It's an invitation for lines to become blurry and that's not how I work."

She shrugs, and a smile so blinding finds her face it makes an unfamiliar feeling spread through my chest. *Shit, she is gorgeous.* "I don't think any lines will get blurry." I put a hand over my eyes and rub my forehead trying to figure out how to be clearer and also to break whatever spell she's just cast over me by smiling at me like that. "Why won't you look at me?"

"Well, for one, because of how you're dressed."

She looks down at herself and then back up at me. "What's wrong with how I'm dressed?"

I shoot her a glare. "Don't."

She frowns, lowering her eyebrows and pursing her lips. "I'm in my bedroom, in my house, that I pay for. I can dress however I like."

"True, but if you're going to summon me here to kill a spider the size of your pinky nail, put on some clothes." She scowls at me and I resist the urge to let a chuckle fall from my lips. "Shay—"

"I've seen the way you look at me, you know," she blurts out and I freeze.

"What? I'm not looking at you in any way that's inappropriate." I don't know what she's seen. I do my very best not to let my eyes linger on her too long or to stare at her with anything but my blank, vacant expression I use while on duty.

"A woman knows when a man is looking at her." She looks up at me through those full lashes and I know at this moment I have to resign. She's too fucking tempting. All I want is to sink my teeth into her and bend her over every surface in this room.

I'll wait until next week to resign so that she doesn't think it's in direct relation to this. At the end of the day, I don't want her to be embarrassed for something I feel just as strongly about as she does. I'll sit her and her parents down and thank them for the opportunity and offer to help them find my replacement but tell them I ultimately need to step away. I'll make up something that won't hurt her feelings. I'll tell them I'm going back overseas. They'll never know. But I can't keep being her bodyguard. I want her too fucking much, and clearly, she wants me too.

Next week, I'll be done.

The next day, Shay Eastwood lost both of her parents.

Present Day

That day still haunts me. I had to be the one to tell her because news reports got leaked before the police could even get to her, and the last thing I wanted was for the internet to tell her that her parents were dead. I get up from the bench and make my way toward her heated pool. The lights on her pool are always on and I walk around it once. I had planned to quit, but there was no way I could leave her then. Not when her whole life changed in the blink of an eye and she felt like I was one of the few people she could depend on.

There was an instance or two that she'd tried again that I know stemmed from grief given that one of the times was the day of their funerals, but after that, she stopped. Things were polite and appropriate and then she met Paxton which seemed to also halt my feelings as well. She seemed happy and I couldn't have her, so I forced myself not to look at her. Not to think about her. Not to touch my dick to thoughts of her riding me. I stopped all of it. *As much as I could.* But now she's single again and she's older and stronger…and *still off limits.*

My thoughts are interrupted by her voice. "I thought you had things to do?" The sound of her flip-flops scraping against the pavement comes closer as she drops her towel down on the chair next to where I'm sitting. She's wearing a crocheted bathing suit cover-up and I can see scraps of red beneath it and the strings tied around her neck. Her hair is pulled into a sleek bun at the top of her head and though it's dark, the light from the pool allows me to see that her face is free from makeup.

Fuck me. If I see this girl in a red bikini right now, I will want to gauge my own eyes out. Her bathing suits rarely have any coverage over her ass and even less over what I assume to be very round and very perfect C-cup tits. "I don't blame you, my pool is pretty nice." She pulls her cover up over her head and tosses it to the chair.

Fuck. I try to remain unfazed but her bathing suit leaves very little to the imagination.

The throb in my dick has me shifting in my seat to relieve the ache. I'm trying to keep my gaze just on her face and not let it focus on her body, but it's hard to miss. Hard to miss the tiny triangles that cover her tits or the even tinier one between her legs. "You've had a little bit to drink tonight; you sure you should be getting in the water?"

She looks at me as if to say, *seriously?* "Well, I guess it's a good thing my lifeguard is on duty." She heads towards the water and I stifle a groan when she turns around and I see that her bikini bottoms are a thong style highlighting her perfect ass.

"Isn't Veronica coming?"

"She has a phone." She giggles. "And a way into my house for that matter."

I glare at her. "The main gate is one thing, but I told you not to share the code to the house with anyone."

"It's V."

"I don't care. I said no one. I'm changing it again," I bark at her, already planning for what the new six digit code will be and I'm grateful for this new irritation so I can stop focusing on how bad I want to run my hands over her gorgeous curves.

"You think I can't trust V?" She's wading through the water slowly, the ripples barely grazing her breasts and my gaze flits back to them. She cocks her head to the side and gives me an innocent look that has my previous irritation melting away.

Don't look at her tits.

"I think if she's coming into the house intoxicated with Derek, she won't have enough discretion to not let him see what she's typing in, and I am not around Derek enough to know whether I trust him or not."

She huffs. "Fine. Make it something easy for me to remember though."

"That's not the point." I shake my head.

"Like your birthday." She raises a hand. "Backwards."

"How is that easy? You don't even know what that is."

"Of course, I do! Seven, eight, three, one, four, zero. April thirteenth, nineteen-eighty-seven but backwards." She gestures like she's typing it into her keypad.

I blink at her. "You remember my birthday?"

"Of course. I'm good at birthdays though."

"Yes but…even the year?"

"I'm good at math and you're thirty—five."

"You're terrible at math." I correct and the thought that she's able to rattle off my birthday so easily lingers in my brain longer than it should.

She huffs. "Can we use that or not?"

I smile at her because technically, yes. It's obscure and difficult and an intruder only has about thirty seconds to get it right. I also have it wired that two wrong tries immediately alert the police. Which is why I don't let her do it when she's been drinking after more than a few visits from the police department when she'd gotten it wrong.

"Fine. When Veronica comes in and I'm sure you two are in for the night, I'll change it."

She nods and continues to move around the pool. I let my feet stretch out in front of me and look up at the sky. We sit in a comfortable silence, just the sounds of her splashing around in the water when she speaks up.

"Did you love her?"

I raise my head and look at Shay who's moved a little further into the water so more of her breasts are covered. "What?"

"Your ex-girlfriend. You said she loved you. But…did you love her?"

"We are back on this?" I should have known that revealing details of my past would send Shay down a rabbit hole of wanting information.

"Well, you know everything about me and my past relationship. Thought we could even the playing field some."

I want to tell her that is not how this works. While, yes, I know a lot about her because it's my job, she doesn't need to know anything about me, so I'm shocked that different words come out. "At the time, I thought so."

"You're not sure anymore?"

"No." My lips form a line. "She was loyal and I valued that but I'm not sure that I loved her."

"Loyalty is pretty important," she says and I'm sure her recent experience is going to make her question everyone moving forward.

"Yes, of course. Probably the top of the list, but I wasn't in love with her and that's pretty important too."

"Fair. Have you ever been in love?"

"I don't think so."

She nods. "Where are your parents? You don't talk about them much. Or anyone in your family. Do you have siblings?"

"I do have parents, yes." I nod. "Well, a father and a stepmother."

She cocks her head to the side in question. "Where's your mom?"

"She left when I was young."

"I'm sorry, Damian," she murmurs. "That's tough. Were you old enough to remember her?"

I never talk about my mother. *Ever*. I didn't even talk to Simone about her. She knew the basic details but talking about her in depth made me feel like shit.

"I wasn't ready to be a mother. I can't do this. I love you but I don't want this," she'd told my father before she left that night.

Even though I was only five years old, those words haunt me thirty years later. That the 'this' she didn't want was *me*.

"Yes. I was five when she left."

"I'm sorry, that's really tough."

"I don't want to talk about it," I say far harsher than I intend and her eyes widen in surprise. She probably assumes we'd be able to bond over not having our mothers around, and not that I'm probably more triggered about the loss of my mother than she is. Through meditation and a brief stint with every religion under the sun that had something to say regarding mortality, Shay has found some peace in her parents' untimely death. *That and a very dark sense of humor.* I, however, have not worked through my mommy issues.

"Oh. Sorry." She frowns.

"I didn't mean to snap at you, I just…don't talk about her to anyone." She nods and wades into deeper water but still stays above it. She moves around for a while and though the silence stretches between us, it's comfortable. The sounds of the trees rustling and the faint sounds of her pool make me feel calm despite the recent thoughts about my mother.

She makes her way to the steps and gets out of the pool in what looks like slow motion. She adjusts her bottoms and I have to resist the urge to do the same to my dick. Her towel is on the chaise lounge to the right of me so I'm surprised that she moves to my left side. I reach for her towel assuming that she's going to ask me to hand it to her when I feel drops of water and her body hovering over my lap as she stretches across me to grab her towel. I don't move an inch while she tries to tempt me by flaunting her body. My eyes dart down for a second, seeing her body in a position over my lap that would be perfect for me to spank her. Slap her barely-covered ass for trying to tempt me when I'm trying to do the right thing.

Is that what this is? Temptation? Is this about me? Or just a cry for a man's attention after Paxton treated her like shit? Maybe her ego is bruised and she wants to feel like it's not her fault that Paxton looked outside of their relationship for sex.

I hope she knows it's not.

I can't pry my eyes away from her even as she *thankfully* wraps the towel around herself. She wipes at her wet skin and I try to ignore the way the water slides down her slender figure.

She takes the seat next to me, stretches her long legs in front of her on the lounge, and lets the towel fall from around her. It's a warmer summer, so it's still about seventy-five degrees even this late at night and her pool is heated so she's probably not too cold yet.

Like always, my eyes are drawn to her legs. They sweep up slowly to her torso, not letting my eyes feast for too long on her breasts but long enough that the image is ingrained in my brain. I make it to her eyes and they're locked on mine. I know I can't pretend I wasn't just shamelessly staring at her. She gives me a smile so sexy and sinful before sinking her teeth into that bottom lip and I can feel the rest of my resolve withering.

I clear my throat, shaking the thoughts from my head, and stand to my feet. "Are you done swimming?" I ask her.

"Damian—" Her eyes follow me and I can already hear the question in her voice.

She's interrupted by sounds from inside of the house and I turn my head just as Veronica comes out of her back door.

"Shay!" she squeals, and sure enough, I see Derek behind her— *and* Jeremy.

"Pool party!" she squeals as she comes skipping towards us. She passes me and makes it to the edge of the pool, wobbling slightly, and for a second, I think she might fall in. I take the few steps to reach her and grab her arm before she falls, keeping her steady and backing her away from the side.

"Uh uh," I tell her. "Max will kill me if I let you drown." Max usually camped out in front of the house whenever she was here so he isn't super close by.

Veronica giggles before turning towards Shay, and when I turn to look at her, I see her eyes fixed on where my hand is wrapped around Veronica's elbow.

I already know what she's thinking. That it's so easy for me to touch Veronica when I rarely touch her. She blinks and the look is gone but I can sense what my instincts are telling me are jealousy and probably a little bit of annoyance towards her friend for popping the intimate bubble Shay and I have been in tonight.

"You guys want to swim?" Veronica calls out to Jeremy and Derek and when they both tell her no, she rolls her eyes. "Well fine!" She looks at Shay. "What happened with Paxton?" She looks back at me and smiles at me. "I've got her now." I don't think she means to be dismissive. If anything, she's probably a little mad at me for leaving without her because I know she wants to be there for Shay. "Thank you for getting her out of that."

"Sure, let's go in," Shay says, standing up, and again, I run my gaze over her…quicker this time since we are in mixed company. "I'll see you in the morning, Damian."

"Are Derek and Jeremy staying?" I ask. I know nothing is going on between Shay and Jeremy but I can't help but feel a little spike of jealousy if he's staying here with her because I have seen the way his eyes run over her when she's not looking. Maybe it's just a general appreciation for how beautiful she is, but she's newly single and he's probably her closest male friend.

I know how these things go.

"I'll let you know," Shay says and the look she's giving me makes me wonder if she can sense the reason I asked has nothing to do with her safety. "V?"

"Derek, yes, obviously. Is that okay?"

"Mmmhmmm," she says, her eyes not leaving mine as she grabs her towel.

She turns away from me and links her arm with Veronica as they move into the house, giving me a perfect view of her round ass and the red fabric nestled between her cheeks. She looks over her shoulder, catching me, and when my eyes dart up to meet hers, she gives me a wicked smirk.

I am so fucked.

Chapter
SEVEN

Shay

*W*HAT THE FUCK, SHAY? WHY ARE YOU TRYING TO GO *down this road again?* Tempting Damian, for what? He's not interested.

I'm back in my room, having left Derek, Jeremy, and Veronica in the living room while I change out of my bathing suit. I pull on a pair of leggings and a cropped sweater that lands just above my navel. I'm taking my hair down out of my bun just as the door opens and Veronica comes in drinking a glass of wine that I'm sure she'll regret in the morning after all the alcohol she's already consumed tonight.

"Okay, so what happened? I assume you don't want to discuss anything around them." She hitches a thumb over her shoulder to refer to Derek and Jeremy.

"Nothing! Oh my God, V, we were just talking," I tell her.

She narrows her eyes, her eyebrows pinching together and a smile slowly slides across her red-painted lips. "I meant between you and your boyfriend you just broke up with? Not your bodyguard, but let's put a pin in Paxton for a second because you're clearly thinking about Damian if that's where your mind went."

Fuck.

"Sorry, I thought you meant—"

"Yes, I'm aware that's what you thought. What I'm wondering is *why*." Even though I'm sure she's consumed a slew of drinks, I know she's not going to let this go. The alcohol will probably make her more annoyingly relentless.

"I don't know. He's been more protective than usual and this whole thing with Paxton just has me feeling, I don't know, insecure?" I let out a breath as I prepare to tell Veronica what happened. "Knowing he fucked every woman in Hollywood?"

"Whoa, what?" Her hazel eyes widen in shock.

"He's fucked multiple women. The one I caught him with is just one of many. He couldn't give me an exact number."

She chokes on her wine. "What the fuck? He said that?"

"Yep," I tell her popping the p. "If that gets out…" I let out a breath. "My God, I can already see the articles. I'm bad in bed. I'm a prude. I don't give head. I really am the girl next door." I tick off the reasons on my fingers. Disgust washes over me over how crude the tabloids can be. "If he'd fallen for some other woman that's one thing, but him fucking everything in a skirt will become me not being able to keep him satisfied or whatever the fuck."

"Or that he's a serial cheater and a fucking asshole," she argues.

"Right, but you and I both know that won't be the only story." I sigh angrily. "I've worked so hard to stay out of the drama. I'm not messy and I mind my business and yet here I am in the middle of my first heartbreak that has the ingredients to become a PR nightmare."

"I am shocked he's been able to fly under the radar about this for so long. Surely someone had to have talked. My god, was he issuing NDAs while she was still coming down from her orgasm?"

I roll my eyes and the petty words leave my mouth like a reflex. "Right, like she came."

Veronica's eyes widen as she giggles. "Oooh. Really now? You always talked about how great the sex was?"

"Women tell all kinds of lies when they're in love," I say in the most dead-panned tone with an expression to match. "I'd give it a six out of ten."

"Ah a D for the D." She giggles.

I sigh and make my way towards the door hoping she won't circle back to her question about Damian. I don't have any answers for her because I barely have answers for myself.

Yes, I'm attracted to him and I'd purposefully put on my tiniest bikini and strutted around him like I was presenting food to a starving man. Yes, I've always had a tiny crush on him that's never gone away.

That's it. He's made it clear that nothing can ever happen between us. But tonight…

We make it to the bottom steps where I see Damian standing in front of my door, staring down at his phone. His eyes immediately flit to me, and in the brief moment before his eyes move behind me to Veronica, I could have sworn he was looking at me differently. Like maybe he *shouldn't* be looking at me.

It's nearing two in the morning. Jeremy just left and Derek and Veronica have just escaped to their bedroom to "sleep," *but Veronica is not quiet and I can already tell they're doing anything but sleeping.* I'm sitting on my couch, finishing up the last bit of wine from the bottle that Veronica opened when the familiar sounds of the porno movie being shot in my guest room right now reminds me that I haven't had sex in quite some time. *And also, that I definitely do not want to listen to that.*

It's been over a month since Paxton and I had sex, and to my knowledge, it was for no other reason than geography. *In light of new events, who the fuck knows.*

But I like sex. *A lot.* Even when I didn't come, *which happened more often than I would have liked,* I still loved the intimacy of sex.

Touching. Tasting. The moans and how slick and wet everything becomes as you glide against each other.

Fuck, I am horny.

And slightly drunk.

Which is a very dangerous combination.

The sounds of Derek grunting snaps me from those feelings and irritation blazes through me. I wasn't a stranger to hearing Veronica have sex, *unfortunately*. Our dressing rooms on set shared a wall and she and Derek often retreated to her dressing room to fuck after the on-screen couple they portrayed had gotten hot and heavy.

I take another sip of my wine when a wicked thought floats through my mind.

No.

Go masturbate or something because seeking out Damian while you're this horny is just going to get you into trouble.

I swallow thinking about the man who has been in the back of my mind for the past five years and in the front of it for the past few hours.

"A rebound is normal," I say out loud to no one because I'm still alone. A sexy sound penetrates the air and I take that as an agreement. I roll my eyes at my justification.

You cannot rebound with Damian.

Why not?

Because it will make things awkward as fuck and that's if he even wants to go down this road with you at all.

I go to the front of my house and peek out the front window that faces the guesthouse, noting his lights are still on. I tap my red manicured nail against the glass in rapid succession while my mind goes back and forth over whether I'm going to do this.

Okay relax, it's not like I'm going to go over there in a trench coat with nothing underneath. Let's just feel out the situation and see where it goes.

I down the rest of the glass and set it down before moving towards my security system on the wall to disarm it, slip on my outdoor slippers, and move out the front door before I can stop myself. I don't feel nervous walking out here alone despite it being almost two in the morning; my gate is securely monitored twenty-four-seven as is the gate wrapped around the entire community. I'm a few steps from Damian's door when it flies open and his piercing blue eyes that are darker than usual land on me.

Eyes that are confused. Angry. *Maybe something else.*

My gaze drops down on instinct because *fuuuuuck* he's wearing gray sweatpants and it's doing little to nothing to hide what's beneath them. My eyes dart away quickly and into his which are narrowed at me. He's close enough for me to smell him and he smells so fucking good. I don't detect any cologne, it's just his natural essence which I don't know how to describe as anything other than just raw sex.

"What are you doing out of the house at two in the morning, Shay?" I'm pulled from the thoughts of how to get his scent ingrained in my skin by his biting tone.

"I—"

"When I set the alarm that means there shouldn't be anyone entering or leaving," he interrupts.

"I disarmed it," I say guiltily, feeling like I'm being scolded. "I'm not a prisoner, Damian. I can come and go as I please, you know." I cross my arms over my chest defiantly and briefly scold myself for not changing into something that showed a little more skin. The sweater shows off my stomach but my tits and my legs are some of my best features and neither of them are on display.

"You told me you weren't leaving."

"I'm not!"

"Then what are you doing here?" He crosses his own arms over his chest allowing me to see a hint of his tattoo just over his bicep. I know he has quite a few all over his body. A beautiful and intricately designed compass on his chest, a wolf on his arm, a lion on his back, and a cross with some initials on his upper arm that I've been too nervous to ever ask who they're for in case it's related to a painful memory. The words *Dum vita est, spes est* are on his forearm which I researched after I first saw them and it means, *while there is life, there is hope*, and several others scattered over his body.

Realizing that this isn't happening the way I envisioned it, I opt for the truth. "Well, Veronica and Derek are breaking the rules of their arrangement and I can hear it. So, I…was wondering if you were awake and if I could hang out here for a little bit. Jeremy left," I tell him, though I'm sure he's already aware of that. He narrows his eyes at me like he's not totally buying what I'm selling so I continue. "Can I come in?"

I can tell he wants to protest but he steps to the side and lets me in before slowly shutting the door behind him.

"We need to get something straight, Shay," he says and I already know he's about to call me out for attempting to seduce him. Part of what makes Damian so good at his job is his ability to read a situation very quickly, so I'm sure he's figured out why I'm really here. Besides the fact that I've got noise-canceling headphones that I could use to drown out the sounds of Veronica and Derek, I'm a heavy sleeper who can sleep through most anything, especially after I've been drinking. Two facts that Damian is well aware of.

I turn around to face him and he's standing in front of the door, taking up most of the space with his large frame.

"Okay?" I tuck a wavy hair behind my ear and take a deep breath when something I hadn't noticed when I first entered the guesthouse hits me in the face. I turn my head to the side, scrunching my nose as I try to make sense of what I've noticed when the words leave my mouth before he can speak. "Did you have a woman here tonight?" There isn't a rule that he can't have a woman over and he does have days off, so I suppose he could have a girlfriend or a fuck-buddy, but I assumed I would know that. Yet, I smell perfume. It's fresh like someone was just here and I showered after the pool and didn't put…*wait…*

"No." He grunts and he takes a step closer to me. "Shay—"

"It smells like…me? What I wear." I put my nose to my wrist, wondering if maybe I'd absentmindedly sprayed some, but I only smell my moisturizer and the scent of the toner I'd used on my face.

"I don't know what you're talking about," he tells me. "There hasn't been a woman here tonight, and you shouldn't even be here."

"Why?"

"Because I'm not going down this road again with you, Shay." He stomps past me and I spin in a circle to follow him with my eyes as he moves into the kitchen area. His large television, which takes up most of the wall, is still on and I can see he's watching Sports Center. A glass of whiskey is sitting on the coffee table in front of the dark gray sectional couch I'd custom ordered when I designed this room. I didn't originally have a television quite so big but he switched it to this one once he moved in. *Men.*

"What…road?" I ask.

"The road where you," he swallows, leaning against the refrigerator, "try to tempt me."

My sex clenches at his words like they have a direct line to it. "I didn't realize—"

He cuts me off with a look. "I'm a red-blooded man, Shay, and even the most disciplined man has his limits." My heart begins to beat faster because he's never said anything like this to me before. "And now you're—" He stops and clears his throat. "You should go."

I feel a flash of cold and then hot made worse by all of the clothes I'm wearing. It makes me want to shed them all. "I'm what?"

"Feeling vulnerable because of Paxton and you trust me and I get that but I can't fill that void, Shay."

"This isn't about that." I correct him. *It isn't?*

"Oh?"

"There's always been something here. The way you look at me…" I remember Veronica's words about how he looks at me and her ongoing theory that he has feelings for me. "I'm not the only one that's noticed."

When he rubs a hand over his jaw and looks away from me, I notice a slight pink tint in his cheeks. I wonder if he's embarrassed that I'm calling him out or if it's the alcohol catching up with him. "Looking isn't touching, Shay."

"So, you admit you're looking, and that you want to…" I whisper, "touch."

"No." His voice is deep and gravelly and again has a direct line to the space between my legs that throbs for attention, reminding me why I came over here in the first place.

I take a step closer and drag my index finger along the dining table as I make my way around it to get closer to him. "You're telling me, as disciplined as you are, that you wouldn't be able to separate your job from…" I bite my bottom lip and raise an eyebrow, "something else you could do for me?" I'm now in the kitchen with him and I don't even attempt to hide the way my eyes move slowly down his body to his groin and back up. I move closer and when he makes no effort to move, I wonder if I've got him. "It must be tough. Finding someone to…take care of things."

His eyes trace my face and down my body and part of me wants to take off my sweater to expose my sheer red lacy bra but I worry that might kill the moment we're in.

He doesn't respond to my statement so I continue.

"Has it been very long?" There's still about three feet between us and I inch slightly closer to him. He doesn't respond again. "It's been a minute for me." I bite my lip. "Six weeks or so. Even longer if we're talking about…if it was really good." I chuckle and I hate that it makes me feel inadequate. Like it was *my fault* that Paxton never made my orgasms a priority like I made his.

His jaw ticks and he narrows his gaze. "He didn't make it good for you?" Something that looks like concern flashes in his blue eyes and it makes my toes curl. As if he could somehow protect me sexually the way he protects me physically.

"It wasn't usually his main concern in bed. I mean don't get me wrong, there were times I *did* but—"

"Every time." He grunts and the two words hang in the air like what I hope to be a promise.

"What?" I ask, desperately needing clarification.

"A woman needs to come every time." My heart picks up speed again listening to him talk about a woman's climax. "Preferably before I do." He shrugs. "And after." A spark shoots through me and congregates between my legs. It begins to throb in time with my racing heart.

"Oh." I let out a breath, the alcohol and this conversation making my skin prickle and my cunt get slicker with each passing second. "You didn't say how long it's been for you."

"A while." He stares at me, and then, just when I think he's going to take a step closer to me, he breaks our gaze and moves to his living area to pick up his glass of whiskey. He drains the entire contents before slamming it down on the coffee table so hard I'm surprised it doesn't break. I jump at the noise and then he's moving back towards me fast, crossing every line he's drawn between us, and on instinct, I take a few steps back until I feel his kitchen counter at my lower back.

"I would make you come every. Fucking. Time," he whispers and my sex clenches at his words and at how close he's standing. We're about as close as two people can get without touching as he peers down at me.

I drag my eyes over the hard planes of his chest and his arms, willing him closer, willing his hands to touch me, his arms to wrap around me. There are so few times I remember him touching me and I only recall his arms around me twice. Both times occurred the week my parents died so there wasn't anything to those touches besides sympathy and comfort.

I draw in a short breath trying to stifle the moan sitting in the back of my throat. "How?"

"How would I make you come?" I nod, words escaping me and a smile pulls at his lips. "Well, that depends."

I swallow. "On?"

He shrugs. "What you want first."

"First?" I whisper. "Touch me." This whole time I've been here, through this entire erotic dance he hasn't touched me once and I'm ready to jump out of my skin. "You never touch me."

"There's a reason for that."

It's as if his words click and suddenly, I'm wondering if Veronica's theory isn't totally off base. "Because you want to."

His index finger starts at my wrist and drags up my arm to my shoulder leaving goosebumps in its wake. Then he takes another step closer so he's right against me. My breasts are pressed against his torso and I angle my head to look up at him. His other hand finds my hip, tracing up before dragging his finger across my stomach, circling my navel lightly and I feel like I'd sell my soul to the devil in this moment to feel his hand drag over my pussy in the same way. His touch is so light, and yet, I'm hyper-aware of every place he's touched in the past two minutes. "I can't...touch you out there." He motions towards the door and I nod in understanding.

"Can...I touch you?" He nods once and I run my hands up his torso and his chest, rubbing him with both hands. I drag my hands up his abs, feeling each one of the hard ridges. "I want to come..." My buzz is starting to wear off and my boldness leaves with it but the high of this space with Damian fuels me. I'm high on this and him and his scent and the way he's looking at me and the fact that he's still got his hand on my hip, gripping me tightly. "On your tongue." And then I remember some men don't do that and while Paxton did, it wasn't that often. *Certainly not as often as I did*. I bite my lip but hold his gaze. "I mean...if you do that kind of thing."

His eyes haven't left mine as he raises his hand higher and rubs the skin just beneath my breast. "I do that kind of thing."

Fuck. Me.

His hand drops from under my sweater and finds the waistband of my leggings. He pulls them gently before letting them snap against my skin and I whimper. "Damian, don't tease me."

"Oh? You mean the way you've been teasing me the past five years?"

A smile tugs at my lips at his playfulness. "I didn't...think you noticed."

His hands drag up the sides of my body, sliding up the slope of my neck and then his thumb drags across my bottom lip, dipping slightly into my mouth. "I fucking noticed, Shay." His thumb falls from my lip and then his head is moving slowly towards mine. I reach up on my toes to meet him halfway and just before our lips touch, Damian's phone beeps just as I hear the sound of a door slamming. It breaks the sensual haze we are in and we both snap our gazes towards the interruptions.

I hear the distant sound of Veronica yelling just as Damian pulls his phone from his pocket. "Are you fucking kidding me?" he growls, storming towards the door. I scurry behind him but he turns around to glare at me. "No."

"What do you mean no?" I ask. "If something is wrong with Veronica…"

"You and I both know she and Derek just got into a drunken argument. So no, you do not need to go out there. You stay here," he says and I can hear the implication. *How would we explain this?*

I watch from the window as Damian walks outside and Veronica looks at him, points at Derek, and makes a motion with her hands that is probably along the lines of *we're through*.

For tonight, I automatically think and mentally curse my best friend and her fuck-buddy slash boyfriend for being on their usual bullshit and ruining everything Damian and I were working towards. *Especially since they'll be fine in two days, if not tomorrow.*

Derek and Damian talk for a few moments before I see one of Derek's security's cars. He gets in and heads down my long driveway. I'm waiting for my phone to beep with a text from Veronica, and I suppose I should probably go back to the main house before she realizes I'm not there.

Damian comes back in and lets out a sigh. "Who knows what they're even arguing about." He waves me over. "Let's go, I'll walk you back."

"But—"

"No." He pins me with a glare. "This…I let things get too far, and I'm sorry." He clears his throat. "This is why I like to keep lines clear and I don't drink and I certainly don't need you here." He points around the guesthouse.

"So that's it? I understand that maybe with Veronica here it isn't the best idea but…not…ever?"

He takes a deep breath and looks around the room avoiding my gaze. "No."

"You're kidding."

"No, let's go." He stands at the open door waiting for me to leave.

"Damian—"

"Shay," he barks and I frown at the tone he's taking with me. Especially after everything that's transpired here. I feel humiliated and rejected, and his attitude towards me like this is all my fault is not helping. I move towards the door, my eyes narrowed at him because now I'm fucking pissed. He grabs my elbow, keeping me in place. "I'm sorry." His tone is soft and they match his eyes that seem as sorrowful as his words.

I shut the door behind me and stand in front of it. "Don't make me leave."

He puts his hands over his eyes. "What are you going to do about Veronica?"

"If she hasn't texted me by now, she's probably asleep."

"It's too risky," he argues.

"So? Don't you ever take risks?" I counter.

"When it comes to you? No."

I don't know why the words warm me but they do, and I feel them in my chest and between my legs as they wrap around me. "Tell me this isn't over."

He sighs. "I don't know, Shay."

I swallow and take a step closer to him, running my hand up his torso again and then back down, allowing it to graze over his groin *twice*. My knuckles drag down his shaft and then I place my palm flat against his dick that's slightly hard and I squeeze. "Are you sure?"

His nostrils flare and then he's pushed me against the door, his arms on either side of me, his face a mere inch from mine and I wonder why he hasn't kissed me yet. "Next time you touch my dick, it's going in your mouth." He takes a step back and I struggle to breathe after having him in my space. He shrugs cockily. "If you do that kind of thing," he says repeating my words back to me.

I open the door behind me, realizing my best game plan is to keep him wanting more and maybe not while Veronica is sleeping over. "Oh, I do all kinds of things." I give him a wicked smirk before I'm out the door without another look back, despite the fact that I know he's right behind me.

Chapter EIGHT

Shay

Me: Can we go for a run?

Damian: Of course, when will you be ready?

Me: 20 minutes?

Damian: So, by that you mean 35?

Me: *middle finger emoji*

Damian: I'll be ready in 20.

I really don't want to go for a run but I *do* want to parade around Damian in tight spandex shorts and a sports bra. I'm still buzzing from the events of last night. My skin tingles from where he touched me, and the spaces where he alluded to touching me ache with the thought of him there.

Goddamn, he is so fine.

"Next time you touch my dick it's going in your mouth." I squeeze my eyes shut thinking about the delicious orgasm I gave myself last night when I got back to my room. I was wound up so tight by my night with Damian that I was ready to come the second I glided my finger over my clit. I didn't even need my vibrator.

Okay, I did use it after, but it only helped marginally. At this point, I don't think I'm going to know true relief until Damian Hunt is between my legs.

"I do that kind of thing." My mind remembers. In reference to my pussy. *Him eating it.*

I wave a hand over my face trying to calm myself *and my pussy* down. I pull on the pale purple spandex shorts and sports bra that matches because this color makes my skin glow and the shorts make my ass look fantastic.

And Damian runs behind me so…

I pull my hair up into a high ponytail, grateful for the natural wave it's sporting today from my curls from yesterday. I put on a headband to keep any stray hairs out of my face and protect my edges and grab my phone and my AirPods. Sometimes I run in silence, but I feel like music today to drown out the roaring thoughts of wanting my bodyguard to fuck me until I don't know my own name.

I stare at the mirror and notice my nipples are hard, easily visible through my top. I'm not cold but sometimes I can't hide them—*it probably doesn't help that I'm still very horny despite my three orgasms last night*, and while most of the time I change into something that conceals them better, I decide against it for obvious reasons.

I make my way down the hall, peeking my head into the guest room knowing for sure that Veronica is still asleep, and sure enough, the blackout curtains are drawn and I hear her softly snoring. Not that Veronica would go running. She hates it and prefers literally any other form of working out. I send her a text that I'm going for a run just in case she wakes up and wonders where I am. I make my way down the staircase and a smile finds my face when I see Damian waiting at the door looking like temptation in basketball shorts.

He chuckles and raises an eyebrow as soon as he sees me. "So that's how you're playing it, huh?"

"Playing what?" His eyes move off of my face to my chest and then down the rest of my body lingering on my legs before moving up again. His gaze heats my skin and I shift, trying to relieve some of the ache between my legs. "Are you telling me I look good, Mr. Hunt?"

He pulls a baseball hat onto his head opting to leave it forward, thank God. A man in a backwards hat is my fucking weakness. Damian in a backwards hat? I might faint. "Something like that," he says as he walks out the front door.

I slide my phone in the right pocket on my thigh meant to keep my phone snug and look up at him. It's only about eight in the morning, but it's July in LA which means it's already hot and only going to get hotter in the next hour.

"Once around the community?" he asks, and I nod. It's about three miles and I usually jog the first mile, walk the second, and jog the third, ending with a sprint.

To be honest, I wouldn't mind if we walked the whole three miles today so we can talk.

We start our run once we're out of my front gate and begin our silent jog down the street. We don't usually talk; I'm not in the kind of shape that allows me to have a whole conversation while running. Damian, on the other hand, is a machine and could probably have a full-fledged argument while sprinting. It's a nice morning, and I note some of the non-gated houses have set up their sprinklers. Some people are already out by their pools. Kids are outside playing. About ten minutes later, we finish the first mile and we slow to a stop.

"I have to start pushing you harder. You barely broke a sweat," he says and I pull the AirPods out of my ear, holding them in my hand as we continue walking.

"Excuse you, I liked that pace. And there are other ways you could push me that will make me break a sweat. Probably more enjoyable too."

"I don't know, it's pretty enjoyable for me running behind you." I shake my head, turning back towards the road as a smile slowly finds my face. "I can't stop thinking about last night." *Oh, this is almost too easy.* Part of me thought he wouldn't be up for talking about it, but he's openly flirting with me?

"Oh?"

"I pride myself on keeping it together. Not losing control and yet...all I want to do is lose myself in you." My eyes widen at his confession and I reach for his hand when he pulls away slightly and shakes his head. "Forget we're in public?"

"Right. Yes." I let out a breath because there are always eyes watching. Even in this gated community, where there aren't usually a ton of paparazzi. Even fellow celebrities have big mouths. It's fucking annoying.

"I can't stop thinking about you either. I thought about you all last night," I tell him.

"What did you think about?" His voice lowers, like he knows what he's asking is private.

"What it would feel like. You and me. My imagination and my vibrator didn't really do it justice." He groans, picking his hat up and moving it backwards to rub a hand over his face, scrubbing a hand over his stubbled jaw which sounds almost as sexy as it looks. "Are you fucking kidding me?" I mutter and he chuckles.

"Your nipples are poking through your top, those shorts give your ass so much definition, they're basically molded to you, and you just gave me a visual of you fucking a vibrator while you thought about me, and you can't handle how I wear my hat?"

I glare at him. "Correct. Unless of course, you want me to try to mount you in front of all of the gated community of Lakeland?"

He shoots me a smile, revealing all of his teeth and I swear my heart skips a beat. "I have your itinerary for the day," he starts, and I note he still hasn't moved his hat. *Tease.* "I see you have a party downtown tonight?"

"Unfortunately. I'm supposed to go with Paxton." I shake my head. "I am so fucking angry with him." He doesn't respond. "I trusted him." I sigh. "It's weird though; I feel nothing for him. It's like he's a totally different person to me now. Learning about that kind of betrayal—" I scrunch my nose. "I'm disgusted. How will I ever trust anyone again?"

"Not all men cheat."

A smile ghosts over my face, but I don't look at him. "Never cheated on anyone?"

"No," he answers instantly.

"Not even emotionally? Maybe when you were overseas and a little bit homesick?" I probe, putting my thumb and index finger an inch apart.

"No. When I'm with a woman, I only have eyes for her." I turn to look at him and our eyes meet. Dark, intense eyes that I can't look away from. My heart flutters thinking about him with his eyes on me. *Only for me.*

I nod and turn back towards the road. "Good to know."

"If there's any point that you want to go," he starts, "you let me know." I cock my head to the side wondering what he means when he clarifies. "Tonight?"

"Oh. Right."

I want to say something about us or what later tonight after the party could mean for him and me or what any of this means for him and me, but he speaks before I can figure out how to phrase it. "Race you the last mile?" He looks at his watch before turning to me. "Come on, I'll go slow."

I put my middle finger up although it wasn't a dig. He can run a mile in six minutes and it takes me somewhere around ten.

"Fine." I narrow my gaze at him, and just before he finishes his countdown from one, I take off back towards my house.

I spend most of the day getting ready for Lorenzo DiLaurenti's party, the *It* director in Hollywood and the director of Paxton's most recent film. It's my first time being invited and I'll admit I am excited. The *Enzo Gala* is the event of the summer and will have dozens of directors in attendance. With it being my final season of the show, and as I'm staring into the abyss of the unknown, it would be nice to see what else is out there. What else *this* world can offer me. Lorenzo's movie is anticipated to sweep the Oscars with nominations in all five major categories and several others. This party is the whole reason my PR team advised that I not end things with Paxton and yet I'm dreading going. I don't want to fake anything. I don't want to be on Paxton's arm. I knew there would have to be some pleasantries and despite my anger last night, I knew there would be touching and perhaps even a kiss.

My hair and makeup team are just finishing up and I'm extremely pleased with how I look as I twirl in my full-length mirror. A floor-length champagne-beaded gown hugs me in all the right places giving me an even more cinched waist and tasteful cleavage with its sweetheart neckline. The back is completely open and goes down to a few inches above my butt and I am so grateful for all of the yoga and Pilates I've been doing recently to give me such a toned back. There is a slit that goes up to just above my knee and I hope it's enough to still catch Damian's attention. My hair is pulled off to one side, falling over my left shoulder and I can't help picturing Damian's mouth running over the skin exposed on the right side of my neck and shoulder. His teeth sinking into the flesh when we get back later tonight.

That is absolutely the plan.

I'm not planning to have any house guests tonight but I'm planning to have Damian in my bed. My lips are painted red but that is the boldest thing about my makeup; my eyes are covered with a mix of gold and bronze to complement my dress and my complexion.

Usually, Paxton and I would be arriving at something like this together but I told him there was zero chance of that happening and that I would meet him there. This isn't a red carpet event, so it's not as if we need to take pictures together. My manager, Cooper, did order a limousine for me tonight and I'll admit, a wicked thought floats through me about what Damian and I could do once the privacy screen goes up. Usually, he rides in the front, but there have been times when he's ridden in the back with me if he wants to go over any precautions or if it's a club I haven't been to and he wants to let me know where he'll be stationed.

He would actually get blueprints of where we'd be and mark it like a treasure map. X's for where he'd be and dotted lines of routes I should take if anything happens and I can't find him.

I make my way downstairs and am surprised I don't see Damian waiting for me at the bottom of the stairs like he always does. I'm just about to text him to let him know I'm ready when I hear a sharp intake of breath followed by a *"fuck"* from behind me.

I turn towards the source of the sound and see him coming towards me in a full black tuxedo with a glass of champagne in his hand and my mouth drops open in shock. "*You're* having a drink?"

He doesn't respond; he just runs his gaze all over me like he doesn't know where to look first. His eyes ping-pong between my breasts and my legs and my face—more specifically my mouth—then my eyes then my mouth again. He hands me the flute of champagne and I realize it's for me to calm my nerves. "You look…breathtaking. My God, you're a vision."

I gently graze my bottom lip with my teeth, grateful I'm wearing a lip stain that won't move. "Thank you." I move towards him and run my finger over his black tie beneath his vest and jacket. "You look very nice as well." I rove my eyes over him the same way he did to me. "You didn't have to wear a tux."

He shrugs. "It was the safest option and you know I like to blend in as best as possible."

I nod as he reaches for my hand and spins me around slowly. I shiver when his hand finds the bare space of my lower back. When I'm facing him again, his eyes are on mine, and if he doesn't stop staring at me like he wants to devour me, I am not going anywhere.

"Stop looking at me like that." I take a sip of my champagne, tipping my head back but still keeping my eyes on him. My cheeks are heating and the tiny thong I'm wearing is already getting wet at all of the sexy fantasies flying through my head.

He takes a step towards me. "I can't look at you like *this* out there, so I have to get it out of my system now."

He lightly runs his knuckles over my cheek and down the side of my neck that's exposed and then between the valley of my breasts, dragging his finger along both slopes. Goosebumps erupt all over and I gasp before taking a step back. "Damian." My nipples pucker against the fabric and all I have to do is slide the dress gently off one shoulder and he could be staring at my naked breasts. I contemplate doing it, giving him a glimpse of what's to come later but his phone beeps, breaking the tension.

"The limo is here," he says moving away from me and towards the door.

I take a larger sip of my champagne and the words leave my lips before I can stop them. "You haven't kissed me."

He turns around and tilts his head to the side. "Come again?"

"You haven't kissed me."

He stares at me as if he doesn't understand what I'm saying. "And now is the time to do that for the first time?" He moves back towards me. "You think now, while the driver is waiting outside to take you to a party, is the time for me to put my lips on yours for the first time? While I have to be careful about your lipstick and your makeup and can't slide my tongue between your lips? What, you're expecting a nice, simple, and polite kiss on the lips? You don't think I'll want to rip this dress off? You really think the first time we kiss should be…now?"

The words die on my tongue and I'm at a loss. I guess I agree and maybe I should have phrased the question as "*when* are you going to kiss me?" I finish the rest of my champagne before setting the flute on the credenza in my entryway and grabbing the clutch I'd set down.

"Later," I tell him as I walk by and I feel his warm hand on the small of my back all the way to the door before he drops it.

The driver is already outside and he opens the door just as I start down my walkway. I can hear Damian behind me, and when I get to the door, I look up at him. "Can you ride in the back with me?" I ask and he nods once before darting his eyes to the driver who appears unfazed. Limo drivers exercise the most discretion. They all sign strict NDAs so they can't share whatever they see or hear or think with anyone. I lift my dress and sit in the seat closest to the door so I don't have to move around too much. Damian walks around the other side so I don't have to move and sits next to me. Immediately, I press the button to raise the privacy screen and Damian's hand tries to swat mine away to keep it down.

"You know he won't say anything," I whisper. "You vet all the drivers too." The screen gets to the top and I turn to face him. "Did you see my shoes?" I turn to rest my back against the door and lift one of my feet adorned with a glittery ankle-strapped stiletto to rest on his knee, careful not to let the bottom of my shoe touch his pants. He glares at me knowing what I'm doing and yet his hand finds the strap wrapped around my ankle and rubs the skin there before trailing slowly up my leg.

"I love your legs," he says, not pulling his gaze away from my legs, letting his eyes drag up along with his hand.

"I know," I tell him and his eyes snap to mine at my response.

"You know?"

"Yes, did you know you're never exactly discreet with how your eyes devour my legs when they're on display?"

He lifts my leg and I sink further in my seat as his lips find my ankle and trail up my leg. "Is that so?" His tongue darts out and trails up my leg almost to my knee and I bite my bottom lip, hoping and praying that his tongue will make it higher.

"I don't want to go anymore," I blurt out. I know we are probably almost there as Lorenzo doesn't live that far from me, but suddenly, I care less about the party that could potentially help my career and more about this man's tongue on my clit.

"Yes, you do," he grunts.

"No. I want you," I argue, reaching for the switch to lower the privacy screen to tell the driver to turn around, but Damian swats my hand away.

"You need to go. More importantly, you want to go. Stop thinking with your pussy, Shay." He sets my leg back across his lap but makes no effort to move it.

I scoff even though the vulgar words falling from his lips make me shudder. "Excuse you? I was doing fine. You're the one that started eye fucking me and touching me the second I walked down the stairs. Maybe *you* should stop thinking with your dick until you decide you're ready to use it."

"Who says I'm not?" He gives me an inquisitive look. "We haven't exactly had a lot of time since last night."

I roll my eyes petulantly even though he's right. We've only had a small window where we've truly been alone and I know that we need more time to explore whatever this is. *We need all night.*

"Will you stay in the main house tonight?" I ask him.

"Are you planning for any house guests?" I shake my head and give him a devilish grin.

"No. Just me."

He licks his lips as he traces his eyes down my body. "I think that can be arranged."

"Please," I push, wanting something to look forward to as I prepare for a night of fake pleasantries and making nice with Paxton.

His blue eyes trail back up my legs and settle on the apex of my thighs that's barely covered by my dress and licks his lips. "So, about that kiss…" he says as his eyes slowly move up to mine.

"You can't be serious. NOW? You said there wasn't enough time when we were at the house, but now, minutes before we arrive is the time?"

"I didn't mean *those* lips." My mouth drops open and a whimper leaves my lips at the thought of his hot mouth pressed against my wet cunt.

"Now?"

"Now." His eyes are dark and they flair wickedly as he moves in front of me to the floor of the limo. He raises my dress just as the limo slows. "Fuck," he grits out as his eyes drop to his watch. "I thought we had more time." Then his face is between my thighs, his stubble rubbing deliciously against the skin as his mouth inches closer to my pussy and his breath against my wet flesh has the beginnings of my orgasm dancing beneath my skin. I feel the limo slowing further and just before it comes to a stop, he presses a kiss to my satin-covered pussy, so light and so gentle that I convulse.

"Oh my god, Damian." My clit is hard and pulsing and desperate for his lips to wrap around the sensitive flesh. I raise my hips closer to his mouth for more contact when he chuckles and pushes my hips back down.

"Later," he grunts as he helps me to pull my dress back down.

Chapter NINE

DAMIAN

I DON'T KNOW WHAT POSSESSED ME TO DO THAT, TEASE US both just before we arrived, and I know she's just as frustrated with my actions. I get out of the car and make my way around the limo to open the door for Shay, when Paxton, dressed in a tuxedo and holding a single red rose, appears standing next to her door preparing to open it. "Thanks for getting her here." He nods at me though I sense something dismissive in his tone as he opens the door.

From my vantage point, I can't see her face but when he holds his hand out for her, I can see her shoo him away. She gets out of the car on her own even though I know she needs some help with the way the dress conforms to her.

Her eyes find mine immediately, holding my gaze for a second before she blinks away and a detached look moves up over her face as she settles back on Paxton.

"You look gorgeous," he tells her, holding out the flower for her. The party is being held at Lorenzo DiLaurenti's house, so there aren't any paparazzi lurking around but there are some people out front;

guests and waitstaff are walking around with drinks and there are a number of men running the valet, so she puts on a smile for any potential onlookers and takes the flower before running it under her nose gently.

"Thank you. You look nice." She runs her gaze over him once, not quite the same way she looked me over, but enough to trigger just a spike of jealousy in my memory that she used to date this man and she does find him attractive. His hand finds the small of her bare back as they move up the walkway covered with a red velvet carpet. The house is enormous and there is a huge tent set up behind the house where the party is going to be held. While she was getting ready, I left her with a member of my team that I have in place for events and scoped out the location. It's been a while since anything worried me, but there are times, especially at parties like this, when I can't be sure of everyone who'll be in attendance and it requires me to be extra vigilant. There aren't any overt threats at the moment, but you never know who could be hiding in plain sight.

We make it to the tent and Paxton picks two flutes off the tray, handing one to her, and I hate the picture he's painting of the doting boyfriend. Thoughts of him trying to liquor her up and charm his way into her bed tonight flash through my brain and an irrational anger moves through me.

She's not mine.

I'm casually walking through the tent when I hear my last name being called from behind me. I turn to see Paxton's head of security, Brent Jackson, dressed in a black suit versus a tuxedo. He nods towards me, nursing a glass of whiskey in a highball glass.

"Jackson." I nod at him as I continue walking. We aren't particularly friends, and now I'm wondering just how much he knew about Paxton's extra-curricular women and it pisses me off that he probably enabled that bullshit.

"She looks great." He nods towards Shay and my eyes follow his line of sight.

She's talking to a group of people, commanding their attention just as she always does. When Shay is in a room, all eyes find her.

Even if it's just for a moment. People want to be near her. She's got this energy that's intoxicating and sexy that draws you in. A boisterous laugh leaves the crowd and I see Paxton wrap his arm around her waist and press a kiss to her temple. I wait for her to tense or appear uncomfortable but she doesn't and though I know why, *because she's got ten sets of eyes on her*, it bothers me more than I care to admit that he can touch her so freely.

Get your shit together, Hunt.

"He wants her back, I know. But he's going to have to do better than this, I told him." Brent tucks a hand in his pocket. "He thinks that they'll just fall back into old patterns if they fake it long enough."

The crowd somewhat disperses and Paxton and Shay make their way to the dance floor to begin a slow dance around the space. There are several other couples dancing and pictures are being snapped from all angles. I watch as he spins her effortlessly before dipping her and a giggle leaves her.

She looked so beautiful and carefree. I hate that he gets to see it after everything he's put her through. Even if it is just for show.

I turn my head back to Brent who now has a plate of bacon-wrapped scallops.

"After he fucked every woman in Hollywood? He can't possibly be that foolish. Shay is not going to forgive him," I tell him and I'm not sure if I'm trying to convince him or myself of that.

"He's thinking of taking her on a trip. Maybe Paris or somewhere tropical. He's going to ask her tonight. Somewhere they can fall off the face of the Earth for a few days and they can talk and be alone."

"A trip isn't going to move her. She goes to Paris any time she wants to go shopping and she's been to every tropical destination on the planet at least twice." *That girl will use any excuse to be in a bathing suit on a beach with a margarita.*

"Not with a Harry Winston diamond on her finger."

I jerk my head towards him. "Excuse me?"

"Don't say anything, yeah?" He downs the rest of his drink and puts it on a tray of a server passing by like he's a guest and not someone on duty. *He's such a fucking prick.* "But yeah, he's going to ask her to marry him."

I rub a hand over my forehead as I stare at his security in disbelief. "You cannot be serious. She doesn't trust him. She's not going to say yes."

"I tried to tell him that." He shrugs. "He can't force her down the aisle and obviously she doesn't trust him, but he's hoping that a ring will buy him some time and at the very least some good press."

Fuck, is he going to spring a ring in public to force her to keep up appearances? I'll fucking kill him.

"When?" I grit out, trying my best to keep my anger in check, but Brent's words coupled with Paxton's hand moving down too close to her ass for my taste as they move around the dance floor has the word coming out harsh and clipped.

"I don't know."

"In public?"

"Probably."

Fuck.

"Why is he doing this? Trying to trap her into a relationship he doesn't want to be in himself?"

"What makes you think he doesn't? Because he's cheated on her a few times? Come on, Hunt you can't be that naive. He cares a great deal for Shay." He chuckles like it's the most common thing in the world. "Shay is coming up fast. Do you know the kind of power couple they'd make? She's good for his image."

"And what about hers?" I ask.

"He's not bad for hers either. They're good for each other."

"He's the cliché Hollywood playboy and they think the girl next door is good for his image, but he is *not* good for her."

"No one knows he's a playboy, Hunt. Relax. Look at how everyone has been falling at her feet all night." He gestures towards the crowd and the circle of people that are watching them float around the dance floor.

"That's not Paxton's doing. She's always been charming," I argue, hating that he's trying to allude that this asshole is why she's so successful.

"No, but he's the reason she's where she is *tonight*. Why *those* people," he points, "those directors, more importantly, are falling at her feet. I know you're smart enough to know it's not what you know, it's who you know. And more importantly, in this business, who you're fucking."

The thought of his hands on her after mine just were irritates the fuck out of me. Infuriates me that she's so beautiful even on the arm of a man that doesn't deserve her.

"I gotta take a leak, I'll catch you later, Hunt." He reaches out to shake my hand and I oblige, my eyes not leaving Shay who's managed to break away from Paxton, and is over by the buffet table getting a small plate of food. Grateful for Brent's exit, I pull out my phone and pull up her contact.

Me: You look stunning. I can't take my eyes off of you.

I watch as she must feel the vibration because she sets her plate down and pulls her phone out of her clutch. A tiny smile slowly moves onto her face. I see her typing and then she slides it back into her purse so she can pick up her plate before moving to an open table to sit down. She doesn't look my way even though I know she knows where I'm standing and I'm not surprised when I feel the buzz in my hand.

Winter: I wish I had a reason to keep my eyes on you. You look so handsome tonight. I can't wait to get you out of that tux.

A surge of confidence moves through me. I wasn't a stranger to female attention. Even some of Shay's friends have let their eyes roam over me shamelessly, but attention from Shay is an entirely different high.

Paxton sits next to her at the table and pulls a piece of cheese off her plate and whispers something in her ear. Her eyes shift from side to side before turning to look at him and I want to turn away. I don't want to be privy to their intimacies and yet I have to focus on

Shay. *And therein lies the problem with getting involved with the person you're protecting.*

My eyes on her will mean something different when I've touched her, kissed her, fucked her. I'll be staring more at her curves and her smile and how beautiful she looks and I'll be less aware of what's going on around her.

And then I remember the ring he very well may have in his pocket. *He wouldn't ask her here, right?* That would just be awkward and tacky and Shay would hate that even if they were in an actual relationship.

If he really wanted her back then he absolutely would try to whisk her away on some romantic vacation, I'd be forced to witness.

My teeth grit at the thought of his hands on her, his lips on her, his tongue inside of her. My dick hardens thinking about me doing all of those things to her and I turn away in an attempt to will it back down.

"Actor or model?" I hear from next to me and when I turn my gaze, I see a short busty brunette with long wavy hair in a turquoise dress with eyes that match it staring up at me. She flutters her eyelashes seductively as she moves her martini pick around her glass in a circle.

"Excuse me, Miss?" I ask, even though I heard every word.

"Are you an actor or a model?" She puts the stick to her mouth and pulls the olive off with her teeth. "And more importantly, your place or mine later?" I raise an eyebrow at her and she giggles. "Don't be so serious. I'm kidding!" She giggles before touching my arm. "Well, sort of." I take a step back, out of reach.

"I'm neither. I'm on duty."

"Oh, you must be someone's security then." She runs her eyes up and down my body and sinks her teeth into her lips. My eyes move to Shay hearing her reference my job and I'm surprised to see her eyes on me, an eyebrow raised sexily like I'd been caught doing something. I turn to look at the woman who's begun talking about what it is she does, *something about film editing which is just a stepping stone into acting,* and then back to Shay as if to say: *you can't possibly be jealous.*

Her eyes dart to the woman next to me and then back to me before she cocks her head to the side. *Watch me*, I can practically hear her thoughts in response to mine and then she's moving out of her chair towards us.

I cross my arms over my chest as I watch her curiously because I'm not sure what she's planning to do given that she can't exactly let this woman know that the only woman I plan to take home tonight is her.

"Hi, Damian." She smiles, her eyes sparkling as she approaches us. "Who's your friend?"

"Oh my, Shay Eastwood! The life of tonight's party, it seems." She beams and looks up at me to explain why she'd be over here seemingly ruining her chances with me.

I clear my throat. "I'm sorry, I didn't get your name, Miss?"

"It's Annabelle." She nods. "How do you two know each other?"

"Oh, we are very well acquainted." Shay scrunches her nose and moves closer to me and her scent mixed with her territoriality is making me want to drag her into the nearest room and fuck the jealousy out of her. "The man I trust more than anyone."

"Oh, so he must be your bodyguard." She giggles. "Lucky you."

Shay rolls her eyes. "Yes, and he's seeing someone who I'm actually quite fond of," she says matter of factly and I try not to react to her lie or the thought that I'm seeing *her*.

"Shame." She pouts. "Well, lovely to meet you," she says, giving Shay a pleasant smile and then she's gone without another word.

"I'm seeing someone?" I ask.

"Aren't you?" She frowns, casting her gaze to the room, smiling at someone, and giving them a small wave. "Or was your mouth on my pussy in the limo earlier tonight a figment of my imagination?" She turns to look up at me and I can see the lust in her eyes as she lets her eyes sweep down my body quickly.

"Jealous?" I ask.

"No," she says with a dramatic eye roll before she purses her lips. "Maybe."

"You're here with another man, you know," I remind her.

"But he's not going to touch me tonight."

"And you thought I'd touch her? My mouth on your pussy was *not* a figment of your imagination." It's been playing through my mind on a loop since my lips touched the delicate satin.

She shrugs. "Maybe you thought you could have both. Me and then her later." She rolls her eyes.

"I'm not Paxton."

Her eyes flash to mine angrily. "Not fair."

"Neither is assuming I'm going to fuck anyone other than you tonight," I snap, and widen my stance, crossing my arms over my chest.

I know my words affect her but she doesn't respond to them. She licks her lips and turns her gaze towards the table behind us. "Did you eat anything?"

I'm about to respond when Paxton makes his way over. "Mind if I steal my woman back, Hunt?" He tips his chin towards me and wraps a hand around her shoulder, pressing a kiss to her cheek, and the narrowed look he gives me makes me think he's trying to send me a message.

"Not your woman and stop being so touchy," she grits out and slides away without drawing any attention.

"Shay, baby…"

"What did I tell you?" she starts.

"You said in public—"

"That doesn't give you permission to feel me up."

"Shay—" He looks at me, giving me a look. "You mind? I don't think you need to be present for this conversation. No threats here."

"Are you sure about that?" she snaps before turning her eyes to me. "I'm good, D."

I nod and move away from them but stay close enough that I can still see their body language. He seems to be nervous and is trying his best to keep her from exploding. I know Shay doesn't want to either. She prides herself on maintaining her composure. His hands find hers, clasping them in his and bringing them to his lips before rubbing his thumbs across her skin. "I'm sorry, Shay." I see his lips move and then his hands find her cheeks, stroking the skin. I frown, watching her nod and then he presses a kiss to her forehead. I watch her walk away from him and back towards the house and a cocky smile finds his face as he fiddles with his cufflinks and walks in the opposite direction.

What the hell?

I follow her and watch her walk into the bathroom. I stand out front and pull out my phone to text her only to be surprised by a message from her.

> **Winter: I'm alone in here.**
>
> **Me: Okay?**
>
> **Winter: Come in please.**
>
> **Me: You sure that's a good idea?**
>
> **Winter: No, but you're hot when you're jealous and I thought your dick in my mouth might calm you down.**

My dick pulses in my slacks.

> **Me: Terrible idea.**

I want to ask what's going on with her and Paxton but a part of me wonders if I'm not entitled to that information. Maybe I'm just an itch she wants to scratch or something she just wants to get out of her system before she goes back to her boyfriend.

Potential future husband.

I push through the door, letting my dick and my curiosity cloud my judgment to find her running her fingers through her hair in the mirror. Her eyes catch mine in the reflection and she turns around giving me a wicked smirk. "I thought this was a terrible idea?"

I walk towards her until I'm pressed up against her with her back against my front. "It is." I run both of my hands down her sides gently and settle on her hips, gripping them, and she shivers.

"I love the way your hands feel on me." She turns in my arms and runs her hands up my torso. "Every time he touches me, I wish it was you."

I reach up to cup her face and she wets her lips instantly. I take it as an invitation when her eyes drop to my lips and then flutter closed for just a second before they slowly open. She's staring up at me through her thick full lashes and I can honestly say I've never seen anything sexier than the way she's looking at me. I lean down and brush my lips across hers lightly and she lets out the sexiest sigh. I take another step closer, pushing her against the sink, and press my dick into her stomach. I push my lips to hers slightly harder, but not too aggressively because she can't leave this room with her lipstick ruined without raising questions as to how that happened while her boyfriend was not with her. She tries to deepen it when I pull back and she frowns.

"More," she whines, grabbing me by my jacket and pulling me closer to her.

I shake my head. "Not here," I tell her, although I wish I could rip this dress off of her and impale her on my dick.

"Can we go?"

"Whenever you're ready, gorgeous."

A smile crosses her face that would make an atheist believe in God before she looks at the door and then back to me and then slowly, she bends over. It takes me a second to realize that she's sliding her underwear down her legs. She holds them up and then slips them in my hand and they're fucking damp.

She gives me a wicked smirk as she backs up towards the door. I finger them gently, running my thumb over the damp fabric. Her eyes are still on mine, so I hold them under my nose and inhale her sexy scent, never breaking our gaze.

"Damian," she whispers.

"Yes, Miss Eastwood?" I say as I slip her panties into my pocket after one final inhale.

"I cannot wait to fuck you."

Chapter TEN

DAMIAN

I'M RELIEVED THAT THERE ISN'T ANYONE LINGERING OUTSIDE of the bathroom when she leaves because I'm only a few steps behind her. I watch as she makes her way over to Paxton, touches his arm, pulling him away from the crowd, and whispers something in his ear. My hand grips the panties that are in my pocket, still fingering the crotch of them as I try to recall the scent. God, she smelled so sweet. The mixture of her perfume and that sexy earthy scent is making me wild. *Reckless*. It's making me want to walk over to where she's standing with Paxton and tell him she doesn't owe him any explanations. That they're finished and that I planned to spend the rest of the night reminding her what orgasms—*yes, plural*—feel like.

I can tell he's annoyed, his stance is combative, his arms are crossed over his chest, and his eyes are slightly narrowed. We've only been here about an hour and a half, but my guess is she's talked to everyone that she's needed to and she wants to leave them wanting more. I'm sure he's pissed that she's not only leaving early but that he's not invited to leave with her.

I see him guiding her somewhere assumedly so they can be alone and I follow so that she's not out of my sight. I don't think Paxton would ever manhandle her, but she's also trying to end their relationship much to his disappointment, so I can't be sure. I'm only about twenty feet from them, my back turned to try to give them some privacy when all I want to do is stand behind her and dare him to touch her.

It isn't until I hear her call my name that I turn around to see that he has her against the wall, with his hand wrapped around her wrist. She doesn't seem like she's in pain, but for her to call for me, I know that means she doesn't want to be in this situation anymore. I'm next to her in an instant, putting myself between him and her forcing Paxton to release her wrist and stare him down.

"What's going on?" He furrows his brow and begins to speak when I cut him off, raising a hand. "Not you." I turn my head to the side enough to see her hand resting on her hip. "Eastwood," I grunt. I use her last name from time to time, and right now I'm trying to remain as professional as I can. Using her last name is keeping me from showing this asshole how I feel about him putting his hands on the woman that—*somewhat*—belongs to me.

"He's throwing a tantrum because I'm leaving and don't want to go on his bullshit fake vacation."

"It's not fake," Paxton counters.

"It's fake in the sense that you want to do it for pictures. I'm over it. I don't want to be with you." She stomps. "If we have to fake it for a few months at things like this, *for work*," she stresses, "fine, but if you think I'm going to fake it beyond what is absolutely necessary, you're crazy."

"Why was your hand on her?" I ask him.

"I didn't hurt her," he says instantly.

I'm about to respond that it doesn't answer my question when she interjects.

"No, but I told you to let go and you didn't."

I glower at him. "Is that true?" I suddenly want to break his hand for thinking that she owed him anything.

"Because she wasn't listening!"

"Listening to what?" Shay exclaims. "You fucked up, Paxton! It's over. There's nothing you can say to make this right. There are a million girls out there, probably that you've already fucked that will gladly take my place. Go find one of them."

He runs a hand through his hair and lets out a sigh of exasperation. "I don't want one of them. I want you."

I can tell he's getting irritated with the fact that I'm still standing between them and he's having to speak around me.

"Would have been great if you felt that way before you cheated on me."

His eyes snap to mine angrily like I'm the reason this conversation isn't going the way he wants it to. "I still don't understand why you're here. She's not in any danger. She's safe with me, Hunt. Can't you back off?" I want to respond that based on his actions she is definitely not safe with him, but I refrain as the sound of a camera taking a picture cuts through the tension and my eyes flit to the source of the noise to see someone scurrying around the corner.

"See, you're causing a scene," Paxton groans.

"ME!?" Shay exclaims. "You couldn't just let me go."

"Great, now who knows what's going to come out. Shay, you're fucking unbelievable, you know that? Us staying together benefits you too." He glares at her and I take a step closer to him, forcing him to take a step back.

"Watch your language," I warn him, and it's one I hope he heeds because I don't give more than one.

He groans, knowing he's not going to get anywhere. "This is fucking ridiculous. Your PR team said you were on board."

Shay moves from behind me. "I am! There was never any talk about a vacation and I was *very* clear last night with you about what I wouldn't tolerate. Seems *you* are not on board." She turns to look at me. "I'm ready to leave. *Now*." She walks away, moving to the main room towards the exit, and I follow closely behind her. She stops to talk to a few people and I keep walking towards the exit as I send a message to the driver to have the limo brought around.

After she says her goodbyes, we leave the party in silence as we make our way to the limo. The tension crackles between us and my dick hardens with every passing second at the thought of what's to come. I want my hands on her so badly I know there's no way I can wait until we get back to her house.

"I got it." I nod at the driver before we get to the door and he makes his way to the driver's seat. I look down at her before I open the door and do a quick scan of who is around, how close they are, and if they'll be able to hear what I say before I lean down close to her face. "I'm not letting you out of this limo until you come."

She gasps and her eyes light up with excitement as I open the door for her. She slides in and I close the door behind us, grateful the privacy screen is still up to avoid me having to raise it again. She reaches for my belt the second we begin moving but I grab her hands and pull them to my lips, shaking my head. "No."

Her brown eyes widen expressively. "No?"

I drop to my knees on the floor of the limo and run my hands up her thighs, pulling her down so her ass is on the edge of the seat. "No." My voice is low and I can hear how gravelly it sounds in my own ears. I push her dress to her waist exposing her hairless cunt and I let out a breath because I wasn't expecting her pussy to look as good as it smelled.

I know we should talk about what just happened. I should see if she's okay about the interaction with Paxton but I can't go another fucking second without tasting her.

She'd spent quite a bit of time by her pool recently reminding me that every inch of her is exposed to the sun except for the tiny triangle between her legs and a small area surrounding her nipples. These areas are slightly lighter than the rest of her rich brown skin and the thought that I'm seeing something that no one else in the world gets to see sends a feeling of possession through me. The tan lines are so sexy, like a line drawn on her skin of what I shouldn't touch or taste or kiss.

"Oh." The word leaves her lips with a gush of air and her lips part allowing her tongue to peek through, reminding me that I haven't tasted her mouth because I was trying to avoid ruining her lipstick.

I grip her thighs to hold her in place, my thumbs moving back and forth softly on her inner thighs, and I move up to her face. I drop my eyes to her mouth letting her know what I want and she leans forward to connect our lips. Her hands find my cheeks just as both of our mouths open and my tongue slides through her lips to find hers which she meets with such an urgency my cock jerks in my pants. She moans, holding me closer to her as she moves her hands from my cheeks to the back of my neck to play with the hair there.

There is something about a woman's hands in my hair that drives me insane.

I pull back, remembering how desperately I want to eat her cunt and drop my lips to her neck, peppering a trail of kisses down her chest and between her breasts. I move one hand from where I'm gripping her thighs and gently pull the cup of her dress down and circle her nipple with my tongue, my eyes still on her even though I'm desperate to see what her nipples look like. I want to know if they're dusty pink or brown or a mix between the two. She whimpers and I feel her trying to close her legs, but I drop my hand to keep them apart.

I feel like a man possessed, with my hand between her legs, my mouth on her nipple, and my eyes on hers. I feel desperate to taste every inch of her in the span of this ride home like I don't have all night to explore her body with my mouth.

When I look down at her cunt, she's wetter. Her sex is slick and slightly parted from holding her open so I can see her clit peeking out and my mouth fucking waters for a taste of her. I drop my face, hovering just above her pussy and blow gently. "Damian." She shivers and I watch as the goosebumps erupt on her flesh and her fingers dig into the leather seats. "Don't tease me. God, I've wanted this for so long." She's staring down at me, her breast still exposed and her breathing labored and shaky as she waits for the moment we're both anticipating.

"So have I," I grunt, telling her the truth and she gasps just as I flatten my tongue and run it through her slit and swirl it on her clit.

The sexiest moan leaves her lips and then her hands are in my hair. Her moan vibrates through me and has a direct line to my cock, and fuck, I wish I had the space to take my dick out and grip it while I do this. There is something about eating a woman's pussy that turns me hard as a rock and Shay has the sexiest tasting cunt. I roll my tongue over her clit in circles, fast and then slower when I feel she is getting to the edge based on her moans. I cast my gaze up at her and her eyes are closed, her bottom lip pulled between her teeth and her back arched as best as she can with how she's seated. I slide away from her clit, and lap up every drop of wetness in my quest to the entrance of her sex before I push my tongue inside of her.

"Oh my godddddd." She groans as she pushes me harder against her and grinds her pussy against my face, forcing my tongue further inside of her. I smile inwardly at her body's desperation for a climax as she raises her hips in time with how I make love to her cunt. I slide my tongue back to her clit because I can sense we are nearing her house based on the turns we are making and I was going to make good on my promise of not letting us out of this limo until she'd come all over my face.

I suckle her clit, using my lips to suck her into my mouth. "Jesus Christ, Damian." I slide my hands under her dress to grip her ass and pull her closer and her legs slide over my shoulders as I eat her faster and lap at her making her melt against my tongue.

"Time is running out, if you don't want the driver to know I have my head between your legs back here," I grunt against her.

"Mmmm, I'm close."

I feel us slowing to a stop and I can sense her climax looming. I hear the driver get out of the car and before he can think about opening the door, I reach to the door locking it from the inside before doing the same to the other. "I need you to come all over my face, gorgeous," I tell her. "You know all those nights you touched yourself thinking about me?" I whisper against her wet skin, giving sloppy, wet kisses to her cunt. "I touched my dick just as many times," I confess. "Jacked my dick fucking raw thinking about my tongue stuffed in your cunt." I growl and then she shakes, pushing her hands further into my hair and her pussy harder into my mouth. She lets out a low sexy moan that sounds like my name, making me painfully hard.

"Fuck, I'm going to come," she moans. Her pussy quivers against my tongue and she gets wetter letting me know she's doing exactly that. "Oh my God, right there. Yes!" she shakes as cries out. She pulls her hands from my hair and puts them next to her on either side to keep her upright because when I look up at her she looks like she's going to collapse.

Her eyes drop to mine and they're slightly glassy but she blinks them away as I move back up so that we are face to face. She lunges forward, putting her lips back on mine and her arms around my neck as she kisses me like she can't get enough. She pulls back after a moment and drags her nose down my jawline. "I always loved the way you smell and I can still smell you…along with me." I move off the floor and sit next to her, running a hand through my hair and then along my jaw to collect some of her juices that are covering the area around my mouth.

I unlock the door. "You ready?" I raise an eyebrow at her hoping she hears both meanings in my question. Ready for me to open the door and also for all the things I plan to do to her tonight.

The smile that finds her face tells me she knows exactly what I meant. "Absolutely."

Chapter ELEVEN

Shay

MY BODY IS STILL RECOVERING FROM THE SOUL-shattering orgasm Damian gave me in the back of the limo and now we're in my bedroom like we're a couple that just got back from a night out, and I let myself fantasize about what that would actually be like. A night out with him followed by a sex-filled night in. Dinner and dancing and pictures on the red carpet with the television star and her security-turned-beau. *Could that actually happen?* I allow myself to think about positive news reports and interviews and people shipping us because it's *the cutest fucking story.*

I'm brought out of my fantasy by the sound of a champagne pop and I see Damian setting a bottle in a bucket of ice that he'd brought up from downstairs.

He turned down the lights and lit the fireplace and now his tie is off and he's undone the top few buttons leaving the top of his chest exposed. I can see a sliver of ink and I'm excited to see the tattoos I haven't seen before. I'm still in my dress, knowing it'll take little to no effort to take it off and I want to tease him a little since he knows I'm completely nude underneath. A flash of his lips wrapped around my nipple comes charging into my brain and even though it was brief, it sent a delicious surge through me. "I've never had an orgasm like that." I slowly pull some of the pins out of my hair that are keeping it to the side as he moves towards me, removing his jacket and loosening his cufflinks. His hands reach up to hold my face and the smile he gives me almost stops my heart.

"I want to give you more orgasms like that," he tells me and my sex pulses in anticipation. "I want every orgasm I give you to be better than the last," he whispers against my skin as he reaches under the strap of my dress and lets it fall off my body to pool at my feet. He takes a step back and scans me from my feet to my face and I thank every Pilates and yoga class and every miserable hour spent with my trainer because of the look of hunger and desire in his eyes. "You're the most beautiful woman I've ever laid eyes on." His hand rubs his dick and I lick my lips, wanting to feel him in my mouth because I know I'll enjoy giving him head as much as he loves eating my pussy. I move towards him reaching for his belt when he grabs my hands and I frown.

"This is the second time you've stopped me. Damian, you can't fuck me with your clothes on." I groan as he walks backwards, my hands still in his, and sits down on my gray sitting chair in front of the fireplace. He spreads his legs and pats his thigh giving me a look that heats my entire body. I cock my head to the side before sliding my fingers through my sex that is still wet from his assault. "I'm going to make a mess on your tux."

"Oh, I fucking hope so."

"Don't you want to fuck me?" I ask as I slide onto his lap, straddling him and opening up my sex. The cool air tickles the wet flesh and when his covered dick rubs against my clit, I whimper in response to all the stimulation.

"There are so many ways I can fuck you before I even get my clothes off." His hand slides down between us to my pussy and drags two fingers through my slit slowly. I grip his shoulders to try and tether myself to this moment. He slowly slides his fingers away from me and his tongue darts out to lick them lasciviously.

Jesus Christ, this man is going to kill me.

He nods his chin towards me in that sexy way that men do. "Make yourself come."

I blink at him. "What…? How?"

He shrugs. "However you want. Tell me what you want." He reaches up and grips my chin. "Take what you want."

"Well, take your dick out for starters."

He smiles a dazzling smile that makes my stomach flip and my clit pulse and I hate that he seems to have a hold on my heart and my sex right now and both are fucking dangerous.

"Nice try, gorgeous. Rub your cunt against my dick."

"Through your clothes?"

"You've never dry humped before?" His words are sinful and sexy and low and they rumble through my body. I swallow thinking about pressing my cunt to his covered dick trying to make out every ridge through his clothes.

"Not since I was sixteen with one of my Dad's client's sons." I roll my eyes before a flare of guilt runs through me when I remember where—*the back of my Dad's Maserati*—and when—*my Dad's birthday*. I look up towards the heavens and wince. "Sorry about that." I turn back to him. "Nevertheless, it was not fun."

He chuckles and rubs his thumbs over my nipples. "You didn't do it right." He grips my thighs and moving me back and forth over himself aggressively. A shiver dances up my legs and slides up my back as I roll my cunt over the hardness between us.

"Can we at least do it through your briefs?" I ask him as I begin unbuttoning his shirt. I've seen him shirtless a few times at the beach or when we've been on a private yacht when I've basically begged him but it hasn't been nearly enough times. I gasp when I see his chest, because there are more tattoos than I remember, and fuck it's a turn on. "You are so fucking sexy, Damian. Just looking at you makes me wet." I moan into his ear as I grind my wet cunt on him. His hands find my naked ass and he squeezes. "My heart is pounding right now and I can feel it between my legs." I nibble on his neck and move up his jaw still smelling the scent of my cunt as I begin rubbing against him again. I run my tongue over his pulse point and press a hot wet kiss there that makes his cock jerk beneath me. "Please fuck me, Damian. I need to feel your dick inside of me." I'm trying to break him and I think I know how to do it. "Do you want to know how I know it's big?" He pulls me away and gives me a look that says I might be in trouble for what I have to tell him.

"Tell me," he says through gritted teeth, his voice husky, and his eyes blazing with something between lust and fury.

"I walked in…I didn't realize anyone was in the shower and I saw…" I drop my head back remembering the way my mouth dropped open when I saw how hung he was. "I hadn't meant to."

When I raise my head to meet his eyes, his blue eyes are almost black. "Where?"

"When we spent those few days sailing in Greece last year."

"Was I jacking off?"

A flash of his hand wrapped around his dick crosses my mind. *I wish.* I shake my head. "No."

"I jacked off a lot that trip. It was as if you refused to put on clothes the whole time we were on the boat." He groans in what I assume to be a sexually tortuous memory. I remember that I did spend a lot of time in a very tiny white bikini that left little to the imagination because I didn't have to worry too much about the paparazzi while we were out on the water.

"You think of me when you touch your dick?" I ask him as I rub my cunt against him and I feel myself building as he moves me back and forth over his dick. I grind my pussy against him and I've never felt so sexy and wanton. Me naked and grinding my wet cunt all over a fully clothed man in a three thousand-dollar tuxedo.

"Yes." He grunts as he pulls my face close to his so we're nose to nose. He has one hand on my cheek and the other on my ass. He slows his ministrations but continues fast enough that he could still make me come this way. "Do you think about me while you touch your pussy?"

"Yes," I tell him. "Even when I was with someone else," I whisper. "You've been the star of so many of my fantasies ever since I met you. I felt guilty at times, but I couldn't help it." I gasp as he hits my clit at just the perfect angle. "And now it's real." I grab his face. "Tell me I'm not dreaming."

"No." He grunts and then we're up and moving, with my naked body wrapped around his fully clothed one. He kneels on the bed and pushes me down into it. I'm grateful I unbuttoned his shirt so it comes off with ease. I reach for his belt and he doesn't stop me this time and then his pants are down his legs. I move up the bed and he moves with me but I press my foot against his shoulder, preventing him from coming closer.

"Take the rest of your clothes off," I command and his eyes drop to my pussy, like he's angry at me for stopping him from coming for what he wants. I hadn't realized his shoes were still on until I hear them drop to the floor and then his pants and the clink of his belt and then his briefs are gone leaving him naked and flawless. There's a thatch of neatly trimmed dark hair surrounding the base of his long, thick dick and I swallow with nervous yet excited anticipation as I think about deep-throating him. I stare up at him on his knees and my sex aches with the need for his dick. I've never felt such a primal urge to fuck someone as I do in this moment. My legs fall open in invitation and his eyes drop to my sex and then back to my face and then he's on top of me, his mouth attached to mine and one leg hitched over his hip. I raise my hips to attempt to get closer to his dick. "Fuck. Wait. Baby." His words are strained like he's struggling to get them out and I'm sure it's because his dick just brushed between my wet slit. My heart flips at the term of endearment and I look up at him questioningly. "Should I use a condom?"

My eyes blink several times because I wasn't expecting him to ask and the carnal blur of the night has made me forget all reason. "I—I'm on the shot and I got tested after…well…you went with me to the Doctor, so you know," I whisper, not wanting to have to relive the humiliation of getting tested after learning of Paxton's betrayal.

"That wasn't why I was asking. I just don't want to do anything you're not comfortable with." His blue eyes are so sincere and although it's the least sexy thing we've said to each other all night, I find myself getting wetter.

"I want to fuck you without one," I tell him. "Because you have the nicest dick I've ever seen." I rub my nose against his. "And I trust you more than anyone."

"You know you can trust me." He leans down, pressing a kiss to my lips before he drags his tongue down my body and back to my sex.

"Damian, I'm already wet. I'm ready, *please*," I beg.

"Just give me another taste." His tongue rubs over my clit again and again and again and just as his thumbs reach up and strum gently over my nipples, the build-up of everything we've done since we got out of the limo comes exploding out of me.

"DAMIAN!" I cry out as he licks me to another climax. "Oh my God, right there. Oh God, I'm coming. Yes yes yessss." I put a hand over my eyes as I come down from another roaring orgasm and a giggle leaves my lips as he places gentle feather-like kisses all over the slick flesh.

"Now," he grits out. "Now I'm going to fuck this pretty cunt." He drags his hand over his dick from root to tip as he hovers above me and I watch in fascination as his pre-cum drips onto my sex. "That means you're mine now." He grits out and the thought of being his renders me speechless so I nod in agreement.

Yes, please.

He holds his dick against my sex, not pushing inside, just rubbing against my clit before he taps it three times in rapid succession. "Oh my God, please, Damian," I beg and finally he pushes himself inside of me. I let out a moan as he hits a spot I've never felt. "That feels," a gush of air leaves me, like the wind was just knocked out of me, "really good."

"Yeah?" he asks as his lips crash to mine and he begins fucking me harder with each thrust. "Fuck," he growls as he rotates his hips, forcing my eyes closed as stars explode behind them. He pulls away from my mouth and grunts in my ear as we continue our frenzied fucking, our skin slapping against each other with every thrust. "How the fuck do you feel this good?"

"I don't know, but one taste, and I'm already addicted to how this feels," I moan.

"And you haven't even had a taste." He smirks and I bite my bottom lip.

"You wouldn't let me."

"Trust me, I cannot wait to have you on your knees and those perfect lips wrapped around my dick."

His filthy words ignite something inside me and I feel my orgasm starting in my toes and sliding up my body. "God, I think I'm going to come." My eyes flutter closed.

"Eyes open. I want to see the moment you come all over my cock."

I open them as best as I can, but the feeling is too good and I feel like a tidal wave is pulling me under. "Damian," I moan. "My God, I don't want this to ever end." I think I hear him say *never*, but my eyes slam shut, just as the best orgasm of my life shoots through me touching every inch of my body and making me feel like I'm vibrating. I'm vaguely aware there is skin under my fingertips and I drag my fingernails down something hard and firm, doing my best to pull him closer to me and then I hear him groan as his thrusts get more erratic.

"Fuck, Shay. I'm fucking there, gorgeous. Fuck." I'm still coming down from the high of my orgasm when he finishes, pumping every bit of frustration he's had over the last five years into me. His lips are back on mine as he comes down and I wrap my arms around his neck and legs around his waist, locking my ankles to keep him in place. He pulls back when he finishes coming and looks down at me almost angrily. I frown, wondering why he's looking at me like that when he drops down and kisses my neck and mutters, "The way your pussy just gripped my cock, you'll never marry anyone else."

Chapter
TWELVE

Shay

WHAT DID HE JUST SAY?

My mouth drops open as he slides out of me and lays on his back staring up at the ceiling before turning his head to meet mine. I'm lying on my back as well, but I move instantly to cuddle against him, resting my chin on the hard planes of his chest and sliding my leg through his. My knee bumps against his dick gently and he tightens his hold around me.

"Was that a very weird way of asking me to marry you?" Butterflies flutter in my stomach despite the absurdity of my question.

He loosens his grip to rub my back gently and shakes his head. "No."

The word comes out clipped and although it would be fucking insane if that was what he meant, I can't escape the small part of me that also feels rejected by his no. He sits up on an elbow, forcing me off his chest and I already hate the loss of his warm skin underneath me. "Seems your boyfriend has a ring."

"Ex-boyfriend," I correct reflexively.

"That's what you're focusing on?" He lowers his gaze and it takes a second to realize what the second part of his sentence was. I was so focused on correcting the fact that Paxton is not my boyfriend, especially after what we'd just done, that I missed everything else he said.

"A WHAT?" I sit up. "Who told you that?"

He puts a hand over his eyes and drags it down his face scratching his jaw in the process. "Brent," he grunts, referring to Paxton's security who I swear never really liked me. "I don't know if he was planning to ask you on the vacation he wants to take you on or maybe before you go as a way to get you to go on said vacation, but evidently, there's a Harry Winston diamond with your name on it."

I blink at him several times. "I don't want it."

He looks at me like he doesn't believe me. Like the promise of a proposal or expensive jewelry would be enough to forget about what we'd just done and go running back to Paxton. "You sure?"

"Okay, I'm only going to say this once and then I'm going to need you to trust me because I'm not going to stroke your male ego," I tell him with a cheeky smirk as I climb on top of him. "I don't make it a habit to just sleep with anyone. I'm twenty-three and you're the third man I've ever slept with, which means that *this*," I tell him pointing back and forth between our naked bodies, and more importantly, his hard dick that I'm sitting on, "means something to me. It also means I wouldn't have crossed this line with you if things weren't completely over with Paxton." I roll my eyes. "Yes, of course it doesn't exactly seem like that to everyone but just give it some time, okay? Publicly, Paxton and I have an expiration date. Behind closed doors, it's passed. We are over." I cock my head to the side, remembering his words. I lean down, letting my nipples graze his chest and run my lips down his jaw. "Does the idea of me marrying someone else drive you crazy?"

He grips my hips and pulls me over his dick, rubbing me against it. I let out a moan that sounds pornographic as his dick slides over my clit. "Yes," he says and I'll admit I'm a little shocked at his honesty. "I've spent the last five years doing my best to keep things professional and you broke me down in the two weeks it's been since you've been unattached. Now that you've given me a taste, the thought of anyone touching this," he grips my pussy hard and I let out a gasp at his possessive words, "makes me crazy. I know you have to play a certain part out there but in *here*, you belong to me."

"Yes," I moan out and he sits up, with his back against the headboard, pulling me onto his lap with his dick in front of me. I look down and see it's standing at attention. "You're ready to go again?"

He runs his tongue over his bottom lip and a tremor moves through me thinking about what it can do. "Arguably the sexiest woman in the world is naked, sitting on top of me, rubbing her wet cunt against me. Yeah, baby, I'm ready."

I lean closer, running my lips across his gently. "Does this work both ways?" He looks at me curiously waiting for my explanation. "Do you belong to me?"

"Fuck yes." He doesn't wait for my response before he presses his lips to mine, kissing me so deeply that I feel it everywhere. "Ride this dick, baby. I want to play with your sexy tits while they bounce." His hands reach around me pulling me to him just as he lowers his mouth to suck one of my nipples into his mouth, and I groan as I slide up and hold him at my entrance.

I hold myself up on my knees, rubbing the tip of his cock against my clit as I feel the gentle nibble of his teeth and I whimper at the slight pain coupled with immense pleasure. "When is the first time you've thought about this?" I ask him. "About me like this?" I breathe out as I begin to slide down on him slowly.

I grind myself against him, and I let out a whimper every time I hit the base of his dick and my clit grazes his skin. I pull his mouth away from my breast and raise his chin to look at me.

"A while ago." His blue eyes are sincere but hooded and the way he's looking at me is making my heart flutter in my chest.

"I love that I drive you crazy." I let my eyes flutter closed as I move up and down on him and I don't mistake a low animalistic groan that leaves his lips. His hands tighten on my hips, helping me to move up and down faster on him. I wrap my arms around his neck, grateful for my thigh muscles that allow me to bounce on his thick and hard cock with ease.

His hand finds its way into my hair and he pulls, lowering my mouth to his, fucking me with his tongue in a similar way that he's fucking my cunt. My body begins to build again and I don't think I've ever had four orgasms in one night. The position of me being on top, Damian hitting a spot that no one has been able to reach, and the rubbing of my clit with every thrust, I feel myself moving towards another. "You're going to come again, aren't you?" he whispers against my throat, as he drags his tongue along the skin. "Your pussy is so hot and tight, Jesus Christ, how am I ever going to get anything done knowing what you feel like?"

He smacks one of my ass cheeks and I can feel the sting of his palm in my clit. I gasp, "Do that again." I tell him and he complies, smacking me slightly harder than the last and alternating between each ass cheek. I drop my forehead to his shoulder as I fuck him harder and he gives as good as he takes, thrusting his dick into my needy cunt that's desperate to come all over him.

I've never needed a climax as badly as I do right now. Maybe because I know it'll be powerful or because I haven't had orgasms like the ones he's given me tonight and I'm already greedy for more, or maybe it's because every time he looks at me or kisses me or touches me I get uncontrollable flutters in my stomach.

"I need you to come, baby." He grunts low in my ear. "Take what you need from me." He grits out as his thrusts become more erratic and I know he's hanging on by a thread waiting for me to climax before he loses control. "No one has ever fucked me like you do," he says as he slams me down one final time and his words force me closer to the edge. The thought that this sex god that's fucked me to four roaring orgasms has enjoyed *this* as much as I have is a high I've never experienced. That he'll want more. That this isn't the end. That I'll get another night or *multiple nights* of multiple orgasms.

Fuck yes.

The thought of more triggers my release and sends me over the edge. "Oh my god, I'm coming!" I cry out, burying my face back in his neck as he lets go, with a roar of expletives and my name and baby and something else I can't make out because I'm trying to regain my equilibrium over the most intense orgasm of my life. He slows his strokes and I don't move, resting at the base of his dick as he softens inside of me with each passing second. I slowly pull back to look at him.

His blue eyes are dark and piercing and I feel like they can see every single thought that I have or have ever had. I blink a few times, trying to break the trance we both seem to be in but his hands find my face and his face grows serious like he can feel the shift as deeply as I do.

"Hi," I whisper, pushing his hair back and wiping his forehead that's slick with a layer of sweat. I'm not sure what else to say and he's still staring at me and still inside of me and I feel overwhelmed and overstimulated.

He chuckles before dragging his hands from my face down my body and resting them on my hips. "Hi."

The sound of my phone ringing breaks the intimate bubble, and I'm partially glad for the intrusion because I feel drunk on this, and god only knows what I might blurt out while I'm still feeling the effects of this sex high. "I should probably get that."

He nods, helping me off of him and I watch in fascination as he falls out of me, noticing that he's still slightly hard. I stare at his dick, wet and glistening from my cunt, and then back to his eyes that are staring at my tits with his teeth digging into his lips like he wishes they were on my nipples.

The gasp that leaves my lips sends his eyes to mine and then I'm underneath him, my hands being held above my head. His lips find mine and he murmurs between kisses. "You can't look at me like that."

"You were looking at *me* like that first."

I don't know how long we are like this, our limbs intertwined, our mouths attached like we were never going to see each other again, but eventually, he pulls back, both of us out of breath because we value kissing more than oxygen.

He drops his forehead to mine as our breathing slows. "Clearly we need some ground rules." His hands are still holding mine down above my head and it feels so sexy being restrained by this big and powerful man that also protects me with his life. It was a heady feeling that the way he protected me was suddenly very different. He moves his face to my neck and nibbles at the skin there and I moan in response.

He pulls back and I stare up at him. "I have to be able to focus out there," he says, and his face is serious despite his dick hardening against my leg.

Jesus, this man is a machine.

"Okay."

He sits up pulling me with him and into his lap. "No looking at me like you want to sneak off to a bathroom."

"Okay," I repeat

"No sexting me either." He gives me a look, reminding me of what I had said to him earlier and also that I had yet to taste his dick.

"I don't agree to that." I smirk and he narrows his eyes at me.

"Your safety is the most important thing. If I'm distracted, that allows things to…happen. I don't want to make any mistakes where you're concerned."

I swallow, knowing that he's always been over the top about my safety, and a part of me wonders if he's about to become even more intense.

My phone begins to ring again and I'm brought out of the moment by the fact that this is probably the same person calling from earlier and if I don't want that person to send a search party, I should probably answer. I get out of his lap to see Cooper's name on my phone and I can only imagine the number of things he's calling to freak out about. It's almost midnight and Cooper doesn't usually harass me after ten unless it's an emergency.

"Yes?" I ask.

"Where are you and why aren't you answering my calls?"

"Home and because I do like to shower after a night out," I lie effortlessly.

"Why are there pictures of you and Paxton looking less than friendly?"

I groan remembering the pictures that were snapped while we were at the gala. "It's not my fault. Paxton is pressing taking a trip together and according to his big mouth security, he has a ring that I do not want. I swear to god, Cooper, if he asks me to marry him the answer is no so you need to tell his team not to even try it because he'll get embarrassed." He groans and I continue. "There are fake relationships all over Hollywood that are mutually beneficial and require no trips or fake engagements. Why is Paxton so pressed on keeping me under his thumb?"

He sighs. "My guess is he still has feelings for you."

"That's not my problem, Coop. I'm almost ready to release the truth. You need to put him in check or I will."

Another sigh. "I heard tonight went well. I've gotten quite a few calls..."

Excitement courses through me at the thought that I generated some buzz tonight. Lorenzo had a lot of questions regarding how I wanted to transition from a TV star to something bigger. If I felt that I was ready for movies. The kind of roles I'd want to play. The kind of roles *he* could see *me* playing. They were the kind of questions that directors asked when they're interested in casting you *or* if they have you in mind for a specific role. Producers flocked to me all night with questions about whether I had time for breakfast or dinner or coffee and to chat about my future.

My back has been to Damian this whole time and when I turn around, I notice him staring at what would have been my ass because he's staring at my pussy. His eyes shoot to mine at having been caught checking me out and I shake my head. His eyes are hungry and I can see the tension in his sharp jaw as he runs his eyes slowly down my body.

"Yeah, it was great." I cut him off as he's been talking for the past thirty seconds. "Coop, I'm tired. Can we talk about this tomorrow?"

"That's fine. I'm going to call Paxton's manager in the meantime and try and straighten this out. I think those pictures are going to be online by morning."

"Okay?" I say, without a care in the world about what happens. I'm hoping at this point they out us, so I can be done with it.

"Why is Damian between you two anyway?" he questions.

"I called him over."

"Because?"

I let out a sound of annoyance. "He wouldn't let go of me."

"Are you serious?" he barks and I can already hear Cooper's slight parental instincts he has regarding me coming out.

"It didn't hurt but he wasn't listening and I just wanted him off me."

Damian's eyes go from sexy to angry when he realizes what I'm talking about. He's on his feet, holding his hand out for me to hand him the phone when I shake my head. *No.* I mouth, because what reason would I have for Damian to be hanging out with me at midnight? It could be completely innocent, but I don't need Cooper on my case about keeping things *professional* with Damian. My eyes drop down to his dick that's swaying between his legs as he gets closer to me. I feel my skin heating and my sex tingles with the need to feel him there.

Not now though!

I hold my hand out to stop him from coming closer.

"This fucker is really making it difficult for me to sell you on this ruse," he says and I take a step back as Damian takes another step closer.

"I'll come by tomorrow and we can talk about it." I want him off the phone before Damian takes it from me. *Although, he could if he wanted to.* "I'm going to bed," I say before he has a chance to bring up anything else he wanted to talk about.

"Alright, you okay, Shay?"

"Fine, just tired."

Damian's arms wrap around me and he lifts me off the floor. I hold in the moan sitting in the back of my throat as we end the call and I glare at him.

"Okay, not doing that while I'm on the phone is a part of the ground rules."

He carries me into the bathroom and sets me on my feet. He reaches for my makeup remover from my small vanity I have on the counter and pours some onto a cotton pad before rubbing it along my face.

"You should have let me talk to him." He rubs the makeup from my skin gently and I'll admit there's something sexy about having a man do this for me.

Something a man has never done.

"I could do this myself, you know."

"There's a lot of things you can do yourself that I like doing for you."

I can't hide the smile from finding my face as he pours some on a new cotton pad and continues his task. "Letting you talk to Cooper at midnight would just raise a whole bunch of questions about what we're doing this late. Especially because until recently you never spent much time alone with me."

He nods in understanding and it makes me wonder if he wasn't thinking clearly earlier. Was it a knee-jerk overprotective reaction? "I'm sorry if my being in the picture makes things difficult."

"Why are you sorry? I called you over."

"I hate that you felt you had to." I shrug and he nods towards my huge walk-in shower. "You mentioned showering while you were on the phone."

I nod, knowing where he's going with this. We are both still naked and I smile at the look he's giving me. He opens the glass and reaches in to turn on the water and it shoots down from the rain showerhead. He moves around me and grabs where I usually keep my shower caps and hands them to me.

"Okay first, how do you know how to find my things so quickly?" He cocks his head to the side, shooting me a look, and I roll my eyes realizing that he probably has every inch of my bedroom and bathroom memorized in case anything is ever out of place. "I'm never going to be able to keep anything from you." I take the shower caps from him and set them on the counter. "Normally yes, but I have to wash all the product out of my hair that my stylist put in for the gala and I'd like the first time we shower together to not feature the unsexiness of a shower cap. Give me a break."

I'm through the glass door when I feel a hand around my wrist and I'm yanked against a hard chest. "You are sexy in everything." He takes a step and runs his gaze down my body for the hundredth time tonight and then back up. "And nothing, god damn."

I watch as the water hits the muscles of his chest and glides down his body to his dick. "I could say the same thing about you." My eyes dart to each of his tattoos and I move around him, running my fingers along all of the ink on his back as well before moving to his front again. "I have a thing for guys with tattoos." I bite my lip. "Will you tell me what they all mean to you?"

"A lot of them date back to when I was in the military." He swallows. "They represent people or times. Some of them don't have much meaning." He grabs my hand and presses it to his chest to the compass. "Mine points North, which means you're on the right path. North will always guide you home." He drags my hand to his shoulder where there's a wolf. "Wolves mean protection and loyalty." He moves to his forearm to the Latin words.

"Where there is life, there is hope," I whisper and he smiles before giving me a nod. "I looked it up when I saw it. I love that." I run my fingertips over it. "I spent a lot of time thinking about what that means in the context of what I've been through…" I trail off. "Someone who has dealt with so much loss."

He nods. "Do you want to talk about it?"

I shake my head. "No." I look up at him. "And I don't mean I don't want to talk to you about it, I just mean not now."

He nods again and moves to his other arm to the cross and gives me a sad smile. "The two initials are for men we lost in my last tour overseas."

"I'm sorry." I rub the ink and push my body into his, wrapping my arms around him and giving him a tight hug.

I feel his chin rest on the top of my head and then he moves my face and presses a soft kiss to my forehead. "I'm sorry that you understand this feeling. That you understand loss on such a visceral level. I wouldn't wish it on anyone." He pushes me against the tile and I hiss as the cool marble hits my back. The steam in the shower clouds the air. "I was planning to leave you," He tells me and I frown at his words. "Before you lost them, I was planning to resign as your head of security."

Tears spring to my eyes at the thought of not having him for the past five years. "Why?"

"Because of this." He points back and forth between us. "There was an attraction between us and I was worried what that meant for being able to protect you efficiently. But then you lost your parents and the way you clung to me the day you found out and the weeks following…you didn't want anyone within three feet of you except for me, and I just couldn't leave you. Not like that." He swallows and hearing *what could have been* has me shivering despite the warm temperature of the shower.

"You wanted to…leave?" The water slides down his body and I follow the trails, unable to look him in the eyes while I'm feeling this vulnerable.

He rubs my upper arms gently before his index finger finds my chin and gently raises my face. "But then things changed between us. I saw you as this person that I wanted to protect for more reasons than it was my job, and I didn't trust anyone to keep you safe." He cups my face and rubs his nose against mine. "I put my feelings aside because you needed someone you could depend on." He swallows.

"And…now?"

"You can still depend on me but I don't think I can put my feelings aside anymore."

"Why didn't you ever tell me how you felt?"

"Because I still worry about how I'm going to protect you. How this…changes everything."

Chapter Thirteen

DAMIAN

MY USUAL ALARM FOR FIVE-THIRTY IN THE MORNING GOES off, and normally, I'm someone that gets up immediately. I rarely need the snooze button, but given that I'd slipped out of Shay probably only an hour ago, the thought of prying my eyes open right now is the last thing I want to do. Shay moans in my arms and I can feel her waking up. "Turn it off," she groans into my chest while simultaneously pushing herself closer to me. We are in the center of her king-sized bed and I look at my phone that's not exactly within arm's reach on her nightstand. I try to move and she whimpers and pulls me closer. "No."

"Let me get my phone."

One eye opens and she lets me out of her grasp so I can grab it and silence it before moving back to her. "I need to get up."

"No, you don't." She presses her hand to her mouth to stifle a yawn. "What time is it anyway?"

"Five-thirty."

"What!" She groans and snuggles further into her white duvet that, to be fair, is very comfortable. "What are you doing up this early?"

"I always get up around this time and check a few things on the property, go over camera footage from the night before, and go for a run."

"Okay, but we've been asleep an hour; surely you can't do all those things properly on an hour of sleep."

"I've done more on less," I tell her.

"I have to get up in a few hours to go to the set. We start the press tour in a few days and they want us to come in to prepare for our interviews and take some promotional pictures." She sighs. "I already know they're going to be pissed about these bags under my eyes from staying up all night."

"You look beautiful as always," I tell her and she fucking does, even minutes after waking up she's still the most gorgeous woman I've ever seen.

"Keep talking like that and looking at me that way and you're going to have to fuck me before you get up." She sits up on her elbow and reaches below the blanket to grab my dick when my alarm goes off again. I reach for my phone, turning it off this time before I grab her hand that is wrapped around my dick and bring it to my lips.

"As much as I would love to, I need to do a few things." There are things I have to do every morning. Things that put me at ease. She frowns before nodding and then I'm off the bed, pulling on my briefs and my slacks and sliding on my shirt before buttoning the buttons in record time. Shay has her blanket wrapped around her and I can tell she has something on her mind. I kneel on the bed and cup her face, raising it to meet my gaze. "What is it?"

She opens her mouth but no words come out and then she lets out a breath. "At the risk of sounding needy or clingy, I just…you're leaving and I wasn't sure if the high of last night wore off? Or if maybe you're regretting what we did and you don't know how to tell me?" She fidgets with her fingers in her lap. I've rarely seen her nervous. Shay is confident and quite frankly a ball buster so it does something to me that she's allowing herself to be vulnerable and soft with me.

"No." I shake my head. "I don't know if the high of you will ever wear off." I hate the words as soon as I hear them out loud but the small smile that finds her lips makes it worth me sounding like a pussy. I lean down and press my lips to hers gently and maybe that's what she needed, a kiss or the promise of more before I left her bed. That there would be more kisses and more *us* later.

A few minutes later, I'm jogging down her stairs and moving towards the exit. I am confused when I notice that the alarm has been disabled and instantly, I'm aware that I'm not alone on the floor. *There is no way I forgot to set the alarm and Annette, her house manager, is off this weekend. Who the fuck is in the house?*

A familiar face appears in the hall with a Starbucks cup in her hand and her eyes widen when she sees me.

"OH MY GOD, SHAY CELESTE EASTWOOD!" she screams, *yes screams,* and I watch as Veronica goes through a hundred different emotions as it dawns on her why I would be upstairs at five in the morning, not to mention with half of my shirt unbuttoned. Even when I do stay in the main house, I stay in the guest rooms downstairs.

"Veronica? What are you doing here? How did you get in?" I press a hand over my eyes regretfully as I remember I never changed the code the other night. It also doesn't escape me that the other night was when things started to change between Shay and me.

Fuck, what else have I missed while my mind has been preoccupied?

"This is precisely why she doesn't need the code to the house," I tell Shay who makes it halfway down the stairs clad only in a robe, her eyes wide as she looks at Veronica who glares at me for my comment.

"What are you doing here!?" Shay asks her best friend.

"Catching you in the act evidently. How long has this been going on? Oh my God! I knew you were into her!" She giggles and turns to Shay. "I want to know all the details."

"Okay, I was going to tell you anyway, you didn't need to break into my house." She rolls her eyes as she moves down the rest of the stairs. "But what are you doing here at five-thirty in the morning?"

"Hello, we have to be on set at eight, and since when is there a time I can't show up at your house?"

Shay looks up at me and I'm annoyed that all it's taken is one night with Shay to miss something like the front door opening. Even if she did have a code, I usually get an alert to my phone when the front door opens and somehow, I missed it or slept through it.

"How long have you been here?" I ask her.

"My question first!" she shrieks and I glare angrily at her, hoping she realizes now is not the time but she smacks Shay in the shoulder. "Call off your guard dog."

"Okay both of you, no." She shakes her head as she points between the two of us. "You two are not going to put me in the middle. Be nice to each other."

I let out a huff and run a hand through my hair annoyed that I still haven't gotten any of the answers I've asked for.

"V, I'll tell you everything. Don't antagonize him." She purses her lips. "He wants to know when you got here because it's freaking him out that he didn't know the front door opened."

"Yeah, I'll bet he didn't." She raises her eyes up and down and scrunches her nose and I feel like I'm on the verge of exploding.

"Damian," she says, turning her back to the current pain in my ass and looks up at me. Her hand reaches up and strokes my face. "I'll figure out what you need to know. Okay? Don't be grumpy." She smiles at me and just seeing her stare at me like that has the tension leaving me slowly. She stands on her tiptoes and puckers her lips and I look over her head to see Veronica beaming at us with excitement. It makes me slightly less irritated that she seems to be happy with this new development between us. I lean down and press a kiss to Shay's lips that lasts no more than a second knowing that if I let it go on for too long, I'll drag her back to bed.

After I made my morning rounds, went on a quick run, and took a shower, I do my usual security footage scans, and I notice that her bedroom light was on until three in the morning. Even after we turned the lights out, we made out for at least another hour, our bodies rubbing against each other like they didn't ever want to part. I explored every inch of her with my lips, and my god, she sucked my dick better than anyone ever has, getting accustomed to my size quickly and deep-throating me with every thrust. I couldn't even come in her mouth, I was too desperate to feel her cunt again, so I pulled out and finished inside of her much to her disappointment.

I don't think I'd ever been with a woman that was annoyed that I hadn't come in her mouth.

It has been some time since I've been with a woman; not since Simone, but one-night stands were few and far between. Shay has been my focus. I've spent my nights off sleeping or reading or sometimes at the gun range. I don't frequent bars or the nightlife scene and the few times I had friends in the area whose visit happened to coincide with some time off, I spent it catching up with them, not looking for someone to fuck. I'm not a stranger to meaningless sex. I spent the majority of my early twenties before Simone doing just that and now, I'm over it.

Especially now that I know what Shay feels like.

She's submissive in bed in so many ways, letting me do all the things I want to do. She's eager to please; I can spot a praise kink a mile away and she gets off on it. *A lot.*

But she also tells me what she wants and when she wants more and harder and faster. It turns me on that she wants me so much and can't get enough of me. Even this morning, leaving her bed without being inside her just one more time was more difficult than I'd let on.

I've never been a big cuddler but waking up with her body intertwined with mine, her head resting on my chest like she'd been doing it for years, felt so fucking *right*.

I'd woken up feeling content and it wasn't just because I'd spent the night having the best sex of my life but because of who I'd had it with.

God, I'm fucked.

I turn my eyes back to the footage noting everything looks normal. I roll my eyes when I see Veronica pulling up in her Mercedes and letting herself into the house around five.

I'd also gotten a stack of fan mail from Cooper the other day that he'd wanted me to go through. Typically, that's a job for her assistant and her publicist but he said there were a few pieces that worried him and asked if I'd take a look. She got a lot of fan mail from adoring and borderline obsessed fans. The only times we took them seriously were when they seemed to have too much information, speaking on things that weren't reported to the public. There was someone last year that sent pictures that were far too close and inside her gated neighborhood telling her he loved her. I was a nervous fucking wreck until we figured out who it was and filed a restraining order.

Usually, when we figure out who it is and *I* personally deliver a restraining order to them, they tend to back off and Shay is none the wiser. The last thing I want is for her to worry or be afraid to live her life. This is what I'm here for; to allow her to live her life while I shield her from anything that could interfere with that. It's a job I take very seriously.

I open the unsealed envelope and when I spot the typed words, I'm immediately on edge. Most fan letters come handwritten. *Even the ones that are over the top and require me to get involved.*

SHAY—
I KNOW YOUR RELATIONSHIP WITH PAXTON IS OVER.
I KNEW HE DIDN'T DESERVE YOU.
I TRIED TO TELL YOU HE WASN'T GOOD ENOUGH.
THAT HE WOULD HURT YOU.
YOU IGNORED MY LETTERS!
NO ONE WILL EVER LOVE YOU LIKE I DO.
PLEASE LET ME.
I'VE BEEN WAITING FOR YOU. FOR US!
I CAN'T WAIT UNTIL WE CAN BE TOGETHER.

I grit my teeth thinking about how much this person knows. Could it be someone fucking with her? Trying to scare her? Maybe someone from Paxton's team in hopes it will send her running back to him in fear?

No, it couldn't be that. His team couldn't be that desperate.

I clench my hand into a fist already wanting my eyes or my hands on her as I fear the worst. I scratch my jaw as I put it to the side and open another one that I believe to be from the same person. More of the same sentiments. There are four letters in total. All of them typed in the same block font and all referencing the demise of her and Paxton's relationship.

I look at the envelopes and all of them are addressed to Cooper's office and my blood runs cold thinking about the next one showing up here somehow.

> **Me: I'm changing the code to the house. Please do not disclose it to Veronica.**
>
> **Winter: Okay, I think you're overreacting though. She's sorry she scared you! To be fair, she did tell me last week she'd come over early today. I've just had other things on my mind :)**
>
> **Me: That's fine. And I'm not saying I don't trust her, I would just feel better if the only people that had it were the people that absolutely need it.**
>
> **Winter: Understood. We are going to leave in about an hour, okay? I'm going to ride with V.**
>
> **Me: Okay, I'll be behind you.**

I want to tell her that I'd feel better driving her myself, but I can't. I have to be able to separate the role of her bodyguard and the man that she's sleeping with, and if the two begin to blur together I'll become an unhinged caveman that won't let anyone within a mile of her.

This is exactly why you don't get involved with your client, Hunt.

I look down at my phone and see that she's sent me an emoji with a kiss and I smile wishing that she was in front of me to give her a real one. There isn't anything else I can do about these letters right now. I don't even know how long ago they were sent. It's possible they were sent before Shay even learned of Paxton's betrayal and he was sending these in hopes that Paxton was cheating on her. Or maybe this person knew before Shay even knew. There are too many unknowns and it's pissing me off that I have nowhere to start. I type out a message to Cooper.

> **Me:** Keep an eye out for any other letters.
>
> **Cooper Jennings:** You got it. What happened with Paxton last night? Pictures are starting to circulate of you in the middle of them. We and P's team both tried to buy them but they leaked too fast.
>
> **Me:** She's just over it. She feels like she's backed into a corner with him and he's acting like they're actually together even in private and this isn't all a ruse.
>
> **Cooper Jennings:** Got it. Alright, well we have a call with the head of his PR team later today.
>
> **Me:** Get it sorted out.

I stare at my words and shake my head before I pull up the alerts I have set up for her and sure enough I see the picture of me in the middle of them. From the angle, luckily it doesn't seem like they're arguing because I'm more in front of her and the pap wasn't close enough to get a clear shot of Paxton's face. The fact that I'm there is why there's a question. Am I protecting her from him? Did he do something to her? Was I breaking up an argument? All of these are speculation but the questions are out there, and I'm sure Paxton's team is not pleased with how this looks.

A knock on my door breaks me out of my thoughts and when I peek out of the window, I see Shay standing there dressed in a black halter mid-length dress and her hair that was previously wet from the shower we took last night, blow-dried and curled. I open the door and she pushes her way inside and then she's in my arms, wrapped around me like ivy. Her lips connect with mine and I'm reminded of the way she kisses, like she can't get close enough to me, and I groan at the taste of her toothpaste and the scent of her shampoo and her perfume as my tongue moves against hers.

"You smell good," I tell her and she presses her nose into my neck.

"So do you. We are ready to go but I just wanted to give you a kiss before I can't for the rest of the day."

The thought that I won't be able to touch her irritates me more than I expected. I set her on her feet and tuck her hair behind her ear.

"Well, I think I should be able to give you a kiss as well." She raises an eyebrow knowingly and then I'm on one knee in front of her, raising her dress to her waist revealing a silky black pair of panties. "Hold your dress up," I command her as I press my lips to the fabric before moving it to the side and sliding my tongue through her slit. I look up and see the look she's giving me, brown eyes clouded with lust and her mouth slightly open making me want to force her to her knees and push my dick through those full pouty lips again. She must not be wearing a bra because I can see her hard nipples pebbling against the fabric of her dress and god these legs. Legs that I wish could be wrapped around my neck right now. I slide one hand up her leg and squeeze her thigh as the other is still holding her panties to the side.

"Damian."

"Yes, baby." I lick and suck at her clit, lapping at her and swirling my tongue around the space. "Tell me what you need."

"You." She moans. "I need *you.*" She groans as she runs her hands through my hair and scores my scalp with her nails.

I need you, too. I want to tell her but I can't get the words out.

I need you safe. Alive. Mine.

Chapter FOURTEEN

Shay

GOD, I'VE MISSED BEING ON SET.

I slide my Dior sunglasses to my head and let out a sigh of relief as I push through the door to the *LA Dreams* set. Returning to the life of Ashley Anderson feels like coming home. I've been playing her for almost ten years across two television shows so in many ways, she's become a part of me. There have been so many instances I had *what would Ashley do* moments. She has parents, a boyfriend—soon-to-be husband—that adored her, and, quite honestly, the perfect life so I love stepping into her shoes for several months out of the year and getting to pretend everything is fine. Ashley Anderson has her life together, whereas Shay Eastwood feels like a mess half the time.

"I cannot believe you and Damian," Veronica says as we make our way down the long hallway lined with headshots of actors and actresses that have worked on this very stage. I drag my fingertips over my six-foot headshot like I always do in hopes that it reminds me that I can do this. I am talented and worthy of being here.

"*You* can't? Miss *oh my god he's so hot for you?*" I raise my eyebrow at her.

"I didn't think he'd act on it!" I chuckle because neither did I to be honest. "I support this one hundred percent." She turns around because a lot of times Damian will walk me in to make sure I get settled, but he's not behind us. I can't help the smile on my lips thinking about what her support means.

Are we just sleeping together? Dating? More than that? The idea that I could potentially be falling for Damian hits me hard.

"When are you calling it off with Pax?"

"I don't know. I kind of hope the paparazzi figure out the truth and it'll end this ruse once and for all. Right now, I have to be careful or else I'm going to come off looking like *I* betrayed *him*. Isn't that ironic?"

She snorts. "People love you, Shay, they'll believe you."

"They love Paxton too," I argue as we make it to the set and it seems we are the last to arrive because I see Jeremy and Derek and the rest of our co-stars along with producers and the director. They scream both Veronica's and my names and surround us pulling us into respective circles, and I'm reminded again how much I love it here. These are my people. People I trust more than most. We've been together so long that we know almost everything about each other. These are people that were there when my parents died, when Jeremy ended his long-term relationship, when Veronica's parents went through their divorce, and when Derek lost his mother. There was something to be said for the people that were there when shit went down.

"What is going on with you and Paxton?" Denise, one of the executive producers that I've known since I was fourteen asks me from over her glasses. "You do not seem like you guys are on good terms?" She reminds me in so many ways of my mother, her gaze warm and simultaneously like I better not lie to her. I wrap my arms around her like I haven't seen her in years and not the two months since we went on hiatus.

"A mess," I tell her honestly because a long time ago, she vowed to take a thousand and one of my secrets to the grave. *Though I'm not ready to tell her about Damian.* "We'll talk."

Hours later we've been to hair and makeup to prepare for pictures when my mind drifts to the man sitting outside waiting for me.

> **Me:** What are you doing?

He answers almost instantly.

> **Damian:** Going through emails, you okay?
>
> **Me:** Yes. We are about to start taking promo pics and I was thinking about you. Why didn't you come in?
>
> **Damian:** I thought maybe you'd want some space
>
> **Me:** From you? No. And aren't you supposed to have your eyes on me at all times?
>
> **Damian:** I wish. Besides, you don't normally need me in there while you're shooting. What's changed?
>
> **Me:** What's changed? Really!?
>
> **Damian:** I mean what's changed in regards to me being your bodyguard?
>
> **Me:** Maybe I WANT your eyes on me at all times.
>
> **Damian:** Ah now I get it. I think being near you for no real reason might be against the ground rules.
>
> **Me:** Fine :(
>
> **Damian:** I'll see you after.

I make my way out of my dressing room towards the set, leaving my phone in my room since there is nowhere for me to keep it when Jeremy comes out of his room and gives me a smile.

"Hey hey." He's wearing a perfectly tailored gray Brunello Cucinelli suit; a typical look for the sexy billionaire Ashley's in love with.

I gently tug on the green tie that brings out the color of his eyes and give him a smile. "Hey."

He wraps a hand around my shoulder as we walk down the hall towards the set. "You good, Shay?" He stops walking, reaching for my hand and stopping me in my tracks.

"What do you mean?"

"I've known you for a long time and I don't know…" He runs a hand through his hair and shrugs. "Seems like something is off."

"Liiike?" I ask as I begin walking backwards because I'm definitely not about to disclose this new revelation with Damian to Jeremy. We're close but I'm not ready for that.

He looks around and moves closer to me like he believes I've got a secret to tell him. "I don't know. Everything good with you and Pax? Things seemed weird the other night at Rush."

I scoff and roll my eyes hearing his name. "Vault?"

He nods, hearing our code word. "Vault. You know you can trust me, Shay."

"We aren't together…anymore," I tell him. "He cheated on me with a thousand different women and I found out." I wave my hand as if to say et cetera. I begin dancing as I hear the music they've turned on for set pictures to get us in the mood trying not to let this conversation bring me down.

His eyebrows shoot to his hairline. "A thousand? And you're okay?" I can hear the unspoken part of his question in his voice. *How are you okay after three years?*

"I don't know the exact number but evidently he doesn't either, so yeah, I'm going to assume it's a large number." I scrunch my nose as a vision of them together flashes through my brain. "I caught him in the moment and it kind of just turned me off to it. Like balls deep, J." I scrunch my nose, thinking about the visual I'll probably have for the rest of my life.

He shakes his head. "I'm sorry, Shay." He reaches for my hand and laces it with his dragging his thumb over my knuckles. I know he's probably recalling his own experiences with an unfaithful partner. "I'm here if you need to talk."

I nod. "Thank you. Just don't tell anyone. Our PR teams want to keep us together through our award seasons," I tell him.

"Vault." He nods, crossing an X over his heart just as Veronica emerges from her room and skips towards us.

She knocks her hip with mine and slides between us, linking her arms with mine and Jeremy's. "Can you believe this is our final season? Six seasons, what a ride. Jeremy, what are you going to do without me and Shay to keep you young, old man?" She chuckles as we make it to the set they've set up for our pictures.

He rolls his eyes. "Fuck off, V. I'm sure you'll still be sending me a thousand TikToks a day."

We're rounding the fourth hour of pictures. We've changed outfits, and hairstyles—*namely me*—and we're on our final set of pictures.

We took a break for lunch and I forced Damian to come inside because I knew he had to be hungry and the spread that the production team puts out is phenomenal. But it was like an equally fun and nerve-wracking game having Damian so close to me amidst so many people that didn't know something is going on between us. I couldn't stare at him, he couldn't stare at me, and the few times our eyes locked, it could be for no more than a second to avoid raising questions. At one point though, I started eating a banana and Damian started coughing out of nowhere.

I'm going to pay for that later, I'm sure, especially because I don't even particularly like bananas.

Damian lingered after lunch and despite the bright lights in my face, I knew he was behind the cameras watching. This wasn't the first time he'd been on set while I was doing something, but it was the first time since we'd crossed certain lines. It felt different, him being here, like he was watching me through different eyes and it made me feel infinitely sexier.

The final pictures being taken are of me by myself in front of a green screen that they'll Photoshop a variety of pictures into for promotion like the LA skyline or the *LA Dreams* logo. They're using a fan to give my hair a windblown look so it's drowning out the sounds of anything besides the faint music still playing. I can't even really hear Lucas, the director, or any of the executive producers. The sudden banging sounds of something overhead breaks through the hum of the fan, and I resist the urge to look up because I know the cameras are rolling and I don't want to ruin the shot. It sounds like metal grinding against metal and it's getting louder so I finally do look up. My eyes widen as I see a light fixture falling and in the split second it takes for it to register that it's going to land on top of me, I've been knocked to the ground out of the way just as it hits the very place I was standing with a loud and very hard crash.

My heart is beating a million times a minute and when I open my eyes, Damian is on top of me, his eyes wide with shock, like he can't believe he got to me in time. We are surrounded instantly by everyone on set, and they're all asking a million questions. I vaguely hear the director screaming, *"Who the fuck can tell me what just happened?"* but the voices are all being drowned out by the blood rushing to my ears to the beat of my pounding heart.

I can't answer if I'm okay or if anything hurts. I think I'm in shock, and then Damian's voice roars over everyone to be quiet. He sits up, pulling me with him, his eyes still on me like if he looks away, I'll disappear. I realize my hands are still wrapped around his biceps and I grip them tighter as fear stays wrapped tightly around me.

"Are you okay?" he asks, his voice laced with concern and his eyes full of worry.

I nod, my eyes still wide and unblinking, still unable to find the words as I look behind him at the very large, sharp metal light fixture that very well may have killed me if he was just a second later.

"I…"

"Honey, here." Denise kneels next to me, handing me a glass of water. "Do you want to stand up? Guys, give her some air." She shoos everyone away and I'm grateful for her because it instantly feels like I can breathe now that people have taken a few steps back. I take the water with one shaky hand, still gripping Damian's arm with the other, not wanting to let him go for anything.

I take a slow sip just as Lucas lowers to his knee in front of me. "You okay? Jesus Christ, I am so sorry." He looks to where I was just standing and there's a crowd from the tech team surrounding it and looking up from where it fell. "We're going to call it quits for the day," he says, his brown eyes wide and worried behind tortoise horn-rimmed glasses.

"No shit," Damian snaps at him and Lucas shoots him a glare before removing his glasses and pinching the bridge of his nose.

"East, you good? Do you need to go to the hospital?" he asks using his nickname for me.

"N—no." I shake my head. "It didn't get me. Just scared me." I swallow hard, still trying to calm my racing heart.

"Oh my god, what happened?!" I hear Veronica's voice moving towards me, the neat braid that she'd had for pictures, is no longer neat—*or in a braid for that matter*—letting me know what she's been doing when she drops to her knees next to me and wraps her arms around me. "Are you okay? They said…" She trails off and looks behind Damian and then looks up and then at me and then back to Damian and then to where my hand is still wrapped around him.

"You were here." Tears spring to her eyes, probably having drawn the same conclusion that I did.

He nods once before turning back to me. "Do you want to stand? Or…do you want me to carry you?"

Heat fills me thinking about him carrying me out of here and I shake my head not wanting anyone to see that side of our relationship knowing that I won't be able to hide it the second I'm in his arms after what just happened.

"I can walk." He stands up first, helping me to my feet, and I wince when I feel a sharp pain shoot through me. Damian is a big guy and although he didn't put all of his weight on me, the way we landed was not ideal.

"Shit, are you okay?"

"Yes, my back just hurts a little." I shake my head at the look he's giving me. "You saved my life. Relax please." I give him a small smile despite the pain shooting up my back and I look at Veronica as we start towards the exit.

"I'm fine. I'm just going to go home and rest."

"I'm coming with you," she says. "Let me just go get my stuff."

"V—" I start but she's already out of earshot and jogging towards her dressing room.

I'm able to get off of the set pretty easily, but now I'm walking a bit slower with the adrenaline wearing off and the aches starting to flare up everywhere.

"For fuck's sake," Damian growls, lifting me into his arms in a fireman's hold once we're somewhat alone and continues walking down the long corridor. He pushes his way outside and I'm grateful that I rode with Veronica so it'll just be Damian and me in his truck on the way home. He unlocks the car and slides me onto the back seat.

"Wait, can't I sit up front with you?" I want him to hold my hand or just be closer than he'll be with me sitting in the back.

"No."

"But—"

"No, Shay." He closes the door before I can protest any further. We make it off the lot and are driving towards my house just as the sky begins to darken. It wasn't calling for rain and it's only two in the afternoon, so I'm surprised by the ominous dark clouds. Damian hasn't said anything and I'm not sure what to make of it.

"Are you going to say anything?"

"Not while I'm driving, no." His voice is even and he doesn't even look at me.

I frown. "Why?"

"Because that was the scariest moment of my life and I can't relive it and operate a vehicle at the same time."

"I'm okay though. You got to me in time."

"By a fucking millisecond. Now quiet." I'm sitting behind the passenger's side so I can see that he's got a death grip on the steering wheel. His knuckles are turning white and I can hear them cracking. He goes the speed limit the whole time, adhering to every traffic law like he's afraid something might happen again. I watch relief wash over every inch of him the second we are inside my community and driving up to my house. He drives through my private gate and when he pulls to a stop in front of my house, his shoulders sag and he puts a hand on his forehead before he unbuckles his seatbelt. He turns to look at me and a sad smile finds his face.

"No one would have been able to get to you that fast. If I hadn't been there…" His nostrils flare. "I'm going to be a nightmare on that set once you start shooting."

I bite my bottom lip, "Damian, it was an accident."

"I don't fucking do accidents. Not where you're concerned."

Lust flares through me and my sex clenches despite the dull ache everywhere else.

"Can you come get me out of the car, so you can kiss me already?" I cock my head to the side.

He nods, gets out of the car, and opens the door for me before he stops and looks behind him at the house and then back at me. He takes a step back. "I would feel better if I checked out the house first."

I lower my arms that were previously outstretched for him to lift me into his arms. "What? Damian…"

"No, just…until I'm one hundred percent sure what just happened was an accident, I'm taking extra precautions." I gasp thinking that he suspects that maybe what happened was intentional and a chill snakes down my spine. "I don't want to scare you." His hands find my face and he presses a gentle kiss to my forehead that I desperately wish was on my lips. I whimper when he pulls back. "Ten minutes. You remember the drill."

I roll my eyes remembering all the nights I couldn't even get into my own house until he'd searched it top to bottom and my house isn't exactly small. I let out an annoyed sigh and shift uncomfortably in my seat figuring now is the best time to call Veronica and tell her not to come over because I want some alone time with Damian.

"I'm going to be there in five," she says the second she answers the phone. "Do you want me to bring anything?"

"V—"

"No. You can ride his dick later. I'm coming over."

"I'm fine, I swear, and yes I would like to ride his dick without you in the house."

"You can barely walk, how are you going to do that?"

I mentally shoot her my middle finger. "Okay, maybe he'll do most of the work. The point is, can you not?"

She huffs and I can hear the sounds of her turn signal. "Shay, that was really freaking scary. Not many things could stop me and Derek by the way, but I heard the crash and everyone screaming your name."

"I know and I appreciate it, but I swear I'm fine, and you know Damian will take care of me. He's pretty shaken up too, so I think he might want to be alone with me."

"Fiiiiine…" she trails off. "Okay, I'll give you guys some space now, but maybe I'll swing by later?"

"Okay," I relent.

We get off the phone and after a few more minutes Damian comes outside and I can tell his body is still tense from the events of the day. He pulls me into his arms and presses a kiss to my neck. "All good." We make it inside and then up the stairs and I hear water running. "I'm running you a bath. It'll help with your muscles and any aches and pains," he answers in response to the look I'm giving him.

"Are you going to join me?"

He sets me on my feet because I'm in a dress that needs to be unbuttoned. He does so quickly before setting me gently on the bed. "No."

"Why?"

"Because you're sore and if I'm in a bath with you, I'm going to want to fuck you, and that will not help." He drops to his knees and slowly peels my underwear off of me. "I am also still a little on edge by what happened and I don't know how gentle I'll be."

I'm wearing a strapless bra and he reaches behind me to unsnap it allowing it to fall from around me and my breasts spring free within very close reach of his mouth. I move forward slightly, pressing my breasts closer to him, and as if there's a string tethering him to me, his lips find my nipple, flicking it with the tip of his tongue before sucking it to his mouth.

"That feels..." I let out a sigh because I don't have a word for what he's making me feel right now. My nipples are very sensitive and he's the first man to pay them a lot of attention.

His stubble scratches against my skin and I tremble under the gentle mixed with rough sensations. He lets it fall after a few minutes before rising to stand in front of me. I pull my hair up into a bun as he walks back to my bathroom and shuts off the running water before making his way back into the bedroom.

He gently pulls my head back to look up at him and then his lips are on mine, licking at the seam and then pushing his tongue into my mouth. His mouth is warm and comforting and makes me feel safe. It makes me want to crawl inside his skin. I moan in response to his kiss, wanting more, and I'm grateful when he puts an arm behind me and slowly lowers me to the bed. He's supporting the majority of his weight but I still feel him on top of me and I shiver at the thought of being completely naked underneath him. I try my best to reach for his belt, but he pushes my hand away and gets off the bed, pulling me into his arms and walking me into the bathroom. He sets me gently on the side of the tub and makes me test the water with my foot to make sure it's not too hot before lowering me into the huge tub full of bubbles.

He sits on the floor next to the tub, his elbows resting on his knees, and stares at me.

"What happened?" I ask him.

"It all happened so fast," he says. His blue eyes narrow and then he leans his head back, running a hand through his dark hair. "I heard something overhead and I moved closer to the set and I remember someone saying I couldn't be that close but I ignored them because something didn't feel right." My body goes rigid as anxiety moves through me. "And then I heard it and I saw it and I saw *you* and I just started running." He moves closer and grips my face, resting his forehead against mine. "If I hadn't been there..."

"But you were."

"Only because you begged me to come in for lunch. I'm not usually there, Shay." He clears his throat and his eyebrows lower. "And now we're…" he says. "I'm already overprotective when it comes to you, and now I know what your cunt tastes like, so…" His lips form a straight line and I can't help the chuckle that leaves me in response to his dark humor. "I hope you like having a shadow." He rubs his head and lets out a sigh.

"You're more worked up than I am. Can you lighten up?" He shoots me a glare and I give him an innocent smile. "Will you just join me? You'll feel better."

He reaches behind his head to pull off his shirt in that sexy way men do and I smile thinking I'm about to get my way when he only moves closer to me while not making an effort to get in the tub. "Lean back."

"Aren't you—"

"No," he says cutting off my question of whether he's getting in as he reaches for my loofah and begins washing me. He does this for a few minutes, actually bathing me before he drops it into the water and his fingers move beneath the water to my sex. My eyes float to his and he stares at me through hooded eyes as his fingers play with my clit.

"I can't think about something happening to you." He frowns as he strengthens the pressure of his fingers on my clit. "It…fucks with me."

I nod, not knowing what to say at this moment and he continues to stroke me harder.

"Please," I whimper, though I'm not sure what I'm asking for. An orgasm or for him to join me or to kiss me. His lips rest against my shoulder as he fingers me and I grip the sides of the tub. I begin slowly rocking against him and then his fingers leave me and I notice he grabs the retractable shower head I have for the bathtub. He turns it on and sets it to my favorite jet setting. I give him a look and he gives me a wicked smirk.

"Is this the setting you use?"

"I don't know what you're talking about," I say feigning innocence.

"When you soak in your tub and rest this against your pussy, how hard do you like it?"

I swallow and nod towards the water shooting out of the spoke at the speed I like. "That one."

He lowers it under the water and instantly I feel the water shooting against my pussy and *fuuuuuck it feels good.*

"Oh yes." My head falls back as I let the feelings take me under.

"You like that? God, you're fucking incredible, baby."

I bite my bottom lip, trying my best not to come yet but the angle that the water is hitting my clit has me building quickly towards my climax.

"I...I don't want to come like this," I whimper.

"No? The water doesn't feel good?" *God, yes.*

"I want...you." I pant. "Please. I *need* you," I beg. "Don't you want me to come while my pussy is wrapped around your dick?" A devilish smirk crosses my face. "Don't *you* want to come while my pussy is wrapped around your dick?" I purr and my eyes flutter open when the pressure disappears from between my legs and then he's standing to unbuckle his slacks and toe off his shoes fast and then he's in the tub, slowly sliding down in front of me and pulling me into his lap. His arms wrap around me, gripping my ass cheeks as he positions himself at my entrance.

His eyes are stormy and filled with heat as I slowly move down his shaft. The water moves around us and I can only imagine the mess we will have to clean up when water is all over the floor but I don't care because he's finally inside of me and I feel safe and like nothing can touch me. His lips move against mine as he moves me up and down his dick and my heart begins to pound in time with his thrusts. I feel like he's pulling me in deeper, making me crave him, and this and us and I can only hope this doesn't end with me getting my heart broken. He pulls away from my mouth and runs his tongue along my pulse point and I'm pulled from the negative thoughts when he bites down on my shoulder.

"When you talk like that, I'll give you whatever you want."

Fuck me.

"Whatever I want, huh?" I clench my sex hard around him and he closes his eyes and lets out a groan that's so sexy it speaks to the most primal parts of my soul. The parts that make me want to crawl inside his skin and take up residence there.

"Careful," he warns. "Having this power over me comes at a price. Now ride this dick and come all over it like a good girl."

I moan and shiver in his arms hearing those magic words I loved to hear in bed. I hadn't told him that and I'm glad I didn't have to. *Training a guy to say it could be such a buzz kill.*

He stares up at me, running his tongue over his bottom lip as his eyes bore into mine like he knows those words have a direct line to my pussy. "Are you my good girl?"

I nod, my clit splintering and the words tumble out of my mouth at the high of my orgasm. I drop my forehead to his shoulder. "Yes, Daddy! Oh my god, I'm coming." My eyes flutter shut as I ride him harder, the water sloshing all around us.

"Fuck," he grits out and I can feel him pumping up into me, his hands on my hips pulling me harder against him as our orgasms move through us. Somehow in the midst of it, our mouths find each other, our tongues intertwining as his cock pulses and my pussy flutters in perfect rhythm.

Our bodies slow to a stop and our lips pull apart with a sexy sound and again we're eye to eye while he's still inside of me.

Will it always be like this? So intense and passionate? I feel like I can't breathe sometimes it's so overwhelming and I feel like I'm going to say something crazy.

Don't. You. Dare.

I bite down on my bottom lip to stop the intense feelings brought on by the high of the equally intense sex from spilling out of my mouth and I blink away from him. He turns my face back to meet his deep blue gaze. "You are so beautiful." His voice is low and I feel the words washing over my skin and burrowing deep within.

I fucking melt.

I feel the tingles in my cheeks over his praise. "Thank you." I try to move away but he holds me in place, my sex still wrapped around his dick.

"Daddy?" He raises an eyebrow and I'm glad he's broken through the tension.

The tingles turn to flames and I feel them heat for a second before I narrow my eyes. "You didn't like it?" I ask, even though I know the answer.

He laughs and slides me off of him but keeps me in his arms. "You're sexy as fuck, you know that? Of course, I fucking liked it." He nuzzles my cheek. "We should get out though. You need to rest."

"Will you stay with me?" I ask, still feeling slightly shook up from earlier, though sated and maybe a tad bit clingy over the man that has learned things about me and my body in two days that no one *including myself* knew.

He nods. "Nothing could keep me away from you right now."

Chapter FIFTEEN

DAMIAN

WHAT A FUCKING DAY.

I'm trying not to even think about it because it makes me so fucking irate. That fallen light fixture was heavy and sharp and could have killed someone.

Killed Shay.

I squeeze the woman in my arms tighter and she sighs in her sleep. I haven't been able to fall asleep even though it claimed her within seconds of resting her head on my chest. I've just been staring at the ceiling listening to the sounds of her breathing, ensuring me that she's alive.

I'd gone to the guesthouse to get some clothes, and per her request, brought one of my t-shirts for her to sleep in. Now she's pressed up against me in my clothes and no panties much to my dick's appreciation. Her hair is splayed out over the pillow behind her and her lips have formed a pout, pressed against my bare chest. I cup her face, pressing a kiss to her forehead, and she scrunches her nose before snuggling against me more.

I could hold her in my arms forever.

Flashes of what could have happened play through my mind on a loop. More importantly, I don't miss the weight in the pit of my stomach at the thought of anything happening to Shay. She'd always meant more to me than anyone I protected, but now...

I look down at her, thinking about how much everything has changed and is still changing between us. *What does she want from us? From this?*

What do I want?

She and I can't work long-term. She deserves someone in her lifestyle, someone like Paxton—*but not at all like Paxton.*

Is all of this about Paxton? Am I just her rebound?

We come from two different worlds and even though I'd burn mine to the ground for her, I couldn't ask her to do the same.

But I would. I would crawl to her through the wreckage if only she asked.

I want to believe what happened today was an accident. I want to be absolutely sure that there is no connection between the ominous letters she's been getting and what happened earlier. It seems like the obvious conclusion is that it wouldn't be because the person in the letters seems like he or she is obsessed with her. But, they could become angry over the fact that she won't be with them and it becomes a situation of *if I can't have you no one can.* Right now, I'm not discounting anything until I have proof, which means right now, I trust fucking no one that hasn't been thoroughly vetted by me.

The sounds of her phone ringing and my phone pinging breaks me out of my thoughts alerting me that someone has just gotten through her front gate and is on the property.

Fuck. Who's here?

I expect it to be Veronica, but Shay made it seem like we still had a few hours before she showed up and Shay has only been asleep for about an hour. She stirs, wiping her eyes, and groans, probably from a new pain or stiffness she hadn't felt before she went to sleep. She blindly reaches for her phone just as I reach for mine and my blood runs cold when I see what car and more specifically *who* is coming up the driveway.

She groans as I'm sure that person is calling her. "What, Paxton?" I'm off the bed instantly and Shay moves to look at me. I can tell she's about to tell me not to move when her eyes widen and she sits up wincing from doing it too quickly. "What the fuck, why?" She rolls her eyes as I pull on my shirt and sweatpants. "I'm fine. You can't just show up at my house whenever you feel like it, Paxton." She points at her bottom half and I go to her closet to grab her a pair of joggers which earns a smile from her. "Because we're not together!" she shrieks as she pulls her pants up and reaches for her discarded bra to put on under my shirt. She looks down at herself realizing what she's wearing and pulls off my shirt to replace it with one of her own.

The sound of the doorbell chimes and I get an alert that he's tried the code. I scoff at the audacity of this asshole.

"I'm coming. Did you honestly think you could just walk into my house?" she says when I show her the alert on my phone of one failed attempt to enter. She hangs up and we both make our way out of the bedroom and down the hall.

"Maybe you shouldn't be around while I talk to him. Do you want to just wait here?"

I eye her warily because not only does the thought of not having her in my sight cause a wave of uneasiness, but a twinge of jealousy is creeping into my senses at what her ex-boyfriend might say to her.

"Damian," she looks up at me with those big brown eyes and flutters her eyelashes, "don't be jealous. You have no reason to be."

"I'll wait downstairs. It's not so strange that I would be in the house with you after what happened. Especially if you're here alone." She nods and makes her way down the stairs. I move out of sight but still close enough that I can hear what he says and be close if she needs me.

"Yes?" Her voice is laced with irritation as she opens the door.

He lets out a sigh. "Jesus, Shay, are you okay? I heard what happened and I freaked the fuck out. Can I do anything for you?" I hear the sound of the door shutting.

Great, so he's staying.

"No, I'm okay."

"You shouldn't be here by yourself, you're even limping a little."

"I hurt my back and my ankle is a little swollen, but it's okay. I'm fine. Ice and heat. I'm not here alone. Damian is here."

There's a pause. "He's here? Like in the house?"

Sure am. Don't make me have to prove it, asshole.

"Yes. He was worried about leaving me alone."

"Well, he could go and I could stay with you?"

"Why would you do that?"

"Because I've been your boyfriend for three years and I'm worried about you? The woman I love almost got seriously hurt? Take your pick?"

"Paxton, I appreciate the concern, however, I'm no longer *your* concern. I'm fine and I don't feel comfortable having you here. Besides, Veronica is coming over soon and she might actually murder you if she sees you."

"I can handle Veronica." He chuckles and I can hear them getting closer which means they must be walking towards the kitchen.

"Paxton, we aren't together. The sooner you accept that, the easier it'll be for all of us." I raise an eyebrow, wondering if I'm included in this "all" she speaks of.

"It doesn't matter if we're together. I still want to be here for you."

She doesn't need you.

I hear her let out a sigh.

Just say the word, baby and he's gone.

"Paxton..."

"Is there someone else?" he asks and I do not miss the scoff that leaves her lips.

"The audacity you have." I hear her opening her refrigerator and setting something on the counter. "You sleep with countless women but you have the nerve to ask if *I* was unfaithful? The answer is no by the way, not that I owe you shit."

Good for you. I don't miss the fact that she only reiterated that she hadn't cheated on him and not that there isn't anyone else.

Because there is definitely someone else.

"Shay, I'm sorry."

"And I believe you but I said that wasn't enough. Not even close."

"Why are you being like this? So cold, like we meant nothing."

This guy cannot be serious.

"*I'm* acting like we meant nothing? But you cheating on me was supposed to show me, what? That I meant everything? Seriously? You cheated, you got caught, and I ended it."

I don't hear a response and I wonder if it's time that I make my presence known so I can see him out. I make my way towards the kitchen and I see Paxton standing a little too close to Shay for my taste and they both turn to look at me.

"Paxton, I think you should go." I would have asked Shay if everything was okay like I usually do but I don't want any more blame to fall on her. I'll gladly play the bad guy that's making him leave.

"Excuse me?" He looks at me in shock. "I'm fairly certain that's not your call."

I make my way towards them. "She said she wasn't comfortable having you here and that you should leave and you aren't listening. It is my call if you're bothering her." I don't move to stand between them, although I want to because it's pissing me the fuck off that he's closer to her than I am right now.

"We are talking."

"No, we aren't. There's nothing to talk about," Shay interjects and takes a few steps back, away from him. "Please stop making this so difficult."

"I made a mistake."

"A mistake usually indicates one, maybe two, but from what I hear it sounds like you made hundreds of mistakes," I say and his eyes snap from mine to Shay's angrily.

"What the fuck, Shay? I didn't realize you were sharing our business with anyone."

"He's a part of my team, all of whom are very well versed on what's going on," Shay argues.

"And I don't want to have to keep telling you about your language," I tell him.

God this guy is a tool and worse, he lacks any fucking self-awareness. How can he not understand why Shay doesn't want to be with him anymore?

He scoffs and puts a hand over his eyes. "Jesus Christ, you've always been so fucking up her ass." He drops his hand and shakes his head in what seems like disgust or maybe pity. "She's not going to fuck you, man. You think having me out of the way is your *in* or something?" He chuckles and runs a hand through his hair. "Women like Shay don't fuck guys like you."

Shay's mouth drops open and I can see the anger cross her features. "Get out." Her voice is low and her eyes are filled with rage. His smug eyes leave mine and move to hers softening dramatically.

"Shay, I'm sorr—" He starts, probably already regretting going off like that in response to feeling territorial. I'm sure the vibes I'm giving off right now are making him feel insecure.

Good.

Shay is mine, maybe she won't be forever, but right now she is and he can fuck off if he thinks he has any chance at getting her back.

"Get the fuck out of my house." She moves towards the entrance of the house and I go to move behind him so he gets the point that he needs to follow her. "I was willing to make nice and do what our teams wanted us to do but you had to push it. Push *me*," she growls and even though her voice is even, I can see she's ready to explode. "Now, you get nothing. I'm calling all of this shit off and I don't care what they choose to report. You hurt *me*, you humiliated *me*, Paxton, and you're continuing to do so. You don't deserve my compliance for another fucking day." She opens the door and he makes his way through it but stands in front of it. "If you're not off my property in ten minutes, I'm calling the police, and in case you forgot who you're dealing with, the police getting called to my house will be on every news outlet in the country within the hour."

Before he can reply, she slams the door in his face.

Chapter SIXTEEN

Shay

I AM SO ANGRY, I'M SHAKING. FURY RACES THROUGH ME IN A way that it never has before. I'm still facing the door after slamming it in Paxton's face and I've yet to turn around to face the man behind me. The man Paxton had hurled such hurtful and ugly and *very untrue* things towards. Tears pool in my eyes as humiliation washes over me.

"Shay." His voice is even and calm and it slices through me because of course, he's the calm one. Of course, he understands. I feel his heat at my back. "Turn around and look at me, baby." His voice is soft and wraps around me like a warm hug and I turn to look up at him. In the distance, I hear Paxton's car start and I'm hoping he heeds my warning and gets the fuck off my property.

I don't say anything, I just grab him by his t-shirt and move him to lean against the door and then my hands are in his sweatpants and pushing them to his ankles. "Shay."

"Quiet," I growl at him and his eyes widen, his eyebrows shooting to his hairline before they lower curiously.

"Excuse me?"

I grab his dick and begin to move my hand up and down a few times, grateful that he'd forgone underwear in his haste to get dressed. I start to move his shirt over his head but he keeps his arms firmly planted at his sides. "Don't be difficult," I grit out.

"Tell me what you're doing."

"Showing you how much I want you. How much women like me want men like you." I press up against him, wrapping my hand around his dick again and squeezing, making him harden more in my hand. "Shirt off."

He obliges, taking his shirt off without another word, and I lower myself to my knees, grateful for my area rug here so I'm not kneeling on the hardwood floors. When I run my tongue up his shaft, his dick jolts and I see the moment a tremor moves through him. "Do I need to tell you that what he said was bullshit?"

"It doesn't hurt to hear it," he says, and when I look up he's staring down at me, lips parted, a smile ghosting over them, blue eyes wide and sexy, and *fuck!* How could anyone say that a woman wouldn't want him?

Strong and protective and gorgeous. He's everything I want in a man. Eighteen-year-old Shay knew it. It had just taken him a little bit longer to catch up. And now I have this man and there's no way I'm letting him go. I feel an ache begin to build between my legs and I can't tell if that wayward thought is in response to the lust or if I really don't want to let him go.

Maybe I don't want to just fuck him. Maybe I want to *keep* him.
I just hope he feels the same.

"I want you." I run my tongue along the tip of his dick and when I already taste a hint of salt from his precum, my pussy gets slicker as I prepare to fuck this man with my mouth. "You've already fucked me about a half a dozen times and given me double the amount of orgasms so his theory is very false." I stick out my tongue and drag my hand over my palm lasciviously before wrapping it around his dick and begin pumping it, dragging my hand from root to tip. "I love playing with your dick." I place a kiss on the head. "It's so perfect..." I let my eyes flutter closed as I suck the tip into my mouth and swirl my tongue around it. "I've spent more time than I care to admit thinking about your dick."

"Fuck," he growls as I suck him inside, letting my tongue rub the underside of his shaft slowly. "God, your mouth."

"You better come in my mouth this time," I command. "I want to swallow everything your dick has to offer me." I wrap my lips around him and move slowly down his shaft, opening up my throat and moving until I reach the base and he lets out a growl that's so low and gravelly, I shiver.

"Fuuuuuck, baby. That feels so fucking good." Just like before, his hands hang by his sides and I reach for one, lacing our fingers and dragging them towards my head, letting him know that it's okay. "Okay?" His voice isn't higher than a whisper and I can tell it's strained. He's breathing hard already from just a few strokes of my tongue over his dick.

I nod and he begins moving with me, pumping into my mouth as I deep-throat him. "You are so fucking beautiful on your knees, with a mouth full of my dick, baby." I look up just as he looks down at me and our eyes lock. "What are you doing to me, huh?" His eyes shut and his head falls back against the door. "I don't think I'm ever going to be ready to give you up," he says and I frown and shake my head.

"Who says you have to?" I raise an eyebrow before going back to what I was doing not wanting to get into the heaviness of this conversation while I'm choking on his cock. I suck harder and force his entire dick—which is definitely the largest I've had—into my mouth and my eyes start to water.

I feel his thumb under my eye collecting the stray tears. "Too much?"

I shake my head. "No," I mumble around his dick and the vibrations must have done something to him because he slams his palm against the door behind him and begins working his hips against my mouth.

Damian is a sex god that knows my body inside and out already. He's fucked me in countless positions and I've gotten off every time. He eats my pussy like I'm his last meal and sixty-nineing with him was the first time I actually enjoyed it. It feels good that I can do this and make him feel as good as he's made me feel. His hand pulls my hair into a makeshift ponytail at the top of my head and stares down at me as I feel his orgasm looming.

"Baby, I'm going to come. You still want it in your mouth? If not, tell me now." I can hear the urgency in his voice. His breathing is ragged and his strokes have become faster and harder and more aggressive. "Shay."

"Mmmhmmm," I moan and he groans.

"Fuck, I'm going to come. Right there," he grits out. "Yessss, oh fuck." His hand tightens on my hair as he releases in my mouth. He pumps rope after rope of hot, salty cum into my mouth and I swallow it down, milking his cock for every drop. I move back and forth, still sucking him even as he jolts in my mouth. "Baby, stop…" I don't. I continue sucking him, feeling him shudder under my lips. "Shay," he grits and then I feel his hand on my chin and his dick is out of my mouth. A stream of cum connects his dick to my lips as he falls out of me and I watch it with fascination until it breaks. My tongue darts out to lick my mouth clean and he groans before letting out a deep sigh. When he opens his eyes, he looks down at me and narrows them. "You're one of those women, huh?"

"What do you mean?" I ask with a coy smile.

"The kind that keeps going after we come because you want to kill us." His eyes drift shut again and he lets his head lean back against the door.

"I don't know what you're talking about." I drag my tongue up his shaft again and place a kiss on the tip of his dick. His dick pulses and a hand moves in front of his dick to prevent me from kissing it again. I slide his sweatpants up his legs and he helps me to my feet.

"You are incredible. My god, you suck my dick like you were made to do it."

My pussy clenches in response because holy fuck that might be the most vulgar thing anyone's ever said to me. "That's…hot." He picks me up in his arms and carries me into the living room where he sits on the couch, draping my legs over his lap. "How many women have you been with?"

His eyes flit to me and he raises an eyebrow. "What brought that on?"

"You saying what you said about how I suck your dick. I assume that meant I was one of the best and it got me thinking about other women that may have done it better or just as good."

"Definitely not better. Nobody has ever sucked my dick like you have." He lets out a breath. "I've slept with…more people than you have, but sex with you is the best I've had by a mile."

"You're just saying that." I roll my eyes because *of course, what else would he say? Oh yeah, Simone let me fuck her in the ass twice a week and gave me head every hour on the hour.* Speaking of which…

"No, I'm not, but I'm sure you won't believe that. I just wish you would."

"Do you want to have anal sex?" I blurt out not even responding to his last comment. *Smooth.*

His head is tilted back, resting against the back of the couch and a surge of pride moves through me because damn, maybe I did take it out of him. He turns his head to look at me. "Ummm, right now?"

"In general."

"I would not be opposed to fucking your tight little ass, Shay," he says in a way that sounds like *of course I do, just give me a second.*

"I just…haven't ever, so…you'll need to be careful…gentle…slow." I give him a nod and a point of my finger. "Just an FYI."

He smiles. "Noted. Anything else?"

"That I haven't done?" He nods again. "Like what?" He doesn't say anything. "No threesomes. Or sex tapes!" I add, my voice going up an octave. "God knows, I can't replicate what Kim did. I don't have the energy." I laugh rubbing a hand over my eyes.

"You really think I'd share you with anyone? I'd lose my fucking shit. I could never share you." His lips form a straight line. "Fair on the sex tape, though I feel like that has something to do with you not trusting me, but I understand."

"No…I just…"

"I get it."

"Do you?"

"Yeah, you're not like other women I've dated. Every decision you make potentially affects the rest of your life. I respect that."

"Dated?" The word blares in my head like a neon light.

"What would you like to call this? Don't say fucking because you and I both know it's more than that."

"Well, we are fucking," I tease.

"Shay Celeste." His voice is low yet even but I can hear the irritation.

I smirk at the use of my middle name. "Yes, Daddy?"

He can't stop smiling in response and he moves to position me onto his lap. "Answer me."

"Well, I would say that." His lips bite my nipple through my shirt and my bra and I let out a sound that's part moan, part whine. "Are you saying you want to be my boyfriend?"

"Do *you* want me to be your boyfriend?"

"Yes," I whisper as I push my lips to his.

He grunts and accepts my lips, kissing me like we're sealing the deal on our new relationship. His tongue licks into my mouth, coaxing mine into his and we kiss like old lovers that have been doing it for years. His hands are on my face, mine playing with the hair at the nape of his neck, and I move around in his lap, feeling his dick harden beneath me. He lets out a guttural groan and I pull back, remembering my unanswered question.

I narrow my eyes. "You still haven't said how many women you've been with."

He clears his throat and part of me wonders, *is he nervous?* "I had a busy start to my early twenties."

"Ugh." I scoff, hearing the underlying meaning. "You men are all the same."

"Don't." He glowers at me and grips my face.

"You'd be about ready to lose your shit if my number was any higher than two before you. Don't be a hypocrite."

"I'm not a hypocrite. I'm a caveman. There's a difference. And for the record, since meeting you my number is much closer to yours."

"Oh?"

"Since Simone and I broke up, the number is far less." I blink my eyes as if to say, *well?* He sighs. "Five."

"Including me?" He nods. "Well, that's not bad."

"Glad I have your approval," he says sarcastically.

"Don't be like that, I just mean I'm glad you're not a manwhore," I tease. I tilt my head to the side. "Was it bad, when you and Simone broke up?"

"I don't think break-ups are ever really good."

"I just mean was it amicable?"

He sighs in a way that alerts me that maybe it wasn't amicable and he doesn't want to talk about it. "I guess. Like I said, she wanted kids and when I told her I wasn't open to them right then, it didn't go over that well. She felt like she was wasting her time and that I was too intense. I worried too much about her safety, especially while I was away. It was just not the right time for me to have a girlfriend."

I frown, thinking about what we decided just minutes ago. "And now?" I ask and I hate that I did. Hate that I sound like the needy girl who needs a man to tell her *she's* different and *this* is different from the woman that came before her, but *how is this different?*

Other than the fact that he's on my payroll. I internally cringe at the thought.

"Now what?"

"You said it wasn't the right time to have a girlfriend then but now…? You're doing the same thing you were doing then." I'm still in his lap and I try to move while we continue what seems to be turning into an uncomfortable conversation, but he squeezes my hips to keep me in place.

"How do you want me to answer that?" He narrows his eyes but they're still soft like he knows what I'm asking and he doesn't want to say the wrong thing. He lets out a breath when I don't respond. "I don't know what this is between us. I like the way it feels. How *we* feel." His hand reaches up to my cheek and rubs it gently. "I won't hurt you, Shay." He's quiet for a moment before he speaks again. "Do you trust me?"

I nod, instantly because frankly, I do. Even if there comes a time that he and I aren't here, I know he won't hurt me. I know it will be because the timing isn't right or *it* just couldn't work not because *we* couldn't work.

"Can that be enough for now?" he asks and I can hear the unsaid question lurking beneath. *I don't know where this can go but can we just figure it out as we go?*

"Yes." A smile pulls at his lips and then they are on mine kissing me like he wants a round two of what we did in the bathtub despite the fact that he said I needed to rest.

"For what it's worth," he says as he pulls away from my lips, "my feelings for you are different than I've had for anyone else and I admit that what Paxton said has crossed my mind. I mean look at you." He gives me a sad smile and I know where this is going and I hate that he's about to put me on this pedestal that makes him feel like he's not good enough for me. "He's not completely wrong. There are plenty of times when I haven't felt good enough," he shrugs. "Plenty of times where I feel like I failed someone. I would hate if I failed you or couldn't give you what you needed."

I hear the self-loathing in his words and I can't believe anyone has made him feel this way. I climb onto his lap and hold his face in my hands forcing him to look at me. "Look, I know it can be tough to be with someone like me. I know I can be a little high maintenance and a little spoiled. But at the end of the day, I'm still *just* a woman and what people see out there isn't the same person you see. You've never failed me before and I don't think you will now. You are good enough for me Damian. You might even be the best person for me."

Chapter
SEVENTEEN

Shay

DAMIAN FOLLOWED ME CLOSELY FOR THE NEXT FEW DAYS. I had a fitting, where he sat literally outside the room while I tried on clothes from every designer under the sun as we planned out what I was going to wear all season. *I even tried to entice him more than once to join me in the dressing room. But discretion or whatever.*

I had an afternoon at the spa with Veronica because I desperately needed a massage after what happened, a meeting with my trainer, a spin class all with him no more than a few feet away. I'll admit even I think he's overdoing it a little and maybe being a little intense, but whenever we get back to my house, he fucks me so long and just as intensely that I haven't broached the subject. I know what happened really shook him up. *Hell, it shook me up.* And he's just being extra vigilant. I'm sure once he realizes that it really was just an accident and no one is out to hurt me, he'll relax. For now, I'm enjoying all the extra attention *particularly on my pussy.*

"Are you listening to me?" I blink out of the daze I'm in by staring at the man in question behind my dark Dolce and Gabbana sunglasses and turn my focus to Veronica who's sitting on the other side of the table. Veronica and I are having a boozy lunch after a meeting this morning with the producers. She dragged me out after and ordered us a bottle of our favorite rosé the second we sat down.

Veronica pushes her sunglasses into her hair and tucks a strand behind her ears before taking another sip of her drink. "I've never seen you like this." She turns her head slightly to look over her shoulder at the man she's about to talk about. He's not close enough to hear us, but I assume she's checking to see if he's moved closer. "Even with Paxton, you weren't this…" she looks up in the air as if she's looking for the word, "sprung."

"Sprung? Come on." I don't remove my sunglasses because one look in my eyes will confirm Veronica's theory.

I'm falling for Damian really fast and really hard.

I pick up my fork and begin picking through my salad in hopes I can avoid more of her questions but I doubt it when I see the huge smile that makes her eyes sparkle with mischief. "It's good seeing you happy." She leans back in her chair and crosses her legs.

"Thanks, V." I smile and she lets out a sigh that is laced with questions and opinions.

"But…"

"Oh, here we go."

"I'm just wondering where this is going?"

"What do you mean?"

"You just got out of a very long-term relationship that the world doesn't even know has ended yet, and now you're jumping into… this? If it's just sex that's one thing, but I know you." She leans forward and lowers her voice. "And the way you're looking at him and the way you're acting, this is not just sex for you and I don't want you to get hurt."

"Damian wouldn't hurt me," I respond.

"Okay, maybe not but realizing that *this* can't work long term and ending it, would still hurt you even if it wasn't on his terms." She picks up a chip from the plate and moves it through the fresh tableside guacamole.

"Who said it can't work long term?"

"No one." She shrugs. "But how long are you planning to fly under the radar with this? What's going on with Paxton? I know you said you're done pretending, but nothing has come out yet, and all it takes is one picture, one time and then you're forced to go public and I just...are you thinking about going public with this? Does he even want to? Have you guys talked about all of this?"

"Not...really."

"Okay, well, these are conversations you need to have. Maybe even with your PR team," she says.

"We aren't doing anything in public, V." My thoughts float back to the gala when we were very alone in a public restroom with his hard body pressed against mine and my panties in his pocket. I look past Veronica again and see him staring straight at me. Even with his sunglasses, I can feel his eyes on me. On my chest. On my legs that are on display based on how I'm sitting.

"Yeah, now it's easy because you're not shooting and you're more accessible to each other. When you're having sixteen-hour days and you hear me and Derek going at it in the adjacent dressing room, your vagina might think differently." She puts her hands under her chin and flutters her eyelashes. I don't respond and she shrugs. "I'm not telling you what to do or what not to do."

The telltale sound of my phone letting me know that news *about me* has broken interrupts our conversation and I'm wondering if it's the news of the crash on set. I'm surprised nothing leaked up until now but I assume that's all it is when I see Damian stand and move closer to our table. I frown, wondering what's wrong when I open my phone to see the alert staring at me. A picture of me and Paxton with a line between us like a picture being torn in half indicating a breakup. "Fuck," I whisper, just as the sound of a bunch of cameras begin to click around me.

We are sitting outside and now all of a sudden, the area feels so much smaller as a group of paparazzi is standing just beyond the perimeter of the restaurant snapping photos of me and Veronica through the metal gate. Damian has his back to me, standing as much as he can in front of me to block the cameras but there's only so much he can do while we're out in the open.

"Sources close to the former couple say Paxton Copeland and Shay Eastwood have called it quits," Veronica quickly reads. She reads it faster than I can even process and I almost choke when I get to the part about him cheating on me with multiple women. "Oh my god." Veronica's eyes find mine.

My mouth drops open thinking about how this leaked and then Damian is at my table, staring at me with a look that says it's time to go.

My phone buzzes with a text and I'm almost afraid to look when I see his words.

Cooper: My office. Now.

"What the hell happened? This was not the plan." The head of my PR team, Gabe Watson paces the length of Cooper's office like a caged animal, his thumbs furiously tapping on his phone. "We talked about this, you knew what a messy breakup would do. Did you tell someone? Who knew about this?"

I frown because who the hell is he talking to?

"Okay enough!" I slam my hand down on Cooper's desk. Cooper leans back in his chair, his index finger over his mouth which is his tell that he's just as pissed off about all of this as I am. My lawyer, Mark Gibbs, who took over my account after my father passed away, is here as well despite the fact that he didn't really need to be but he was my dad's best friend and has taken a more personal investment in my career.

"Shay, we had a plan, and now we're two weeks away from Emmy nominations and you start filming *LA Dreams* in a few days. This is not the press we wanted for you right now." Gabe pulls his eyes from his screen and looks at me.

"AND? What does that have to do with anything? If I'm getting nominated, I'm getting nominated. Breaking up with my asshole boyfriend really shouldn't make a difference. This was all a ruse to keep Paxton looking cute for Oscar nomination season when it shouldn't have mattered." I cross my arms over my chest. "He cheated on *me*." I shake my head. "And you asking me who I told is ridiculous when he slept with god knows how many women." Gabe's eyes widen, because even though it was reported, I know he's not well-versed on this part of the story. "That's right. It wasn't just who I caught him with. There were *many* women. Any one of them could have told someone. I told Veronica and Jeremy, and Derek probably figured it out because Paxton showed up to the bar we were at last week and tried to corner me into talking to him and *my friends* picked up on it. He wasn't playing by the rules you put in place." I scoff. "And honestly, I don't owe you any explanations. This isn't *my* fault or *my* problem, and if you think I'm going along with some bullshit story that he apologized and I took him back, the answer is no." I pick at my cuticles showcasing how bored I am with this conversation. Paxton has done nothing over the past few weeks but hurt me and piss me off and I'm done playing nice. I want to move on.

Preferably with the man sitting in the waiting room potentially a little jealous over the idea that even after this, Paxton and I still may not be over in everyone's eyes.

"Listen, as far as I'm concerned, I think this breakup is good for her if Paxton is going to be whoring around Hollywood. And as far as Paxton is concerned, he'll be okay. People forgave Brad Pitt." Cooper shrugs as he takes a sip of his coffee that I'm sure is spiked with something in response to this chaos.

I snort. "Paxton isn't as fine or as good of an actor as Brad Pitt."

"Are you prepared to make a statement?" Gabe asks with a deep sigh.

I nod. "Been ready. How soon can I do it?"

Moments later, we're heading out of the conference room, Cooper talking a mile a minute about my first press tour for the show, but I'm not paying attention. I'm working on a social media post. "Hold on a second, let me give you something," he says, breaking me out of my train of thought of wishing Paxton well in everything he does in the future. I look up to see he's talking to Damian who's seated in his usual spot on the couch, leaning back with one finger resting above his top lip and his jaw tight. His eyes avoid me and more importantly, my legs that are still on display.

"What?" I look up at Cooper as he hands Damian a file and I look back and forth between them as I reach for the folder. Damian holds it out of reach and I frown.

"More?" Damian asks, and he looks worried about whatever there's potentially *more* of.

"What is that?" I ask. Damian and Cooper share a look and I look back and forth between them. "Okay, someone start talking." My voice is laced with irritation.

"It's just—" Cooper starts when Damian cuts him off.

"No." Damian gives him a look that I know means not to test him. His posture tenses and his sharp jaw is taut. All I want to do is climb into his arms and pepper kisses along it until he relaxes. *After he tells me what the hell is going on.*

"She has a right to know," Cooper says.

"KNOW WHAT?" I stomp and Damian turns his attention to me, raising an eyebrow like he's not going to entertain my outburst. *Yeah, we'll see.*

"I'll tell her."

"Tell me what?" I ask as soon as we're in the car alone. I'm seated in the back, *again*, as he drives us to my house.

"There's just been…some letters."

I roll my eyes, knowing what he means. "That's all? I always get letters." His eyes find mine in the rearview mirror.

"These are different."

"How so?"

"They knew about you and Paxton before this leaked. Said that they knew he wasn't good for you and now that you're over you two can be together. They're also typed, not handwritten, which is not what we're used to seeing. It may be nothing but there have been a few and all within the past week or so, I just want to be careful."

I lean forward between the two front seats. "You're so tense." I rub my hand down his arm gently and squeeze his bicep, feeling his muscle through his button-down shirt and suit jacket. "Is there anything I can do to fix that?"

He side-eyes me and doesn't even crack a smile. "Put your seatbelt on."

I ignore him and move forward, sliding my hand to his thigh and moving towards his dick. He grabs it instantly, preventing me from going further. "Shay. There could be anyone taking pictures from the front. Yes, your side and back windows are tinted but if anyone is in front of us they could see."

"So? In case you haven't been paying attention, I'm a free agent. I don't have a boyfriend, and I'm not suggesting I fuck you while you're driving. No one would be able to tell what I'm doing."

He loosens his grip but still holds it in place against his leg. He drags his thumb over my knuckles gently and tingles shoot through me. *God, I want him.* And not just sexually but in the ways that make those gentle touches mean something. I don't know how much time has passed as I stare at him with almost a dream-like expression when we pull to a stop in front of my gate. I frown when I realize he's not typing in the code to let us onto my property but unbuckling his seatbelt.

"Stay here." He commands and then he's out of the car and jogging to the gate. I try to sit up to see what he's picking up, which seems to be a large envelope taped to my gate. He opens it immediately, staring down at it with a look of worry and anger. Curiosity gets the best of me so I hop out of the car and start making my way towards him. "What part of stay in the car didn't you understand?"

he barks at me. Long gone is the gentle boyfriend who'd just been caressing my hand and in his place is my bossy bodyguard who is less than pleased that I didn't listen to his order.

"All of it. What is that?" I nod towards what's in his hands.

"Get back in the car."

I put my hands on my hips and glare at him. "No, don't leave me in the dark, Damian."

"Shay…" His eyes scan our surroundings before he ushers me back and into the car against my protests and gets into the driver's seat. He doesn't say anything for the entire drive to my house and then he's pulling me out of the car and dragging me to his guesthouse.

He slams the door behind him and tosses the file on the table. I'm just about to ask him again what's going on when his lips crash on mine. He backs me up against the wall, caging me in with one hand behind my back, lifting me into his arms forcing me to wrap my legs around his waist. His hand slides under my ass to hold me up, while one hand is against the wall. "You have to fucking listen to me, Shay," he says between kisses as his tongue licks its way into my mouth. "If I tell you to do something, it's for your safety." He pulls away and stares up at me.

"But you weren't telling me anything. Since we left Cooper's office, you've told me nothing and you're freaking me out a little."

"Not everything is for you to know right away. I don't want you to be scared, baby. Don't you trust me to protect you?"

"Yes," I answer instantly.

"That means, sometimes you're on a need-to-know basis. And I'm certainly not going to let you look at something I haven't read over first." He gently rubs his nose against mine and then down my cheek and into the crook of my neck. I moan when his tongue darts out to lick the flesh and I tighten my hold around his neck. "Some of the things I've seen…letters you've gotten, I wouldn't want in your head. Not everything is for you to see firsthand."

I swallow. "Do you really think I'm in danger?"

"No." He shakes his head. "I'd never let you be in danger. I'll do anything to keep you safe."

Chapter EIGHTEEN

Shay

EVEN THOUGH DAMIAN HAS BEEN ON EDGE ALL DAY, HE doesn't seem that tense over the fact that I am going out tonight. The main cast of *LA Dreams* is set for a scheduled appearance at a very popular nightclub. We'd sign some autographs, take pictures, and stay for a few drinks. Veronica has already planted the idea of wanting to continue the night out after to somewhere more private and exclusive, but we'll see how drunk I get and more importantly how horny I get. I expect there to be several questions about me and Paxton, but my PR team advised me to ignore them. *Just keep smiling. Don't respond.* I haven't posted my statement yet, and Gabe wants us to try the silent route at first to see what Paxton releases first. Honestly, I don't care. There is speculation that the arrangement was fake and that I have someone or several someones on the side also, but for the most part, people seem to believe that Paxton cheated on me *a lot*.

Pictures are starting to surface and faceless Instagram pages are gaining traction of women claiming he'd slept with them. Pictures of him at clubs and on vacations that I knew nothing about were plastered all over every gossip site in the world. Some of them were clearly doctored but some of them look legitimate enough to make me wonder just how long he'd been cheating on me.

"I want you to wear this tonight," Damian says as he enters my bedroom while I'm still getting ready. I'm wearing a black backless jumpsuit that shows more than a little cleavage that Damian seems to appreciate from the way his eyes devour me. "You're gorgeous," he says as he snaps a delicate chain bracelet around my wrist. He hasn't had me wear the tiny chain that's actually a tracker in some time. He must still be feeling a little anxious about everything.

"Really?"

"Really." He gives me a pointed look. "This club is going to get crowded. This isn't like when you guys go to *Rush*. There's going to be a lot of people there. There's already an hour-long wait to get in because people want a chance to meet you. You're going to be taking pictures and signing autographs and..." he chuckles, "if I was your boyfriend, I could be closer." He takes a step closer to me and pulls me into his arms. "I could keep you in my lap the whole night, and no one would dare fuck with you."

"Is that something you want?" I sigh, as his lips trace down my neck and between my breasts. His tongue darts out and traces the same trail. "Oh god," I moan when I feel my nipple between his teeth. I'm not wearing a bra and when I look down, I see he's pushed the fabric to the side, exposing my breast, and his lips are wrapped around it. "To go...public?"

"No." He grunts, letting my breast fall from his mouth as he moves back to his feet. "I know the kind of pressure that puts on you right now, and I know we aren't ready for that." He swallows and takes a step back, and I frown because things are getting icy despite the heat that was previously building between my legs. "We're moving really fast."

"Maybe because it's five years of tension finally breaking," I say, trying my best to argue that it's not really all that fast. *Both of us have been wanting the other this whole time.* "I thought you wanted this?"

"I do." He nods, scratching his beard. "It doesn't mean we are ready to tell the world."

"I didn't say we should."

He nods. "So, we agree then." He backs up slowly. "I'm ready to go when you are."

"Wait." I don't miss the longing in my own voice when he stops walking towards the door and turns to look at me. "Why do I feel like we just took a step back?"

He sighs and closes the space between us. "I need to be your bodyguard tonight. I can't worry about kissing you or touching or fucking you. If it seems like I'm shutting down on you, it's because I need to be able to do my job, Shay. I have to put that part of me that knows what you feel like out of my head."

Club Euphoria is such pure chaos from the time we enter that even I'm slightly overwhelmed. Even though we have our own section, fans have flocked to us. They have the entire area surrounded, crowding around the red velvet rope separating us from the rest of the club. Women trying their best to get Derek and Jeremy's attention for a potential fling and a few minutes of fame. The ones that aren't, are just taking selfies with their backs to our section to try and get us in the frame.

We signed autographs and took pictures when we first arrived, but it would be mayhem if we tried to now. Damian is in our section with us but he is doing his best to stay out of sight. Yet, I'm hyper-aware of every time he moves. Every time he asks someone to take a step back and returns to his stance, wrists crossed in front of his groin, the heartbeat between my legs intensifies.

He's so protective and dominant and sexy and it makes my knees weak.

Seated in the booth, I take a long sip of my vodka soda when I feel like I'm being watched. I'm used to having eyes on me, but something about this feels odd. Unnerving.

My eyes dart up to look around the club, but it's dark. The only lights are the neon ones bouncing along the walls. Pinks and purples and blues swirl around the club in time with the bass of the speakers.

Damian is getting in my head. Everything is fine.

I stand up, trying to catch Damian's eyes, and I don't have to look hard because I see him staring at me, his phone in hand, pointing at the screen.

I grab my phone and I see his text as soon as I open it.

> **Damian: You okay?**

I smile thinking about how well he knows me, how well he can read me. I know if I tell him about my moment of slight panic where I felt like someone was watching me *he'd* panic, so I lie.

> **Me: Yes. Just wish you could dance with me**
>
> **Damian: You could dance for me**
>
> **Me: What do you mean?**
>
> **Damian: Pretend I'm behind you. Touching you. My hands wrapped around your waist as you grind that sexy ass of yours against me.**

My mouth drops open and I squeeze my legs together as the carnal urge to run to him so we could do all of those things takes over. I slip my phone back into my purse, glad that I'm starting to feel my drinks and my inhibitions have lowered. My eyes find his and though I know I can't hold his gaze the whole time without potentially causing questions, I hold them for long enough for him to know that I saw his text and I'm doing this for him. I raise my hands up above my head and bring them down, moving my hips in time with the beat that has slowed down and is now sexy and sensual and the kind of music you want to make love to. I drag my hands down the sides of my body and then up again, grabbing my breasts before running my hands through my hair, as my eyes flutter shut.

I turn my gaze back to him and drag my index finger down the valley of my breasts and I watch his eyes follow it, probably remembering the same trail he made with his tongue and lips earlier tonight. Our eyes haven't left each other for several moments and I can tell it's taking every ounce of control for him not to stomp over here and pull me into his lap so I can grind against him.

Lap dance on the way home. Got it.

He runs his tongue over his bottom lip and then his jaw clenches before he runs his hand over his beard dragging his thumb over his bottom lip.

My cunt flutters in memory of his beard dragging across the skin between my thighs, a delicious pierce as he fucks me with his tongue.

I continue moving to the beat, grateful that we're in our own section and no one has tried to get behind me to dance. It's crowded enough that no one probably notices Damian and me eye fucking each other but not so much that he can't see every inch of me. His eyes, usually stone cold, have nothing but heat in them as he drags them over me in a way that lets me know he wants me.

He desires me.

I've never felt this way under a man's gaze. Even Paxton's. Maybe because at times he treated me like a trophy he'd won. One half of the power couple that was taking Hollywood by storm, whereas Damian looks at me like... *I dart my eyes to Veronica who's grinding against Derek like she has zero plans to adhere to their no fucking agreement tonight,* and I recall something she said not too long ago.

"*He looks at you like you're his reason for breathing.*"

I turn back to look at Damian, but when I do, someone is right in front of me, startling me. I look up to see Jeremy smiling down at me. His hands grab my hips as I take a step back and stumble slightly. "Easy there, you good?" He looks nice in his suit, a gray Tom Ford that makes him look worthy of a GQ magazine cover.

Fitting I guess, since he was on the cover last month.

"Yes!" I nod, trying to look around him to see Damian but Jeremy is too big, his shoulders too broad and I can't see around him without making it too obvious.

"I'm glad we both have a second. How are you doing…with everything with Paxton?" Concern finds his face, the areas next to his eyes crinkling in that familiar way they always do. His green eyes are warm and comforting and I press a hand to his chest.

"I'm fine. All good."

"I hope you know I didn't say anything…"

"I know, J. You're my vault." I wrap my arms around him in a hug. He holds me tighter and drops a kiss on my forehead before letting me go with a final squeeze and moving into the crowd. I turn my gaze back to Damian who looks at me and then towards the crowd where Jeremy disappeared and then back to me.

I shake my head as discreetly as I can because he can't possibly be jealous. *Of Jeremy?*

I reach for my phone planning to text him when Veronica grabs my arm and pulls me into a hug. "Let's go dance in the crowd," she shouts into my ear. She smells like her signature Prada perfume and what is that—*Fireball?* I blanche at the smell. *Oh God, she's going to be puking by the end of the night.*

I look towards the very crowded dance floor and then back at Damian who's looking at me like he knows what Veronica suggested.

No, he mouths.

"One sec," I tell Veronica, without looking at her. I make my way through the section, passing through other tables filled with other TV and movie stars and social media influencers with the number of followers they might as well be considered celebrities until I make my way to where Damian is standing.

I pull my hair over one shoulder and fan myself. "I can't go dance?"

He looks towards the crowd. "Jeremy seemed a little handsy." He's still looking away from me and I hate that I don't know what he's thinking.

"Damian, look at me."

"No."

"Why?"

"You know why. I wear my feelings for you all over my face."

Oh? "And what feelings are those?"

"This is not the time for this conversation. Can you answer my question?" he asks through gritted teeth.

"Are you jealous?"

"I think he has feelings for you."

This isn't the first time I've heard this theory. There were times Paxton shared a similar sentiment.

"Jeremy? No. You're just feeling territorial." I take a step closer. "Do you need to mark me to make a point?" His eyes snap to mine and drag slowly down my frame, letting his eyes linger on my breasts before moving back up and over my head to scan the room.

"I don't think going in the crowd without me is a good idea."

"Do you want to come dance with me then?" I already know his answer but I want to tease him.

"Also, not a good idea."

"You're being difficult."

"This place is a madhouse," he retorts.

The back to back shots of tequila I took with Veronica are starting to hit me and it's making me feel a little reckless so I turn on my heel without another thought and make my way to the entrance of our section. I feel him right behind me and then his arm reaches out to shield me from the people attempting to touch me. A path somewhat clears and I make my way through the crowd smiling and waving through all of the flashes.

Jeremy appears, standing in front of me and people go wild at the fact that they're so close to their favorite on-screen couple. I hear people chanting for us to kiss or for him to propose or some equally romantic gesture. I roll my eyes playfully at the cheers when he leans down and whispers in my ear, "What do you want me to do?"

I shake my head. "Nothing." I laugh because Jeremy and I never engaged in any fake PDA and I'm not about to start now. "I have to go to the ladies' room." I'm filled with excitement knowing that the VIP bathrooms are private and one stall and it would allow me some alone time with my man.

Jeremy looks over my head assumedly at Damian, "I've got it. I'll take her," he says, and Damian steps between us probably because he doesn't know what Jeremy is talking about or more importantly where he's taking me.

"No, you don't. I think you've forgotten how this works," Damian says.

Despite the dull roar of the club, I hear the bite in his tone and if I wasn't starting to feel a little drunk, I might try to diffuse the situation. *But I want him a little keyed up. I want him to not care that we're in public and fuck me in the restroom because he's jealous and wants to remind me who I belong to.*

I didn't forget but I love his caveman side and I'm happy to see him starting to surface.

"Relax, Hunt. She's just using the bathroom."

"It's fine, J. I'm good. I don't need two escorts." I laugh, trying to insert comedy into the situation when I know Damian is feeling anything but humorous.

He nods, looking at Damian and then back to me. Five years of friendship, and close to five drinks tonight and I'm not totally sure I understand the look he's giving me. Luckily, I don't have to give it too much thought when Derek shows up with a beer for him and says something in his ear that I don't hear.

"They want us for pictures. Can I steal your man for a bit?" Derek jokes and I roll my eyes, trying to bite back the smile that Damian is probably seething behind me.

"Go, please. Get out of my hair." I wave them off.

Some of the crowd follows them, and though some follow me as I make my way towards the restroom, they stop once Damian closes the curtain behind us that has its own security in front.

I don't say anything as we make our way down the long hallway of one stall unisex bathrooms. The bathrooms all have doors that go from floor to ceiling *for a reason*, and I open a vacant one and walk inside. It's not huge but large enough for a toilet, sink, and a small loveseat in the corner. It's clean and smells of lavender. Damian settles in front of the door, his back to me and I let out a loud sigh.

"Get in here!"

"No," he grunts.

I grab his arm and tug as hard as I can but he doesn't move an inch. "Please, *Daddy?*" I purr, hoping this will break him and sure enough he tenses before looking around, probably to make sure the hallway is empty before he slips inside the dimly lit bathroom with me.

"Hi," I say, locking the door behind him, and then I'm in his arms.

"Jeremy is *not* your man." He leans down and growls in my ear, pressing a kiss to the space behind it that causes a delicious shiver to move through me.

I pull back and stare up at him. "I know, Derek sometimes calls him that when we're all together because we're together on the show. Derek is also hammered by the way."

"I don't give a fuck about what Derek said. Jeremy's acting like he's your man. Touching you," he unties the bow at the back of my neck and the front falls forward revealing my naked breasts. "He kissed you." He wraps his arms around me and rests them on my ass, pulling me harder against him, digging his erection into my stomach. "And then tried to press it about bringing you to the bathroom?" He grunts. "That's my job."

I let out a breath because the air is getting thick and hot between us and I know I'm not getting out of this room without an orgasm. "He's not your man or your fucking bodyguard." He pulls the rest of my jumpsuit down my legs and helps me step out of the pants, leaving me in nothing but four-inch Valentinos and black sheer La Perla underwear. His mouth drags up my left leg, nibbling the skin gently before his tongue darts out to draw circles on my inner thigh. "I'm both and it's my fucking job to keep you safe."

His words make me wetter and I squeal when he snaps my panties that are getting damper with each passing second against me. "Take them off," I whisper and he does without hesitation, dragging the silky fabric slowly down my legs, careful not to snag them on my pumps before pocketing the wet material. He drags his nose through my slit and takes a deep breath, inhaling my scent and then allows his tongue to follow suit. "Fuck me," I pant. "Please. Your dick."

"You don't want my tongue first?" His husky voice feels like honey in my veins. "Your needy little clit doesn't want it? I think it does. It's pulsing."

He spreads my lips and blows gently against my wet flesh and I don't know if it's the tequila or the sexual tension between us, but I'm feeling drunker with each passing second. He presses a wet kiss to me, rubbing his tongue all over me and the sounds that he's making are so carnal and sexy it takes my breath away. "This is mine," he murmurs and I hear the urgency in his voice and the gruffness of his tone.

I need him to fuck me; I want him to fuck his aggression into me.

"Damian, I want your dick. Please," I beg.

He stands to his feet. "Take it out."

I reach for his belt, unbuckling it, and releasing the button on his slacks, sending them down his legs. I rub my hand over him, the hard, thick dick behind gray Calvin Klein briefs that allow me to make out every ridge of him. My mouth waters and I bite my bottom lip, wanting it in my mouth when he reaches under my chin forcing my gaze gently upwards.

"We don't have time for that. Someone will be looking for you soon."

"Veronica will cover for me."

He shakes his head and turns me around to lean over the loveseat, facing the full-length mirror that shows our reflections. His lips move to rest on my neck and I watch us through hooded eyes in the mirror. *God, we looked good together.* This tall, gorgeous man wrapped around me like he wants to devour me. He's still wearing his suit jacket, with his pants around his ankles, but I'm completely naked. "I'll never let anyone get to you, you know that right? I'll do whatever it takes to keep you safe." I shudder at his words. That he would go to great lengths to not only make me feel good but to protect me. It makes me feel safe in more ways than one.

His dick brushes my ass and it sends a shiver through me thinking about him inside me, stretching me. "I'm going to fuck you from behind, and you're going to watch us." He reaches between my legs and cups my pussy. "You're going to watch as you come apart in my arms with my dick inside you."

He pushes me down over the arm of the couch and lines his dick up with my entrance, grazing my clit tortuously. "Damian," I sigh breathily, which sounds more like a plea. I look up and our eyes meet in the mirror, and I'm wondering if the placement of this mirror three feet in front of us was purposeful. He grips my hips and slides into me with so much force I'm pushed forward. I arch my back, pressing my hands into the cushion, and with the second thrust I already see stars dancing in my periphery.

"Don't you dare come yet," he grunts as he drags a hand down my spine and continues to thrust.

"But..."

"Hold it, baby," he commands.

"Damian, oh my God." My orgasm starts to brew low in my belly despite his warnings and I clench trying to slow it down. "You fuck me so good." I stare at us and watch as one hand reaches up to grip my shoulder as he tightens the other's grip on my hip.

"Yeah?" he asks. He pulls back slowly and slides back in and I see him looking down.

"Are you...watching?"

"Watching you take me? Yeah." His nostrils flare. "Fuck you're wet. You should see my dick right now. Shiny and wet and covered in *you*."

"Let me see," I whine.

"Later," he grunts. "Later tonight you'll watch me fuck you with my tongue and then with my dick." He picks up the pace, fucking me harder and more frenzied than before. "Shay, your ass is fucking fantastic. The way it moves against me when I fuck you from behind." His hand drops to one cheek with a smack and I cry out.

"Oh my god," I moan, the bite of his palm pushing me closer to the edge. "Can I come now please?" I ask, not sure I can hold off much longer but wanting to obey him.

"What a good girl you are for listening," he says, his voice even but sexy. "Come for me, baby." I push back against him, meeting him thrust for thrust as I chase my orgasm. "You're fucking perfect, Shay. I want you so much." His words send me over the edge. I love the way he fucks me, what he says, and how cherished he makes me feel when we're like this.

"Damian. Right there!" I cry out when my orgasm crests and I feel like the wind has been knocked out of me as I struggle to catch my breath. My eyes flutter closed and I drop my head to the cushion just as I feel his tongue drag up my spine and a hand reaches around my neck. He squeezes gently, continuing to fuck me through my orgasm and then I feel his dick pulse inside me and his groan. "Come, baby, please come inside me," I beg, feeling him nearing the edge based on how he's thrusting and then he pushes inside me one final time.

"Fuck, take it, baby. Take everything," he says as he fucks me through his orgasm. He hauls me against his chest, letting himself fall out of me, feeding me his tongue, and gripping one of my breasts. He spins me around so that I'm facing him and then his lips are back on mine, his hands are in my hair and mine are around the back of his neck. I pull him closer, pressing my chest against his torso and I purr in satisfaction when my nipples rub against his suit.

He pulls back, holding my face in his hands, and then drags them down my body. His eyes don't leave mine and for once I don't look away. "Why are you looking at me like that?"

"Like what? Like I'm falling for you?"

My lips part and I inhale a sharp breath because I was not expecting that. "What did you say?"

He tucks a hair behind my ear and reaches for the towels stacked neatly in the corner. He dabs at the sweat on my brow and I'm pleased he didn't wipe. He grabs another and drags it gently between my legs and his words coupled with this sweet aftercare has me wanting to repeat the same words he'd just uttered.

He swallows. "We should go. You've been gone awhile." He picks up my jumpsuit.

"No. Don't run away from me. Not after this."

"Sex in a bathroom?"

"You know what I mean," I argue because this was more than that.

"Yes, but I shouldn't have chosen now to say it."

"Say what?" I smirk. He doesn't respond; he just kneels in front of me and helps me into my jumpsuit, sliding it up my body, and turns me around to tie it behind my neck. "Damian," I push.

"Baby, can we talk about it when we get home and you're more sober?"

"Fine. Let me just touch up my makeup. I'll be right out." He nods before pressing a kiss to my forehead. I cross my arms as he reaches for the door. "I feel the same by the way."

Chapter NINETEEN

DAMIAN

My cock, which is still semi-hard from what just happened in the bathroom including the words Shay had uttered just before I walked out the door, softens dramatically when I see Jeremy standing at the end of the hallway looking down at his phone. *This fucking guy, again?*

Why is he so pressed on Shay all of a sudden? Has he always been this way and I'm just taking notice? My theory that now that Paxton is out of the picture he might be interested crosses my mind again and it's already grating on my nerves.

His eyes find mine from down the hall and they narrow, having not seen me standing here previously and it makes me wonder how long he's been standing here waiting for Shay.

"Hunt?" He walks towards me, holding his drink in one hand and the other casually in his pocket before turning to look back towards the entrance of the hallway. "I am not that drunk. Did you walk by me?" He frowns like he's confused by how I appeared, not having put two and two together when Shay emerges from the bathroom looking sexy and gorgeous and not like she'd just been fucked in a bathroom. Her makeup is still perfect. *I'm grateful she'd forgone lipstick tonight and settled for a tinted lip gloss that tasted like cake mixed with liquor,* and thankfully, I hadn't pulled on her hair, so it's still sleek and shiny.

"Jeremy?" Her eyes widen and then she looks up at me and then back at him and I yield to her not knowing how she wants to play it.

He looks at Shay and then at me and then the bathroom door behind us and it's as if a light bulb goes off and he chuckles. "Really?"

"Why are you even back here?" Shay asks, not responding to his snarky question.

"I was checking on you. You'd been gone for a while and now I see why." He snorts as he takes a sip of the whiskey in his highball glass. "This been going on for a while?" he asks, pointing back and forth between us.

"Not that it's your business, but no. It's…new. No one knows but Veronica, and if you weren't following me around like a creep, you wouldn't know either!" She puts her hands on her hips and I can't tell if she's actually annoyed or trying to be funny. I'm thinking somewhere between the two.

He chuckles and rubs a hand behind his neck. "Well, excuse me for being worried about you."

"You don't need to worry about her," I interject. "You've *never* needed to worry about her when she's with me. You certainly don't need to start now."

A scoff leaves his mouth and I shoot him a look warning him to be careful of what he says next. Jeremy's around my height and similar in build but he doesn't have my training and I have no problem putting him in his place if he steps out of it. "Relax, tough guy. Shay and I have been friends a long time and I'm allowed to care about her well-being."

"J, enough." She shakes her head. "I'm good. I'm…" she looks up at me and gives me a smile that makes my heart pound against my ribcage, "really happy." She turns away from me and holds his gaze. "But you can't tell anyone. I'm not ready for people to know yet, and while I didn't cheat on Paxton, if it comes out now, it'll be hard to sell that I didn't." She sighs. "Whenever we go public, it's going to be hard anyway given our history together, but I certainly don't need it the day after Paxton and I publicly ended things."

"Public? Wait…this is serious?" He looks at Shay like she's grown another head.

Annoyance flares through me at another dickhead response like Paxton's. I know I'm not worthy of someone like Shay. Women like her date other movie or television stars and not their bodyguards who live in their guesthouses, but it won't stop me from showing her how much better I am for her. How I'll protect her and care for her and never hurt her. How she can show me the side of herself she can't show everyone else. How I've been slowly falling in love with her over the past five years and now that I have the chance I'm not going to fuck it up.

"Jeremy, this isn't a conversation I want to have right now, okay? We'll talk Monday when we're back on set." I try to ignore the pang of jealousy thinking about her and Jeremy's love scenes. I've watched her show since the first season and Jeremy and Shay are no strangers to love scenes. They aren't HBO level, but he's touched every part of her in some way and it's already pissing me off.

"Fine." He looks at me like he's sizing me up in the way a father or older brother would look at her boyfriend before walking away from us without another word. *This guy can't be serious.*

"He's not going to say anything," Shay says once he's out of earshot. We're still alone in the hallway and I turn to look at her.

"I don't care about that."

"What *do* you care about?" She presses.

"You," I tell her without another thought and she smiles before leaning her head back and presenting her lip for me to take. I oblige, giving her a peck before we make our way back into the club.

I don't want to keep bringing up my thoughts about Jeremy. She believes he doesn't have feelings for her, and while I'm not certain, I'm definitely getting a vibe that's more than just him being "protective." But I also don't want this to be a source of tension between Shay and me. I know what her job entails and I don't want her to think I can't handle it.

We make our way back into the main area of the club, and I follow her through the throngs of people. In situations with crowds, I always prefer her to walk in front of me so I can protect her from all sides. I don't have to worry about someone touching her or grabbing her from behind and I know she feels safest this way. I'll never forget the reason I always walk behind her in these situations.

One night shortly after I first started, Shay was out at a club and I hadn't been the one to go with her to the bathroom. I wasn't the head of her security yet and he was far more lax than I've ever been. *I suppose that's why they replaced him with me.*

The club was still pretty loud and he was walking in front of her but somehow they got separated and he didn't hear her call for him when some guy came up behind her and reached his hand under her skirt. She'd spun around angrily, prepared to yell at him when he met her with an equally angry expression. Like she didn't have a reason to be upset. I'd watched the whole thing happen and I was on the move instantly moving towards her and wrapping a hand around her wrist to pull her into my side. *"I will blow you away if you even breathe the same air as her again, you got me?"* I'd told him and when he fled from my sight, she was still shaking like a leaf next to me. I'd wrapped my arms around her to try and calm her fear and anxiety and had felt what I assumed to be a sigh of relief.

It was one of the few times I'd touched her.

"I want you so much," I whisper against her lips, my hands tangled in her hair as I pull her harder against me. We're in the back of the limousine she has for the night and she's straddling my lap, moving around far too much for someone who said she wanted to wait until we got home for me to fuck her. She lets out the sexiest sigh as she continues to bounce up and down on me like she's riding me as our kissing becomes more aggressive.

She drives me insane in the best way. In a way that makes me crave more and more of her.

I pull away from her mouth and press my lips to her neck, using my teeth and tongue to mark her. I bite down and then soothe the bite of my teeth with my tongue causing her to moan. "Damian," she whimpers. We continue kissing the rest of the way home, our mouths almost frantic and our bodies trying to get closer to each other despite the clothes between us. "I love the way you kiss me."

I nibble on her bottom lip, sucking it into my mouth and dragging my tongue across it. "Is that so? Wait till you see the way I plan to kiss your pussy tonight."

She giggles, reaching for the door as we pull up to her house when I see a car in her driveway and I pull her hand from the door and hold it in my hands.

She's still in my lap as I squint trying to figure out who the fuck that is and more importantly, why I didn't know someone had gained access to her property.

She turns around to see what I'm looking at and groans. "Fuck. It's Paxton." She sighs. "What the hell?"

"You've got to be fucking kidding me," I growl as I move her off of me and I'm out of the car before it's even stopped moving. "Stay," I growl at her, ignoring her pleas to *wait*.

"What the fuck are you doing here? This is trespassing," I spit at the man with the angry expression staring back at me.

"With my own code. Get a fucking grip." He rolls his eyes. "Where the fuck is she?" He narrows his eyes as he looks me over, taking in my disheveled suit and my loosened tie that Shay had undone in her haste to lick and kiss the skin at the base of my throat. It's now untied and slung around my neck. My hair is slightly messy and I run a hand through it, pushing it out of my eyes. "Are you kidding me right now? Shay, get the fuck out here." He makes a move towards the back door of the limousine and I step in front of it stopping him from opening the door or Shay from getting out. I harden my gaze and surprisingly he takes a step back probably realizing that given what he's figured out regarding my relationship with Shay, he should definitely not fuck with me right now.

"What the fuck are you doing here?" I ask him.

He chuckles. "She been fucking you this whole time?"

"Answer me," I grit out.

"I want to talk to her about how the fuck all of my business got out. I knew she was pissed but I didn't expect her to stoop this low!" he yells and I feel Shay push gently on the door, letting herself out. Her shoes are still off, making her much shorter than both of us. Her jumpsuit is equally wrinkled, her hair bigger from my pulling on it, and she has very visible hickeys forming on her neck and one of her breasts. *God, she's beautiful.*

I fucking hate that she's on the ground barefoot. My eyes immediately go to her feet to make sure she hasn't stepped in or on anything. If we were alone, I'd be scooping her into my arms so she wouldn't have to walk on the concrete.

"You talked all that shit about cheating—" he starts when she interrupts putting a hand up to silence him.

"I didn't cheat on you, Paxton."

"Bullshit," he barks. "You think I didn't notice how wet you got for him all the time? There were times you would just stare at him. In front of me! Like I wouldn't fucking notice!"

"Paxton, lay off. Since, you know, there's no point in being diplomatic, talk to her like you have some sense or we're going to have a very big problem." I don't need a reason to hit my woman's ex-boyfriend after everything he put her through, but I would fucking love one.

Is she your woman though? my subconscious asks.

"You don't have to believe me but what reason would I have to lie? You've cheated on me with countless women."

"Because you know if you cheated too, then you can't play the victim." He points at her. "God, what is that? A hickey?" He makes a move towards her and I'm immediately in front of her blocking him from her.

"I will fucking end you, Paxton." I drop my hand to his shoulder, gripping it tightly and I give him a look that I hope shakes him because I'm done messing around. "Your interactions with Shay are over. Do you understand me? You two broke up. It happens. Stop embarrassing yourself." I grip his shoulder harder and he winces. "Shay isn't playing the victim. Even if she didn't have me in her bed fucking her better than you ever did, she doesn't care. What you do, who you do, she doesn't care because she doesn't want you anymore. She wants *me*." I hear her gasp and if I'm not mistaken, it's more out of lust than shock. I want to tell her to just give me five minutes to get rid of this asshole and I'll spend the rest of the night giving in to every *want* she's ever had.

His eyes are cold but I decide to dig the knife deeper wanting him to get fed up with this conversation and leave. "And Shay has spent more time in bed with me the last few days than out of it. She didn't leak the news of your cheating." His nostrils flare and his eyes dart to Shay who's now standing next to me. "Did you ever think maybe it's someone from your camp? I can't imagine all the women you've fucked are particularly happy with having to be kept quiet or in the dark and being treated with little to no respect. Maybe one of them outed you. Or hell, maybe one of the workers on the secret vacations you were taking. A flight attendant, a driver, a bartender. You think everyone values discretion or *doesn't* want to sell the information they have on celebrities because maybe you left them a decent tip once? Grow up."

He narrows his eyes and then looks at Shay. "Fuck you, both."

"Pax…" Shay starts. I can see the tears in her eyes and I'm not sure what it's about. "I know you're angry and I know you think I did this, but I didn't, and I've never cheated on you. Please don't leak this." I realize now she's thinking about her career or her image. She doesn't care about him being angry, but what his anger might mean if he sits too long with it.

"That's all you care about? Fuck my feelings, right?" he barks at her.

"No. I didn't say that. I don't think you can really play that card though because you cheated on me…" she says. *Does he keep forgetting that?*

"Not with anyone that I cared about."

"Okay, so I'm the asshole because I started dating someone after you that I do care about? I'm the problem because this isn't meaningless sex?"

"If this were any other guy on the planet, I'd say no, but I knew you always had feelings for him and you fucked around with me anyway. You used me because you thought you couldn't have him."

"That's not at all what this was, Paxton. I did care about you! I did love you! You broke my heart! You don't get to judge me for how or when I moved on!" I'll admit it stings hearing that she loved him but I ignore it because she's over it and him and wants to move on.

The intrusive thought that I'm just her rebound hits me like a fucking train. Something fun and sexy and exciting before she goes back to her life of glamour and rich men that can give her the world and not one whose only pro is keeping her safe in it.

He scoffs and puts his hand up silencing her and I resist the urge to break it. "Fucking please. You moved on in five minutes. Look me in the face and tell me you didn't have feelings for him. Tell me that you didn't ask him out and he said no."

"I didn't ask him out," she snaps.

"Semantics, Shay. You know what the fuck I'm saying."

"And what does that have to do with anything?" I interrupt. "Nothing happened while you and Shay were together."

"I don't know if I believe that," he grumbles. I see the defeated look in his eyes and his demeanor. He knows it's over. That he fucked up and there isn't a chance he's getting another. That Shay Eastwood is one of a kind and yet he treated her like he could find another just like her. "I'll keep your precious secret, Shay. I'll be the bad guy in this story."

"I haven't said anything to any media outlet. I haven't even made a statement. I don't want you to be the bad guy. I just want to move on."

His eyes dart back and forth between me and Shay. "Can I talk to you alone?" he asks her and her eyes flit to mine. They're not looking for approval; Shay rarely asks for approval for anything, except more recently if she could come, but I see everything in just the brief flash of her eyes.

It doesn't mean anything.
Nothing will change.
I want you.

I'm not sure what he wants to talk to her about, and despite my reluctance to leave them alone, I nod and turn towards her house knowing this allows me to do a quick sweep. A soft hand slips into mine, stopping me from walking, and when I turn around, my gaze finds her warm brown eyes as she looks up at me through her lashes. She flashes me a smile that's both sweet and sexy, and reaches up on her toes to presents her lips for me to take. I narrow my eyes curiously wondering why the show for her ex-boyfriend, but I oblige, pressing my lips to hers for no more than a second and then turn to walk towards the house.

As much as I want to stand at the window and watch, I can't figure out if that's the man she's sleeping with or her bodyguard's dilemma. I eventually decide that she's safe with him and begin my walk through, ignoring the pang of jealousy. I'm still making my way through her top floor where her bedroom is when I hear the door open and close. It hasn't even been ten minutes and I'm interested to see what he wanted to talk about and how it ended.

I'm surprised she hasn't called for me or made her way upstairs and when I hear noises in the kitchen and the sounds of ice in a glass I proceed with caution, not sure what kind of mood she's in. When I enter the kitchen, she's leaning against the refrigerator, drinking a glass of clear liquid and I don't know if it's water or vodka.

"Want to talk about it?" I ask her, nodding my head towards the door. "What he said?"

"He told me about the ring."

I stiffen, not expecting that but also not totally surprised. "He asked you?" Thoughts of him down on one knee, selling her on a life of wealth and security and whatever else he could offer her that I can't come charging into my brain before I have a chance to tell myself she'd never marry him.

She winces, scrunching her cheeks. "Not in the traditional, man on one knee, *'I love you and can't live without you'* type of proposal." She sighs. "It was more of a, *'I know I fucked up but how about a marriage of convenience? You can even keep Damian if you want.'*" I blink in shock because how the fuck could he even speak those words aloud. "Did you hear me swooning from in here?"

A ghost of a smile pulls at my lips at her ability to make a joke even when she's tense. She rolls her eyes and moves around the island in the center of her kitchen, hopping up on it like she's done a million times. She grabs the loosened tie still around my neck and tugs gently pulling me closer to her. "I said no," she whispers and I nod, not knowing how to respond and hoping she has more to say. "Do you want to know why?"

"Do you want to tell me why?" I give her a half smile so she knows she doesn't have to tell me, but also if she does, we'll still be okay. Whatever she said or he said, it doesn't mean anything to *us*.

"He doesn't think it'll work…" She frowns. "You and me. That we are too different and eventually those differences will overwhelm our relationship." She scrunches her nose. "He took two psychology classes before he dropped out of college to pursue acting and evidently, he's Dr. Phil." She purses her lips and years of experience tell me she's trying to stop the tears from falling.

"Baby," I rub her cheek, trying to calm the nerves I know are dancing beneath her skin. "It's okay."

"I want us to try." Her hands go to my shoulders. "If you want. I don't want him, I want you. That's why I said no."

I grip her hips and move between her legs for her to wrap them around my waist. "I want."

She shrugs. "It's going to be a little complicated at first, and then when people find out there will be a lot of questions and opinions. I'm used to that but I worry about you. It's a lot for someone who's never had their privacy violated."

I rub my thumb gently over her chin and press my lips to hers. "Can you let me worry about what I can handle?"

"I just don't want *this* to become too much for you."

"Is this all coming from Paxton?"

She winces. "A little, but I've thought about it. It's impossible not to think about." She drops her gaze away from mine, looking down as she fidgets with her hands in her lap. "I have abandonment issues."

I lift her face and the tears in her eyes gut me, transporting me back to a time when she'd sobbed in my arms and begged me to tell her that it was all a mistake and her parents were still alive. "I will never abandon you."

Chapter TWENTY

DAMIAN

I SEAL MY PROMISE WITH MY MOUTH AGAINST HERS AND YANK her off the counter into my arms before carrying her out of her house. I set the alarms without looking with my lips still on hers and then I'm pushing her through the door of my guesthouse. The last few nights we've been in her bed, but I want her in mine. I want her in the bed where I have lain awake and thought about her with my hand wrapped around my dick as her scent clung to the air.

I set her on her feet as I turn on the lights, dimming the harshness of the overhead lights to give the room a warm amber glow.

"Your place is so clean," she says and when I go to respond she's completely nude, having discarded her jumpsuit and her underwear are still in my pocket.

I let out a breath and drop to my sofa, my heart and dick both pounding in tandem, making me feel like I might have a heart attack or come just from seeing her naked. I signal for her to come to me and she moves quickly onto my lap, settling that pert little ass against me. She looks at me innocently like she's not rubbing her wet pussy on me.

"I don't think seeing you naked will ever not render me speechless for a minute." I groan as the sensation of her tight, sexy body moves against me.

"Seeing your body does a number on me too." My cock hardens beneath her in response and her hands reach for my button-down, yanking it from my pants, and sliding her hands up my torso. "How come I'm always naked while you're fully clothed?"

I slide out of my jacket and lift her up, pushing her into the plush suede sofa. "Because I'm always in a rush to put my mouth here." I drag my finger through her wet slit and she moans when I circle her clit. She whimpers and when I look up at her, her eyes are fluttering closed as her head drifts back and a serene smile finds her face as she rolls her hips against my fingers. "Look at me," I tell her, wanting her eyes on me while I put my mouth on her.

Her eyes fly open, finding mine and I wink at her just before I let a stream of spit fall from my mouth to land on her clit.

She gasps, "Oh my god."

I spread her sex, staring at her slick and wet opening. "You have such a pretty pussy, baby. I fucking love it. That's why I can't stop." I grip her thighs and drag my tongue through her pussy slowly. "I'll never want to stop," I tell her as I fuck her with my mouth slowly. I pour everything I'm feeling into it, trying to show her how much I want her. How I've always wanted her, and even though things are different between us now, I will always protect her.

Even if there's a point in time when we aren't doing this.

"Mmmm, tell me you want me again," she says and I groan against her, hoping the vibrations feel good against her clit.

I pull away and lick my lips, collecting her juices that are covering the bottom half of my face. "I want you so fucking much, Shay. You've been driving me wild for years. I trained myself not to look at you." I pull off the remainder of my clothes, letting my hard cock spring free the second it's out of my briefs. "Told myself I couldn't have you."

"Why?" She looks up at me. "You knew I wanted you."

"A lot of reasons, Shay. For one, I thought it would be too complicated. Crossing these lines while I'm protecting you."

"And now? Isn't it still complicated?"

"Yes, but I let myself touch you and now I'm addicted." I don't want to get into this now, while we're both naked and her wet cunt is glistening in the low lighting of the room. I want to take her to my bed and worship her and defile her and fuck her like an animal and then I want to make love to her and show her that no one could ever know her body the way I do.

Unshed tears glisten in her eyes and when she reaches out to me, I lift her into my arms.

Her legs wrap around my waist and her lips find my neck. "I want to be in your bed," she tells me, but I'm already walking back towards my bedroom just off the living room and kicking the door shut behind me. The second her back is on the bed, I'm sliding into her and my lips collide with hers, my tongue finds hers, devouring her mouth. I lace our fingers and drag them over her head as we begin a rhythm of thrusting and writhing against each other.

"Damian," she moans, "fuck me harder."

I let her hands go and wrap a hand around her back and pull her into my lap. I'm sitting back on my heels allowing me to get deeper as I thrust upwards into her. She wraps her arms around my neck and her eyes bore into mine. "It's so deep," she whispers as she slides up and down on me harder.

I grip her hips, drilling harder into her. "You take me so fucking well."

"Do I?" she whispers. "Is my pussy your favorite?" she purrs.

"You know it is." I pull her bottom lip into my mouth and nibble it gently. "Your pussy is my favorite place to be."

"I love the way you look at me while we're like this," she whispers. "Like you can see everything." Her lips find the space behind my ear before she runs her tongue along the shell and nibbles on the lobe. "It's so intense."

She's right. I've never experienced such sexual compatibility with someone. It makes me wonder if there's really something to the term *soulmate* and if she's mine. Because what I feel when I'm inside of her is something so much deeper than an orgasm.

I continue fucking her, moving her up and down harder with each thrust as I feel my balls tingling. "Baby, I need you to get there," I tell her, moving my hand between us to strum my thumb over her clit, stroking that sensitive bundle of nerves that has become one of my favorite things in the world.

"Damian!" she cries out right as her body goes rigid and her eyes flutter shut. "Oh my fucking god, right there baby." Her lips find mine as she lets out the sexiest moan as she begins to shake in my arms. Her entire body vibrates on top of me and it's almost too fucking much.

"Fuck..." I let my head fall back as the feeling takes me under. "The way your pussy clenches around me..." I grit out and just before I come, the overwhelming need to possess her takes over me so I pull out of her. She gasps and I push her onto her back just in time to shoot my orgasm onto her bare, wet cunt. I grip my cock, dragging it from root to tip, letting my cum drip onto her. I drop my cock, still wet from being inside of her and still slightly hard, and put my hands on her, rubbing my cum into her pussy and over her clit.

I drag my gaze to hers to find her watching my hands as they rub my cum into her skin.

"I want to know how we taste together," she says and when I look up at her, she's giving me the sexiest look. Her teeth dig into her bottom lip and her eyes are full of want. I drag my finger through the mess I made on her and slide it through her lips. She sucks it like she would my cock, and my dick jolts in hopes that it gets its turn between her lips. She pulls me out of her mouth and drags her tongue up my finger. "We taste so fucking good."

I raise an eyebrow at her. "Maybe I should try it then," I tell her as I lower my mouth to her cunt and drag my tongue through her slit, tasting both of us from the source.

She lets her head fall back as a sound that sounds part chuckle and part moan leaves her lips. "Damian, you are so hot, Jesus Christ." She lets out a breath as I get up and make my way to the bathroom. I turn on the sink, holding a washcloth under warm running water before going back to the bedroom. She'd propped herself up on her elbow and I can tell she's looking at something but the room is somewhat dark so I'm not sure what's caught her attention.

I get on the bed, grab her ankle, and pull her gently towards me so I can clean her up when her eyes meet mine. "Why do you have women's perfume on your nightstand?" she asks. "More specifically *mine?*"

I continue wiping her, ignoring her question because I really don't want to tell her why and I'm fucking irritated with myself that I didn't have the foresight to move the bottle of perfume.

"Damian." I don't respond, keeping my eyes trained on her sex that's covered in a slick layer of me. She swats my hand away and I swat hers back and continue wiping her even though now she's cleaned of my seed. I just want my hands on her. I press my finger to her pussy, dragging my index finger through her folds and she pushes my hand away despite the tremor that moves through her. "Answer me." I let out a sigh because I know she's not going to let this go. "I knew I wasn't crazy when I smelled my perfume here." She frowns and I wonder what she's thinking.

My eyes lift to meet her curious ones. "Want to tell me what you're thinking?"

"I don't know. I don't think you have another woman." She furrows her brows and I push her into the blankets, resting my body on top of hers without putting too much weight on her.

"Correct." I drop my head to her chest. "It smells like you."

"We've established that." She deadpans and I chuckle.

"I spray it sometimes…" I press a kiss to her nipple letting my tongue dart out to lick the sweat in the valley of her breasts. "When I'm thinking about you and touching my dick."

I reluctantly look up at her, somewhat worried about the look that could be on her face. Her eyes widen in realization and her mouth drops open as goosebumps pop up all over her flesh. "What?"

"I know it's a little insane, but it made me feel like you were really here."

A sexy smile finds her face. "Oh my god, that's the hottest thing I've ever heard. You masturbate to…my scent?" She wraps her legs around me, pulling me closer, and based on how we're positioned, her wet sex presses against my abs and I relish the feeling of her wetness on me.

"I didn't do it often, just on the nights when I was overwhelmed by the fact that you couldn't be mine."

"Well, I am now," she says. I move to my back and pull her into my arms so she can rest her head on my chest. "You said you were falling for me," she whispers, drawing circles on my chest with her index finger.

I nod. "I did."

She pulls away to look up at me and I look down into her warm brown eyes. "Did you mean that?"

"Shay, I've been falling for you for a really long time."

Chapter
TWENTY-ONE

Shay

OVER THE NEXT WEEK, DAMIAN AND I ARE ATTACHED AT the hip whenever I'm not on set. I'm back to shooting fourteen-hour days and when I'm not there, I'm at my house wrapped in his arms or in a bathtub soaking my tired limbs as Damian rubs my feet or my shoulders *or my pussy*. If we're behind closed doors, I'm in his lap. I fall asleep in his arms, wake up in them, and I don't think I've taken a shower by myself since our first one. We have sleepy morning sex before we get up for the day and at midnight when I get home from the set just before I close my eyes. We make love and we fuck hard and it's always passionate and overwhelming and it takes my breath away most times.

He hasn't told me he loves me but I feel things shifting between us. With every passing day, I feel our relationship growing stronger. We've been able to keep our relationship a secret, keeping everything professional while we're in public, but I know it's only a matter of time before I have to tell Cooper and my team about us.

After the light fixture accident, Damian has been on set watching things closely, and I'll admit it's been nice having him close by. *Especially the days I have love scenes with Jeremy.* He fucks me mercilessly those nights almost to the point of exhaustion. I don't know if it's out of jealousy or just his possessive nature, but I fucking love it.

I love him.

And I think he loves me too.

It's seven in the morning, and I'm sitting in the back of my Range Rover behind Damian's seat as he drives us to the set when I notice him darting his eyes between the rearview mirror and the side mirrors every few moments. I narrow my eyes in question. "What's wrong?"

He shakes his head, finding my eyes in the rearview mirror. "Nothing, baby."

"Liar," I say leaning forward. "Tell me."

"Sit back," he tells me, and I notice he picks up speed a little. I turn around, staring behind us. I don't notice anything out of the ordinary, making me wonder if he's being a little paranoid. I stare out the back window, but all I see is a steady stream of cars and I briefly wonder if there's one in particular that's been following us.

I know Damian is a little on edge about the letters I've gotten and apparently that I've been steadily getting the past few weeks. Especially the one that was taped to my gate that one day. He changed all the passcodes that day and now no one can get through the main gate without being buzzed in. I haven't seen any of the letters, but he told me the gist, and I'll admit I'm glad that Damian and Cooper have been screening them all this time.

"Is someone following us?"

"I don't know," he tells me. "Something just doesn't feel right. I've had this uneasy feeling I haven't been able to shake for a couple of weeks and it pisses me off that I can't pinpoint the source. Why do you think I've barely let you out of my sight?"

"Because you're addicted to my pussy?" I blink at him and he gives me a look in the rearview mirror that seems equal parts annoyed and horny.

"Yes," he grunts, "but that's not why I haven't let you out of my sight."

"Baby, do you think you're being a little paranoid because now things are different?"

"No." He shakes his head. "I've always been very cautious and concerned about your safety."

"Yes, but now you have different feelings for me. I'm your girlfriend now and I think that might be messing with your head a little." I hope he focuses on the fact that it's the first time I've referred to myself as his girlfriend and not anything else that might irritate him.

"It's not in my head," he tells me and the way he says it I decide not to push it.

He seems calmer for the rest of the ride and just before we pull onto the lot he stops just like he always does. He scans the area quickly for paparazzi before I lean forward to peck his lips like I always do. There aren't usually a ton of paparazzi around the entrance because security is pretty tough and they figure the chances of catching anyone out here is slim to none.

Little do they know, I've made out with my bodyguard more than a few times at seven in the morning in this very spot.

When he pulls back, he stiffens and I see him looking in the rearview again. When I turn around, I see a car that is about thirty yards behind us pulling out of view.

"Is that…what you were looking at earlier?" I ask and he nods once, his eyes still staring through the mirror at the space behind our car.

I scratch the back of my head, trying to come up with something to say that will calm the very tense man in the car who looks like he's about to break something. "It's probably just paparazzi."

He nods without another word and pulls onto the lot towards our normal parking space.

It's about halfway through the day when there's a knock on my dressing room and Veronica, Derek, and Jeremy come walking in before I even have a chance to respond. We had an hour break for lunch and Damian had gone to the car to check his emails after I promised him that I'd stay in my dressing room and he didn't have to worry.

"Hi!" Veronica says, as she drops to my couch and props her slipper-covered feet on my coffee table. She has rollers in her hair, eye mask patches under her eyes, she's dressed in a fluffy bathrobe, and I'm pretty sure she has whitening strips on her teeth. Derek and Jeremy are both in sweats holding their plastic containers of turkey club sandwiches and French fries. Derek sits next to Veronica and Jeremy sits next to me on the adjacent love seat and three sets of eyes stare at me without saying anything.

"What's up?" I chuckle as I stare around at them. It isn't unheard of for the four of us to have lunch together in one of our dressing rooms but with the way they marched in here, it seems like there's an ulterior motive.

"We need a reason to come hang out in your room? Since when?" Derek jokes as he opens his container and puts his sandwich to his mouth. "You got any drinks in here?"

"In the fridge." I nod towards the one I have in the corner and he grabs my last sparkling water. I narrow my gaze at him.

"I'll get you another one. Relax, Princess."

I turn to Jeremy who's sitting right next to me ignoring Derek and his lack of manners.

"You don't need a reason but…something tells me you have one."

"We just want to talk," Jeremy replies, dropping his hand to my thigh and squeezing gently.

"About?"

"You. What's going on with you? Everything with Pax and now with Damian…how are you?"

I turn my head away from Jeremy to look at my best friend who's staring at me intently.

"What is this?" I ask her.

She leans forward and grabs my hand. "Babe, we're just… concerned."

"About what?"

"It just seems like you're isolating a little," Veronica says. "We basically live together during the season and I haven't seen you in weeks."

"The season just started."

"Okay, and I haven't seen you all week. You haven't come out… you just…hole up in your house." Veronica winces and I can hear the underlying questions and accusations.

"He doesn't let you out of his sight, Shay," Jeremy interjects and when I turn to look at him, his face is laced with concern. "Even when you're out, he doesn't take his eyes off of you."

"Kind of his job," I joke, trying to lighten the mood, but no one laughs.

"Riiiiight," Derek says, "but now it just kind of comes off like the obsessive boyfriend that doesn't want you to have a life outside of him."

"That's not what this is," I say immediately. "He's shaken up about what happened last week and I've been getting a lot of letters. Semi-threatening ones." I wince.

Veronica narrows her gaze. "What? You didn't tell me this."

"I know. I didn't want you to worry, but I'm good. I'm fine. I'm safe and that's the most important thing." They all just stare at me as if they don't believe me. Derek looks down at his food and Veronica looks at me and I can almost hear her thinking *'oh sweetie'*. "Maybe you guys could come over and we could all hang out and you'll see he's different when he doesn't have to be my bodyguard. That's one of the reasons I haven't been out. I can't even kiss my boyfriend in public right now."

"Boyfriend?" Derek asks with a mouthful of food. "We have labels already?"

"Damian and I…are a long time coming." I bite my bottom lip and I see Jeremy giving me a look out of the corner of my eye.

"Oh reeeeally?" Derek laughs. "Well, isn't that special?"

"Have you seen these letters, Shay?" Jeremy asks.

I turn my head back to him. "What?"

"These so-called threatening letters; have you actually seen them? Or did he just tell you they exist?"

"What are you getting at?" I ask.

"J..." Derek starts and Jeremy puts a hand up, to stop him from speaking.

"It's just odd. You've gotten letters before and now suddenly there's this big ass threat and so your bodyguard, who is now coincidentally your boyfriend, won't let you leave the house?" His voice is laced with judgment. His eyes, which are usually a bright emerald, are darker than I've ever seen and I wonder if it's because I've never seen him agitated.

"It's not like that. I'm allowed to leave the house."

"To come to set. Veronica just said she hasn't seen you. He's isolating you, Shay," Jeremy argues.

"No, that's not what this is. I said you guys should come over. Oh my God, we just started dating and I'm sorry that I'm enjoying the sex which means yeah, I don't want houseguests." I look around the circle. "For the record, when you two started dating," I point at Derek and Veronica, "I didn't see you for months, Veronica. And when you two are on again after being *off* for a considerable amount of time, you don't emerge from a bedroom for anything except to hydrate. But do I say he's isolating you? No, I'm supportive." I look at Veronica, my voice full of hurt and irritation. "But by all means, come over! Let's have a party!" I get up off the couch and go to my makeup chair so I don't have to be sitting next to Jeremy anymore. He's pissing me off the most out of all of them.

"Shay," Veronica says and I can already hear the remorse in her tone. Something tells me that this was not her idea in the first place.

"Paxton royally screwed me over. He made me feel like I wasn't enough. Like I wasn't worthy of him. And then when I caught him, he acted like I should just forgive him because who would I find better than him? We were the perfect couple, why ruin that image? As if I didn't have feelings." I take another breath. "You guys are my best friends; I need you to understand that Damian is important to me."

"Hello, *I'm* your best friend," Veronica interjects. "These hooligans are good friends, fine. Not best friends. Just want to clarify," she says pointing at them and back to me and I laugh, feeling some of my annoyance leave me slowly.

"Then be my best friend and get these two in line." I point at Derek and Jeremy and Veronica nods emphatically.

"We are just worried about you," Jeremy says. "And I know you feel connected to Damian because of everything you've been through with him but that doesn't necessarily mean he's the best romantic partner for you. Trauma bonds don't always equate to romance."

"Okay…?" I ask and now I'm annoyed at him for referencing my trauma. I was not prepared for that. "But it doesn't mean he's not either. Jeremy, I appreciate the concern…" I narrow my eyes at him because maybe I don't appreciate it all that much. *He's actually on my nerves and I'm annoyed I have to spend the next hour in a love scene with him.* "I think? But you're overstepping."

"Yeah, J, back off." Veronica gives him her signature look not to fuck with her and he rolls his eyes.

"Do you love him?" he asks.

Yes, but I haven't even told him that. You're certainly not going to hear it first. "I don't think that's your business."

"Shay." He cocks his head to the side. "I care about you and I don't want to see you get hurt."

"What gives you the impression that Damian would hurt me?"

He sighs. "I just know how easy it is to get caught up in the high of someone being all about you. His life revolves around you and it's fun being up on that pedestal until it's not." He gives me a look like he knows a thing or two about it. I know some things about his relationship with his ex-girlfriend, mainly that she wasn't in the limelight which means it's very possible she was obsessed with Jeremy.

"Okay."

"And after Paxton's betrayal, it might be easy for you to feel like you're falling in love with someone who seems to be all about you," he adds.

"I have a shrink, Jeremy, thanks."

"Have you talked to them about this?" he responds immediately and I think I'm officially over what seems to be turning into a lecture.

"No, I've been too busy having mind-numbing orgasms to talk to my shrink about it," I snap. Damian's theory that Jeremy has feelings for me hits me like a train and I wonder if maybe I shouldn't have discounted his feelings so quickly because this feels intense and weird and not at all like our usual friendship. We always supported each other and now it feels…off.

Jeremy rubs his hands on his thighs and stands up nodding at me. "Okay, Shay. You're like a sister to me and I worry about you. That's all this is."

"Fine." I cross my arms not looking at him.

"Are we good?"

"Sure," I say, still avoiding his gaze and he lets out a sigh before he leaves the room.

"What the fuck?" I look at Veronica, my eyes angry and my tone even angrier. I ignore Derek who's still eating because as far as I'm concerned right now, they're a packaged deal and he's equally to blame.

"I'm sorry."

"What was this, an intervention? An ambush? This is bullshit, V. You are my best friend. Why didn't you come to me if you felt some type of way?"

"I…" She lets out a breath. "I didn't realize it until Jeremy brought it up. He said things were weird at the club and Damian was being really intense about you all night and I was drunk and I took his word for it."

"He wasn't! We were horny—actually scratch that, namely *I* was horny because I was drunk and he was sober but we fucked in the bathroom and Jeremy caught us. Big deal!"

"Okay!" she exclaims. "I didn't know that at the time. I only knew anything because Jeremy told me!"

"Of course, he did. What the fuck is up with him?" I look at Derek, and he freezes, mid chewing, and looks at me confused.

"I don't know," he says, his mouth full of food. He swallows and clears his throat. "He's always had a soft spot for you."

"He's acting like it's more than that and it's freaking me out."

He shakes his head. "No. I've asked him numerous times if he has feelings for you. While we're drunk. High. You name it. He's always said no and I know when that asshole is lying. I think he's just genuinely concerned."

"Well, I'm grown and I can take care of myself." I blink at both of them. "Got it?"

Chapter TWENTY-TWO

Shay

THE REST OF THE DAY ON SET WAS AWFUL. EVERYONE could see that I was off and not my usual self. The chemistry between Jeremy and me was severely lacking and it showed. It finally got to the point that Lucas, the director, decided to call it quits early for the day because none of the scenes we were shooting were anything we could use.

It's the first time I've left the set feeling like I didn't give it my best, but I am still annoyed with the events of the day. I slide into the car and slump into the back seat as Damian gets into the front, and I can feel his gaze on me in the mirror.

"Want to talk about it?"

I'm staring out the window, with my chin resting on my fist when I slowly shift my gaze towards him. "Talk about what?" I ask and I hate the attitude in my voice. I hate that Damian is getting the brunt of my anger when he's done nothing but love me. *Wait.* "Do you love me?"

"What?" He turns around in his seat to look at me and his eyes are wide. He even looks a little scared if I'm being honest.

"Do you love me? Yes or no," I snap, my tone angrier than before.

He turns around and pulls off the lot and into traffic, shifting his gaze to the mirror to look at me. "So, you're mad at me? Is that what's happening here?"

"No, I'm just curious. We've been dancing around it and I'm just curious where we stand."

"Seems like a combative way to ask this question, but okay." I hear the sarcasm in his voice that's masking a layer of hurt. "Can we talk when we're at your house? And I'm not driving?"

I nod, feeling like shit for springing this on him because I'm feeling annoyed with my friends and maybe slightly insecure. He hasn't isolated me. I've wanted to be alone with him as much as he has. If anything, his reasoning has been more for safety whereas mine has been because I want to be alone with him. He'd have no problem if I wanted to invite my friends over.

Fifteen minutes and a mind of racing thoughts later, he's pulling up to my house. "Mine or yours?" he asks.

We'd been staying in his guesthouse for a while because it's a smaller space and easier for him to sweep quickly. Now that he's changed all the codes again, he's less anxious about letting me into my house but I know it still makes him wary.

"Yours," I say and he's out of the car instantly to open my door and help me out. He guides me towards his door and unlocks it, pushing me through.

"Did I do something?" he asks me the second he closes the door behind us. "We were fine this morning and now you're pissed at me; for what exactly?"

"I'm not pissed and I'm sorry for how I chose to phrase it but I don't know how you feel about me because you haven't told me."

"I thought even though I haven't said it, you knew where I stand. It's early and I didn't want to rush us by saying *things* too soon. But I thought you knew." He backs me against the wall and puts an arm up on either side of me. "I thought you could feel it when I looked at you or when we're having sex." He takes an arm off the wall and rests it against my chest. "I thought you felt it here."

"Damian." His words warm me all over and it makes me angry all over again at my friends who don't understand. "I love you," I blurt out, not wanting to wait another second to tell him the words that I've been feeling for far longer than I care to admit. His eyes light up like he can't believe I said it and a smile ghosts over his lips, but a frown finds his face just as fast.

"Are you angry with me? Just tell me what I did, baby." His words are quiet and soft and I don't know what on Earth I did to deserve a man like this. A man that treats me this way when I definitely don't deserve it.

"No," I whisper. "I'm sorry about earlier. Do you forgive me?"

He nods. "Can you tell me what that was about?"

"I will. Just...not now."

His hands find my cheeks, stroking the skin beneath my eyes. "I won't push you, but I hope you know you can tell me anything. I'm always here for you, baby."

How is he so perfect?

Tell me you love me too, I beg him with my eyes.

"I love you." I feel his words in my heart and it begins to accelerate as excitement courses through me hearing those words fall from his lips. "Is that what you want to hear?" A smile finds my lips as he leans down and drags his mouth slowly across mine. "That I am so in love with you that it consumes me?" He presses his body against mine, lowering himself to press his knee between my legs and against my mound. "That *you* consume me?" I grind down against him, my body buzzing both from his words and the stimulation on my pussy.

He presses his mouth to mine and feeds me his tongue, licking his way into my mouth, making my knees weak. He knows how to kiss in a way that makes everything fade away around me. I've never been kissed in such a way that makes my whole body buzz with excitement. Kissing Paxton always felt rushed, like something he felt like he had to do before we moved onto other things. A means to an end. Damian kisses me like he could do it forever. I wrap my arms around his neck, holding him to me and he lifts me with one hand. I gasp at how strong he is as I wrap my legs around his waist.

He carries me to his bedroom, one hand under my butt and one tangling in my hair before he drops me on the bed and presses his body into mine. He grabs the hem of my dress and pulls it over my head leaving me in only red panties as I'm not wearing a bra and his lips immediately go to one of my nipples. His hand finds the other and rolls it between his thumb and index finger as he rolls my other around his tongue. He bites down gently, and it feels like a lightning bolt to my clit. I instantly feel myself getting wet between my legs.

"Damian." I let out a sigh and he growls in response.

"Say it again."

"What?"

"My name." He peppers kisses up my chest and neck to my mouth.

"Damian," I repeat. "I want you, *there*." I shiver, thinking about him in a place no one has been.

"You do, huh?" His tongue darts out to lick my pulse point, along my collarbone, and back down my chest. "You want my dick in your sexy little ass?" He reaches underneath me and cups my butt. He digs his nails into my bare flesh before snapping the strap of my thong.

I mewl, trying to get closer to him and wrap all of myself around him like ivy. "Yes yes yes please," I beg. "I need it."

A groan leaves his lips. "You don't know what it does to me hearing you say you need me." He pulls back, dragging my panties down my legs and tossing them to the floor. He gets off the bed and pulls off his jacket and begins to unbutton my shirt at a speed so slow I think he's teasing me. He drops his shirt to the floor, putting his tattoo covered torso on display for me, and I clench at how sexy he is. I drag my eyes over every hard ridge and plane of his body, counting the abs *eight of them*, and trace the firm and cut lines of the V pointing to his dick. He unbuttons his slacks and sends his briefs to the floor with them and I'm immediately moving towards him when he takes a step back, shaking his head.

"Don't move." He tells me.

"But…"

"If you want this, you're going to have to listen." He strokes his dick from root to tip, his voice deep and authoritative. I nod on instinct because even though I'm particularly submissive, I am very interested in getting what I want and know how to get it.

"Yes, Sir." I flutter my eyelashes at him innocently.

"Sir, huh?" He spits in his hand and goes back to masturbating himself, dragging his hand slowly over every ridge.

"Do you prefer daddy?" I bite my bottom lip and his blue eyes darken giving me my answer. "Oh, daddy it is then," I say, raising an eyebrow at him seductively.

He hovers over me, a mere inch from my face. "Whatever you call me makes my dick hard. *You* make my dick hard."

"I love your dick," I tell him. "It's fucking perfect," I purr and I notice his muscles flex and his dick twitches in his hand. I take that to mean, he likes the praise.

"Well, my dick loves you so I'm glad the feeling is mutual." He smirks. I drag my fingers to the space between my legs and begin rubbing my clit in circles causing his nostrils to flare in response. "Does that feel good?"

"It would feel better if you were doing it," I respond, rubbing myself harder. I'm already soaked, my clit throbbing and my body desperate for a release. Our eyes are locked as we continue to touch each other, inching ourselves to our climaxes. He kneels on the bed, his hand still wrapped around his thick cock, his eyes still on me like he wants to devour me.

"Turn over." My body is buzzing with the beginning of my first orgasm and he must realize it because he grabs my wrist and pulls my hand from between my legs as his other hand continues to stroke himself.

"Wait, please," I whine as I try to pull from his grasp.

"Shhh, I'll take care of it." He grunts as he flips me over and pulls me onto my knees. He pushes my legs further apart and then I feel his breath at my entrance no more than a second later.

"Fuck," I moan as I feel his tongue at my sex, eating me aggressively from behind. He fucks me with his mouth mercilessly, his fingers strumming my clit with each stroke. He pushes his tongue further to flick my clit and I cry out as the pleasure takes over. I'm pushing back against his face, feeling his nose probe my asshole as he eats me hungrily like I'm his last meal. I drop my head to the mattress, grabbing a pillow to rest my head on as I force my ass higher in the air and into his face. "God, the things your mouth can do," I moan.

"It doesn't belong anywhere but between your legs," he grunts. "I am addicted to the way your pussy tastes." My mouth drops open and my whole body feels like it's on fire. I move my head to look between my spread legs and see he's still pumping his dick as he eats me out and the visual is enough to spur my orgasm. *He's so turned on from licking my cunt he has to jack off while he's doing it. God, that is so fucking sexy.* "You're going to come on my face and then on my cock and then I'll fuck this," he says gripping my ass. "But I need the taste of your pussy in my mouth and to feel you clench around my dick once before I put it in your ass." He pinches my clit, rubbing it between his fingers like he'd previously done with my nipple and the sexy friction causes me to detonate.

"Fuck fuck fuck, I'm coming!"

"Yes, you fucking are. Come all over my tongue, baby. Let me taste it."

My eyes float shut and I scream out my climax. "Oh god!" I cry out. I try to move away from his tongue because I feel overstimulated but he moves with me, continuing to stroke my clit. "Too... much," I choke out and he pulls his mouth away from me before I feel his dick there and he doesn't even wait before he slides into me. "Fuck!" My eyes flutter closed and I feel myself floating away already as he begins thrusting into my pussy. I reach down between my legs to feel his dick go in and out of me, pounding into me harder with each thrust. I keep going back further to reach his balls and begin fondling them in my palm.

"Fuck," he growls. "You always know what I fucking want. You are so perfect, Shay."

I feel my climax building and I know this one is going to be even more powerful than the last one, but I know it also means I'm going to be loose when he takes my ass for the first time. I clench in excitement thinking about him there. "Daddy?"

"Yes, baby, tell me what you need."

"I need—" I gasp and he growls in response.

"Yes yes yes, I know you need it. Take it baby. Take what you need from Daddy. Take it fucking all. All of it. All of *me*."

I gasp. "Oh my god, I love you so much," I cry as my orgasm grabs hold of my senses. I vaguely hear him telling me he loves me too but there's a buzzing in my ears. I black out momentarily and all I can feel is the tingling feeling shooting through my entire body. "Fuck, I'm coming again," I cry out. "Right there." I let out a sigh as my body begins to float back to Earth.

He pulls out almost immediately and then I turn around because I'm pretty sure he hasn't come yet. "You didn't come?"

"I want to come here," he says before he lays a smack on my ass. I want every drop of cum in this hole." He gets off the bed and grabs something out of the bedside table. I realize it's lubricant and something else I can't make out.

"When you mentioned you wanted to take this step for the first time, I figured I should get some." He presses a line of kisses down my back and on each ass cheek.

"Thank you," I tell him because thank God one of us is prepared.

His hands grip my ass cheeks and then I feel him spreading them and a feeling of shyness takes over me for being so exposed. I breathe a slight sigh of relief that I always shower before I leave the set.

"Have you ever had anything here?" he asks. "A finger?"

"No." My heart begins to pound in my chest at what we're about to do.

"Okay, so we need to work you up to my dick." I feel his fingers there and then a gust of air and I realize what he's about to do.

"Oh my god. Damian…"

"Do you trust me?"

"With my life? Yes. I'm not sure what trust has to do with eating my ass but okay…?"

He chuckles and squeezes my ass harder. "Fine. Do you love me?"

"Mmhmmm…"

He smacks my ass and I clench. "Words."

"Yes."

"Is this too much for you?"

I want to say yes, that never in my wildest dreams *and there were quite a lot featuring him*, did I picture his tongue in my ass, but I take a deep breath instead. "No."

"You tell me to stop and I will."

I nod though I don't know if he can tell based on his vantage point and then I feel his tongue circling the hole. He spreads my cheeks more as he forces his tongue inside me. My toes curl and my mouth drops open as his finger rubs my clit gently and then I hear the buzzing.

"For your clit. I want this to feel good for you. It doesn't always the first time." He rests the vibrator against the sensitive bundle of nerves and I squeeze my eyes shut as pleasure shoots through me. I take it from him, holding it against me and rubbing it in slow circles moving towards my climax slow and steadily.

"Damian, fuck." I bite my bottom lip but I slowly feel myself relaxing with each stroke of his tongue over my hole. Coupled with the vibration on my sex has me moving fast towards another orgasm. His tongue leaves me and then I hear the squirt of the lubricant and something cool at my hole and a finger pushing into me slowly.

"This okay?" he asks and I nod, my mind wiped clean of every single thing I've ever thought about sex. I'm not a prude and I've watched my fair share of porn, but seeing and doing are completely different things. I thought I'd feel dirtier with his mouth and fingers there, but taking this step with someone I trust and love completely makes me feel like this is anything but dirty. It's beautiful and magical and I want to do it again and again for the rest of my life.

My pussy begins to pulse with the beginning of my orgasm so I pull away, wanting to feel the peak of the high when he's in my ass and I don't know that I will have the energy to come again after three strong orgasms. I'm breathing deeply, trying to calm the blood singing in my veins when he adds another finger stretching me.

"You're doing so well, baby. You look so pretty bent over for me with my fingers in this tight hole." He rubs my back gently, his tone soft despite the bite in the words. "Gorgeous," he praises. I shiver and clench around his fingers and he groans. "Fuck, you're going to feel so tight wrapped around my dick." I hear the squirt of more lube as he works what I think to be a third finger in and I turn the vibrator back on.

"I—I think I'm ready," I tell him. "Your fingers can only prepare me for your dick so much." I turn around and meet his eyes. "*Nothing* feels like your cock."

I see the pride on his face and I giggle to myself that men really are all the same when it comes to praise about their dicks. I turn back around. "I'm going to go slow, okay? Fuck, your ass, Shay." He leans down pressing a kiss to each cheek again and then I feel his thick, heavy cock at my hole. He drags it across the skin slowly and then I hear more lubricant both at my hole and I'm assuming on his dick and then he pushes in slowly. I feel like the wind has been knocked out of me because god damn, his fingers feel very different. I feel his hand between my legs and he grabs the vibrator from my hand. "Just focus on breathing," he says as he rests the vibrator on the lowest speed on my clit as he works himself into my ass. He moves back and forth slowly, stretching me.

"Damian," I let out a shaky breath because I feel full and overstimulated. I clench around him and he groans.

"Fuck," he grits out. "Your ass is so fucking tight."

"Does it feel g-good?" Despite the tightness in my ass, the vibrations on my clit are starting to make me feel loose and my body can't decide if the tension coursing through me is because of pain or because of the looming orgasm. *I suppose a little of both.*

"Yes, fuck, it feels like nothing I've ever felt. You are fucking incredible." He goes in a little further, pushing a little harder each time and while I still feel a pinch, it's starting to hurt less and less. He's holding one of my hips with one hand and the vibrator against my clit with the other and I know this can't be particularly easy for him to do. *I guess he doesn't have an eight pack for no reason.*

"I got it." I grab it back from him. "Fuck me."

He reaches down, his cock still half inside of me and presses a kiss to the middle of my back. "You sure?"

"Yes, go faster. Harder," I tell him. "I want your cum in my ass. Fill me up. I want it in me for the rest of the night."

"Shay." He grunts as he begins fucking me a little harder, and pushing himself further into my asshole. The burn is subsiding and I've turned the speed up on the vibrator. I slide it inside, fucking my pussy while he fucks my ass. "Fuck, baby." He's starting to breathe heavily and I wonder if he's about to come after not coming yet tonight.

I turn my head and I see him staring down at where we are connected, his dark chestnut hair fallen slightly over his eyes and his bottom lip drawn between his perfectly straight teeth. *He is so fucking sexy. And fucking mine.* The thought that I've brought this man to his knees for me and he wants me and this as bad as I do makes me feel powerful and sexy and I never want this feeling to end.

"I'm going to come baby." And those words seem to spur my own because I feel the familiar tingle in my toes. "I love you so much, beautiful."

His sweet words coupled with the sinful things he's doing to me and the vibrator in my pussy pushes me over the edge. "Oh my god, I'm coming," I moan out. My breath comes out in tiny puffs because the orgasm has made my chest tight and I'm struggling to breathe. I pull out the vibrator when I feel him moving faster in my ass and then I feel him beginning to pulse.

"Fuck fuck fuck me. Right there," he grits out as his thrusts become harder and his grip tightens on my hips as he pumps into my ass.

My pussy feels like the vibrator is still resting against it the way it still tingles in the wake of my orgasm. He pulls out gently and then I feel his fingers at my asshole rubbing his cum against it and back inside of me.

My arms finally give out and I'm on my stomach. I feel so loose and sexy and high like I'm flying and when my eyes flutter open, he's lying next to me on his stomach staring at me with a serene smile on his face. "You are so beautiful."

He moves closer to me and presses a kiss to my forehead before bringing me to rest my head on his chest. He's on his back now and I'm lying almost completely on top of him as he strokes my back and holds the back of my head. "That was amazing," I say but I can't be sure if I slurred my words at all.

"It was. Did I hurt you?"

"I'm okay," I say, the exhaustion of multiple orgasms and anal sex and a full day on set all hit me at once. I hear him tell me he loves me but I don't think I even respond before I'm asleep.

Chapter

TWENTY-THREE

DAMIAN

THE NEXT DAY, SHAY DOESN'T HAVE TO BE ON SET UNTIL noon, so I spend the morning with her before she goes to set. We're back in her house, and despite her attempts to seduce me, we haven't had sex and I didn't join her in the shower. I'm in her kitchen making her breakfast when she comes downstairs wearing leggings and a flowy v-neck top that shows off her perky breasts, making me regret turning down all of her advances. Her wavy hair falls around her and the smile on her face is so blinding and stunning I can't take my eyes off of her.

"Hi, beautiful."

"Are you cooking for me?" She looks up at me and then down at the pan in shock like she can't believe it.

"Nothing gets by you," I joke as I flip the bread in the pan.

"It smells so good. I love French toast," she squeals before plucking a strawberry from the fruit salad I'd put out for her.

"I know."

"I didn't know you could cook. Where has this hidden talent been all this time?" she asks as she sits at her dining room table.

"I don't cook for anyone," I tell her.

"Oh, I see. So, this is 'thank you for letting me stick my dick in your ass' French toast?" She takes a sip of the orange juice I'd set on the table.

"No this is 'I love you and I want to take care of you which means feeding you more than the protein bars you eat in the morning' French Toast." I crack the eggs on the other skillet knowing that above anything, Shay loves eggs and usually eats them once she gets to set if it's an option.

She picks at her fruit and I can tell she wants to say something. "You're so good to me. What did I do to deserve you? Everything you've done for me even before we were here. You could be saving the world or protecting a president or something and you're just looking after little old me." She gives me a small smile but I can hear the self-deprecation in her tone.

"Protecting you has been the greatest honor of my life, Shay," I tell her and when my eyes meet hers there are tears in them. "I would do anything for you and the job of keeping you safe is one I take very seriously."

She cocks her head to the side and puts a hand to her chest. "Damian…"

I finish cooking her eggs the way she likes them and put them on the plate next to her French toast. I set it in front of her and she's looking at me with those eyes that usually have her naked within seconds. "Don't look at me like that."

"You're just amazing and I hope you know how much I appreciate everything."

"I do. You let me stick my dick in your ass, remember? That is the highest level of appreciation," I tease and she rolls her eyes.

"So, I have something I've been wanting to talk to you about." She takes a bite of her eggs. "Aren't you eating?"

I cross my arms over my chest. "Talk to me."

"Eat with me, please. I am not going to let you watch me eat."

She points towards the stove. "Oh my god," she moans as she takes a bite of the French toast. "No offense, but this might be the best thing you've ever put in my mouth." She winks as I get up and turn the stove back on to make more French toast.

"I'll remember that when you're begging me to come in your mouth later."

"Will you though?" she quips and I give her a look.

"What's on your mind, baby?"

"Well, I was thinking of having some people over. Like a very lowkey cast thing. We do it a few times a season and I thought I'd host the first one."

"Mmmhmm," I say, without looking at her.

"How do you feel about that?"

"What do you mean how do I feel? It's your house, baby. I feel fine with you having people here. Are you planning to invite people you don't know?"

"No, and it might just end up being Derek, Jeremy, and Veronica because…I want you to actually have fun. I want to give my bodyguard the night off."

"I don't want the night off from being that."

"Please, D. They don't really know you aside from being my bodyguard and I would like them to get to know you as my boyfriend. If you're here, I'm safe and you can let your guard down a little." She cuts more of her French toast and swirls it through the syrup letting out another moan worthy of porn. "You're sexy, you have a perfect smile, a big dick, *and* you can cook. You really are god's favorite."

I snort even though I like that she loves these things about me. "Don't try and butter me up."

"I'm not. I just want to hang out with my friends…and you? As much as I love spending time alone, there's going to come a time when you're going to have to be around people in a social setting. I am going to need a date to the Emmys, you know."

My eyes snap away from the pan to hers. "The Emmys are in two months."

"Correct." She nods.

I blink at her in confusion. "You want me to go with you?"

"As opposed to the other man who told me he loved me and spends his night fucking me senseless?" she says and though I know it's a joke, I can hear the irritation in her voice.

"Will you be ready to share *this* with everyone by then?" I ask pointing back and forth between us.

"Why not? You're not my dirty little secret, Damian. I said I didn't want people to know right now because things just ended with Paxton, but in a few months, no one will care. We could even show up on the red carpet for the first time together. Oh my gosh, people will go nuts." She claps her hands and scrunches her nose in that cute way she does when she wants to get her way with me.

Nerves creep up my spine at the thought of being on the red carpet with her. Smiling and taking pictures and being a part of her world in a way I haven't been before. "I don't know about that. I can't be watching out for everything with cameras flashing in my face."

"Well, you wouldn't have to worry about that?" She blinks at me.

"What do you mean by that?"

"Well, I assume at some point you wouldn't be my bodyguard anymore."

I give her a look of confusion as I pull the French toast off the pan and place it on a plate. "Run that by me again."

"Damian, I'm going to need to get another bodyguard at some point. You can't do this forever."

"Says who?"

"Uh, you? You already said it's complicated being with me and protecting me." She frowns. "If you think for one second you're going to break up with me because you would rather protect me than be with me because you don't trust anyone else, think again. I don't accept that."

I move towards the table and sit down at the head of it so we're seated diagonally from each other and pull her feet into my lap. I hate how well she knows me. If I were stronger, I would. I would tell her that keeping her alive is my number one priority and I don't trust anyone to do it as well as I can. Would anyone take a bullet for her? Step in front of a car? Push her out of the way of a heavy light fixture that could have killed me just as easily as it could have killed her? You only have one second to make a decision and if there's any hesitation it could cost Shay her life. I want to tell her that.

But I can't.

"I wasn't suggesting that." I let out a sigh. "I want to do both, baby. I don't want to choose between being the man that makes you come and the one that keeps you safe."

"But…I don't know how you can do both. You can't be that arrogant that you think you're the only man on the planet capable of keeping me safe."

"It's different. I have different vested interests in keeping you alive now."

"I get that, but okay, say we're still here in five years for instance; I would prefer the father of my children not put himself in harm's way."

She can't be serious. And also, kids? "To save the mother of my children? I absolutely would."

"You're missing the point!"

"So are you." I shake my head as I cut into the French toast, slightly more irritated than I was before. "It doesn't matter, even if I'm not officially your bodyguard, if I'm with you socially, I'll be right next to you and that means anyone trying to fuck with you will need to go through *me*."

She sighs and puts her head in her hands. "Okay, let's just take this one day at a time for now. I would like to have people over tonight and I'd like it if you could hang out with us. Maybe have a drink or two?"

I know this is something Shay is absolutely not going to let go of and here would be the best place to do this. "Fine."

She squeals and is in my lap instantly, wrapping her arms around my neck and pressing her lips to my neck. "Thank you!"

I tighten my arms around her and reach for her chin, guiding it to my mouth and pressing a kiss to her lips. "Kids?"

A tiny bit of pink tints her cheeks and she rolls her eyes. "Hypothetically speaking."

I nod, thinking about her round with my child and a baby that looks just like her. My dick hardens thinking about my ring on her finger and I hate thinking about how it would work being with her and also protecting her.

This is why you don't sleep with your mark and you definitely don't fall in love with them.

Shay

Although the three of them had irritated me the day before, I want to prove a point that Damian is not isolating me, so I invite Veronica, Jeremy, and Derek over for dinner after we're done shooting for the day. I momentarily think about inviting more people, but Cooper and my team don't even know about Damian and me yet. I'm not ready to reveal it to some of the cast and crew of *LA Dreams* before I have a chance to tell them. So, it will be an intimate party of five. I ordered a bunch of takeout from our favorite Thai restaurant and even make my signature gin lemonade.

"Can I help you with anything?" Jeremy comes up behind me and puts his hands on my shoulders as I'm pouring the Pad Thai noodles from the container into one of my serving bowls. Derek and Veronica went to put their stuff in my guest room since they already decided they're staying over and Damian had gone to his guesthouse for a minute leaving Jeremy and me alone in my kitchen.

"Nope, I'm good." I move out from under his hands.

I'm still irritated with him and I know he can feel the tension because he's been trying to talk to me since he got here. I give him a smile to let him know that I'm trying despite what happened yesterday.

"Shay…" he starts, "I'm sorry about yesterday, alright?" He lets out a sigh. "Why are you so pissed? I'm just worried about you."

"That didn't feel like worry; it felt like you were inserting your opinion when I didn't ask for it and being a little judgmental, but I don't want to talk about it. I invited you over, I just want to squash it."

"But you're barely talking to me and everything on set is weird and people are starting to notice."

"Things are fine. Today was much better than yesterday," I retort.

He scoffs. "So, that's it? Five years of friendship and now we're just polite co-stars? What the hell, Shay? You're my best friend."

"You certainly didn't act like it yesterday."

The sound of a throat clearing stops our conversation and I see Damian in the entrance to the kitchen. I know I should have told him about what prompted this get-together but I was hoping it wouldn't come up. I assumed the three of them wouldn't bring it up around him and I surely wasn't going to. I smile when I take in the fact that he changed into black jeans and a black t-shirt that makes him look sexy as fuck.

"Hi." I move to him instantly and wrap my arms around him. He does the same, resting his hands on my ass and squeezing it. I'm wearing a black strapless midi dress that highlights my waist and flares out slightly and I'm relishing over how well we match.

"Everything good?" he murmurs against my lips and I nod.

"Now that you're here, yes." I look up at him and I notice he's looking over my head at Jeremy.

"Hey," I say to get his attention and he looks back down at me. I pucker my lips and he takes them instantly, dragging his hands away from my ass to cup my face and kisses me deeply, working his tongue into my mouth and touching mine gently.

God, he can kiss.

A cat call breaks through our kiss as Veronica and Derek enter the kitchen and I pull away with a dramatic eye roll.

"Let's eat, I'm starving," Derek says and we carry the rest of the food to the terrace where we're having dinner. It's a comfortable summer night and I thought eating outside would cut through some of the tension. Except Damian and I are sitting on one side of the table while Veronica, Derek, and Jeremy sit on the other and it kind of feels like a setup for an interview or an interrogation.

We eat in a somewhat comfortable silence even though I can't remember a time when the four of us didn't have a million things to talk about. I look across the table and when I see they're all looking down at their plates, I'm annoyed all over again. Veronica looks up and catches my eye. Over ten years of friendship allow us to speak pretty easily with our eyes and I give her a look telling her to say something.

What do you want me to do?

Anything!

She rolls her eyes. "So, Damian, what are your intentions with our Shay here?" She flutters her eyelashes and gives him a cheesy smile with her hands under her chin.

I choke on my drink and give her my middle finger while I'm trying to get the alcohol down my throat. Damian rubs my back instantly and hands me a glass of water that I take a small sip of. "Veronica!"

"What?" she asks with a look that says *what did I do?* "It's a valid question. It's what Mrs. E would have asked," she says referring to my mother.

I glare at her. "Okay well, Mom, can you not?"

"I love Shay very much," Damian says and I snap my head towards him, not expecting him to respond or to say *that*. "My intentions with her are to give her whatever she wants. To make her happy. I spent a very long time trying to deny my feelings for her and I don't want to do that anymore."

Veronica's eyes snap to mine full of excitement and like she's already thinking about where we are going for my bachelorette party.

SHUT UP!

I know! I smile.

She turns her gaze back to Damian. "That is…so sweet." She sighs dreamily before turning to Derek. "Why don't you say cute stuff like that to me?"

"Don't start," he says, wiping his mouth with a napkin. "You laugh whenever I try to do anything romantic and then just try and get in my pants."

"How is this going to work though?" Jeremy interjects and Veronica and Derek both turn their previously humorous gazes to him. They both frown just as Damian and I turn to him.

"What?" I ask, already annoyed at where this conversation is headed.

"I mean, you have to understand how hard it will be for him to be both?"

"Jeremy, we talked about this," Veronica says, and I hate that there's a conversation that the three of them have had about me and my relationship. "We aren't doing this again."

Damian shifts uncomfortably next to me and I hate that he's probably piecing together that there's already been one conversation regarding us that he knows nothing about.

"Does Cooper even know? Your PR team? How are you spinning this story exactly? Aren't you worried that people are going to think you've been together this whole time? That you were cheating on Paxton?"

"No. People decide to date people that they've known for a while all the time. I didn't cheat on Paxton."

"You can't be so naive that you think people will just buy that nothing was going on while you were with Paxton," Jeremy argues.

"I don't think it's really your business what goes on between us personally or professionally," Damian adds and I wince thinking about how the rest of this evening is going to go.

"I've known Shay just as long as you have, actually a bit longer." I roll my eyes internally at the juvenile thinking. "She's my friend and I care about her."

"And I don't? You're her friend. I'm her man, there's a difference."

Veronica's eyes widen and looks at me with a grin she's trying to hide because she lives for that caveman attitude.

"We should take some shots," Derek says, trying to break through the tension.

"We should absolutely not take some shots until everyone is on the same page," I say looking at Jeremy. "We are getting married this season, J. I am not going to be going back and forth with you about this for the next three months while we are supposed to be disgustingly in love. I won't be able to handle it, and the writers will kill me if I go to them and ask for me to break off our engagement or leave you at the altar in the series' freaking finale. The producers are taking notice that our chemistry is off so I need you to get on board or we are going to have a lot of long nights of reshoots."

Veronica groans. "Please guys, you remember what it's like when we aren't on good terms," she says pointing between herself and Derek.

"I'm fine," Jeremy says.

"No, you're being unsupportive and judgmental and frankly a pain in my ass," I snap.

"Because I don't think you're thinking this through."

"Thinking what through? I'm in love with Damian. We're together. That's it! That's the tweet!" I yell and I look at Derek. "You know what, I will take a shot."

"That's my girl." Derek points at me, before going to the bar cart I'd rolled out when we came outside.

"You and I both know that it's not that simple. When you two go public, everything changes," Jeremy argues. "Are you ready for them to go digging into your past?" He looks at Damian. "Because they'll have a lot of questions about your first wife you were still married to a year ago," he snaps.

Derek drops a shot glass and it clatters against the cart. "Fuck," he grumbles as he tries to clean up the spilled tequila. Veronica chokes on her drink and her eyes snap to Jeremy. "Excuse me?!" Her eyes snap to my shocked ones. "His what?"

"What?" I look at Jeremy and then at Damian. "What?" I shake my head. "Jeremy, what the actual fuck?"

Chapter
TWENTY-FOUR

DAMIAN

I HAVEN'T SPOKEN AND IT'S BECAUSE FURY IS RAGING THROUGH me. I shoot Jeremy a glare and despite the look of contrition that I'm sure is for Shay's benefit, I know he's feeling smug by her reaction, meaning that I hadn't told her.

I knew this was a conversation I needed to have with Shay, but for Jeremy to explode this all over her due to jealousy and resentment over the fact that we're together enrages me. I've never been more certain that he has feelings for her, and this shit ends *now*.

"Shay—" Jeremy starts and she puts a hand up silencing him and turns her gaze to me with wide brown eyes that are looking at me curiously. They don't seem sad but confused and maybe a little angry.

"Inside," she says standing up and I follow behind her. I don't know what I'm walking into when she closes the door to the patio behind her and crosses her arms.

"You've been married? You said you've never been in love, that you didn't want to get married! That's why you broke up with Simone! You lied to my face!" She says all of this within the span of a few seconds, her voice getting progressively louder and more excited with each statement.

"I wasn't married to Simone."

"Oh, that makes it better? Who? When?"

I let out a sigh. "It's not what you're thinking. I was not in love with her. I've never been in love until I met you. It wasn't romantic." I hear Veronica yelling on the patio and I'm surprised that I have somewhat of an ally in her because she sounds like she's letting Jeremy have it.

I grab Shay's hand and gently move her away from the door and I'm grateful she at least lets me touch her. I lead her down the hallway towards her office and shut the glass French doors behind us before guiding her to the couch. I sit on the coffee table in front of her and stroke her knees gently. "Do you trust me?"

"I did. What is going on, Damian?"

I did. Those words sting like shit.

"About six years ago, after Simone and I broke up and a little before I met you, a friend of mine—my best friend's fiancée to be more specific, was diagnosed with cancer. My best friend, Rob, was killed in combat while we were overseas and," I sigh as the pain of losing him resurfaces. "I promised him I would look out for her." A tear rolls down her face and I reach out to wipe under her eyes. "I felt somewhat responsible for what happened for a long time." I wince. "I tried and I just…there was an explosion." The words get caught in my throat and it's as if I'm back there again. It's been almost ten years and I can still be transported back to that moment when I lost my best friend like it's real time. Shay climbs into my lap and wraps her arms around me tightly and I'm grateful for the comfort.

"Why didn't you tell me any of this?" she whispers against my neck. Her lips touch my skin as she speaks and the small touch of her lips on me calms my nerves.

I swallow, wanting to get out of the headspace of the haunting and painful memories. "I was going to tell you, baby. Believe me. I didn't anticipate anyone beating me to it." Anger floods me and I can't believe that motherfucker did this.

How did he even find out? Did he have someone look into this?

"She had lost her job and her insurance lapsed…" I sigh. "I couldn't watch her die."

"Have you ever been involved with her…romantically?"

"Never," I tell her. I know this situation may be difficult to take in but I can ease these fears because I've never touched her. "We were married on paper so she could have access to my medical coverage. That's it. She's in remission and ended up getting a new job and we got divorced last year." She pulls back and moves out of my lap and I already miss the comfort of her body pressed against mine. "Tell me you believe me. I didn't love her. It wasn't romantic."

She leans back against the couch and rubs her forehead. "I believe you, Damian, but it doesn't explain why you didn't tell me this. I would have understood. It makes me wonder what else you're keeping from me. You're such a mystery and now I feel like there's so much I don't know about you. You had a wife for the majority of the time I've known you and I had no idea."

"Because it didn't mean anything. I only talked to her about how she was doing and that was even few and far between. She had a strong support system and I'm across the country. I never even saw her."

She stands up and gives me a hard look that lets me know she's pissed. "That's not the point, Damian."

"What reason would I have had to tell you then?"

She narrows her eyes. "You could have told me when things changed between us."

"I was planning to."

"Easy to say that now." She snaps back.

"Baby, it's been three weeks."

"You told me you love me."

"More than anything," I respond and I see her hard eyes soften slightly at those words.

"And yet, you kept this from me. Something I should know!"

"You're right, which is why I had every intention of telling you. I was going to tell you everything. My marriage to Heather is tied up in a lot of baggage that I don't discuss freely. It's attached to demons I spent years in therapy exorcizing."

She stands up and begins pacing the room, something I know she does when she's worked up and can't sit still. "Damian, is there anything else I need to know? Anything that could come up? Something that paparazzi or gossip rags could find? A secret child somewhere?"

I shake my head. "No. Anything else I would want to tell you would be things that are more personal."

She doesn't say anything, she just leans against her desk, staring at the floor. I stand from the coffee table and make my way towards her and pull her into my arms. She lets me hug her and I begin to rub her back.

"Are we okay?" I murmur in her ear, fearing the worst. Maybe she feels betrayed or like I've lied to her. That she's triggered by all the lies Paxton told her and this is too much that I'm another man that's lied to her even by omission.

She nods. "I don't like being blindsided. I don't like secrets." When her eyes meet mine, they're watery and like the color of caramel, and if she wasn't upset, I'd comment on how beautiful they look highlighted by her tears. "And I know it's irrational to feel jealous but the fact that you've been married before is fucking me up a little."

"I'm sorry. Please don't hate me."

"I could never hate you," she whispers. "I love you." She twists her mouth and lets out a breath. "But I just feel like we jumped into this and I don't know anything about you." She pulls out of my grasp and I already hate the wall she's putting up between us. "Let's just get through tonight and we can talk."

"Maybe it would be best if you continued the night with your friends and I went back to the guesthouse."

"What? No. The whole point was to get to know my friends better." She shakes her head and pinches her brows together.

"So, I'm supposed to deal with your asshole co-star now? Who's another problem by the way. He did this vindictive shit because he has feelings for you, Shay, and he's trying to drive a wedge between you and me."

She can't actually think I'm going back in there to pretend everything is fine. That he hadn't tried to ruin my relationship with her.

"I'll admit, I don't like the way he went about it but he does not have feelings for me."

"You can't be serious."

"He doesn't!" she says with a stomp of her foot and I'd actually think it was adorable if this were any other conversation.

"How do you know?"

"I've known him for years and Derek said he doesn't. He would know!"

"You've known *me* for years and you had no idea about my feelings for you. Men can mask their feelings, though he's really god damn obvious about his."

"Fine. I'll tell him to leave. Happy?"

"No, Shay. Nothing about this makes me happy. Which is why I said this was a line I didn't want to cross."

"It's impossible to not cross this line! What do you expect to be the bodyguard that just fucks me behind closed doors?" she snaps.

"We are more than that and I resent the implication that you're just a fuck to me. That we are just a fuck to each other." I glower at her, because fuck that.

"Can we be more if you're not willing to be with me out there as well?" She points to the window.

I don't say anything because I don't know what to say. This is exactly what I was worried about. Trying to find that line when it's become so blurry. "I'm not suggesting we hide it, but we could be private about our relationship."

"So, that's a no on taking me to the Emmys then, got it." She shakes her head with an eye roll. "Whatever."

There's a knock on the door and Shay snaps her gaze to the sound of the door opening and Veronica popping her head inside. Concerned blue eyes find Shay as she crosses the room and wraps an arm around her shoulder. "I told Jeremy to go. He was being a tool. Derek said he had a few drinks before he got here but like SO?" She looks at me and then back to Shay. "Do you want Derek and I to go too?"

"I don't care," she says and pulls away from her.

"Damian, can you give us a minute?" Veronica asks and I nod, grateful for the time away from Shay so maybe she will calm down a little. I know she's angry and rightfully so, *on some things*.

I make my way out of her office and out the front door and I'm grateful that Jeremy didn't linger because I can't be responsible for what I say to that asshole. I slam the door to my house behind me with such force, the house rattles and a few books tip over on my bookshelf. As much as I want to have a drink, I'm not sure when Shay will want to talk and I don't want to be intoxicated and say something I regret.

Minutes later, there's a knock on the door and my subconscious is already convinced it's Shay when I open it. Irritation washes over me when I see Derek standing at the front door with a bottle of beer in his hand holding it out for me. "Thought you could use this."

I don't take it from him because I'm not about to let him think we are friends when I'm not sure if he was in on Jeremy's fucking ambush. I close the door behind me, as I sign that I'm not letting him in and stand on my porch with my arms crossed.

He's shorter than Jeremy and therefore shorter than me and not as built but still looks like he's spent some time in the gym. He has jet-black hair and hazel eyes and I remember Shay saying that he's the heartthrob of the show despite Jeremy being her co-star.

"I had nothing to do with that," he tells me.

"Why should I believe that?"

"Because Veronica would have my balls if I did anything to hurt Shay and believe me, she had Jeremy's balls," he says and I'm inclined to believe him because I do think he cares about Veronica. From my perspective, it seems the "off again" parts of their relationship are her idea and not his.

"Is she okay?" I nod towards the house. I'm not sure if she's upset or angry, crying or yelling and it's driving me crazy that there's so much distance between us.

"I don't know. Shay and Veronica are still in her office. I didn't hear any crying but," he shrugs, "you sure you're ready for all this drama?" He chuckles.

"There wasn't any until your friend caused it."

"It would have come out."

"I would have told her first. Cooper and her team aren't even aware that we are together. We keep our relationship behind closed doors. Jeremy went digging because he's jealous and he wanted to cause a problem."

"I think he's just worried about her."

"You actually buy that? Tell me something. What would *you* do if Veronica started dating some other guy?"

"That's different. Veronica and I are in a relationship." He snorts. "Or whatever the fuck. You know what I'm saying. Jeremy and Shay have never been together in any capacity."

"That doesn't mean he doesn't want to be or he doesn't have feelings for her. I see everything, Derek. More specifically I see everything in regards to *her*."

He scratches his jaw and looks towards the house. "I get what you're saying, I do, and J was out of line for airing your dirty laundry like that."

"It's not even dirty laundry. I married my deceased best friend's fiancée to give her health insurance. He died in combat, she got sick, that was it. We divorced when she got better and got her own coverage."

"Well, fuck," he says, taking a sip of his beer. "You really are that noble."

"Did he even bother to find out the details when he was attempting to dig up dirt?" I ask him.

He shrugs. "I don't know. I don't even know if he knows all of that. Veronica didn't ask for the details. She just called him an asshole for unleashing that on her and said he needed to leave."

"I love her," I tell him. "This is difficult enough to navigate right now without her feeling like her friends are turning on her or judging her."

"I don't judge her. We've been through a lot together. The four of us," he says. "We've spent eighty percent of the last six years together. Long nights and vacations and all the ups and downs of life."

"And I like that Shay has people that have her back but there's a difference between that and what Jeremy just did today. She is still an adult capable of making her own decisions. And I'm not some random guy. I've been here. I've been through a lot with her too."

I didn't go back to the main house for the rest of the night. I stayed in my guesthouse to give Shay some space. She didn't call or text me so I took that to mean she was fine with my decision. It's nearing one in the morning and I'm sitting on my couch, having just gone through a new stack of mail when my phone beeps indicating someone opened her front door, and then a few moments later there is a knock on my door.

I open it and she's standing there, dressed in one of my t-shirts and a pair of joggers. Her eyes are slightly hazy like maybe she's cried or maybe she's intoxicated. She walks by me without a word and I close the door. I follow behind her and watch as she pulls her pants off and slides under my covers.

I pull off my shirt and my pants and slide in next to her and pull her against my chest, pressing my mouth to her neck.

"You didn't come back over," she says sadly.

"I didn't think you wanted me to."

"I always want to be near you."

Well, that's a good sign. Maybe she's not that angry.

"I'm sorry," I tell her. When she turns around so we are face to face, I can see the defeat all over her perfect features lit by the glow of the light on my nightstand. She sits up, pulls her hair to one side, and begins to play with the ends of it. "What is it, baby?"

"I feel like I'm in the dark." She blinks her eyes a few times. "You're usually my light but…not knowing that you were married before feels big even if you didn't love her. It makes me feel like we took a lot of steps back. Like you telling me you love me somehow means less than it did before."

"It doesn't." I shake my head and sit up so we are face to face. "I love you, Shay. Only you."

"I'm not jealous," she says instantly.

"I know," I tell her and I believe that. I don't think she's jealous of Heather. She shouldn't be. There really was nothing there.

"That doesn't mean I love the fact that you've been married before, but I'm not jealous." She twists her mouth and looks away before turning back to look at me a moment later. "Did you ever think about marrying Simone?"

"Maybe," I tell her honestly. "In an abstract thought when I was thinking about the future, but I think it was more the idea of marriage that I knew I wanted in the future. Not necessarily with her. I also wasn't interested in marriage then, which is one of the reasons we parted, like I told you." A chuckle leaves me as I think about how Simone would have reacted if I told her I was going to start protecting Shay Eastwood. "She would not have liked me being your bodyguard."

She cocks her head to the side innocently and flutters her brown eyes at me. "Why?"

I give her a look because she can't be new to women being jealous of her. "Because you're drop-dead gorgeous, baby, and I've spent the last four years living on your property." She nods in understanding and I can see her mind spinning with another question. I drag my knuckles down her cheek gently in an attempt to calm her nerves. "What else?"

She swallows. "You said you don't typically talk about your mom to anyone. Did you...with any of your past relationships?"

"Is that what this is about?"

"No...maybe? I don't know. You know all my deep dark secrets and I guess it makes me feel like you don't know if you can trust me and maybe that's selfish to think it's about me." She lowers her chin. "I guess I'm just feeling insecure."

"I wish you didn't." She's biting her bottom lip and I reach up to release it from between her teeth, rubbing my thumb over the wet skin. "I know it's not that simple but no one has ever had my heart but you, Shay." Her watery brown eyes meet mine and she shakes her head. I pull her into my arms so her back is against my chest and I interlace our fingers. "I love you."

"I love you too." She looks up at me and gives me her lips. I take them eagerly, kissing her through the discomfort that comes with thinking about my mother.

I pull back and turn my light off, cloaking the room in darkness. "She left when I was five because she didn't want to be a mom. I guess she was scared or thought she wouldn't be good at it and she was worried about screwing me up." I chuckle darkly. "The irony."

"Damian..." she whispers and strokes my arm that's wrapped around her middle.

"She told my dad she loved him but she wasn't ready to be a mom. She didn't even say goodbye to me."

She freezes in my arms and then brings her hand to her lips. "I'm so sorry, baby."

"It's okay. My dad and I...we were great, and then he met my stepmom and she treated me like her own so it was all good after a while. But she is why I struggle with not feeling good enough when it comes to women because I wasn't even good enough for the one that brought me into the world."

She gasps and turns in my arms, and though I can't make out all of her features, I know she's staring at me. "That's absolutely not true. That is not on you, Damian. She left because of *her*, not because of you." She leans in closer and her scent surrounds me as she drags her fingertips over my jaw. "I would never leave you, Damian."

Chapter
TWENTY-FIVE

Shay

IT'S BEEN A FEW DAYS AND I CAN'T SHAKE THE FEELING OF annoyance.

At my friends.

At Damian.

At the world.

I don't know if I'm still a little irritated that he kept something like that from me or I'm feeling territorial that he's been married before or maybe a combination of the two, but I'm in a foul mood and everyone is taking notice.

Maybe it's because I wonder how this is going to work between him and I.

Maybe it's because I've had longer days than usual on set and we haven't really had the time to talk since that night.

I haven't spoken to Jeremy except for on set and I'm glad he's been smart enough to keep his distance. He did leave flowers in my dressing room with a card saying he was sorry the next day but other than that it's been radio silence.

Today, Jeremy and I have an interview as a part of our press tour, so we are at a different studio than usual without any of the rest of the cast or crew. I'm in my assigned dressing room packing up to go home when there's a knock on the door. I frown in confusion because Damian doesn't usually knock, so I have no idea who it is.

"Come in," I call and Jeremy enters with a sad smile on his face, his hands up like he's surrendering.

"I come in peace."

I look him up and down slowly. "Do you?"

He slides his hands into his slacks pockets and leans against the wall. "The interview went well."

"Mmmhmm."

"You were funny. It's nice to see you laughing," he tells me.

"I learned a long time ago how to laugh on command especially when I don't feel like laughing and make it convincing." I give him a fake smile that borders on saccharine before letting it fall with an eye roll.

He nods and the awkward silence stretches between us. "Shay, I'm sorry about how I handled everything."

"How did you even know that? Are you trying to dig up stuff on him?"

"Yes." *What the fuck?*

"Why?"

His lips form a straight line and he shrugs guiltily. "I didn't want a repeat of what happened with Paxton."

"Paxton was a serial cheater."

"I just meant I didn't want to see you get hurt. I didn't want you to be blindsided and the second you went public, people would have gone digging into his past. You know how it works, Shay."

"And the way you chose to tell me was you not wanting me to get hurt? Bullshit. It wasn't your story to tell."

He sighs and sits down running a hand through his hair. "It was never my intention to hurt you. I'm in love with you, for god's sakes," he blurts out like it isn't a huge bomb that's going to change everything. "It bothered me that another man that doesn't deserve you is getting a shot with you."

My mouth drops open because *no fucking way*. "I'm sorry, back up, what?" My mind is moving a mile a minute and my hand immediately goes to my bracelet, knowing it can't do anything but make me feel closer to Damian and hope he can sense that I need him.

"I've been in love with you for years. Since Alex and I broke up. Hell, it's *why* we broke up if you ask her," he continues.

I blink several times in shock. I remember Alex did break up with him and I also remember I never really got a straight answer as to why. I didn't push it because it wasn't my business. I tuck a hair behind my ear nervously trying to figure out what to say and how to say it without potentially ruining what's left of our friendship and potentially the chemistry on our hit television show. *Fuck. Why did he have to tell me this now?* "Jeremy, you can't be serious."

"I was trying to give you time after you and Paxton broke up and then I saw you at the club with Damian and I got pissed, all right?" He stands up and crosses the room. I take a few steps back. "Shay, you know me. You can trust me. We've been through everything together."

"Jeremy..." I put my hands up. *Damian was right all along.* "This whole time?"

He nods and reaches his arm out to touch my face, but I move out of his reach. "We could be so good together. It would be so easy, Shay." I hate that I feel like he's following me around the dressing room because now I'm against a wall with nowhere to move.

"Jeremy, stop," I say.

I want to call for Damian or anyone but I don't want to be dramatic. *Jeremy wouldn't hurt me...right?* After five years of friendship, I hate that I don't know the answer to that question.

He stops walking and looks down at his feet. "Do you feel anything for me?"

I swallow nervously, unsure of how he'll take the truth. "Not beyond a friendship," I tell him. "I...I love Damian. I've loved him for a really long time and maybe that makes me an asshole for staying with Paxton. I just…I thought he wasn't an option for me. I thought he didn't feel the same way about me."

He snorts. "Who wouldn't want you? You're Shay Eastwood."

"That's not why I want her," Damian's voice is low and icy but heats every inch of my skin as he shuts the door behind him and crosses the room. He stands in front of me but for the first time, I don't think it's because he thinks there's a threat to me.

But to him.

"Are we going to have a problem, Gardner?" he asks, referring to Jeremy by his last name. "I know your show requires a lot of specific scenes, but she's acting. She does not want you."

I don't hear him respond so I peer around Damian and see the angry look Jeremy's giving him. I've rarely seen him angry; I've never so much as heard him yell except when we're shooting and our characters are arguing.

"Jeremy…"

He takes a step back. "I'd be much better for you. He won't love you like I do. No one ever will."

Chapter
TWENTY-SIX

DAMIAN

DID HE JUST SAY THAT?
Every red flag shoots up thinking about all of the letters that Shay has been getting that said exactly that.

No fucking way.

My heart pounds in my chest and adrenaline rushes through me at such a level, I feel like I could punch through a wall. I follow behind Jeremy wanting him out of this room and away from Shay. I shut the door with more force than I would normally and lock the door behind him. I need a moment to calm down and more importantly I need to be alone with her before emerging from her dressing room. I leave my hand on the door, trying to quell the fury raging through me thinking about the fact that I was fucking right. I knew he had feelings for her and now they're out there and they work together and it's possible that there's more to it.

I briefly run through all the letters that I've pretty much committed to memory because I've read over them so many times trying to think of any indication that Jeremy could be the author of those letters.

"Damian?" I hear her voice from behind me and then I sense her at my periphery and her hand rests on my bicep. "You're shaking," she says and I dart my gaze to her hand and then to her eyes. "I'm sorry," she says and I can see the sadness and worry in her eyes.

I shake my head hoping she understands that I'm not angry with her. I grab her wrist, remove it from my bicep, and wrap my arms around her. Pushing her against the wall, I seal my mouth over hers.

"I am done," I growl against her lips as I lift her into my arms and tangle my hands in her hair as I continue kissing her like I need her more than air in my lungs.

She pulls back. "Done?" she whispers and I see the tears rushing to her eyes. "What—"

"Done with this fucking distance between us." I know she's still annoyed about what happened with her friends and maybe even at me for keeping such a large secret from her.

Relief floods her face and I realize she thought I meant I was done with her. She nods. "I love you."

"Say it again," I grip her chin, as she claws at my back while I press my dick into her center.

"I love you." She buries her face in my neck and I feel her tears against my neck.

I rub her back, and I swear I can feel her heartbeat pounding against my chest. "Shhh, don't cry."

"I can't believe that happened… and now I have to work with him for the next two months. I had no idea. I swear."

The idea of him touching her, kissing her, doing the intimate scenes of her show all the while I'm not sure if I can even fucking trust him makes me feel almost manic, and before I can think, I've grabbed her travel bag and her hand and I'm pulling her out the door. The car is parked directly in front of the hotel, but there is a swarm of people outside, and I can already hear her name being said under the dull roar of the crowd.

"Do not stop for pictures or autographs," I tell her before I open the door and she frowns at me.

"Why?"

"I just want to get you back to your house."

"Is this about Jeremy?" she asks. "Damian, I can't just ignore them because of what happened. It has nothing to do with them."

"Shay." I shoot her a look and she furrows her brows.

"You can't keep me locked up in a cage. This is why I have a security team."

"Yes, and as the head of it, I make the calls."

"Because you're jealous?"

"This has nothing to do with that. I think Jeremy is unstable and—"

"Because he's in love with me?" I don't want to keep going back and forth with her and she shakes her head before I can respond. "And one has nothing to do with the other. These are my fans, Damian. They know I'm here and I always stop for a few photos. Stop acting brand new."

I grit my teeth and take a deep breath through my nose, knowing that this is not a battle I can win unless I plan to throw her over my shoulder like a caveman and carry her to the car. *Something tells me she might like that.*

"Be quick," I tell her and I can see the face she gives me out of the corner of my eye. I push open the door and everyone is immediately calling her name and holding out small posters and magazines and pictures of her. She smiles and signs everything that is closest to her as I slowly move her through the crowd, holding an arm out so no one gets too close. She poses next to a few girls that look like they may be in their late teens that are all telling her how much they love her and she smiles graciously just as she always does. My eyes are looking everywhere, my entire body on high alert.

Could Jeremy really be behind all the letters? This whole time?

I keep moving her through the throng of people and I'm grateful when we are finally at the car. I open the car door for her and she waves to the crowd one more time and blows a kiss before sliding in the back.

I get in the front.

"I have a driver, you know. You don't have to keep driving me around everywhere. You can sit back here with me and make out," she says and I know that I've been wary about letting anyone drive her around but I'm not sure how skilled her driver is if we're being followed and I don't want to take the chance.

"What are you going to do about Jeremy?" I ask her.

When she leans forward and looks up at me, I resist the urge to tell her to sit back.

"What do you mean? I just have to deal with it."

"Won't kissing him feel different? It won't feel weird doing love scenes with him knowing how he feels about you?"

"Yes, but what am I supposed to do? I'm an actress, Damian. Please tell me you can handle this. Tell me you trust me."

"Of course, I trust you. But there's a big difference between kissing your co-star and kissing one that has been harboring all of these feelings for you. Don't tell me you don't understand that."

"What do you expect me to do, Damian? If I go to my director with this he's going to be like 'okay, and?' I'm an actress. It would be the same situation if we hated each other. I would just have to deal with it. I think this is more about you and me, and I get that, believe me, I do, but I just need you to trust me."

"I do. It's *him* I don't trust."

The second we get back to her house, she goes inside to shower while I go to the guesthouse to change and go through every single letter that has had me on high alert. I even pull out some of the old ones from years ago to cross reference. It's impossible to prove that the letters came from Jeremy, but something just isn't sitting right with me. I heard him say something about his ex-fiancée right before I barged in, and I wonder if his feelings for Shay really started that early. It's like I'm seeing everything in a new light and now I'm running through every major interaction between the two of them that I've witnessed.

Is this all because I'm jealous?

Am I seeing shit that just isn't there?

My phone rings and I narrow my eyes at the name that is on the screen. "Hunt," I answer.

"We need to talk," the voice says instantly without a hello or fuck you.

"Paxton?"

"We need to talk *without* Shay," he adds.

I lean back against the couch wondering what the fuck her ex-boyfriend could want to talk to me about. In a normal situation, he'd probably want to kick my ass, but seeing as how he is definitely not capable of that and he knows that and I know he knows that, I wonder what this is about.

"Now?"

"Preferably."

"Okay, come to Lakeland," I tell him referring to the large community her house sits inside. "I'll meet you at the entrance. Forty minutes. I need to get someone from my team over here."

"Fine," he says and hangs up the phone.

In light of the recent events with Jeremy, I find myself more on edge at the thought of being around yet another man that still holds a candle for my woman. I'm out of my house in an instant, jogging to her house, letting myself in, and then flying up the stairs. The need to have both my eyes and my hands on her overtakes me. I send a text to Kent, a member of my team that I can trust to be here promptly as I enter her bedroom. I still hear the water running and I'm through the bathroom door and yanking open her shower door, suddenly blind with lust and rage that dances at the edge of my senses. I toe off my shoes leaving me barefoot, but I don't bother to take my clothes off, leaving me in jeans and a t-shirt before I'm in the shower with her, one arm across her chest, hauling her against mine and one hand between her legs.

She yelps in surprise but it quickly turns to a moan when she feels my fingers against her clit. "Tell me who this belongs to."

"You."

She spins out of my grasp and stares at my fully clothed form. I think she's about to ask why I chose to get into the shower with all of my clothes on when her eyes meet mine and her teeth find her bottom lip in response to the look I'm giving her. "Tell *me* who *this* belongs to," she says grabbing my dick through my pants and squeezing.

"You," I tell her as I back her against the wall. "It's always belonged to you. You fucking own me, Shay. Every part of me is controlled by you and my need to keep this going," I say putting a hand to her chest, covering her heart. "I fucking live for this." I slide my hand between her legs and drag my hand through her wet slit. "I live for your looks; whether you're irritated with me or happy with me or ready to fuck me, when your eyes are on me, when I have your attention, I feel like I've won the ultimate prize." I continue rubbing her clit and her hips begin to rock against me in time. I push my fingers inside of her fucking her with two fingers slowly while I rub her clit with my thumb. "And this…" I feel my resolve withering with every stroke of my finger over her sweet clit. "I live for this. I could worship this forever and it wouldn't be long enough."

"Damian," she gasps. "Oh my god." Her hands find my wet t-shirt and she grasps the fabric in her fists. "There's no high like your eyes on me. Your hands on me. Your dick inside me. Fuck. You're the only man I want this from *ever*." She looks down at my hand inside of her and then up at me. "There's no one I trust more than I trust you." She swallows and she looks away immediately and when I grab her face with my other hand the look she gives me is full of vulnerability.

"This…" I tell her pointing back and forth between us even as I continue fucking her with my hand, "is real. We talk. Communicate. Nothing comes between us. *Ever*."

She shakes her head. "No. Never."

I feel her sex clenching around my fingers and then her body is against mine, rubbing against me as best as she can while my fingers are inside of her. I increase my efforts, knowing that Kent will be here soon and I am curious about what Paxton has to say. I still need to tell her that I'm leaving. I grab her breast with my other hand and pinch the nipple gently, rolling it to a hardened peak. "You want to come?"

"You know I do." She lets her eyes flutter shut and watching her climb towards her climax while I'm fully clothed with only my fingers touching her has my dick thickening in my jeans. I know cum has to be leaking into my briefs.

"Fuck, I'm there," she says grabbing my wrist to hold it in the position she wants it and begins rocking her hips against it.

That's so fucking hot.

"Oh god!" She drops her head back and I watch as her breasts jiggle in that delicious way they do right before she orgasms and then she does long and hard. Her cunt flutters against my hand and I wish like hell that I had time to feel it around my tongue and my dick. She rides out her orgasm on my hand, writhing and whimpering as she comes down from her high and I slowly pull my hand out of her and lick my fingers clean.

Her eyes are hooded, but when she reaches for the button of my jeans, I take a step back shaking my head. She puts her hands on her hips and cocks her head to the side. "Still like my irritated look?" she sasses and I chuckle in response.

"I have to run out for a bit. Kent is coming to sit outside."

"Wait what? Why? And where?" She takes a step towards me as I get out of the shower. I already know she's going to follow me so I hand her a towel. "Why can't I come?"

I raise an eyebrow at her. "Since when do you want to come with me when I'm just running out?"

"Ummm I follow you to the guesthouse when you're just getting clothes. Are you new here? I'm actually *your* shadow." She begins drying herself, and I resist the urge to do it for her because I know it's the quickest way for my tongue to wind up inside of her.

"Well, no you cannot come, but I'll be quick," I tell her.

"Can you tell me where you're going?" She begins to apply her lotion and I try to avoid looking at her because I'm trying to get my dick to calm down and watching her rub her nipples and her pussy is not the visual I need right now.

"Just on a run. I need to check out a few things."

"Is this about Jeremy?" she asks as she pulls her shower cap off and her hair out of its loose ponytail.

I shake my head "No. It's not. I promise."

"You wouldn't lie to me, would you?"

"No," I tell her and while I may keep things from her, I'd never lie to her face.

"When will you be back?"

"An hour tops."

"Okay…" she gives me her lips and I plant a wet kiss on them. When I pull back, I see the stars in her eyes and I'm glad I affect her as much as she affects me.

She's in as deep as I am.

When I make it to the entrance, Paxton is already there. It's relatively dark and he's not in his usual car nor does he have his security with him which is a huge red flag.

"Where is Jackson?" I ask, referring to his head of security. "He knows you're out with no security?"

"I'm fine. We need to talk about Shay and Jeremy."

I cross my arms over my chest and lean against my truck. "Go on."

"There's been some talk…"

"Okay?"

"Look I don't know how reliable the source is but it got back to me and—"

"Spit it the fuck out." I don't know what he's about to say but I do know that if it's what I'm thinking, I'm going to be longer than the hour I promised Shay.

"Apparently he was drunk the other night at some dive bar across town talking some shit about how he's fucking her or has fucked her, I don't know."

My blood runs cold. Even though I know it's a lie, just the mere thought of another man inside her infuriates me. Even the fact that the man in front of me has slept with her sends a spike of rage through me. "What?"

"It may have just been him talking shit *but* he did say that he couldn't believe she was fucking her bodyguard now." He gives me a look. "So…that might potentially come out because it got back to me. I pretended I didn't know anything when they told me but who knows who else they told."

I shake my head knowing that Shay is going to be crushed that he outed us on top of everything else. "This guy is the fucking worst. You know he told her he's always had feelings for her?"

"I knew it. I fucking knew it." He groans. "At least you had the decency to hide your feelings for the most part." He scoffs. "I always hated that Shay couldn't see through that 'we're just friends' bullshit." He shakes his head. "Look, I want no part of this. I'm sharing what I know, but I don't want it to be said that you heard this from me, okay? I'm telling you so you can get in front of this."

"Why'd you call me instead of Shay?"

He shrugs. "I thought she wouldn't take my call and…above everything I do think you care about her and want the best for her. And I wanted to give *you* the opportunity to handle Jeremy." He sighs. "I fucked up with Shay."

"You're just now realizing that?"

"No, dick." He grumbles. "Don't be stupid like I am."

"Well, I don't plan to stick my dick in anyone besides her, but thank you for the advice," I say sardonically and he narrows his eyes at me.

"You'll see." He snorts. "You're not even famous, but when you go public with Shay, you'll have women lining up to fuck you."

"I don't want that. I want *her*."

"I didn't either." He shrugs. "I just wanted her too, but shit…you get caught up and things just happen and before you know it you're in too deep but it feels too good and you always think the last time is going to be the last time until it's not." He drags a hand through his blonde hair and rubs the back of his neck. "I'm not making excuses. I fucked up. Hard stop. And it cost me her. Just don't trust anyone."

"I don't trust anyone but her."

"Good." He sighs and looks back at his car. "If you hit that asshole Jeremy, hit him once for me too, alright?"

Chapter

TWENTY-SEVEN

Shay

I WAKE UP THE NEXT MORNING TO LIGHT STREAMING THROUGH the curtains. It's a rare Saturday morning when I don't have anything to do, so my alarm didn't go off at the usual seven-thirty. My body immediately knows I'm alone in bed as Damian and I are usually intertwined even in the mornings. *Either he's wrapped around me or I'm practically on top of him.*

I listen for the sounds of him in the bathroom but I don't hear anything and when I reach for my phone, I notice the note on my nightstand.

Morning, gorgeous
Went to get breakfast.
Be back soon.

I mentioned in passing a few days ago that I'd been craving almond croissants from this bakery I used to go to with my mom every Saturday but I stopped going because it reminded me so much of her. I had forgotten about them for a long time until I randomly got a craving for them I haven't been able to shake. I smile because though I'm not sure, I wouldn't be surprised if he showed up with a box of them.

I press the note to my chest thinking about last night. We'd made love until the point of exhaustion, his body on top of mine, his hard dick slowly rocking into me giving me orgasm after orgasm while he whispered how much he loved me in my ear. I'd fallen asleep wrapped in his arms, my head on his chest letting the sounds of his heartbeat lull me to sleep. I've learned it's my favorite place in the world and the place I feel the safest.

I grab my phone, not wanting to wait any longer to hear his voice and dial his number. It rings and rings and I can't remember a time he didn't answer on the first or second ring. It rolls to his voicemail and I end the call before it gives me the option to leave a message.

Me: Morning! Got your note. Can you get a vanilla iced coffee too? Love you thank youuuu

I make my way into the bathroom to do my morning routine but I can't stop the nagging feeling in the back of my mind that he didn't immediately call or text me back.

Is this me being clingy?

I frown because I've never been this girl. With Paxton, we'd gone days without talking when we were on location and while I noticed, I wasn't climbing the walls like I am now.

I pick up the phone and call him again and it rings and rings again before going to voicemail. This time I leave a message. "Hey, I'm not upset or anything but you usually answer right away…I could be lying in a ditch somewhere." I chuckle nervously. "I'm not! But…I'm starting to worry. Should I worry? Can you call me back? I love you."

My fingers immediately start fidgeting and a feeling I haven't felt in years hits me at full force. Before I can convince myself that he's fine and I'm overreacting I'm pressing the call button.

"Do you know what time it is?" Veronica asks with a groan.

"Eight-thirty. Does Max ever not answer you?" I ask immediately.

"Huh?" she says and I know she's still half asleep.

"When you call Max, does he ever not answer?"

"No, of course not. Why? Is Damian not answering?" She yawns. "Did you guys have a fight? Maybe he's just not answering his girlfriend, not the woman he's protecting."

"Veronica…" I warn and I hear talking in the background, assumedly Derek.

"What? Where is he anyway? We have the morning off and we don't have to be at the table read until five so I'm surprised you aren't doing it all over your house."

"He went to get me breakfast and now he's not answering." I take a deep breath realizing it's been twenty minutes since I started calling him. "What if something happened to him?"

"Damian is indestructible. He's fine," she says over the sounds of running water.

"Then why isn't he answering?" My heart is starting to accelerate, growing more aggressive with each passing minute. She doesn't answer and I hate how loud the silence is. I'm trying my best to keep my mind from going there, but the tragedies I've endured make me assume the worst every time. It is fucking exhausting but unavoidable. "There's no reason why he wouldn't take my call, V. He's my bodyguard. Even if he was pissed at me, he'd answer. And he's not pissed at me! He went to get me breakfast!"

"Okay, I'm coming over." Probably in response to the shrill tone of my voice.

That was the thing about Veronica. I never needed to call for her, she just *came*. She knew if she asked me, I'd tell her no. I'd tell her I'd be fine and it's early and I'm sorry for waking her up and she should go back to sleep and not worry about me. Instead, I hear her grabbing her keys. "Let me just get Max and I'll be over in a few." Veronica lives in a different community a few miles away. "Want me to stay on the phone?"

"No." I shake my head. "I am being ridiculous. You don't even need to come." I put her on speaker and drop my phone to my bed as I start going through the list of scenarios that would explain why Damian hasn't answered that *isn't* him lying in a ditch somewhere.

"Shut up, I'll be there in ten minutes, but I swear to god if he shows up, right when I get there, he's making me breakfast."

A beep indicating a news alert about me breaks me from my thoughts and I open it and tears immediately rush to my eyes. "Oh my god. Oh my god."

"What what," Veronica says and I hear the slam of her car door. "Get there fast, I think something's wrong," she says to someone. "Shay, talk to me."

"The…" I stammer, trying to get the words out. I'm suddenly freezing and when my teeth start to chatter I briefly wonder if I'm going into shock.

"Shit," Veronica says and I take it to mean she's seeing what I'm seeing which is a news alert reporting that both me and my bodyguard were in a car accident. There aren't any pictures but it's my Range Rover and there are ambulances and firetrucks and my truck is literally on fire.

"Oh…"

"Come open the door, Shay. I'll be there in five."

I don't know how I move my feet but somehow, I get downstairs and open the door, leaving it wide open. I immediately sink to the floor in front of it and sure enough, Veronica and Max are coming through the door moments later.

"Hey," she says kneeling down in front of me so we're at eye level. "We don't know anything."

"False. We know I wasn't in the car but HE WAS! That's my car and he's the only person that drives it."

My phone starts ringing and I'm glad it's Cooper so he can get a handle on this. "I wasn't in the car," I say instantly, tears forming in the back of my throat. "D—Damian went to get me breakfast." I think I'm still in shock because my entire body feels numb and I'm not in full-blown hysterics like when I lost my parents. *Maybe subconsciously, my body knows he's still alive. Please, baby,* my mind thinks.

"Okay," he lets out a breath. "I'm glad you're okay. You're alone?"

"Veronica just got here."

"Do not leave your house until I call you. Is there any security there?"

"I think Kent is still here. Damian had him stay in the guesthouse last night," I say and I'm glad Cooper doesn't question it because I really don't have the energy for the conversation regarding where Damian slept if Kent was in the guesthouse.

"We're releasing a statement that you're safe and at home. Stay off the internet, Shay, I mean it."

Veronica takes the phone from my hand and stands up. "Find out what is going on, Cooper." she says and I can't hear his response but she looks at me. "I will take her to the scene myself. Damian is...you know how important he is to her." I'm still sitting on the ground and when I look up at her she's looking at me the way a mother would look at their child in pain. She hangs up just as another call comes through.

"It's unknown," she says holding out the phone for me. I answer it, hoping it's Damian but somehow knowing it's not.

"Hello?"

"Shay Eastwood?"

"Ummm, who's calling?" It isn't often I get random calls. My phone number is pretty protected; I've only had to change it a few times over the years, but I still know better than to confirm my identity before I know who's calling.

"This is Nurse Greene from Lakeland Hills Medical Center." My heart drops and Veronica immediately moves to grab my hand.

The tears begin to slide down my face instantly out of fear and sadness or maybe relief that they've figured out that I'm important enough to him to receive this phone call. *How did they find me?* I sniffle. "How is he?"

"First and foremost, Mr. Hunt is alive." Veronica lets out a sigh of relief. I try to but I hear the *but* in her voice. "He was unconscious when they brought him in and he is in surgery." She doesn't say anything further. "Are you there Miss Eastwood?"

"I'm here," I whisper, my mind racing and full of intrusive thoughts that have me believing I'll lose the love of my life on the operating table.

"Can you get yourself here safely?"

I'm immediately moving up the stairs to change into more than just Damian's t-shirt and a pair of sweatpants. "Yes, I have someone that can drive me. May I ask how you knew to call me?"

"Mr. Hunt has you listed in his phone on his emergency contact as his employer." It stings hearing myself referred to as that.

"I see."

"We will see you soon, Miss Eastwood." I quickly brush my teeth, shed the sweatpants, and replace them with leggings, leaving on his t-shirt as I pull on a leather jacket and grab my bag completely forgoing makeup. I grab a pair of sunglasses and a baseball hat and pull it on, knowing that it's the most incognito look I have time for before I'm bolting down the stairs.

Kent is stationed out front and nods at me. "Cooper said he didn't want you leaving."

"Cooper is not the boss, contrary to what he thinks," I tell him. "I need to be with Damian. I know you know we're together. So, you can either drive me, or Max can." I say pointing at Veronica's security.

Kent drags a hand over his goatee and I can tell he's at war over what to do. "Let's go."

Surprisingly, there isn't a bunch of paparazzi around my gate but there's a ton around the gate to the main entrance of the community because people know I live inside. "Get down. You too Veronica." Kent tells us so we aren't spotted through the front windshield that isn't tinted. We make it through the crowd with only a few flashes since they're not sure who's inside.

We make it to the hospital in record time with Kent going much faster than the speed limit and I'm fairly certain he ran more than a few lights. The car has barely stopped before I take off running for the doors and the paparazzi lingering outside go *fucking nuts*. Veronica is right behind me and both of our details trail us, trying to keep the paparazzi out of our faces, but at this moment, I couldn't care less about what I look like or who is taking pictures. I'd leak a sex tape if it could get me to Damian faster or for the promise that he is alive.

Nothing fucking matters but getting to him.

"Damian Hunt, please," I say immediately to the woman sitting at the front desk who looks barely a few years older than me. Her eyes look up and when they widen, I briefly see the stars in them before they flit to Veronica and widen further. I take it to mean she knows who we are. I'm still wearing the hat and sunglasses but Veronica isn't wearing any kind of disguise which makes it pretty obvious who I am.

"Uh uh," Veronica says as if to say *now is really not the time.*

"V," I warn. "We'll give you pictures, autographs, whatever you want. Just please tell me where I can find him."

She nods and looks to her computer remembering herself. "Sorry, I...just a little starstruck." She blushes. "He's still in surgery but he'll be in the intensive care unit. Room 400."

I rub my chest, trying my best to keep the cracks I feel re-forming in my heart from growing. *He's fine. He's fine. He's fine.*

I run up four flights of stairs, not having the patience to wait for the elevator and when I get there, Cooper is already standing in the ICU waiting area. "What—"

He tears his eyes away from his phone and gives me a disgruntled look. "Didn't I tell you to wait at home?" he asks and I glare at him.

"Cooper, lay off," Veronica says.

"Do we know anything?" I ask, ignoring the look he's still giving me.

"Doctors won't disclose anything to me. Since you're his emergency contact, they'll probably share more with you. I've talked to the police officer that was on the scene though; he went downstairs but he'll be back." I put my hand over my mouth to quiet the sobs threatening to break through. "He was conscious on the scene, adrenaline, he thinks that he was able to get himself out of the car. He told the officer he thinks it was a hit-and-run. Someone had been tailing him and then when he thought he lost him, they plowed into his side of the car at an intersection. But Damian was able to get himself out before it caught fire." He clears his throat. "The officer did say he was pretty banged up and shocked he was able to move."

Veronica turns her eyes to me. "This is good. He's okay. He's alive."

Guilt washes over me slowly until I'm sure of it. "They were probably trying to get me or to me. What if they were trying to abduct me or…who would want to hurt Damian?"

Veronica's phone begins to ring. "It's Derek, one sec. I told him I would keep him updated." She walks away leaving Cooper and me alone.

"He has to be okay." I don't say it to anyone in particular, just to the atmosphere in hopes it gets to the right deity that controls this kind of thing. "We just…" I look at Cooper, realizing that he's going to figure it out sooner rather than later the second I'm allowed to see him. "I love him."

Cooper's eyes widen in realization. "You're…together?"

"For a couple weeks now." I nod. "But the feelings have been there for a really long time if I'm being honest. I don't care what you or my PR team think by the way. Everyone is just going to have to figure it out."

A knowing look crosses Cooper's face and he smiles. "Well, it's about time he told you how he felt."

Chapter TWENTY-EIGHT

Shay

MY MOUTH DROPS OPEN AND I MOMENTARILY FORGET about the situation as it sets in that Cooper knew Damian had feelings for me. "Excuse me? You knew?"

"Anyone with eyes could see he had it bad for you."

"Oh my god. Cooper! What?!"

"I mean anyone that spent a lot of time with you had to know. Everything he did for you after your parents passed? He went way beyond the call of duty of a bodyguard. He slept outside your bedroom door for weeks when you were having nightmares."

My mind is spinning with all of this information as I try to think about the past five years through a new different lens. I finally register what Cooper just said and pull my eyes from the ground where I was staring. "What?"

"He'd sleep outside your door so he could hear you and get to you faster. Usually only on the nights that Veronica didn't stay over."

"How do you know that?" There's no way Damian would have told anyone that.

"I came over early in the morning one day and found him there." He gives me a smile. "I knew then."

"Did you say anything? Warn him to stay away from me?" I narrow my eyes at him, daring him to tell me something like that.

"No." He shakes his head. "I always thought if you two ended up together, it would be the real deal and your PR team would have a field day selling your love story."

"It would have been nice if you had shared this theory then."

"ME? Didn't Veronica have the same theory? You ignored her. You definitely would have ignored me."

"Yes, but Veronica thinks everyone is in love with each other. She was convinced you were having an affair with my mother at one point." Cooper's eyes widen and he gives me a guilty look. "ARE YOU KIDDING? Now we are adding childhood trauma to the list right now?"

He shakes his head and puts his hands up. "I'm kidding. I'M KIDDING. I was trying to lighten the mood."

I give him both my middle fingers. "NOT HELPING."

Not long after my conversation with Cooper, Officer Ferguson approaches me. Veronica went to get me some water, Cooper is on a call, and I'm immediately off the uncomfortably hard waiting room couch.

"I'm Shay. I'm Damian's girlfriend." I say before he has a chance to ask who I am.

"I thought he was your bodyguard?"

"Off the record, he's my bodyguard and we are romantically involved."

"Makes sense now. Heard him tell the paramedic to tell you he loved you before…"

My heart thumps painfully in my chest. "Before what?"

"He did lose consciousness on the scene. He was crashing but they got him back in the ambulance."

I nod, knowing most of this information but it still feels like knives to my heart. "Mr. Hunt is a fighter. He was able to give me a few characters of the license plate and the color and the model. We are in the process of running a trace on all of them."

"Did he say who he thought it was?"

"No. He did say you've been getting some letters though. Threatening ones, obsessive ones. It sounds like you may have a stalker," he says. "And if that's the case, they more than likely knew you weren't in the car and that *he* is your boyfriend."

"You think…they were targeting him specifically?"

He shrugs. "This is just my initial thought with a bird's eye view of the situation. I would need to dig deeper. I know you just broke up with someone. Was that amicable?"

"Well…no, but Paxton wouldn't do this."

He pulls out a notepad and looks up at me. "You sure? Does he know about your relationship with Hunt?"

"Yeah, he found out."

He narrows his eyes. "And how did he take it?" I give him a look and he jots some notes down on his pad. "Right. Not well, I assume."

"He thinks I was cheating on him and I wasn't."

"Okay," he says without looking up and I'm sure he's thinking *not my business.*

"Just clarifying."

"Anyone else?"

You know you're thinking it, I hear Damian's voice in my ear. *Tell him.* "I—I don't know."

"Don't know…?"

"My co-star on the show. He's been…different lately. He told me he had feelings for me and I don't feel the same. But it's been weird. He's been *off*, kind of." Though shooting has gone as best as it could go with things being in a weird limbo between us, when the cameras stop rolling it's like he's a totally different person. He's withdrawn and barely talks to me anymore. I thought maybe he was just embarrassed for how he acted or the fact that I don't reciprocate his feelings but now I'm wondering if there's more to it.

"Okay, name?"

"Jeremy Gardner. I'm not saying he did and I don't want to get anyone in trouble…" I stammer.

"If he didn't do anything he has nothing to be in trouble for. I'm not in the business of throwing A-list celebrities into jail, Miss Eastwood, but this is a serious offense. Attempted murder, stalking, harassment, and vehicular assault are all felonies we take very seriously.

"Okay…"

"Now, I didn't get to talk to Damian long at the scene, but when he's out of surgery, I'd like to talk to him again."

"Yes, of course."

He nods before handing me his card. "This has my direct number. You call me if you think of anything else, alright?"

It's been almost four hours since we got to the hospital and he's finally out of surgery and recovering in the ICU. I haven't been able to see him and I'm fucking over it. My lawyer and Gabe from my PR team have long since shown up and Derek got here a few minutes ago. Even Paxton called to make sure I was okay and to see if Damian was okay. He offered to have food sent to the hospital but I was in no mood to eat anything.

Surprisingly nothing from Jeremy.

Or maybe not surprisingly.

I open my messages with Damian, sniffling as I scroll through our messages of the past three weeks. I scroll through dirty texts, sweet ones, and questions about what we're having for our late-night dinner and I just want to fast forward a few weeks where he's asking me what color my panties are and how he can't wait to take them off with his teeth.

The doctor, who's been very kind, has come out several times to keep me informed and I'm grateful for the updates, but I wanted to see Damian. Hold him. Touch him.

Does he know I'm here? Can he feel me?

After what feels like an eternity, the doctor motions for me to follow him and Kent is right behind me much to the doctor's annoyance.

"He stays outside of the room," he says referring to Kent as we follow him back through two sets of double doors. "Now, he's not awake yet but he should wake up within the next few hours. The surgery went well and his vitals are all good. He'll definitely be weak for a little while. He has quite a few broken bones, some swelling in the brain, and a punctured lung. Overall, he was banged up. But we're optimistic that he'll make a full recovery. I just want to warn you because of how he looks."

"Okay." I nod.

He's going to live. He's going to live. It doesn't matter how he looks. He's going to live. Not dying.

He lets me into his room and immediately I just want to crawl onto the bed with him. "Damian," I whisper. I rush to his bedside and press a kiss on his lips before the doctor tells me I can't touch him. "I love you. I love you so much." I press another kiss to his swollen cheek and his forehead. He has a few cuts on his face and a black eye but for the most part, his face is unscathed. I reach for his hand and gently squeeze it. "It's Shay. Can you hear me? If you can, please wake up and talk to me. I'm so scared." I sniffle. "You make all my fears go away." I push his hair back and drag my knuckles down his cheek slowly. "I need you to tell me everything is going to be okay. That you're going to be okay." A tear rolls down my cheek and I feel that familiar pain clawing up my spine and taking hold of my brain.

They said he'll be fine. He's going to live.

Doctors can be wrong, my mind argues.

I don't know how long I sit in silence begging him to wake up with my mind when he makes a noise. They brought in a chair so that I could sit and I'd dragged it next to his bed. I'm holding his hand as best as I can while I rest my head on the bed. My head shoots up when I hear it again, a groan from deep within his chest. "Damian? Baby? Can you hear me?" I can see his eyes moving behind his lids and the tears form in mine at the thought of getting to see his blue eyes. "Can you open your eyes?" His eyes slowly open and the wind is knocked out of me as ours connect for the first time all day. "Damian." I bite my bottom lip before I lightly press my lips to his.

"Mmmm." His eyes which must have been shut while I kissed him open slowly and a ghost of a smile finds his lips. "Shay," he whispers and I feel like my heart could burst just hearing my name fall from his lips. "Are you okay?"

"Dandy," I say sarcastically. "You scared the shit out of me."

"Is Kent here with you?"

"I'm fine. Kent is here. Can we focus on you, please? I'm not the one in the hospital in the ICU. Are you in any pain? Do you want me to get the doctor?"

"No," he says and I'm not sure which question he's answering or if it's a general no to all of them. "I want to be alone with my girl for as long as possible."

"You're not in any pain?"

"Nothing your lips on me can't fix." He whispers, his voice getting quieter and I wonder if it hurts to talk.

I kiss his lips again and then his cheek. "I love you. This really scared me." I let out a breath. "I'm glad you had me listed as your emergency contact. I was worried at first that they wouldn't let me see you."

"It'll be easier when we're married," he says and I don't even hide the smile pulling at my lips in response to the butterflies flapping their wings through me.

"Married?"

"For our hypothetical children." He winks, referencing our conversation we had a few days ago. Despite the lightness of this conversation, his eyes immediately go dark like he's remembering something. "Do they know who it was?"

"I don't think so? Do you?"

"No one I recognized. That motherfucker came out of nowhere. I'm trained for driving in all kinds of situations but that was something different. It was intentional." He closes his eyes slowly and when he opens them, he looks furious. "What if you had been in the car with me?"

"Then you would have saved us both," I tell him with a kiss to his lips. "You're going to be okay."

"Did they think you were with me? I just…" He lets out a deep sigh and winces immediately. "I don't want you out of my sight."

"Good. I don't want you out of mine either."

"I assume you're staying the night?" he asks and I nod knowing there's no way I'm leaving him overnight.

They will have to remove me by force.

"If you're staying, I want someone at the house and Kent here with you. Do you have my phone?"

I shake my head. "You're not doing any work."

"I'm not. I'm making sure the love of my life is being taken care of while I can't do it myself. This is *not* work, Shay."

It's been a week since Damian was released from the hospital with strict instructions not to overdo it while he recovers. They want him off of his feet for most of the day and Damian is not happy about it.

Luckily, the production team of *LA Dreams* is allowing me a brief hiatus and is shooting some of the scenes I'm not in for a few episodes to give me some time because neither I nor Damian feels comfortable being away from the other. We're both a little paranoid about something happening to the other. However, it seems my grace period is over and Damian is having an entire fit.

"Baby, I have to," I tell him as I pull on a short blue sundress. We'd been having this discussion all the way through doing my hair and makeup and now I'm ready to leave and Damian is still adamant that I shouldn't go to set without him.

"No. I don't know where that maniac is. He's probably spooked that I actually lived and I know too much. It's like he vanished. They can't find the car and I don't want you out there unprotected. I don't know what he wants and I can't risk it. I can't risk you. This is the only place I know I can keep you safe." He's sitting upright in my bed.

He's not technically on bed rest and can get up and move around but he's not very mobile and has to move slowly.

"I have a job though and people are depending on me. I was given way more grace than most people get and I have to finish shooting."

"I'm still not convinced Jeremy isn't behind all of this."

"I feel like that's just a very big accusation. It's one thing to be in love with me but to try and kill you out of jealousy?" I wince. I have yet to tell Veronica that he told me he's in love with me because I don't want things to be even more weird on set. Veronica has a terrible poker face.

"What if you guys just did the table reads here?" he offers.

I shake my head in disappointment. "Table reads? No babe, that ship has sailed. They had someone fill in for me while they ran lines. The table reads are done. I have to go do these scenes cold now and pray to God I do them right."

"I can come," he tells me as he tries to get up and I'm immediately next to him putting my hands on his chest.

"No," I tell him. "You absolutely cannot come. I need you to rest and get better." I lean forward and drag my lips across his. "I miss you." I bite my bottom lip and he raises an eyebrow at me before dragging his tongue across his bottom lip.

"I've been trying to put my mouth on your cunt for days, but you won't let me." He leans back and crosses his arms. "I told you to sit on my face and ride it, but you didn't want to."

"It's not that I didn't want to, I just…I don't want to hurt you."

"I told you I'd keep my hands down. My tongue isn't hurt, Shay." He winks and my skin heats under his gaze. "I'm coming," he tells me as he gets up with a wince. "I'll wait in the car, but at least I'll be close. You're going to be gone ten hours and I will go crazy thinking about you being out there that long without me."

"But you're going to wait in the car for that long? Usually, you're walking around and certainly not in pain."

"Either I'm coming or you're not going."

"Damian, you're not being reasonable. The doctors said you need to be lying down, not in a car for most of the day." I don't even want to tell him about the appearance I have at a premiere for my friend's movie at the end of the week. It's not a huge red-carpet event, but I did say I would be there and they've already announced my attendance so I have to show up.

That's tomorrow's problem.

I sit next to him on the bed and put my hands on his shoulders gently. One was dislocated in the crash and I see it on his face every time he moves it. "Stay here, please. I don't want to be worried about you being in pain or something happening while I'm trying to film. It'll just fuck with me and they've already delayed shooting enough for me. I need to be on my A-game." I explain in hopes he can understand. "Annette will be here if you need anything."

"I don't need Annette, Shay. I need to be where you are." He sighs. "But I know I'm no good to you right now." I see the disappointment all over his face, like he feels like he's letting me down. Like it's *his* fault that he got hurt.

"You're always good to me." I brush my lips across his, hoping he understands that I really do just want him to get better. "I'll be fine," I whisper and he nods.

"I'm not happy about it."

"I know. I'm not happy about my boyfriend being hurt either." I frown at him.

He gives me a small smile and strokes my cheek gently with his thumb. "Have a great day, baby. I'm sure you'll do amazing as usual."

I smile at his words because there is nothing like *his* praise. I press my lips to his one final time.

"CUT! Better. Much better. Let's take five," the director, Lucas, says.

I just shot a scene with Jeremy in my apartment where I'm practically in his lap as we discuss our plans for the future unbeknownst to his character that I'm carrying his child. I climb off of him, untangling us in the process when I feel his hand around my wrist.

"Shay."

"Yes?"

"I'm really sorry." I blink at him, not really knowing what to say because I'm not sure I'm buying what he's selling. He switches the microphone tucked into his pants off and I do the same because the crew really can hear our conversations between takes if we don't switch them off. "I know I came off like a dick and Derek told me the circumstances about Damian being married and I feel like a huge asshole for that."

"You should feel like one! That wasn't for you to tell me. Even if his marriage wasn't just a favor and they were consummating like bunnies, it still wasn't okay the way you exploded that all over me. Out of jealousy? Seriously, Jeremy?"

"I know, Shay. I…I guess I just thought if we were ever really single at the same time, we'd give it a try, and with the show ending, I guess I'm just struggling with you not being a main fixture in my life anymore."

My heart softens slightly because I hadn't thought about it that way. It's definitely not the same when you're not filming together anymore. It's like with any new job, sometimes you lose touch with people from your old one unless you really make an effort. "I understand, but that's still not an excuse."

"I know and I hate that I made things awkward and uncomfortable between us." He leans forward, resting his elbows on his knees. "Any chance we can still be friends?"

"Maybe after some time, yes, but you also need to apologize to Damian."

"I know." He nods. "Hopefully he doesn't beat the shit out of me, that would be a bitch to explain to Lucas." He chuckles.

By the time we're done filming for the day, I'm practically climbing the walls to get to Damian. We'd texted a few times throughout the day and we FaceTimed over lunch but I was ready to see him. There's a knock on my dressing room door and then Veronica is coming in with her bag slung over her shoulder. "Hey, are you coming to Nigel's party tonight?" Nigel is another actor on the show who is known to throw absolute ragers once a month at his house.

"No, I'm going home," I tell her as I slide on the blazer I'd worn to set and pick up my purse. "I want to see my man." I smile at her and she groans.

"Shaaaaay, come on."

"He just got out of the hospital, what do you want from me, V?"

"Ummm to come hang out with your best friend? Don't tell me you're on lockdown until he's better." She folds her arms across her chest and gives me a look.

"No! No. And I'm going to Erin's premiere at the end of the week. So, I'll be out then. I just don't feel up to it tonight. You know I won't be able to have fun if I'm just worried about Damian."

"But he's going to be fine."

I shrug. "Still."

"Lay off, V," Jeremy says from the door as he leans against the frame, his eyes surprisingly sincere. "Nigel will have a hundred parties before the year is over; she can miss one."

"Fine." Veronica pouts. "You better not bail tomorrow." She points at me. "I didn't sign up to lose my best friend just because she got a boyfriend. Don't be one of those women."

"I'm not!" Irritation washes over me thinking that maybe I have become one of those women and Damian being obsessed with keeping me safe certainly doesn't make it easier. I wrap my arms around her and kiss her cheek. "See you tomorrow."

That night, I walk into my bedroom to find Damian sitting on my bed with his laptop in his lap staring pensively at the screen. He notices me instantly and the smile that finds his face is so sexy that there's a flutter in my stomach.

"Come here, baby." He closes his laptop and shoves it to the side.

I shed my jacket and make my way to the bed and sit next to

him, careful not to jostle him but I think not seeing me all day has made him on edge so he pulls me into his lap with more force than he probably should have. He doesn't wince but I see him shift and I wonder if he hurt himself in his haste to get closer to me.

"Damian…" I try to move and he grabs my hip with his good arm and holds me in place.

"You are *going* to put your pussy on my face tonight." His voice rumbles in his chest as he lifts the sundress I'm wearing to reveal my lace underwear. He drags his finger over my slit, pushing his finger against my clit through the fabric. He licks his lips and pushes my panties to the side and strokes me lightly and I sigh in response. "It's been over a week since I've made you come and I can't go another day." He pulls his hand out from between my legs and pulls me closer so he can wrap his good arm around me. I'm against his chest but holding myself up to not put any weight on him. "How was your day?" he asks me before he presses a kiss to my forehead.

I move off of his lap and sit next to him but am still pressed up against him. "Good."

"Nothing out of the ordinary?"

"Nope," I tell him, wondering if I should tell him about Jeremy. *Maybe I should as a segue into attending the premiere.* "Jeremy apologized."

He gives me a pointed look and raises an eyebrow. "Did he now?"

"Yes, and before you say anything, I am wary too, but I want to finish out the season strong. I'm nominated for an Emmy this year, but sometimes politics won't let you win if they know you're coming up on a final season and I'm in such a tough category. So, they may hold it to give it to me next year which means every scene has to be perfect now and it can't be perfect if Jeremy and I are in a weird space when we've been so close for five seasons. The chemistry won't be there and the scenes will feel forced. Die-hard fans of the show will be able to spot that a mile away." He gives me a look I don't understand, like he doesn't believe what I'm saying. "What?"

He closes his eyes slowly and when he opens them, they look

defeated, like he knows this isn't an argument he'll win. "I just don't trust him."

"But, don't you trust me?"

"Of course, I do."

"Then nothing else matters. Do you think I'll…leave you for him? Because that's not going to happen. Or cheat on you?" I shake my head. "Is that what you think this is about?"

"No. I know how you feel about me."

I nod because I don't want to argue about Jeremy. As shitty a friend as he's been, I don't think he had anything to do with Damian's accident and I don't think he would do anything to hurt me. I just wish he wasn't feeling insecure about him. "There's a premiere I have to go to at the end of the week," I tell him, trying to change the subject, though I know this isn't necessarily a better one.

He tenses and looks down at me before letting out a sigh. "There's no point in trying to talk you out of it, is there?"

I shake my head. "D…we need to talk about this."

His eyebrows pinch. "Okay?"

I move away from him so that I can face him straight on. "It can't be this constant battle every time I have an appearance."

"It's not, Shay."

"Yes, it is. I've been dreading telling you about this all day because I knew you would try to talk me out of going."

"You do see the state I'm in, right?" he says waving his hand towards his body.

"Yes, but I have security."

"Not the point, Shay. What if you had been with me? What if they do the same thing to Kent while you're in the car? What if it's worse next time?" He rattles off a series of questions like they're all he's thought about all day.

"I don't know, but I can't live my life in fear."

"I don't want you to and when I'm well enough to move around, I won't be as paranoid because at least I can ward off the threats. I know that I can protect you, Shay, but right now, I'm unable to move and yeah, that scares me that you're out there with a very real threat or a potential stalker while I'm stuck in here unable to do shit about it."

"Have there been any more letters?"

"Nothing since the accident." He shakes his head.

"See! Then maybe, it's over?"

"Right," he says, grabbing his computer.

"Maybe he just wanted to scare me." He doesn't respond so I continue. "Damian, the point is I think that even when you're better we should consider hiring someone else."

"I think I've been pretty adamant about how I feel about that," he says without looking away from his screen.

"Okay, but it's not just your decision."

"As the head of your security, I beg to differ."

"Damian, *I* hired *you*. That means I do have the final say in this." Feeling exasperated, I get off the bed and cross my arms over my chest.

"I was told to keep you safe by any means necessary, even if you're throwing a tantrum."

My eyebrows feel like they go to my hairline. "Are you kidding me? I'm throwing a tantrum because I have to go to a premiere and you know, MY JOB?" I can feel myself getting excited and I know I don't want to argue with him but *tantrum*?

"You do a lot of other unnecessary shit too, Shay, and normally it's fine, but circumstances are different right now, and you're either too naïve or immature to see that."

What the fuck? "Immature?"

"I already said I understood about the premiere. Yes, I don't love the fact that you're going out without me, but I get it, it's your job. It doesn't mean I want you running all over California unprotected. If you can't understand why, then yes that makes you immature."

"This is all because of us being together. You've always been intense but this is on another level."

"So, I should care less about your safety because we're together?"

"No, but you're letting your feelings cloud your judgment and it's going to ruin us." I'm starting to fully understand his hesitation about us being together if this is how it's going to be for the rest of my life. "The problem with all of this is I'm used to things being a certain way and now it's like it's changed and you think you have more of a say because we're together. You don't get to just pull rank because you're my boyfriend now."

"Pulling rank how exactly? You're still going to the premiere."

"That wasn't up for debate!"

His nostrils flare and I can tell he's getting angry. "So, you just don't care about my thoughts at all now when it comes to your safety?" His voice is low and growly and if we weren't in an argument, I might find it sexy. I'll admit it still does something to me despite my irritation.

"No, but this seems to stem from jealousy or just you being an overprotective caveman. It needs to still be reasonable, Damian."

"Jealousy?"

"This isn't about Jeremy or Paxton or other men?"

"No, it's about one man—or I suppose woman that seems to be fucking stalking you, Shay. This is a very real situation. Just because you aren't privy to every little threat doesn't mean they aren't there. I work to keep them out of your sight. I lie awake at night so you don't have to and I'm not going to apologize for that."

"And I'm saying now you don't have to. We can hire someone else so you can relax and just…be with me?" My voice sounds weak because I don't feel like arguing anymore. I missed him all day, and I just wanted to cuddle up against him. Arguing with him makes me feel like shit and I'm tired and tense and I don't hate the idea of sitting on his face like he mentioned earlier.

"I already said that wasn't an option and it sure as shit isn't until we figure out what the fuck is going on."

"Fine." I pull off my dress and he narrows his eyes curiously. "You're annoying me, so I thought maybe an orgasm would make me less pissed at you."

He cocks an eyebrow at me but keeps the rest of his face impassive. "I'm not happy with you either. You think I want to make you come after your tantrum?"

I cock my head to the side and give him a smirk as I pull my bra off and let my tits spring free. "Yes."

His eyes trail down my body and between my legs as I slide my panties down them leaving me completely nude. He runs his tongue over his teeth and bites his bottom lip in that sexy way he does that makes my sex pulse. "Come," he says as he moves to lie on his back.

I get on the bed, straddling his neck and I watch as his pulse flickers. "You can't have your eyes on me twenty-four-seven. I know you have this intense need to keep me safe, and believe me, I love it, and I get off on how obsessive you can be about it, but I do still have to work. My job requires me to be out there." I nod towards the window.

"Can't you understand where I'm coming from?"

"Of course, I do." I move up and hold myself over his mouth and his breath on my wet slit forces my eyes shut. I feel the tip of his tongue touching my folds gently, not sliding between them. He tongues the skin there and I move my fingers down to part my sex for him exposing myself to him. "Can't you understand where I'm coming from?" I gasp as he brushes over my clit with the tip of his tongue.

"Damn, you're fucking hot. Lower," he grunts and I oblige, grateful for the squats and thigh workouts I do that will make this easier. I meet his gaze as his tongue begins to lap at me, dragging it against my clit, and I don't think I've ever seen a sexier visual. I lean forward to put both of my hands on each side of his head as he rubs his tongue over and over and the last of the irritation begins to float away.

I briefly wonder how we must look. Me riding his face while he's not touching me at all except for where his tongue meets my pussy.

Fuck, this is hot.

"Oh my god, I love you so much."

"Then let me fucking take care of you, Shay. Stop fighting me," he grits out.

"I'm not," I whine as I rub myself against him. "Ah! Right there. Please, oh my god!"

"You like that?" he asks, while his mouth is still pressed against me. "How's it feel, gorgeous?"

"So good. Yes yes yes." I pull back so that I can watch him and I can see the smile in his eyes when our eyes lock. "Damian, I'm going to come."

"Thank fuck," he growls. "Give it to me, then give me another one."

I bite my bottom lip as I go over the edge. "Fuck, yes I'm coming." I cry out as the orgasm pulls me under. "Damian!" He groans against me. I stay over his face for a moment while I come down from the euphoric feeling and move off his face to the space next to him while I try to catch my breath.

"That was fucking hot." I look over and my mouth drops open when I notice his mouth is shinier than usual. He drags his hand up slowly and wipes his mouth before dragging his tongue over his hand. "I love your taste."

I move down between his legs and rub his cock through his sweatpants. "I want to taste you now."

Chapter
TWENTY-NINE

DAMIAN

I didn't want to tell her that there had been another note. That the note had been at the entrance to the gate *again*. This fucker knows where she lives and is completely covered when he delivers it. This time it was delivered in broad daylight with a bouquet of flowers so the security at the front gate hadn't thought anything of it.

YOU CAN'T PROTECT HER FROM ME.

The six words that were directed at me have been playing through my mind on a loop since I saw it, and now she's supposed to go to a premiere tonight. I've had three of my guys thoroughly sweep the venue of the premiere but there's still a feeling I can't shake. She left about an hour ago, and since then I've watched the security footage of the person leaving the note at her gate no less than a hundred times. I didn't expect it to be the same car that ran me off the fucking road but my intuition makes me believe that everything is linked. I stare down at the pictures of her tonight, both ones she took in the limo for me and from the paparazzi.

Christ, she's pretty. I stare at picture after picture of her in a white strapless dress that makes her look like an angel.

And you're going to lose her if you don't back off about all of this.

I didn't want to scare her, but I feel fucking out of control over not being with her. I wince as I try to get up and do my best to move around the room. Against everyone's advice and direction, I've been pushing myself, walking around her room every once in a while, and even down the stairs. I've seen some improvement in the past week but it isn't enough to be with Shay all day. I'm requiring updates from my team every hour and I'll admit maybe I am going overboard about her safety, but she was right, us being together has made me even more obsessed with keeping her safe. The idea of losing the love of my life over something I could have prevented makes me fucking anxious. *And quite frankly terrified.*

I tried so hard to avoid this. This impossible catch-22 of a bodyguard falling in love with the person they're protecting. Will there ever be a time that I'm not obsessed with her safety? If we get married? Or if she were pregnant? *Yeah, I'd really back off then.*

My phone rings and when I see Kent's name on the screen, I answer immediately. "What do you got?"

"She's fine. The co-star you said to look out for has been a little clingy, by her the whole night, and a bit touchy."

I try to ignore the jealousy and the way my hand flexes with the need to hit something. "It's just for show, I'm sure, but thank you for letting me know. Make sure he doesn't get *too* handsy."

"Got it, boss. Talk to you in a bit."

A few minutes later, it rings again and I see Shay's name on the screen.

"Hi, gorgeous."

"Hi," she says and I can hear that she's somewhere quiet. "I'm in the bathroom."

"How is it going?"

"Good, but I wish you could be here. I actually think I'm going to leave soon."

"Oh?" I look at my watch and note she's only been there about two hours. I know it's supposed to go on for at least five and Shay isn't usually someone that leaves that early when she's invited somewhere.

"Yeah, it's…weird. I don't know. I feel uneasy."

I'm immediately on high alert. "What do you mean?"

"I don't know. You always told me to listen to my intuition when something doesn't feel right. I can't put my finger on it though."

I'm already pulling on my shoes because if she's admitting this to me, it means she's actually scared. "I'm coming there."

She's silent for a moment. "Okay," she says and I can hear the shakiness in her voice.

She's not arguing that? Fuck, something is wrong. "Baby, what happened? Tell me what's going on."

"Jeremy is being weird. I think…I think you might have been right."

FUCK.

"Right about what?" I say trying to keep her calm even though my adrenaline is going through the roof. I'm pretty sure I could kill him on sight if he touches one hair on her head but the last thing I want is to get Shay worked up unnecessarily. I'm sending a text to Kent to not let her out of his sight until I get there as I make my way down the stairs as fast as my body allows and out her front door.

"I'm not sure. It's always been in the back of my mind but so many people have come up to me tonight saying they didn't know Jeremy and I were together. Like when did that rumor start? So, I brought it up to Jeremy he acted like he didn't know what I was talking about."

I remember what Paxton said and I wish I would have told her. "Do not be alone with him."

"I won't."

"Good girl. I'll be there soon, I'm going to stay on the phone with you. How is the night otherwise?" I ask, trying to take her mind off of being scared. I start the car and I'm flying down the driveway when I hear her speak.

"Someone's in here." I don't hear anything and then I hear the sound of a door opening.

"Shay, what's going on?" I push harder on the gas, wanting to get to her faster. "Baby, talk to me," I order her and then I hear her gasp and my name leaves her lips in what sounds like terror before the phone goes dead.

Shay

There's a sound of a stall opening and I'm immediately confused because I could have sworn no one was in here with me. I shake off the weird feeling until there's a light tapping on my stall door. I frown. "Someone's in here," I say, and when I look down at the floor the feet on the other side look like a man's.

I gasp just as the door is forced open and I see Jeremy on the other side. "Damian!" I cry just as he rips the phone from my hand and drops it onto the ground, smashing it.

I go to scream for help when he puts his hand over my mouth and shakes his head. "I wouldn't unless you want to be burying your precious bodyguard in a few weeks."

He pulls something out of his pocket before pressing a knife to my neck just as I hear the door open.

"Get the fuck away from her. I will shoot you," Kent barks.

"I will kill her first. For god's sake, you can't even pee alone?" He looks at me and then at Kent and pushes the knife a little harder into my flesh. I whimper. "I don't want to kill you, baby, but don't push me." Jeremy stares down at me with an angry expression. "I never wanted it to come to this." He pulls his hand away from my mouth and looks at Kent as he pulls me in front of him, using me as a shield. "Drop it," he says looking at the gun in his hand.

My bottom lip trembles. "This whole time?"

"Do you mind? I want to talk to her alone," he says looking at

Kent. He's still got a knife pressed against my neck and I'm standing in front of him so there is not much that Kent can do at the moment.

"I am not leaving her."

Jeremy pushes a little harder and I cry out.

"Just wait outside, Kent," I tell him.

"I'll lower my gun."

"Nope. This is privileged information between me and Shay. Sorry."

"I'll be fine," I tell him and I wish I had the kind of wordless communication with him that I used to have with Damian even before we were together. He leaves the bathroom though I hear him shuffling outside, so I know he's close.

Jeremy lowers his knife and I rub the space on my neck where the knife was. "Did you do...that was you driving? You could have killed Damian."

"That was the plan, Shay," he scoffs. "Had I actually been driving, I would have. It's fucking impossible to find good help, but I couldn't risk getting hurt and fucking up the show. Lucas would have a fit." I blink at him in confusion. *He actually thinks I'm going to continue the show with him?* "Well, I assume the show is going to halt for a few weeks while you and I disappear."

Fear floods me at the words *you, I,* and *disappear*. "Wh—what are you talking about?"

"Well, yeah, you and I are going to Europe."

"For what?"

"To elope obviously. We've discovered our feelings and we knew it would come as a shock to everyone so we fell off the face of the Earth and will resurface as man and wife." He takes a step closer and puts a hand on my cheek and then drags it down my body. "God you're pretty. I can't wait to put a baby in here." He rubs a hand over my stomach and it causes a wave of nausea to move through me.

I feel disgusted with his hands on me and the thought of bringing a child into the world *not to mention, what it takes to make said child*, with this monster has me wanting to throw up everything I've eaten today. "You're crazy."

"I am only crazy about you and you just won't let us be together."

Keep him talking, Shay, I'm almost there, I can practically hear Damian say. "No, you are crazy. Why didn't you just tell me you had feelings for me? What is all of this? You...are you the one sending me letters too?"

"My manager says I do have a flair for dramatics."

"Oh my god, all along?" I shake my head realizing just how much he has everyone fooled. "What if I say no?"

"Then, I keep going until it's done."

My blood runs cold at what he means by that. "What's done?"

"Damian's death."

Tears rush to my eyes at the thought of living in a world without Damian, a world where he wasn't the center of mine. "I'll just go to the police," I tell him. "They'll believe me." I almost tell him that he's already a suspect in the accident but I decide against it.

"Fine." He shrugs. "I'll be in prison, but Damian will still be dead." He gives me a smug grin that quickly turns sinister. "You don't understand, Princess. The only way Damian lives is if *you* marry *me*."

"Oh my god." I let out a breath. *Or I kill him myself.*

"Do you know how long I've waited for this? To have you to myself?" He sighs. "We are going to be so happy. And rich! Oh my gosh, fans are going to lose their shit when they figure out we got married. This season is going to explode. You'll definitely win that Emmy."

He expects us to finish out the season? What the fuck?

"So, we're going to go." He points towards the door.

"What?" I ask.

"We're leaving and your security out there is going to let us go or he'll be my first casualty."

"I'm not leaving here with you."

"Then Damian gets in another accident." He shrugs. "I know he's on his way here. You think I don't have someone camped outside of your house?"

Fuck. "Please. Jeremy...you can't."

"I can and I will if you don't toe the line, baby."

"Why do you want to be with me like this? Against my will? How…?"

"I'll take you however I can get you and if that's by force, then so be it." My blood runs cold thinking about all the ways he probably means that and I'm sure that means he plans to force me to have sex with him too.

"Fine," I tell him. "Just leave Damian alone. You have to promise me," I beg as tears begin to slide down my cheeks at the idea of never seeing the love of my life again. I'd never recover from it but at least he'd be alive.

"Once we're married, I'll never bother him again, so long as he's far away from you."

His phone beeps and he looks at it before looking at me. "Alright, looks like Damian is a little more than fifteen minutes away; time to make our exit."

"But…"

"Tick tock." He touches my nose with the tip of his knife. "If he gets closer than ten, he'll be detained, sweetheart."

"Okay!" I exclaim. "Okay. Let's go."

"Excellent. Now put on a smile," he says as he opens the door and Kent is standing in front of it blocking us from getting through the door. Kent's back is to us and as he turns, Jeremy stabs him in the side causing him to fall to the ground with a thud.

"Takes care of that problem." He says as he drops my smashed phone next to him.

"Oh my god!" I say as Jeremy begins to walk, dragging me along with him. I try to hold the tears in when Jeremy whisks me down a hall and out a back door, preventing us from seeing any paparazzi or anyone besides some kitchen staff that probably just assume we're sneaking off somewhere to hook up.

He pushes me into a black car with dark-tinted windows and just as I go to scream, there's a cloth over my face.

And everything goes black.

Chapter THIRTY

DAMIAN

I can't get Kent on the phone after I told him to go in the bathroom and I'm fucking feral as I weave through the traffic to get to the premiere.

I swear to fucking God if anyone touches one hair on her head.

There's traffic for miles and part of me wants to get out and run, knowing adrenaline will get me to her faster than sitting in this jam. I grab her phone and pull up her tracker and I slam my hand on the dashboard when I realize she's not wearing it because it's reporting that it's at home. I run a hand through my hair angrily.

Why the fuck wouldn't she wear it? Why didn't I make sure she was wearing it?

Her phone's location is still at the premiere but I notice that one of her Airtags is moving. *What the fuck?*

Which one is with her?

If someone has her, he may have made her ditch her phone.

She has Airtags in all of her bags but what if he made her ditch her purse?

I call Veronica and she immediately answers. "Hey, I'm not with Shay."

"Where is she?"

"Walking around, I think? I just texted her but she didn't answer, her location says she's here though."

"She was in the bathroom and then something happened and I can't get her or Kent on the phone. Please…go find her. She has an Airtag moving away from the premiere and I don't know what to follow."

I frown as I see it's going towards a private airport. One that we've used several times.

"Fuck."

"What?" Veronica says and I can hear a dull roar in the background. I hope that means she's moving through the crowd. "I'm in the bathroom and she's not here."

"Could there be more than one?"

"I—I think there's one down the hall. Damian, what's going on?" I can hear the panic in her voice and I don't think I can be the one to ease her fears.

"I can't explain. Call me if you find her."

I'm pretty sure she's moving with her Airtag, so I begin towards the airport. If she's with her phone, I at least know she's still at the premiere, but if she gets on a plane and that tag loses a signal or dies, it'll be harder for me to find her. Thank fuck, the traffic isn't bad as I move away from the congestion around the premiere, and I continue moving through the streets. I text the rest of my team other than Kent who I hope hasn't been hurt, and tell them to meet me at the airport before calling the police. I'm fairly certain it's the same person who ran me off the road and after warning me to stand down, I end the call.

Stand down? Fuck that. Whoever has my girl is going the fuck down.

The airport isn't that far and I know a back way, allowing me to arrive before whoever has the Airtag. I'm out of my car instantly, ignoring the pain slicing through me with every step, praying that each of those steps is another closer to Shay. I move towards the entrance, scanning my badge that allows me access when I bring her here. I see a private jet on the tarmac ready and I'm up the stairs to the plane. The jet is massive and I know it has to belong to a celebrity which has me convinced that Jeremy or maybe Paxton has to be behind this.

I see a bucket of champagne, two glasses, chocolate-covered strawberries, and two boxes with the word *Cartier* on the top and one looks like a ring box. I open it and my stomach rolls at the large diamond inside and then I see lights on the tarmac and Jeremy gets out of the front seat. I don't see Shay and I have a dark thought that maybe she's in the trunk. My heart is pounding so loud I can hear it in my ears and in all the years I've been a security I've never been so fucking terrified *or uncertain*.

Where is she?

He moves towards the plane and I draw my gun, knowing that I'm probably going to have to shoot him. I move into the bedroom at the back of the plane, leaving the sliding door cracked so I can see what the fuck he's doing. I see him board the plane, drop off two duffel bags and take in his surroundings. He pops the champagne and pours two glasses before moving out of the plane again. I peek my head out of the door and watch him go back to the car where he pulls out an unconscious Shay and hefts her up to carry her in a fireman hold.

Fuck.

I curse myself for not shooting him when I had the chance because now Shay is in his arms and I can't risk hitting her.

"Finally," he says as he gets back on board the plane. "We're alone." She's still unconscious and he sets her in a seat. "I really thought you were going to wake up. It's okay though, we can still have fun, can't we?" he says and I cock my gun just as he presses a kiss to her forehead.

"Over my dead body," I growl at him and his eyes widen when he sees me. He reaches for something, but I'm faster, and I shoot him in the leg and then the arm.

"FUCK!" he screams as blood pours from both wounds. He goes down, but I know he's not dead and I'm on the move instantly as I pick him up, holding his arms behind him and moving him off the plane. He's moving in and out of consciousness murmuring something about Shay and killing me. I want nothing more than to go be with her, but I want to make sure this asshole is arrested first. My team is pulling up just as I make it to the bottom step and I yell at them to bring cuffs or a rope or something to subdue him and one of them tosses me the cuffs.

"He stabbed Kent at the premiere," one of them tells me as I put the handcuffs around his wrists. "He's going to be okay though."

"You'll never be good enough for her," Jeremy spits out.

"Yeah, well you'll never fucking have her," I grit out before kicking him in the side. "Watch him. He did something to Shay. She's unconscious," I tell them, so they'll send help up here as soon as they arrive.

The adrenaline is wearing off now that Jeremy is restrained and I know Shay is about to be in my arms, but it still knocks the wind out of me when I find Shay still passed out.

"Fuck," I growl as I drop to my knees in front of where he laid her on the seats. I feel around her body, looking for any rips in her dress and I breathe a sigh of relief when I don't feel anything. Her dress is floor length but it's flowy, and I want to be sick at the thought that he touched her while she was unconscious. I lift her dress and I'm grateful to see her underwear intact and I just have to pray that nothing happened.

I should have killed him. I think regretfully.

I drop her dress and when I look out the window, I see the police have arrived. I turn back to Shay, just as she starts to stir, and I rub her forehead gently before pressing a kiss to her lips. "Wake up for me, baby, let me see those pretty brown eyes." Her eyes flutter open slowly and her pupils look hazy and unfocused. "Hi, gorgeous."

I ignore the incessant pings of her phone as we head back to her house the next morning. She spent the night in the hospital for observation which was just enough time for hundreds of paparazzi to set up outside in preparation for her exit. An exit that featured me carrying her to the car and then following in behind her.

Now, she's sitting in my lap, her head resting on my shoulder and her nose pressed against my neck as we make our way to her house. She hasn't said much since last night. She spoke to the doctor and they did a brief, minimally invasive pelvic exam just in case Jeremy had done something to her while she was unconscious. She'd squeezed my hand the whole time and breathed the deepest sigh of relief when she came back with the all-clear. I'd slept with her in her hospital bed, her small body pressed against mine, and I woke to her practically climbing on top of me in her sleep to get closer to me and away from whatever was scaring her in her nightmare.

"Are you coming in?" she asks, breaking me from my thoughts as we approach her house.

I shoot her a look. "What do you think?"

"I think I want to take a shower." She scrunches her nose. "I smell like a hospital."

I press my nose into her hair and drag it down her neck. I smell a hint of her natural scent that drives me wild and if this had been a ride home from anywhere other than a hospital my mouth would have been on her cunt. "You smell good, baby, but I do think a shower will make you feel better." I want to ask her if she wants my help, but I don't want her to think it's solely for sex no matter how much I crave her. I could have lost her and I would be lying if I said I wasn't fucking desperate to touch her.

The car slows to a stop and I open the door, pull her into my arms and carry her up the walkway to her door. Her assistant had brought a change of clothes to the hospital for her, so luckily, she isn't in that tight gown from the premiere. She immediately goes up the stairs while I lock up and set the alarm. I follow behind her, and by the time she reaches the top, she's shedding her clothing and dropping them to the ground, creating a trail to her bedroom. I pick up the discarded articles and by the time I pick up her panties, I hear the water running. I'm just putting her clothes in her laundry basket when I hear her voice.

"Are you coming?" I turn around and see she's standing in the entrance to her bathroom completely naked and I ball my hands into fists to try and temper the ache in my dick.

I cross the room towards her. "I didn't want to press it if you needed space."

"I don't need space. I need *you*." She grabs my hand and pulls me into the bathroom and steps into the shower. She runs her eyes all over me as I strip out of my clothing and make my way into the shower with her.

She exhales the second the door closes behind me like she was holding her breath and now she feels like she can breathe.

"Tell me what you're thinking," I urge her.

"I'm scared and I hate being scared," she whispers as tears well in her eyes. "I trusted him…he was someone I considered a really good friend, and now I feel like I don't know who I can trust. I feel like I can't even trust my own instincts." She didn't cry once at the hospital and I think now that we're alone, the events of yesterday are setting in. "How did I not know?"

It turned out that Jeremy had been obsessed with her for a very long time after the police found a locked room in his basement that he had made into a shrine to her. Thousands of pictures taped to the walls. Things she'd touched, clothes she'd worn; I think there had even been pairs of her underwear. *A fact that I have kept from Shay.*

I can't believe I had let my guard down and he'd gotten to her. I'd almost lost her forever. *That is never going to happen again.*

"He deceived you, baby. He deceived everyone. You believed what he showed you. You can't blame yourself for that."

"He didn't deceive *you*. I should have listened to you." Her eyes find the floor of the shower as she takes a step back and I feel like I'm witnessing the walls go up around her heart. I can only hope that I'm already in there so she can't close it off to me.

"Hey," I say and her eyes snap to mine. "Things happen sometimes. He preyed on you years ago and spent years laying the groundwork. No one could have known."

"I guess he really was a good actor." I can hear a hint of sarcasm, but mostly her tone is laced with sadness.

I push her gently against the wall as I prepare to remind her that although a very shitty thing happened, she's okay and more importantly alive. "I got to you," I tell her. "I will always get to you." I rub her face and push her hair back gently. "You're safe."

"Because of you. What if you didn't have the instinct to follow my Airtag?" She shivers even though the water is practically scalding and scrunches her nose. "What if he had gotten me to Europe?" I also learned that he had gotten a fake passport made for Shay so there wouldn't be any issues at customs.

He had planned for everything.

Except for the fact that I'd stop at nothing to protect her.

"I'll always find you, baby."

"I'm sorry for…I don't know, not listening to you when you said something wasn't right."

"Hey, it's okay. I don't want you to ever be scared. That's why I'm here." I tell her as I pull her into my arms as she succumbs to more tears.

Shay fell asleep shortly after we got out of the shower and despite the two men I had outside and her physically in my arms, sleep never finds me. She'd moved out of my arms at some point while she was sleeping which allowed me to do a bit of work. I'd begun combing through all the pictures of us and all the stories that were starting to report about Jeremy and what this meant for the television show. The picture of me carrying her out of the hospital spread like wildfire and while her team hasn't made a statement, I know it's only a matter of time before the romance rumors about Shay and I are confirmed.

Shay begins to stir and a whimper leaves her. I'm just about to wake her when she sits up and looks around frantically. The room is dark except for the light of my phone and the moonlight peeking through her curtains. "I'm here," I murmur and she's in my arms instantly. "You're safe."

"You stayed."

"Of course, I stayed. You haven't gotten it yet? Right next to you is the only place I need to be."

The room is quiet so I hear her breath hitch in her throat and she grips me tighter like she's afraid I'll disappear or maybe like *she'll* disappear.

"How long have I been out?"

"A while." *About six hours.* "Are you hungry?"

"I think so."

"Let's get you some food." I lift her into my arms and make my way out of her bedroom turning on the lights as I go.

"I could get used to you carrying me around."

"That's good. The paps already seem to love it. There's a video of me carrying you out of the hospital."

"They think we're together?"

"Some, yes. Some are more concerned with reporting about Jeremy."

"You ready for the chaos? It's going to be different once they figure out you're not *just* my bodyguard."

"For you? I'm ready for anything," I tell her as I make it to the bottom of the stairs. I take a peek outside and see the two black cars stationed there.

"Will they have to be out there all the time?"

"Until I don't think they're needed, but for now yes." She nods and I can see she wants to say something but I change the subject. "What do you want to eat?" I ask her as I set her in a chair. I grab her a water from the fridge and begin pouring it into a glass. "You want something harder?" I ask and she nods. I still hand her the water but I also grab a bottle of whiskey and pour us both two glasses.

"Grilled cheese?" she asks.

"Really?" I chuckle at the simplicity of her request and she frowns.

"Okay how about a steak?" she says sarcastically and I'm happy to see a bit of her attitude coming back.

"I just wasn't expecting you to say that."

Ten minutes later, we're sitting on her couch drinking whiskey and eating grilled cheese sandwiches when she turns to me. "Move in with me."

I cock my head to the side because though I want her with me all the time, it worries me that she's so frightened.

"Because of what happened? Baby, I'm just right there." I point towards my guesthouse. "I'll never be far away." I don't want her to think I have to sleep in her bed with her to keep her safe.

"No." She shakes her head. "Because I love you and I can't imagine waking up in the morning and your face not being the first thing I see." She moves into my lap, straddling me, and puts her hands on my cheeks. "I want you and I want us." She presses her lips to mine for the first time since yesterday and it's as if her body just realizes it because she moans the second her tongue sweeps against mine. I don't know how long our lips are attached but when she pulls away her eyes are filled with lust and with the way she was moving on my lap, I'm going to guess that she's wet and wants me to do something about that.

"What do you want?" I whisper as I grip her harder against me.

"To tell me you want to live with me and then fuck me on this couch."

"I'll do you one better. How about I want to be with you forever?" Her eyes widen and her mouth drops open. "Now, I'm going to fuck you on this couch."

"Yes please. I was worried you weren't going to want to fuck me." She responds as she climbs off my lap and slides her shorts down her legs.

"I *always* want to fuck you." I tell her as I pull off my sweatpants followed by my briefs.

I pull my shirt off and watch in fascination as she does the same, making those sexy tits of hers spring free and I reach out and run my fingers over her. She shivers and I watch as goosebumps pop up everywhere.

"I love how much you affect me."

"You affect me too, baby. You have for so long." I tell her honestly. "Part of it was just being your bodyguard and understanding your body language but for so long it's been deeper than that. You've owned me for longer than you know, Shay." I pull her naked body back into my lap. She starts to slide down when I stop her, cupping her pussy. "Are you wet for me?"

"I'm always wet for you." She says and I slide a finger between her slit and see that she is wet but not as much as I'd like. Not like when I've run my tongue over her clit. "I know that look." She gives me a wicked smirk. "And as much as I love your tongue in my cunt, I'd rather it be in my mouth right now while you fuck me."

"Fuuuuck." I drag my dick through her slit and rub it against her clit as I prepare to slide inside of her. *Because there is no arguing with what she wants right now.*

I spit on two fingers and swipe them through her slit just to make her even wetter before I line my cock up with her entrance and she pushes herself down. Her lips crash against mine and her tongue snakes into my mouth and moves against mine with fucking urgency. She moves up and down, grinding her clit against me every time she hits the base of my dick. "That feel good?"

She lets out a moan so sexy and pornographic, I almost come. "It always feels fucking good, Damian. You're the only man that's ever made me feel this way."

"Yeah?" I pull away from her mouth and reach for one of her lush tits, sucking it into my mouth while my hand palms the other. I want to beat my chest with pride that I'm able to make her feel this good and that she wants this from me. *Only fucking me.*

Her head falls back as she continues to move up and down on me, our bodies moving together in perfect synchronization. The sounds of our bodies slapping together along with her sexy moans are the only noises to be heard and it's the sexiest fucking sound.

Her hands find my shoulders, digging her nails in to the flesh and my cock hardens inside of her. I reach behind her neck, guiding her mouth back to me just as her hand reaches behind her and touches my balls. I groan in her mouth and my dick jerks inside her slick cunt.

"Fucking perfect." I grit out against her mouth. "Baby, I need you to get there. Please," I tell her, because I need to feel her spasm around my dick before I come.

"Touch me." She pants. "*There.*"

The thought that she enjoyed the ass play as much as I did has me gritting my teeth to stop myself from coming right this second. I reach around her and put a finger there, pressing against that ring and massaging the area.

"I love that it's something only you've ever had." She whispers in my ear. "I love *you.*"

And those three words, words that have become my favorite words when uttered by her almost has me coming again.

"I love you too, so fucking much."

I bite down on her shoulder as I continue to bounce her up and down harder on my dick while my finger rims her asshole. "Fuck I'm going to come." She moans just as I drag my tongue up the slim slope of her neck.

"Please." I beg her again. "I need it."

Her eyes squeeze shut and then I know the second she starts to climax because her cunt clamps down on my dick and squeezes just as her head falls back and her mouth opens but no sound comes out.

"Fuck, yes. There it is." I groan as my orgasm pulls me under and I begin pumping ropes of hot cum into her.

After a few moments her eyes find mine and her skin is sweaty and her hair is a mess from my light pulling at one point.

She's so fucking beautiful.

"I could get used to doing this forever." She whispers before her lips find mine.

Shay

It's been three weeks since the incident and I have not wanted to leave Damian's side which is fine because there's a temporary filming hiatus while writers scramble to rewrite a script that no longer includes Jeremy, eliminating my character's fiancé.

Jeremy is being held without bail for a list of felonies. It was confirmed that he was behind Damian's accident and had a hit out on him. With all the evidence stacking up against Jeremy, it is predicted that he will be in prison for a long time.

The only person who has not been okay with me not leaving my house is my best friend who is lying on the lounger next to me as we sunbathe by the pool. Damian is just across the pool so he can see us and I can see him but he probably can't hear what we are saying. I'll admit I am having a bit of separation anxiety and I'm not sure if it's from my bodyguard or my boyfriend. *Probably both.*

I start seeing my therapist again on Monday and I am sure she's going to have plenty to say.

"I lost you to a boyfriend and then almost lost you to the man who was stalking you. You're coming out tonight." She sits up and pushes her sunglasses into her hair revealing teary blue eyes that I'm not sure is because of the mimosas or something else. "You're my best friend, and I can't believe…" She shakes her head like she wants to rid the thoughts from her brain of what could have happened. "How did he fool all of us? Even Derek."

"How's he doing anyway?" Derek probably took the news hardest after me and spent two days not speaking to anyone before getting blackout drunk and showing up at Veronica's house. He was barely able to stand as he broke down and cried in fear that Veronica and I believed he knew something or was possibly in on everything with Jeremy and that he'd lose us too.

He started seeing a therapist the next morning.

"Better now," she says but I can see the sadness in her eyes. Both Derek and I, two of the people closest to her are taking this hard and I worry that she's so concerned with us that she's not dealing with her feelings regarding her own relationship with Jeremy.

"We all need this," she says and I sigh because maybe this is Veronica's way of coping. A night out with the three of us because for so long it had been the four of us and it's time to start a new normal.

"Maybe this was a bad idea." I wince and adjust the strapless corseted dress I'm wearing as I see all of the flashes of cameras surrounding the car. Damian's blue eyes find mine and he narrows them curiously.

"I think you want to do this but you're scared. You're always going to be scared the first time."

I look out into the sea of flashes, listening to the sounds of people calling my name, and nod in agreement. "Am I ready for this?"

"Of course, you are." He tucks a dark curl behind my ear. "I'll be right there next to you. I won't let anyone get to you, baby." The news has been relentless with their reports about whether Damian and I are in a relationship and tonight will probably be all the confirmation they need when they see the way he touches me. I can't imagine him wanting to keep his distance tonight.

"You ready?"

I nod, letting out a deep breath just as he opens the door. I put on a smile and when I reach for Damian's outstretched hand everyone goes fucking *nuts*. Thousands of questions are being thrown at me from every direction about us and about Jeremy and the show and I just smile and wave and sign a few autographs as I make my way through the crowd. Damian still holds an arm out, in that same way he always does to clear a path for me, but now his other arm is holding me securely around my waist. We make it to the entrance and just before we turn to go inside, I grab his hand and pull him closer. I tilt my chin up, letting him know what I want and he gives me a smile that makes my knees weak before pressing his lips to mine. He wraps his arms around my back, pulling me closer and dipping me at the same time. I vaguely hear the sounds of the cameras and the screams and cheers but everything fades away as I sink into our kiss. I wrap my arms around his neck pulling him closer and just as I try to deepen it, he pulls back giving me a hungry look.

Fuck, but I'll have you later. I can practically hear him thinking.

I turn towards everyone standing outside the club and give them a wink and a final wave before moving inside with Damian right behind me.

"I didn't know we were doing that."

"I figured I'd give them something." I shrug. It had been a snap decision brought on by the way his arms felt around me.

We make our way to our section and I already see Veronica and Derek and several of the extended cast and crew. Veronica squeals as pictures of Damian and me from just moments ago are already circulating and she holds her phone up to show us. "Really? God, you guys are hot." From the angle of one of the pictures, you can see my other two security that Damian had follow us tonight because he knew I would probably beg him to have a drink or three and dance with me and he wanted to have all bases covered. I'll admit though, we did look hot. The picture looked like it belonged on the cover of a romance novel or a movie poster.

Damian takes a seat in the booth and I immediately sit in his lap, reminded instantly of the fantasy I've always had and I can't believe that it's finally coming to life. His arms wrap around me, pulling me hard against his chest and he bites down on my bare shoulder gently before brushing his lips against my skin.

"Is this what you wanted to talk to me about, young lady?" Denise, one of my favorite executive producers from the show asks as she approaches our table and sits down next to Damian and me.

"I meant to tell you. Things just got a little...hectic."

"I'll give you a pass this once." She chuckles before she pushes her glasses on her nose and takes a sip of her martini. "I'm happy for you." She nods at Damian. "Take care of our girl."

"Of course."

I melt in his arms, inhaling his cologne, and letting his scent calm me from the chaos swirling around us. "Do you want to dance?" he murmurs in my ear and I spin to look at him in shock.

"Umm yes? Have we met? We can...out there?" I point towards the crowd of people.

"Yeah, I don't think anyone will fuck with you with my arms around you." He kisses my neck and I hear squeals and *oh my Gods* in the distance. "Besides, I would do anything to make you happy." His words melt me and I press my lips to his. His eyes dart around the crowd on instinct and he nods once. When I follow his gaze, I see Luke and the new guy he'd just brought on as a trial run stationed fairly close by.

"I'm glad you're willing to bring on more help."

"I'll do whatever I can to keep you safe. Your safety is my number one priority." I quirk an eyebrow at him. "Well, until our hypothetical children come around."

Epilogue

Shay

One Year Later

"Give it to me, baby. Come on," Damian whispers against my clit. He's in his favorite position, on his knees in front of me in the back of a limousine, his mouth attached to my pussy as we make our way to my biggest award ceremony of the year. I'm up for an Emmy again for my final season of *LA Dreams*, and after the year I've had—particularly the final episodes of the show that really put my acting to the test with the very drastic exit of Jeremy's character—everyone is already calling me as the winner.

Especially since I lost the Emmy last year.

Jeremy was convicted of attempted kidnapping, murder for hire, two counts of attempted murder, vehicular assault, and stalking. He received a life sentence without parole so the writers decided just to kill his character to not completely alter the tone of the show by making him "a bad guy." But it made for some very intense scenes requiring me to do *a lot* of hysterical crying.

And the board lives for that shit.

Damian's hands rub over my swollen belly, stroking the skin above my belly button in time with the strokes over my clit and I feel the swift kick from within in response. I'm seven months pregnant, a surprise neither of us saw coming, and Damian has been obsessed with my pregnancy and the thought of being a father.

I want to grip his hair, but we're minutes from arriving at the show and I don't want us looking like we're sexed up like we always are.

The moment the paparazzi found out about Damian and me, they started following us around relentlessly and have shared hundreds of pictures of us engaged in *all* kinds of public displays of affection. Kissing, touching, dancing at clubs, making out in the front seat of my new Range Rover, me sitting in his lap any time we're out to dinner alone. There was one stray shot of us leaving the doctor where he was on his knees in front of me with his lips on my stomach that made it onto every news outlet in the country within an hour. He'd gotten me a puppy for Christmas because I wanted a dog for years that he refuses to let me walk by myself so there are dozens of pictures of us walking our Cavalier King Charles Spaniel, Hunter.

"That feels good," I moan, feeling my orgasm hovering over me.

"Mmm, then give me what I want," he growls. "Come on my face." He inserts two fingers into my slick wet channel and finds that spot that has become even more sensitive during my pregnancy. He curls his finger to reach it and my climax washes over me.

"Oh fuck, baby right there," I cry out.

"Right there?" He closes his lips around my clit and sucks as I come against his lips. "Oh fuck yes. Come for me, baby." He holds me in place as he licks up every drop before he slowly slides my panties back up and underneath my black gown. He wipes his face with the facial wipes we now keep in the limo since he can't seem to ride back here with me without eating my pussy. He presses a light kiss to my stomach before taking the seat next to me. "What are you thinking about?" he murmurs and I turn to look up at him.

"I don't know if I'm more nervous to lose again or to actually win."

He grabs my hand and locks our fingers together. "No matter

what happens, Shay, I am so proud of you. Despite everything you've been through, you are the most remarkable woman I've ever met."

"Don't." I point at him as I feel tears prickling in my eyes and he smiles before pressing a kiss to my lips, light enough to not ruin my lipstick. *The whole reason we didn't have sex back here.*

"*They* would be so proud of you too." He says referencing my parents.

We are sitting in our seats in the audience, waiting anxiously for my category. Damian is seated next to me with his hand on my knee to keep it from incessantly bouncing. I do technically have a new bodyguard, but as Damian predicted, he barely gets to do his job because Damian is no more than a few feet away from me at all times. There are even times that Damian acts more like my bodyguard than my man and I have to remind him that he's on the red carpet to take pictures *with* me and not to keep people back.

I watch Veronica and an actor from another hit show make their way onto the stage to present the award for best actress in a television drama. She looks gorgeous in a strapless floor-length silver gown that looks like tiny diamonds with the way the light hits it. I beam with excitement knowing it will look perfect with the very large diamond ring Derek plans to give her tonight.

"Remember to breathe," I hear in my ear and then he presses a sweet kiss on my cheek.

"He seems more excited than I am." I rub my stomach as I feel a kick from inside and Damian's hand rests on top of mine.

"He knows his mother is a star."

I turn back just in time to hear Veronica finish listing the names of the nominees. "And the Emmy goes to…" She opens up the envelope and squeals instantly. "Oh my god! Damian, bring our girl up here!" She jumps up and down and presses the envelope to her chest. "Shay Eastwood-Hunt!"

The theme song of *LA Dreams* starts blaring through the entire auditorium as the room erupts in applause and cameras surround me as Damian helps me to my feet. I hug Cooper and Derek and a few members of the crew on the way up to the stage, my arm linked with Damian's as he guides me.

"You okay?" he whispers in my ear and I nod as we make it to the stairs. He kisses me for no more than a second, but it's enough for the room to get even louder with their screams and a few stray cat calls. "I'll be here," he says.

I love you, I mouth at him as I make my way up the stairs and Veronica rushes toward me to pull me into a hug.

"You fucking did it!" she squeals in my ear. "Love you so much."

"Love you more," I whisper back as I make my way to the podium.

I let out a breath. "I don't know how many people can say their best friend handed them their Emmy. On a show they were on with you, no less." I look at her and she's staring at me like a proud mom still bouncing with excitement. The tears have already started to form as I think about the speech I sort of practiced *just in case*. "Wow, thank you so much. I've been playing Ashley Anderson for over a decade and to close the chapter on this part of my life…to say goodbye to her on this kind of high is unbelievable." I hold the Emmy up and look at the gold statue *that's heavier than I anticipated*. "Six years ago, I started this show and then immediately went into the worst period of my life, so in a lot of ways being Ashley Anderson saved me. It showed me that I was resilient and that I was tough enough to get through the worst. It showed me that," I dart my gaze to where Damian is standing and give him a wink, "where there is life, there is hope." I laugh through my tears. "There are so many people I want to thank before they kick me off the stage." I go through my laundry list of people and when I get to the end I turn towards Damian. "And of course, to my husband, thank you for everything, for always being my light in the dark. I love you. And finally," I look up and hold the Emmy over my head, "Mom, Dad, this is for you." I blow a kiss upward and then towards the cameras as everyone applauds and music indicates a commercial.

"You always know how to deliver a monologue," Veronica chuckles when we get backstage and we've removed our microphones. She pulls me into a hug and when she pulls back the tears are moving down her face again. "That was really good."

"Thanks, V." She nods behind me and I turn to see Damian standing there with the sexiest smile on his face and then I'm in his arms the best I can be with my stomach between us.

"Fuck, I'm proud of you. You are amazing and I am so honored to be your husband." His eyes are a bit glazed and I wonder if he got a little emotional during my speech especially when I referenced his tattoo. "That is *not* the speech you practiced for me."

"Sorry." I giggle. His lips crash against mine and we stay like that for a few seconds before a throat clearing interrupts us.

"How did you get back here before I did?" my bodyguard, Luke, says to Damian.

My husband shrugs. "They know me."

"Okay, well it would have been nice if you let me in on the secrets. I am her head security, Hunt."

Damian gives him a look of derision before turning his gaze back to me with a look that says, *can you believe this guy?*

I press a hand over my lips to stop the giggle from expelling from me and shake my head. *Be nice,* I tell him with my eyes.

He wraps an arm around me and presses a kiss to my temple as he walks me towards the refreshments table. "Yeah, sure. Keep telling yourself that."

The End.

Want to know what to read next?
Check out *What Was Meant to Be*, an age gap, second chance, Dad's best friend romance!

Acknowledgments

If you follow me on Instagram, then you know this story was born from a stray picture of a very famous woman and her bodyguard that was rumored to be the father to one of her children (the scandal!) If you've been following me for longer than I've been publishing, then you remember my first ever fanfiction was a bodyguard romance. I've wanted to write and publish one for ages and I am so happy with Shay and Damian's story. I hope you guys loved it too! The Bodyguard is still one of my favorite movies to this day, minus the ending because why couldn't they end up together!? So, in some ways, this book felt like a love letter to myself.

This book could not have come together without so many amazing women in this community who I feel so lucky to also call my friends. I couldn't possibly name them all and I want to take a moment to acknowledge all the women that reach out to me every day. The people that check in to chat about more than just spicy books. *I see you. I remember you. Thank you. I love you.*

Tanya Baker, Melissa Spence and Erica Marselas, thank you for your feedback and your insight. Thank you for always reading all the versions of my books and listening to my lengthy voice messages or rants *where I'm really talking to myself.* I could write a novel about how grateful I am for your friendship. Thank you for everything. I love you guys.

Becca Mysoor, I hope you know you're stuck with me now. Thank you for all of your help with this book. Thank you for knowing what I'm trying to say without me having to say it. Thank you for understanding my wants and needs and working with my crazy schedule. I appreciate you so much. You're just a positive ray of sunshine and I feel so lucky that I have you. Thank you for being you.

Kristen Portillo and Logan Chisholm, thank you for helping make this book perfect! One day I'll get my tenses and my timelines right the first time around. Until then, I'm grateful I have you guys to catch them. I appreciate you both immensely!

Stacey Blake, thank you for always making the interiors so gorgeous and exactly what I want! I love the way you make my books sparkle.

Ari Basulto, I would be lost without you. Thank you for all that you do to keep me organized! Thank you for running all of my teams and overall Q.B.'s life better than I could. A million thank yous.

Emily Wittig, somehow you always know what I want and I am obsessed with my paperback covers! They are so perfect and I love them. Thank you for always understanding my vision. You're the best!

Pang Thao, thank you for all of my gorgeous teasers and all of my last minute promo things and all the things I ask you to make me all the time. You're so good to me and I appreciate everything you do! And thank you for designing this e-book cover! I love it!

Rachel and Alexandra, thank you for being my sounding boards about everything. For stepping up and helping me with so many things. For your advice and your support. Endless thank yous and so much love.

To the ladies at the Author Agency, Becca and Shauna, I am so excited to work with you guys. I feel like this is just the beginning and I'm super excited! Thank you for everything!

To the babes on my street team and ARC team, thank you for your excitement! Thank you for your love for me and my books and that you're always willing to let me take you over a cliff. The reason I can do what I do is because of you guys in my corner. Thank you for always clapping the loudest. I love you guys so big.

To all of the bloggers and bookstagrammers and TikTokers, thank you for your edits and your reels and your videos and always sharing my books! For still talking about books I wrote two and three years ago and loving them so much. For sharing with your friends (and sometimes your family? Ha) Thank you for everything you do. (Because seriously? Videos are so hard.)

And finally, and most importantly to YOU, to the readers, thank you for letting me into your minds and your hearts again with another book. I hope you enjoyed it! I love you all. Let's do this again soon—maybe more taboo next time?

Also by
Q.B. TYLER

STANDALONES

My Best Friend's Sister
Unconditional
Forget Me Not
Love Unexpected
Always Been You
What Was Meant to Be

BITTERSWEET UNIVERSE

Bittersweet Surrender
Bittersweet Addiction
Bittersweet Love

CAMPUS TALES SERIES

First Semester
Second Semester
Spring Semester

Available through the Read Me Romance Audio Podcast

Fantasy with a Felon

About the
AUTHOR

Bestselling author and lover of forbidden romances, tacos, coffee, and wine. Q.B. Tyler gives readers sometimes angsty, sometimes emotional but always deliciously steamy romances featuring sassy heroines and the heroes that worship them. She's known for writing forbidden (and sometimes taboo) romances, so if that's your thing, you've come to the right place. When she's not writing, you can usually find her on Instagram (definitely procrastinating), shopping or at brunch.

Sign up for her newsletter to stay in touch! (https://view.flodesk.com/pages/6195b59a839edddd7aa02f8f)

Qbtyler03@gmail.com

Facebook: Q.B. Tyler
Reader Group: Q.B.'s Hive
Instagram @qbtyler.author
Bookbub: Q.B. Tyler
Twitter: @qbtyler
Goodreads: Q.B. Tyler
Tik Tok: author.qbtyler

Printed in Great Britain
by Amazon